SIDE SHOW
1995

An Anthology of Contemporary Fiction

Edited by
Shelley Anderson
Marjorie K. Jacobs
Kathe Stolz

somersault press

Acknowledgments: Special thanks to Gerald M. Winer for his always valuable production assistance and to Jean Schiffman for her editorial skills.

MANUSCRIPT AND EDITORIAL CORRESPONDENCE:
All submissions and correspondence should be addressed to: Somersault Press, P.O. Box 1428, El Cerrito, CA 94530-1428. Manuscripts are accepted between November and June of each year. A $10.00 entry fee is required with your first submission (multiple submissions are encouraged but only one entry fee is required per writer for the year in question). THERE ARE NO GUIDELINES. The entry fee includes a subscription to the next annual. Always enclose SASE if you wish a response. Submissions are critiqued if desired. Small cash prizes are awarded for the best three stories as selected by the editors. All accepted writers will be paid $5.00 per printed page at the time of publication (October 1995).

For ordering, see the order form at the end of the book.

The stories herein have not been published elsewhere.

International Standard Book Number
0-9630563-3-6

Cover painting by Electra Long; cover design by Lawrence Cannon

Foreword

From "The Responsibility of Writers"

The essential characteristic of the first half of the twentieth century is the growing weakness, and almost the disappearance, of the idea of value. This is one of those rare phenomena which seem, as far as one can tell, to be really new in human history, though it may be, of course, that it has occurred before during periods which have since vanished in oblivion, as may also happen to our own period. It has appeared in many domains outside literature, and even in all of them. In industry, the substitution of quantity for quality; among the workers, the discrediting of skilled workmanship; among students, the substitution of diplomas for culture as the aim of education. Even in science there is no longer any criterion of value since classical science was discarded. But above all it was the writers who were the guardians of the treasure that has been lost; and some of them now take pride in having lost it.

... The good is the pole towards which the human spirit is necessarily oriented, not only in action but in every effort, including the effort of pure intelligence. The [Modernists] have set up non-oriented thought as a model; they have chosen the total absence of value as their supreme value. Men have always been intoxicated by license, which is why, throughout history, towns have been sacked. But there has not always been a literary equivalent for the sacking of towns. [Modernism] is such an equivalent.

The other writers of the same and the preceding period have gone less far, but almost all of them — with perhaps three or four exceptions — have been more or less affected by the same disease, the enfeeblement of a sense of value. Such words as spontaneity, sincerity, gratuitousness, richness, enrichment — words which imply an almost total indifference to contrast of value — have come more often from their pens than words which contain a reference to good and evil. Moreover, this latter class of words has become degraded, especially those which refer to the good, as Valery remarked some years ago. Words like virtue, nobility, honor, honesty, generosity, have become almost impossible to use or else they have acquired bastard meanings;

language is no longer equipped for legitimately praising a man's character. It is slightly, but only slightly, better equipped for praising a mind; the very word mind, and the words intelligence, intelligent, and others like them, have also become degraded. The fate of words is a touchstone of the progressive weakening of the idea of value, and although the fate of words does not depend upon writers one cannot help attributing a special responsibility to them, since words are their business.

- Simone Weil

Philosopher and visionary, Simone Weil, wrote the above sometime before the Second World War.

Permission granted to reprint from *Simone Weil Reader* edited by George A. Panichas (Moyer Bell Ltd. 1977)

CONTENTS

SECOND PRIZE STORY
There was an old woman
Lived under a hill;
And if she's not gone,
She lives there still. - Nursery Rhyme

MEETING OLD LADY COLDWATER

by Lee Blackcrow

1.

Before the new blacktop road, before the electric pole, when the way was muddy and crooked, when few visitors walked the three miles in to the cedar log cabin, when snow meant a five-day blizzard with ten-foot high drifts — in those days out on the prairie near the Badlands of Redstone Basin, there was silence.

In the middle of the silence, eighteen-wheelers chug-shift-chugged coming up Horseshoe Bend and Redcloud Hill five miles away. And at the far end of the silence, spirit buffalo and Indian ponies plunged down to Branding Iron Creek over the hill.

When Suzanne Stone married Selo Blackcrow in March 1976, and moved to his family's deserted 1918 "Sioux benefit" cabin, she moved back in time. She touched the thick protective walls, enchanted by the silvery rough-hewn cedars, so warm in winter, yet so cool in summer, amazed at the hard gloss on the smooth earthen floor. She had sought and found a change of worlds.

About a month later, she woke up one crisp morning to the drip-drip-drip of winter snows beginning to melt from the eaves. Out the small south window she saw patches of delicate new grass in the corral encircling the cabin.

1

Suddenly the big room with its windowless north and west walls felt dark and oppressive, crowded with furniture, saddles and tires. In the middle of the floor sat Selo's 26" color TV, unplugged, of course, a wedding present from urban Indian relatives. Her brother-in-law Milo was using it as a work table for making braided bridles and hackamores from old hides. Maybe its insides had survived the minus 30 degree March weather.

Without a supply of firewood, they'd been forced to heat the cabin with broken fence posts and old tires cut into slices. Fortunately Milo had come out to help, but then he'd been caught by the blizzard and had stayed, while Peter, her son, boarding at Holy Rosary Mission High School 100 miles away, couldn't make it home through the drifts.

After pancakes, Selo and Milo finished their coffee, then put on army parkas and navy wool caps and went outside to work on the '64 red Ford station wagon that hadn't started since the blizzard.

Quickly Suzanne finished the breakfast dishes, opened the door and tossed the grey dishwater outside, drowning the night peehole in the nearest drift. The horses whinnied from the sheltered side of the cabin, rounding the corner and shuffling to reach the open door. First her roan mare and newborn pinto colt, then Selo's gelding quarterhorse Red Walker, and nuzzling in closer, her son Peter's newly arrived Appaloosa stud, Bloketu, a beauty. Even Milo the rodeo rider had noticed him. She had taken over the chore of feeding them commodity oats every morning, and they remembered. She didn't even have to shake the bag.

Then, filling a pot of sorted black beans with water from a dipper in the cream can by the door, she set it on the woodstove to simmer for dinner, noonmeal. She shifted the enamel coffeepot with the sign *wakalyape* taped on it to the rear to keep warm.

She didn't care if Selo laughed, she was going to learn Lakota. She had tacked signs everywhere, *mini* on the cream can, *tiyopa* on the door. He wasn't helping her, got too impatient with her interruptions. "Besides," he'd said, "You don't want to talk like

2

a man, do you? Men teach men, women teach women. Different words, different endings." The priests' dictionary hadn't told her that, but he was probably right.

She checked her woodpile, added a few sticks to the fire. Still enough kindling to last for awhile. Then outside to breathe the sunshine. Such a fine day, an outside day. Crisp air warmed by the sun made her eyes squinch. Blinding snowdrifts still, and no sunglasses. She tied her long blonde hair up in a head scarf, put on her ski jacket and waterproof hiking boots, and went out to join them.

The two brothers, Milo and Selo, were so different, Milo tall and broad, Selo short and wiry. Their faces, too, Milo's grey-black hair wavy in a ponytail, Selo's straight in two braids. Milo's broad forehead and nose set in a round face, Selo's high cheekbones and hawk nose set in a fine-featured face. Hardly seemed like brothers.

She heard Milo's guttural Lakota from behind the cabin over by the engine hoist, where they worked without gloves on the engine, surrounded by rusted car bodies, worn plyboards, and baling wire. He was cranking something heavy up on the hoist while Selo, bent under the open hood with a ratchet, was muttering. It looked major.

"You told me it was just the carburetor," she said.

Selo looked up. "Worse. Cracked block." As he cranked the ratchet, it dropped through the engine to the ground. "Damn, don't bother us."

She winced. He was so curt with her now. OK, she'd go away and do something useful, too. Beyond the melting drifts, across the creek, the sundance grounds were bare. She went over to the lean-to built against the cabin's north wall, and picked out a rake. Hoisting it on her shoulder, she stomped through the slush down to the creek on her way to the round grassy arbor. In the center stood the sacred tree. Sanctuary. She'd clear off the old dried pine boughs so new grass could get a headstart for this year's sundance.

At the bottom of the footpath she turned right to cross the shallow spot in Branding Iron Creek, where it rattled over coarse gravel, near the old spring bubbling up from a pool close to the bank of Badlands shale.

Suzanne hesitated. Bending over the spring was an old woman in black — black headscarf, black shapeless long-sleeved dress, her feet hidden in the dry weeds of the winter creekbed. She was dipping a wooden pail into the pool. A neighbor! But her back was to Suzanne. Should she disturb her? What was Lakota for a woman greeting a woman? *Maash-ke*? Suzanne waited. Maybe she'd remember. It was so still and peaceful here. The old woman hadn't moved. Oh well, leave her alone, too. Suzanne slowly waded across the creek and up past the young cedars and sweat lodge firepit to the sundance arbor.

2.

At lunch, Suzanne spread the table with beans and an iron skillet full of sliced fried potatoes mixed with commodity beef. Selo and Milo came in and washed their oil-black hands in the washbasin, sat and ate silently. Lakota men ate first, talked later.

As she brought them a plate of fresh *kabuk* bread, she asked, "How goes it?"

"Bad," replied Selo, tearing off a piece of thick pan-fried bread. "Need a head gasket."

"Gonna make one after noonmeal," Milo said, "out of tar paper." She looked up. He was waving his mug at the loft overhead, where her son slept when he was home. Sure enough, a black roll of roofing was wedged in a corner.

When they had finished eating, she refilled their coffee mugs from the enamel pot on the woodstove and asked, "By the way, who's that old lady dressed in black?"

Milo looked up, paused, mug in mid-air. "What old lady?"

"The old lady getting water down at the spring."

4

"Enhh?" Selo turned and stared at her. "When did you see her?"

"Just this morning, on the way down to rake the sundance grounds." Suzanne dumped coffee grounds in the slop pail and rinsed the pot. "I thought you said there weren't any relatives around for miles. Just Old Pat McCoy on this side of the creek."

"Wearing black, you say?" Selo asked. "And old?"

He was starting to interrogate her again. What now? "I don't know." She shrugged. "I couldn't see much. She was wearing a black scarf, like Auntie Nellie does, and a long black dress."

"And what was she doing?"

Suzanne cleared the tin plates off the table and dumped them in the big dishpan. "Dipping an old wooden bucket in the spring, you know, just at the edge of the creek where it bubbles up in the gravel."

"Did she talk to you?"

"No. Her back was turned." Suzanne began pouring boiling water on the dirty dishes. "It was very still, and I didn't want to intrude. So I just went on by."

"And she wasn't there when you came back up?"

"No. So what?" He was exasperating.

Selo pushed back his chair, took out his Bull Durham from his vest pocket, rolled two cigarettes, and offered one to Milo.

She hated cigarettes, but put up with their roll-your-own smoke. After all, tobacco, *knick-knick*, was part of their culture.

"So who *is* she?" Suzanne demanded.

Selo lit up and took a puff. "Are you sure you saw someone?"

"Of course, Selo. Who is she? What's the matter?"

Milo hesitated, taking a long drag before speaking in the slow traditional style. "You probably saw Old Lady Coldwater. Our grandmother. Sounds like it. It's her land, her spring."

"Oh. Well, why didn't she stop in?" Surely she'd heard the mechanics, or seen the cabin's chimney smoke.

"She died in the flu epidemic." Milo paused. "Back in 1919."

"What?" Suzanne turned around and looked directly at him, even though she knew that was rude. "Wait a minute, Milo, who

5

I saw down there was as real as you or me! Or that Appaloosa stud whinnying outside!"

The men listened to the restless horses. Did they feel it too? No one moved. Did they think she was nuts? "You think I saw a ghost?" she turned and looked at Selo now.

"Seems so." Selo ground out his cigarette.

"What? I did *not* see a ghost! I saw a real person! I don't even believe in ghosts!" She banged the tin plates in the dish rack. How could he not believe her?

"Oh, yeah." Selo could be harsh, cynical. "Is she there now?"

Suzanne looked at him. She'd just said the old lady was gone by the time she'd come back up to cook noonmeal.

"Not there, enhh?"

"I know what I saw," she repeated. No one was going to make her deny that. "That doesn't mean that she wasn't really there when I *did* see her." She stopped. He'd got her going again. Arguing was pointless. She knew what she'd seen, and nobody could change that.

"That's her spring," Milo continued slowly. "Only spring for miles around — that's drinkable. Those sulphur springs in the Badlands are no good." He shifted on his chair and propped his bum leg out on the kerosene can. He'd broken it steer-wrestling in the first All-Indian rodeo years ago at Rosebud Fair.

"That's why she moved away from her band at Cheyenne Creek and lived here, with the *Wajajes*, the outcasts, that spring. And why we still stay way out here."

"Look, did either of *you* ever see her? I mean, she died before any of us were born, right?" The two looked away. Maddening. Why was it they just didn't answer a direct question?

Milo continued, as if she hadn't spoken. "Got her name from it, Rattling Water. She had a voice like water over gravel, strong. Strong person, too. The land agent wrote it down as Annie Coldwater, though." Milo was off in memoryland.

She was still angry. "I don't believe it! I could've gone right over and touched her, if I'd wanted to."

"Good thing you didn't," Selo said, frowning.

"Why?" What now? She could hear the fresh coffee grounds boiling. Then the newborn pinto colt whinnied to its mother. "Why won't anybody answer my questions? What's the matter?" "You have to stop asking so many questions," Selo said. "It's un-Indian." But how else could she learn? He turned slowly to Milo. "We'd better get over to Henry Steed's tonight, enhh? Can we get that engine in and running before dark?" "Looks like we gonna try. Get Edna to make the food and tobacco ties. If we wait till dark, the gumbo'll freeze over and we can make it on those back roads over to Ring Thunder in time for night meeting."

3.

Selo walked Suzanne over the soft snow to Pat McCoy's trailer in the next quarter section, hoping to hitch a ride into town nine miles away. The old man had a high-center four-wheeler that could make it out to the road and into Eagle Nest, into the BIA housing circle where Edna Burning Breast, Suzanne's sister-in-law, lived in an AIM house, its brick sidewall painted with the AIM flag—a Red Power fist in the center of an upside-down US flag—next to the Oglala Sioux tribal flag, red with eight white tipis forming a circle in the center.

"You help Edna make some frybread," Selo said. "We'll need lots and she'll teach you." As they went in the door and past the blaring TV with six kids sitting on a couch, he waved, "Hi, takozhas!"

In the small but modern kitchen Edna stood in front of the stove wearing a flour-dusted print apron, boiling potatoes. Her long dark hair was tied up in a red headscarf, topped by black-framed reading glasses kept nearby for doing beadwork.

Suzanne shook her wet hand. "Glad to see you." Perhaps she would explain what was going on. But maybe not. She knew Edna didn't like her long blonde hair, hadn't wanted her youngest brother marrying White. When all the relatives had

7

been talking about the wedding plans in Lakota, Edna had said in English, "Oh, if you *really* want to!"

Selo spoke rapidly to his oldest sister in Lakota. She looked sideways at Suzanne and frowned.

"*I-nach-ni, i-nach-ni,*" she heard Edna reply with that heavy German guttural sound. Hah, she'd learned that one already. That meant, "Hurry up."

Selo bent close to Suzanne, as close as he'd ever get in public, and said softly, "Take care. I've got to get over to George Swift Hawk's and get a car part, then hitch back." Then he pulled back, opened the kitchen door, turned and waved. "See you later. Wish us luck." For some reason he was instantly in a better mood. She knew he enjoyed talking with Edna.

"Have him send me over some deer meat for the soup. Can't use that commodity beef." Edna, who'd been angry a moment ago, now smiled. "Good to see you. Not easy, out in the country."

"Oh, but I love it! The space! Do you know you can see thirty miles in all four directions? And the sunsets! They ring the sky so you can even see rosy clouds in the *east!*" She stopped abruptly. Selo had told her not to gush over sunsets. "Please tell me what's going on."

"Oh, we're going over to Ring Thunder for a night meeting." Edna said. "Selo wants to introduce you to Henry Steed." She was stirring a steaming pot of small purple berries. "Here, you stir, while I mix up frybread dough. He's an old family friend. That way, things will be all right."

"But what's wrong?" The berry pudding was beginning to thicken. "I don't understand."

"Oh, not too good to see *wanaghi,*" Edna said, kneading flour in a big enamel pan. "But we'll fix you up OK, so it'll be safe for you to stay out in the country all alone."

"But I don't mind. I like it. It's peaceful."

Edna patted and rolled the dough, deftly slicing off squares for her to fry. "Not supposed to see ghosts. Not even White people."

"Why not?" Suzanne poked the puffy browning dough with a fork and flipped them over, sizzling in the heavy iron skillet. It's not good to eat such greasy, heavy food, she thought. Diabetes and heart attack food. The treaty issue rations used to be buffalo. "Whites don't believe. Not in our world. They don't believe in them." She looked at Suzanne. "You don't believe, do you, eh?"

Suzanne didn't answer. She just kept on forking brown frybread into a paper bag on the floor.

Edna wiped her floured hands on her apron, left the kitchen, and came out from the back bedroom with a battered red family album. "You finished? Time to take a break." They sat at the kitchen table and drank strong coffee. In the front of the album lay two 9 x 12 glossy portraits of an old Indian man and woman.

Edna put on her glasses. "Ellis Blackcrow and Annie Coldwater. Taken in 1907 in Washington, D.C. Part of the Black Hills Claim delegation. Some museum photographed them. See his medal?"

But Suzanne was staring at the old lady. Trapped in a turn-of-the-century high-necked long-sleeved dress, she looked so much like Selo. The same falling-down eyebrows! Except her braids hung to her waist.

Edna noticed her stare. "Yes, she was a strong one. Small but tough. She claimed the 800 acres given her, even though she had to move away from her family at Cheyenne Creek way out here to keep them. She kept her five sections whole. Never sold out. We'll do the same."

Suzanne sucked her finger, burned by spattering fat while turning frybread.

Edna continued remembering. "She used to ride horseback over to Old Lady Little Thunder's, three miles away, just to *visit*. Every day! In those days people had to visit, not like now, 'Hello-goodbye!'" She reached over and fished two frybreads out of a basket. "Can't eat ceremony food, but I set these out for us."

"She was smart, too," Edna continued. "Always won at bone games. You know, gambling. And they say once she won a Spanish barb. One of those thick buckskin horses with a black stripe down their backs and cream-colored rings around the eyes."

"Yes, Selo showed me one at Austin Two Moon's."

Edna rose stiffly from the table. "Well, time to make the offerings. Red tobacco ties. Not so good to talk about the dead. Leave 'em to rest."

Suzanne was stubborn. "Who I saw was alive. Maybe the old lady in black down by the spring was Old Lady Coldwater. I don't know, but she's real."

"*Wanaghi*, they're real too."

4.

Just after dusk, they heard the sputter of a badly missing engine roar into the driveway. Quickly they loaded the six pots of ceremony food, lids tied on with cloth strips, and two bags of frybread, into the back of the station wagon. In the front seats they put army blankets and denim quilts for the long cold ride.

"You can't sit next to Selo," Edna told her. "He's driving, and Uncle Delbert needs to sit in front."

"Well, I could squeeze in the middle."

Edna looked annoyed. "No, men sit in front. Besides, you can't sit next to Uncle Delbert. He's your father-in-law."

"Oh. Why's Uncle Delbert going?"

"He needs to be doctored, too."

"Oh. Who else is being doctored?"

"Get in! Let's go," Selo said, gently easing the frail old man into the front seat. "We're late."

"Sit in the back with me," Edna said.

Suzanne peered in. There was Auntie Nellie, already in the car. So she quietly climbed in and sat between her and Edna, and the six of them were off. She was still puzzling over how Selo's uncle could be her father-in-law. Night meetings must be like an outing or expedition for the old folks. Oh well.

10

She slept in the packed car, lulled by the dust and washboard ruts as Selo drove over dirt back roads to the next reservation, Rosebud, and onto the paved two-lane hilly road into the Spotted Tail Agency. Ring Thunder lay beyond, out in the country. They said that anyone who had made it out to the old log ceremony cabin through the mud ruts was supposed to be there.

When the car bumped to a stop, she stumbled out in the darkness and into a small log cabin. This one had a plyboard floor, and although smaller than her cabin, two log posts in the center held up the roof.

Selo sat her on one of the long benches lining the walls, one right near the door. "I've got to sit over with the men by the singers," he said. "Stay awake! And no English once it starts! They'll tell you what to do." He gestured at Edna and Aunt Nellie, who were sitting down next to her.

A small wizened man in pearl-buttoned pink cowboy shirt and beaded reservation hat stood and shook her hand. "First *washichu* I heard of seen spirit people. You come to see more?" His lips smiled, his palm paper-thin. "Welcome! We give you the best seat in the house."

Suzanne smiled back. Selo had told her he was a "ghost medicine man," very powerful, because he used the ancestors for his doctoring. "But I didn't see a ghost, I saw a real person. An old lady." She knew she wasn't supposed to answer a medicine man back, but this was getting ridiculous.

"Ohanh," he replied, "*Mini Hlayela.* How lucky."

"Sit still and keep your feet tucked in," Edna whispered in her ear, "so the spirit people won't trip as they come by."

After they nailed blankets over the windows and pounded the door shut, Suzanne drifted off even while trying to stay alert, almost before the kerosene lamp was blown out and the slow steady deep drumbeat began. The room was close and stuffy.

Suddenly the door beside her began to shake. Someone was pounding on it. From the inside, or outside? She should be able to tell, but she didn't move. Then thumps shook the floor.

11

Thumps going around in the darkness. But finally the ancient Lakota songs lulled her, filled her, Lakota prayers blurred in her ears, and she dozed off.

Sometime in the middle of the darkness, Edna shook her awake and told her to stand. Now the air was cold, an old musty smell on the breeze. Soon she heard rattling near her ears, like someone shaking a gourd. Could she be seeing little blue sparks?

Finally Edna tugged her to sit down. Near morning the kerosene lamp was lit again, people stretched and talked and ate. She ate what Edna put in front of her, a bowl of warm beef soup, frybread, potato salad, chocolate cake, *wozhapi*, sliced ham, cold black coffee.

It was over. She knew no one would tell her what had happened while she slept. But everyone seemed happy. Now they could drive home in the pale pre-dawn, frost etching every field and pasture.

5.

Two weeks later Henry Steed and his singer, Larry Black Thunder, came in a pickup pulling a horse trailer. To get Peter's Appaloosa stud. "A fine horse!" he'd said, deciding.

Suzanne didn't understand. She said to Selo, "But that's Peter's horse! You can't give it away! That's our stud! Our only stud. What about all those Appaloosa ponies we're going to breed?"

"That's the one he picked, that's the one he gets."

"But why are we giving him a horse? Why can't we give him that useless color TV?"

"For the doctoring, that's what we owe, a horse."

"What doctoring?"

"You ask too many questions. Don't you remember, the night we went over to Ring Thunder? The night you were doctored?"

"I was doctored?" Suzanne had known something was going on, but not that. "Why have *me* doctored? I told you I saw a real person!"

Selo put his arm around her and walked her over to the creek bank away from the cabin while they caught and loaded Bloketu onto the trailer.

"You mean we have to give the Appaloosa to Henry Steed because he doctored *me*? So I wouldn't see ghosts any more? I can't believe this."

6.

That weekend her son Peter came home from Holy Rosary. Selo and Milo had gone into town for gas. Although she had missed her tall, rangy son growing up so fast, she dreaded seeing the four-wheel drive clinic van drop him off at the edge of the mud road. She knew he'd been waiting since the late March blizzard to get home and ride Bloketu.

As soon as he walked into the cabin, he saw her and started in non-stop. "Where's my horse? He's not in the corral. He's gone! Who stole my horse? How could you let someone steal my horse? How could you let him get away? I've been waiting forever to ride him, and he's gone!"

"Henry Steed wanted him. He came and got him this week."

"You gave away my horse?" He paced in front of the TV. "How could you give away my horse? It's *my* horse, not yours!"

She sighed. "I know. I tried, but if we hadn't given it away when he came for it, we'd have lost it anyway. It'd sicken and die, throw somebody or get stolen, spoiled somehow. If a medicine man wants something, you have to give it, or else..."

"Or else what? You believe in that stuff?" He picked up a braided bridle from the TV and wrapped it around his hands.

"Yes, and no. I just know we had no choice. We'll get you another horse."

His hands ruffled through his short blond hair. "I don't want another horse. I want my Appaloosa stud. He was mine! You don't understand. You just did it because Selo made you. You don't even care about me and my feelings! It's the one thing I

13

have here of my own, and now Selo gives it away, and you don't even stop him. Why doesn't Selo give him *his* horse?"

"He didn't want Red Walker, he wanted the Appaloosa."

"Yeah. My horse. The best one." He looked at her. "Mom, I'm not forgiving you! Or *him!*" She could tell he meant Selo.

She turned her head away. The last of her sons always had it the hardest, not the easiest.

He put down the bridle and came over to her. "Hey, what happened, Mom?"

"Oh, I saw somebody who wasn't there."

He stared at her closely. "Mo-om! What's happened to you?"

"I shouldn't have said I saw anybody. Sorry. I didn't know what would happen. I don't know who I saw, but she's not a ghost. I don't believe in ghosts."

"OK, Mom, OK. I don't either." Good. She wasn't going crazy.

"Look, Mom, you believe in the spirit of God. Just call what you saw a spirit, guardian angel, something."

"OK. I'll think about that."

"Still, I lost my horse. So what'm I gonna ride now?"

"My horse."

"With a nursing colt? I hate it here!" But he took his bridle from the wall and went outside.

She hadn't gone crazy. Somehow the doctoring had saved her, protected from the "ghost" she'd seen, a spirit living in the other world she'd come so close to, so close to "the other side," the land of the dead. She knew it wasn't good to see *wanaghi*. Good to know they were around, protecting and watching over the sundance grounds and the vision pit, good to feel their protective spirit, but not good to *see* them, especially in broad daylight.

I know, she thought. I'll call her the Spirit of the Spring.

7.

A week later after supper Suzanne saw Old Lady Coldwater again, down by the spring. Clear and real as the moon just coming up. So this time Suzanne walked ten steps toward her back and pleaded, "You better help me. Tell me what's going on, because nobody else will."

She listened to the rattling water in the creek, and all around her, the silence.

Swift as a shadow, short as any dream ... - Shakespeare

A DELTA *DREAM*

By Charles Fenno

Whear my cue comes, call me, and I will answer. I have had a dream, *past the wit of man to say what dream it was* sounds in my mind as the alarm rings. I'm vaguely aware of the profound darkness of pre-dawn. Things swim to consciousness after they've happened and I know that I must have bathed and dressed only because we're in the car whirring through a vast stillness softly suffused with a pale, pastel glow that suddenly erupts with teenagers electric with energy, pinwheeling into one waiting car after another until the street is empty and I'm again whirring along, an incomprehensible map on my knees.

Colors melt out of the darkness and a strange, flat landscape snaked with elevated waterways emerges, at first hesitantly and then laid bare by a pitiless, blazing sun. The countryside seems desolate and arid— how can we find a beach to do our play on in this strange place where the water flows fourteen feet above the land?—

"Beach? Beaches aren't in the delta— are they?"

"Oh yes— this one is all grassy with woods all around and a tree, upstage— that's where you enter. Listen up, everybody, everybody enters from the tree upstage, all right?—"

16

"Well what about cues? How will we know our cues— there won't be any sound—"

"Yes, yes, we're bringing a ghetto blaster—"

"And *lights*— what about *lights*??"

"There'll be tiki torches and lanterns, and a full moon. That'll be plenty of light. The faerie procession—"

"But we can't do that, can we?"

"Now wait..."

"Yeah— what about aisles? We don't have any aisles to run down do we? Are there aisles on a beach?"

"Yeah! and what about the flashlights— that'd just be dumb. Who's gonna see flashlights in the woods?"

"No, no, not with flashlights. Sparklers— sparklers and flares and you'll run through the woods— that happens when the boats are arriving."

"Boats?"

"Yes. Now will you listen? They're coming in boats— well, barges, really, and while they're coming in to beach, you're all going to run through the woods with sparklers and flares— it'll be pure magic. That's how we open."

"NEAT!!"

"Boy, that's going to be something!"

"Are we going to do the show on the boat?"

"Yes. Well, partly— the comedians— listen, now— comedians are on the boat with Theseus and his party seated amongst the guests— we're doing that part of the play while they're eating dinner."

"Yeah, and we're gonna throw Hermia overboard!"

"Is that right? Is that right? Oh boy, oh boy, we're gonna throw Hermia in the water."

"How're we gonna do that? How're we gonna get her over the sides?"

"The boats are very low— now just calm down a minute, all of you— the boats are just sort of barges— but only if Hermia agrees, is that understood?"

"But you know what? You know what? I bet this is the first time anyone's done *Midsummer Night's Dream* at the summer solstice— huh? Huh? Isn't it?"

"Yeah, and a full moon, too— don't forget that—"

"Well *is* it?"

"I don't know. Now will you listen—"

"Well I bet it's the first time on a beach in the delta—"

We arrive down a long, lumpy dirt road to the foot of some farmer's corn field with the levee rising on the other side of the field. Everyone is loaded with blankets and sleeping bags and picnic baskets, props and costumes, everything anyone thought to bring. We trudge across the furrows of the corn field, climb the steep bank of the levee and then down a steep wash and so onto a tiny scrap of lumpy, weedy beach. Everybody mills about in dismay.

"What!!? This is the stage???"

"Somebody lied to us!!"

"Well where are we supposed to act? In the water?"

"Hey—!, water!!"

"NO! No! Now just hold your horses, there'll be time for that later. Now I want everybody in a circle, sitting, all right? Everybody? In a circle...SIT!! Now I can't be shouting at you all day— I have to have something left for tonight, too, so just listen" and we listen in steep dejection, huddled together on the tiny, weed infested beach while Pat runs through the day's activities. I hold my ghetto blaster mournfully— it's tiny and broken and the sound booth is going to be in the middle of a straggly, bare bush which provides no cover— I'm going to stick out like a sore thumb.

The sun beats everything into wilted defeat. Every time a break is called, exuberant bodies fling themselves into the slough to be called— no, shouted— back, drooping and weary to the run-through.

"What's next? What scene are we working now?"

"Ly-SAN-der!! Come on, will you? You're holding everything up."

"Well it's not my fault— he threw me in and my shoes are wet—" flinging himself to the ground in sudden, desperate despair, "I can't act with wet shoes. I can't."

"Well it was just for a joke."

"ALL RIGHT! That's enough of this bickering. No more throwing anybody in, is that clear? Now take your places— we have to get through this scene so you know the blocking."

Sunset. The levee bank is a fringe of tender gold. The beach is swallowed in shadow. From all sides the high-pitched, mirthful chatter of adolescents mingles with the chirping of birds and the high hum of insects. I see the kids traipsing back and forth on the levee road bedangled in ribbons and full of anxious dismays and rivalries.

"Is this too much make-up?"

"Who cares? They can't see anything anyway."

"How's this?"

"PAT!"

"In a minute!! I'm CHANGING!!"

"Ohh that's right! That's right, just push your faeries in the bushes, Marjorie, see if we care!"

The slough wends away in silver sheen like some path no man can tread. All is calm now— the trees still, birds and bugs quieted, only our urgent preparations breaking the peace of this sunset.

Everything begins to come to life as costumes are donned. The horizon is pastel pink fading to robin's egg blue, all about us is an immense, peaceful silence.

"I hear boats!! I hear boats!!"

"Where's my hat!?! But I have to have my hat!! PAAT!!"

"In the *prop* box— everything is in the *prop* box."

"Hey, it's gonna be all right, isn't it? You think it's gonna be all right, Pat?"

"It's going to be perfect, absolute magic. I know."

"Well where's the moon? Isn't there supposed to be a moon?"

High, pink-hued clouds drift past as night slowly, softly settles. Little airy fillips of fancy twine into the preparations: Bottom

19

stands in straw hat, leaning against a stump, starring across mirror-still waters. Now Changeling and a faerie dip their fingers in the water and send an echo of ripples out to vanish into stillness. The last of the light ebbs like a fast-flowing tide. The pages sit in a circle, applying make-up and Puck, in ribbons and briefs, stops to stare.

"THE MOON!! THE MOON!! COME AND SEE THE MOON!"

Everybody runs up to the levee road where a huge, pale pink moon floats just above the horizon across green fields of corn. Behind us the sunset is all purple hued and vanishing. The kids form a long line on the levee road and stare in silent wonderment on a moon translucent as a bubble.

"Gee there *is* a moon. They didn't lie to us after all."

"Oh my God, the boats are coming!! Here come the boats!!"

"HEY HEY HEY, can't you hear? The boats are coming!!"

Already the moon has changed— now it's gold, still huge, rising into the sky. Everybody races down the side of the levee, back to the beach, back into the shadows— day is gone, taking with it its glaring incredulity.

"COME *ON* EVERYBODY..."

"Naw, it was just a motorboat— it's not them."

Back at the beach dusk lingers in a pale glow along the horizon; the moon is still below the levee. One star shines forth. The moon, when it reaches the beach, will be all a hard silver shinning, small and very bright.

Now my arbor is a dark retreat. I creep into its shadows and know the sound booth will be hidden as it should be. The beach is small and bright, the tiki torches giving it a medieval quality.

"Will somebody tell me if my costume works? Please??"

Oberon holds a flashlight on himself. He's all bedecked with Christmas tinsel and his costume shimmers and glistens as though flock of stars has come to dance about his body.

"Look at Oberon! Look at Oberon! Oh that's cool."

The moon lifts above the levee, and I can see it through my arbor, a shining silver disk through a black lacework of leaves. Still no boats. The actors are sitting in a circle now, holding hands, almost motionless, silent. Snug the joiner stands apart, a lonely sentinel at the water's edge, watching for the boats. What today were dingy aluminum flat-bottom barges are now gloriously improbable ferries of magic festooned with Chinese lanterns. The guests, all in white and sitting about the boat talking, are like substantial ghosts intent on routine occupations. The boats land, the passengers disembark like a line of apparitions descending from the glowing boats onto the dark land, their pale clothes gleaming in the moonlight. The play begins. The tiki torches are already burned out. Only the moon illuminates this convocation of ghosts rejoicing in the antics of shadows. I sit in my bower of blackness intently listening for my cues.

This world is not conclusion;
A sequel stands beyond ... - Emily Dickinson

CAN OF COKE

by Colleen Crangle

So there I was, minding my own business as they say, which in this place means minding *their* business, when she walked up the aisle between Linguistics and the Sociology of Religion and said to me: "I know what you did." I did not want to talk about it, so I climbed down the steps and turned to go, leaving a pile of unshelved books stranded up there among the oversized sociology tomes. "I have to say it," she said. "Thank you, Minezayo."

I stopped in my tracks. Minezayo? Since when have I been Minezayo to her? No longer Sammy, am I? Now I'm Minezayo, my given name but not one whites are inclined to use. It's too difficult they say, they with their Oosthuizens and Urquharts and Viljoens. *Viljoen* — that's a soft *v* like the *f* in *deaf* and a soft *j* like the *y* in *you*. But I did not want to talk about this thank-you business so I, Minezayo, walked away. She — her name is Alice, Miss Alice Hilborn, chief deputy library specialist — she stood there and I, Mr. Minezayo Notile, walked away.

You see, it's not that I've got anything against her but I know her type. Nice, kind, respectful, English-speaking liberal who always treats me right. And then she goes home, five minutes drive to her spruce little flat on the beachfront with a tenth-story view of Algoa Bay — I know because I heard her describe it

22

once. Me, I head home on the bus, three buses to be exact, to a room in my mother's house, and I light a candle, no not to pray, but so I can read my Gilbert Ryle and post my homework to the University of South Africa and eventually, maybe four years from now, get my bachelor's degree. And then come back to work in the morning shelving, sorting, picking up in this place. I know her type. Always proper, no overt offense. Take, for instance, what I heard her say to her boss Gerrit Viljoen last week. They got a word for it now in America I read — *politically correct*. Alice Hilborn is politically correct. (One advantage of working in a university library is you get to read American newspapers. Like yesterday, I was leaning on the table perusing the *San Francisco Chronicle*, sipping a can of Coke I'd slipped in under my jacket. There I discover that the way they know if you're just pretending to be deaf is: you talk into a microphone and it plays back your words through earphones, delayed a fraction of a second. If you can hear, you get confused and start stammering. Interesting things like that I pick up in those newspapers all the time.)

Anyway, as I said, I heard our politically correct Alice say something to her boss Viljoen last week. Viljoen, I know his type too. He's run this library ever since the university opened in the late sixties. A bold new experiment they called it, English and Afrikaans students together in this bilingual country for the first time. Bilingual? Ever heard of Xhosa, of Zulu, of Sotho, I asked them in that way I have of carrying on conversations with myself through my mother who's now sick and tired of having her grown son still living with her. Time you got yourself a wife she always says to me, and stop all this nonsense I don't understand. Don't understand? What I don't understand is how a woman as smart as my mother can marry a man who's called Sixpence, yes that's what they used to call my father, and not say to him, Thembisile, you are not to have that name used anymore.

Well, last week, Gerrit Viljoen was telling Alice what to do. There was a broken shelf, see. Lopsided it was, with all its books slipping, leaning to the left. I was walking nearby selecting worn

23

books for rebinding. Viljoen said to our Miss Alice Hilborn, "See that shelf over there?" He pointed in my direction. "Over there, by the boy. That's the one that must be fixed." The 'boy' is me and Alice said, casually but with emphasis to teach him a lesson, "That shelf by that black gentleman? Who is it, I can't quite see? Oh, it's Mr. Notile." He looked at her funny and she half bowed to rub in the point. Me, I ignored them both and went over to help Raj who was searching again for another biology book. (They have Indian students here these days. The bold experiment recently got bolder.)

That, as I said, was last week. Then this morning things got a lot more complicated. I was doing a massive job near Viljoen's desk, removing all the natural history books and replacing them with all the volumes in the Afrikaner collection. They've got open office plan here now and Viljoen's little desk is against the wall beside those shelves. (He's a large man but he has a little desk.) Alice came over to Viljoen. I could tell it was an appointment by the way she sat down. She saw me but didn't want to say anything to offend me is my guess — such as, excuse me, Mr. Notile, may I talk to Mr Viljoen in private for just a minute? Viljoen, he acted like I wasn't there. Invisible. I was so close, two rungs up on the stepladder, I could have reached out and, with a stretch, tweaked his ear. This is what he ended up saying to her.

"I can't give you that job, dearie. You're a woman." Her face went tight. "You're not ready. Besides, there're men who need it more than you. They got families, you know. And men don't want to report to a woman."

Alice did her best, I'll hand it to her. She said she had seniority (been there 15 years), was better qualified, had a better disposition, and worked longer hours. He just seemed amused. "More spunk too," he said with flimsy condescension that must've stung like a paper cut, almost invisible.

That was when things got complicated. They continued talking, moving on to other matters. I had all these empty boxes to load up with books, right next to his desk. Quite casually, I stepped off the ladder, filled a box with volumes from the bottom shelf, stacked another box on top, and went on packing one carton after another. Viljoen was getting irritated by this time, I could see, but he had ordered this rearrangement of books and I was in no mood to be messed with. I think he knew. His eyes flashed back and forth from Alice to me but they never lingered long on my labors. Alice looked at me once, then averted her eyes.

Finally I was finished, a solid wall of boxes stretching from his little desk to the now quite empty shelves, him on one side of the wall, me and the rest of the world on the other. Viljoen was completely cornered. Jammed up close on the far side of his desk was a deep metal filing cabinet, and to squeeze past there he'd have to sit on the desk and slither along, his feet dangling. That's what I wanted to see, or else him clambering over the top of the desk, or, heaven forbid, actually moving some of the heavy boxes himself. But I didn't stick around to watch. I thought it best to take my leave while he was still in conversation.

Alice knew what I was doing. By the time I left, her grin was as wide as a river. But I didn't think she'd ever talk about it. I certainly don't want to. That's why I walked away just now. Thing is, I didn't know I had it in me to take revenge on her behalf — petty revenge I grant you, but still very satisfying and still revenge. Didn't know I had it in me and I don't want to think about what it means. It feels a little like I'm talking into a mike, trying to prove I'm deaf but finding myself stuttering and having to admit that I, Minezayo Notile, can still hear.

The purpose of punishment is to improve those who punish...
- Nietzsche

THE SHOPLIFTER

by Paul Pekin

There was a young woman examining costume jewelry at the
end of the counter, an attractive young black woman, well
dressed and self-assured with long silky legs and smooth dark
hair pulled back tight, ballerina style, and it was good to see her;
it honestly was; she might have been an advertisement for
America where things really were getting better.

Zinman was that kind of an optimist. Where others saw decay
and decline, he saw hope. History, for all its wars, famines, and
plagues, clearly told a tale of progress, a journey begun in ignorance, savagery, and fear, that led steadily, inevitably, toward
enlightenment.

Then he stole another glance. Just in time to see this attractive
black girl boldly drop something into the bottom of her purse.

At first it almost seemed a trick of the eye, but then she did it
again, and it became very clear what she was about. Zinman
immediately put down a bracelet he had picked up and looked
around, as if expecting to be accused himself.

Several aisles down, a clerk was bent over her counter in conversation with a customer. Both were black women, and for a
moment Zinman felt the peculiar sensation of being the only one

of his kind present. This was not quite true. Other white people were making their way through the store, men as well as women. But the only employee in immediate view was that clerk.

Approaching, he saw that she was not nearly as young or attractive as the shoplifter. Her short straightened hair was cut in a style reminiscent of the Doris Day of those old movies (if, in fact, it were not a wig) and she wore heavy eyeglasses that seemed to bear down unmercifully upon her broad brown nose.

"I beg your pardon," Zinman said. "I beg your pardon, but that young lady over there just dropped something into her purse."

The clerk and the customer both turned. The customer was an older woman with hair dyed a peculiar shade of orange/red. Zinman recognized that shade. Several of the teachers at his school used it, as did the assistant principal.

"What did you say?" the clerk asked.

"I said that young woman over there just dropped something into her purse," Zinman repeated, lowering his voice.

"You say she's stealing something?" the customer asked.

"I believe she is," Zinman said. "I saw her drop several items into her purse."

The clerk turned, picked up a telephone, and began talking into it quietly. Facing the customer, Zinman decided he had never liked any woman, black or white, who wore her hair that shade of red. A moment later he heard a voice on the public address speaker saying:

"Security. Report to aisle eleven."

Obviously the shoplifter heard this too. Without turning, Zinman knew she was looking directly at him. Then a man in uniform appeared at the end of the aisle, walking swiftly.

"Huh," the woman with the red hair said. "He's going to make a name for himself."

The shoplifter placed her purse beneath her arm and started away, slowly, head held high. She was a stunningly handsome girl, Zinman thought. But when his eyes met those of the security guard, he signalled toward her, and the guard nodded. A mo-

27

ment later the guard had the young woman by the arm and was leading her straight to Zinman.

This was not what he had bargained for.

"Is she the one?" the guard asked. The guard was a young Hispanic man with a dark mustache and a slight paunch, and there was something about him that tempted Zinman to drop the whole matter right then and there. But of course it was too late for that.

"Yes," he said. "I saw her put several items into her purse."

"Oh, no sir," the young woman said. "You could not have seen that. I did not put anything in my purse."

"The man says you did," the guard snapped. "Now open up and let's have a look."

"You are not going to look into my purse!" the young woman said with great conviction. "Nobody is going to look in my purse!"

A moment later Zinman found himself and the young woman being escorted by the guard toward a room at the back of the store. It was almost as if they were both under arrest.

"We'll check that purse, don't you worry, lady," the guard promised.

There was another security officer behind a desk in the back room, a black man with dark mirrored glasses hiding his face, and long thin hands that never stopped moving. "What you got here, Angelo?" he asked.

"The gentleman saw this lady put something in her purse."

"Nobody is going to look in my purse," the young woman repeated with considerable force.

"Come on, baby," the black man with the long thin hands said. "You know I don't allow no bitch to talk to me like that." He snatched the purse from her grip, and dumped the contents upon his desk. Zinman was both startled and relieved to see an entire collection of costume jewelry, complete with price tags, glittering before his eyes. The black man snapped his fingers. "Now look at that! What would anybody want with all this trash? You bitches ain't got no sense at all."

"I paid for that," the young woman cried.

"Tell that stuff to somebody else, baby. Don't tell it to me." The black man picked up a telephone and began talking in a low voice.

"I can prove it," the young woman insisted.

"So go prove it," the black man said. "Show us the receipts."

"I don't carry around receipts. I bought those things last week, and I got witnesses to prove it."

"Wait till your witnesses find out they can get five years for perjury!"

The young woman turned upon Zinman. "Mister! You never saw me put anything in my purse! Why do you say such a thing?"

"I'm sorry," Zinman said. "I saw what I saw."

"You're sorry? *You're* sorry? You got a lot to be sorry about!"

She would have made an excellent actress. If Zinman had not actually seen her put the jewelry into her purse, he would have believed her every word.

* * *

That night Zinman told the story to Joanne, the woman he lived with. Joanne was tall and pale and slightly older than himself with a daughter of twelve who did not get along with people. He had not known Joanne before his divorce, and probably would not have made much of her if he had. They'd met at Parents Without Partners and chosen each other with less deliberation than most people give to the purchase of a new appliance. Probably he was a man who could not live without a woman; undoubtedly she had needs of her own. Why should either be ashamed of that?

"You called the police?" Joanne did not like the police; her ex-husband had stalked her for over a year and the police had, if anything, taken his side.

"Not the police," Zinman explained. "I just reported it to a clerk, and she called security. Then *they* called the police."

29

If Zinman were an optimist, the same could not be said of Joanne. For her the world did not at all seem to be getting better, and she had scars on her body to prove it. The apartment they shared, and the furnishings in it, were hers, all she had left from her marriage, other than these scars. In his divorce, Zinman had lost even more, but things were getting better. Since his wife had taken the boy out of state contrary to the agreement, he was no longer paying child support. It was an ugly situation that filled him with shame, but financially, at least, he was on his way back.

"You should never get yourself involved in something like that," Joanne insisted. "All you had to do was look the other way. It frightens me to think what might happen. People like that. They always find a way to get even."

"Oh, don't worry about that," Zinman said. "She's just a young woman. How would she even know where I live?"

"Where *we* live," Joanne corrected. "And young women often have young men for friends. People like that always know how to find out what they wish to know."

She busied herself at the sink and Zinman, who was setting the table, wondered if he ought to wrap his arms around her and offer such comfort as he could.

"I suppose you're right," he conceded. "Of course you are. The girl only took a few trinkets. She certainly didn't look as if she needed them. There are people like that, they can't help them-selves ..."

"Kleptomaniacs," Joanne said. "But that's not what she is. She's a criminal."

"Well, I never expected they would involve me."

It was the best he could do.

Except for the salad, dinner was pretty much a prefabricated affair, microwave pasta, ham slices, oven warmed rolls. Joanne had little interest in cooking, or eating either for that matter. Life for her was a matter of putting one foot in front of another and doing what you had to do. As soon as the plates were set, she called her daughter away from the television.

30

Nicole was as unlike her mother as a daughter possibly could be, dark, brooding and broad shouldered with thick black brows that almost grew together. Looking at this girl who, if not attractive, was swelling with adolescent sexuality, Zinman could easily imagine the father he had never seen. She dropped heavily into her chair and pushed the salad bowl away.

"You know I don't eat this stuff."

"More for me," Zinman said mildly.

"I heard you guys talking. Did you really turn that girl over to the police?"

"You shouldn't be eavesdropping on adults," Joanne said.

"What am I supposed to do? Put on ear muffs?"

"It's all right," Zinman said quickly. "She has every right in the world to ask." He repeated the story of the shoplifter to Joanne's daughter, adding several details he had missed in the first telling.

As soon as he was finished Nicole said, "I think that's terrible. That's just a terrible thing to do."

"But she was stealing. What if she were stealing something that belonged to you?"

"That'd be different. But she was stealing from the store. They'd never even miss that stuff."

"Maybe not," Zinman conceded. "But in the end we all pay for it in the form of higher prices."

"Big deal," Nicole said, poking at her plate. She ate almost nothing at home, and yet managed to be a dozen pounds overweight. "Big big deal. I suppose if it were one of your students you'd turn him in too. What if it were me? Would you turn me in?"

"Nicole!" Joanne did not like the tone of this talk. Zinman was flattered to see how carefully she protected their relationship. But the girl had asked a legitimate question, and it deserved an answer.

"If it had been you," he said. "I would have asked you to put the things back."

"So why didn't you ask her?"

This was something that had not occurred to Zinman. Now that he thought of it, he saw how foolish it would have been. Caught red handed with the stolen goods spread out on the desk before her, the young woman had still denied her guilt.

"Let's just hope no trouble comes of this," Joanne said.

"You don't have to worry," Zinman assured her. "We probably won't hear another thing on the subject."

"But you'll have to go to court!"

"Yes," Zinman sighed. "Next time, I guess I will look the other way."

Weeks went by and there were no mysterious phone calls, no shadowy figures outside the building, no unusual vehicles cruising the block. Instead the school year began and Zinman found himself once again involved in life's familiar routines.

Zinman taught English and English Literature at a mid-sized suburban high school that, in a sense, was on the wrong side of the tracks. In recent years the Hispanic population of the district had increased dramatically, and this was reflected in the student body. Some of his colleagues viewed these newcomers as a burden, but Zinman welcomed the challenge. Perhaps because he was that kind of a person, the administration had asked him to take on a Social Science class this fall, even though he had never taught the subject before. "Just go by the book," he was told. But as soon as he read the book he saw it was dry and outdated, and he immediately began researching Latin American history and literature. If so many of his students were to be Mexican, it seemed only right he learn something of their culture and incorporate it into this class.

Zinman honestly liked to teach. Each fall he was caught up in the excitement of new classes and new faces, and now a new subject. The shoplifter slipped into the back of his thoughts, even as the day he was to accuse her in court drew near. Nothing would come of it, he decided. The lawyers would offer some slap-on-the-wrist plea bargain, the shoplifter would agree, the judge would go along, and he would not even be called to the stand. Recalling the stories of courtroom justice Joanne had told him, Zinman confidently believed this.

Because he was home every afternoon before Joanne, he usually found himself in charge of her daughter several hours every day. Nicole was not pleasant company. For the most part she simply sat in front of the television, flipping channels, no better satisfied with what she found there than with her companions at school. But there were occasions when she would lift her dark head and seek him out in the dining room which he used as a study.

He would be at work on his students' papers, carefully marking the margins with red ink.

"Why do you do that?" she would say.

"It's my job."

"They're not going to read that stuff, you know."

"What makes you say that?"

"Because I know how kids are. All they're interested in is one thing."

"Which is?"

"You know."

This was not a subject Zinman wanted to discuss with Joanne's daughter. "I'm teaching them about Mexican history," he said.

"I thought you were an English teacher."

"English *and* Social Science this year. Did you know that the Indians in Mexico lived in cities the same as we do?"

"Why did your wife divorce you?"

"I —" Zinman caught himself up short. Did this girl really expect him to discuss his marriage with her?

"Did you cheat on her?"

What kind of a question was that? "I can see why you don't have any friends!" he snapped.

Zinman regretted these words instantly, but they did not seem to upset Nicole, who said:

"I don't want any friends. I'm my own friends."

She was a troubled child. Young people needed stability in their lives. You could see that at school when you were forced to trust

33

your students to a substitute. Sometimes it took a week to undo the confusion of a single day.

On the morning he was to appear in court, Zinman made sure he had left carefully detailed lesson plans for those who would take his place while he was off. It was always less upsetting if the substitute had some written assignment she could busy the kids with, rather than launching off into something of her own. The best way to avoid problems was to anticipate them in advance.

At the courthouse entrance, he was stopped and checked, presumably for firearms, by a uniformed blonde woman who passed an electronic device along his body until she found metal — his house keys which he removed from his pocket sheepishly, almost as if he believed himself guilty of some infraction. He remembered this drill from the divorce — there had been a courtroom shooting several months earlier and new security regulations were its legacy. One afternoon his lawyer had pointed out the very room where it had happened, another lawyer gunned down by a sore loser. "They always blame the attorney," Zinman's lawyer complained, and then added, wickedly, "And sometimes they're right!"

The woman at the information desk directed him down the hall and around a corner. A crowd of very disreputable people filled the passage outside the courtroom. With an uneasy little thrill, Zinman realized that many of them must be defendants in some criminal case or another. He looked for the shoplifter — his jewel thief — but did not see her.

Inside the courtroom several clerks were huddled behind the barrier, studying some kind of document. Zinman went to them with the papers the police had given him. "Am I even in the right place?"

"You'll have to wait," the older of the two women said. "Can't you see we're busy here?"

Both wore that identical shade of orange/red hair coloring that Zinman so disliked.

Then a young man — he could not have been older than 25 —
showed up and introduced himself as the assistant state's attorney. "Take a seat, Mr. Zinman," he advised. "We'll call your
name when the case comes up."
Zinman was confused. "Shouldn't we talk about it first?"
"What for?" the young man said, glancing at the sheaf of papers
he was carrying in his left hand. "Just grab a seat. I'll see if I
can get the case moved up so you aren't here all day."
This was something the young man was not successful in
doing. Court did not even start for another 45 minutes, and when
the shoplifter's name finally was called, no one responded.
"Your honor," he said. "The defendant is not here. The state
requests that her bond be forfeited and the court issue a warrant
... "
"Does it now?" the judge said. "When the court decides to issue
a warrant, the court will issue a warrant. Meanwhile, we'll just
move that case back and see if she shows up."
The state's attorney turned to Zinman who by now was sitting
between two large women. "We have a witness who's been ..."
"I said, we'll wait!"
The state's attorney shrugged for Zinman's benefit.
But Zinman was not in the least upset. He had already taken
the day off, and this opportunity to sit through a criminal court
session, so different from divorce court proceedings, promised
to be a valuable experience, something he might even incorporate into his classes. Here in the United States, the wealthiest
and most progressive nation of the world, even the most obviously flawed of its citizens was given the full protection of the
law. That would be something he could talk about.
The proceedings were not easy to follow. In most cases Zinman
was unable to determine what people were even charged with,
usually some violation of chapter such and such, section such
and such as read off by the clerk, and the defendants clarified
nothing, standing before the bench with hands clasped behind
backs as if still in manacles, speaking in hushed voices obviously
meant to be heard by as few ears as possible. Straining to make

sense out of what was before him, Zinman wondered if the people who wrote those courtroom dramas ever visited an actual trial. When he opened his notebook and uncapped a pen, a deputy immediately leaned around one of the large women and informed him that note taking was not permitted while court was in session.

Shortly before noon, the clerk called the shoplifter's name for the second time and a voice somewhere in the rear of the room answered.

"Mary Brown?" The clerk repeated. "Step forward."

By now Zinman, smothered between the two large women, had almost dozed off. It took him a moment to accept that the thin young black woman in blue jeans moving toward the bench was Mary Brown, and that Mary Brown was in fact the shoplifter he was about to accuse. She seemed younger, and not nearly as tall as she had been in Fielding's, and her hair was entirely different, kinky and short, and there was a slump in her shoulders he had never expected to see.

The judge, frowning at the document he held in his hands, seemed profoundly disturbed by something in these proceedings. He was an older man, perhaps a veteran of too many sloppily prepared trials. "I do not see," he said to the state's attorney, "your complaining witness."

"He's here, he's here!" the state's attorney cried.

"Well, let him step up then!" the judge snapped back. Zinman was forced to stand next to the shoplifter. For some reason he could not bring himself to think of her as Mary Brown. They both looked straight forward and tried to pretend the other did not exist.

"Well what is this all about?" the judge asked in exasperation. "Are you an employee of Fielding's?"

He was speaking to Zinman.

"No, your honor," Zinman replied.

"Then why are you here? Where is the representative of the store? Where is the arresting officer? What am I supposed to do with this?" He tossed the complaint angrily aside and glared at Zinman, as if he were the one expected to provide the answers.

Zinman turned to the state's attorney who was reading his copy of the complaint as rapidly as he could.

"Your honor," the young man said. "The defendant is charged with retail theft."

"I know what the defendant is charged with. I can read as well as you. I asked this man a question."

"Your honor," Zinman said, his heart suddenly pounding. "They made me sign the complaint. I simply reported what ..."

"Who made you sign a complaint!"

"The store security guards."

"They held a gun to your head?"

"No, sir. They just said I had to sign it."

"I see you're easily influenced. Mary Brown!" The judge now turned his attention to the shoplifter.

"Yes, sir."

"Do you have an attorney?"

"No, sir."

"You're charged with a Class A Misdemeanor. You could spend a year in the House of Correction. Is that what you want?"

"No, sir."

"Then you need an attorney."

"I can't afford one."

"Has anyone told you the court will appoint a public defender to represent you if you cannot afford your own attorney?"

"I guess so."

"You guess so." The judge turned to the state's attorney. "Does the state have any suggestions?"

"Ahhhh," the young man fumbled. "The state requests a continuance."

The judge now looked to his clerk who, running her polished fingernail over the calendar, found an open date. "October 17."

"October 17 it is," the judge said. "Mr. State's Attorney, please see to it that you have your case in order. Miss Brown, we have a public defender here who will talk to you. I advise you to pay

37

attention to what he says. The court will recess." Before Zinman could react, the judge and his long black robes had swept out of the room.

"What are we supposed to do now?" Zinman asked the woman standing next to him.

"I have no idea," Mary Brown said.

* * *

That evening at the dinner table Zinman told his story to Joanne. "I'm sorry I signed that complaint," he confessed. "It turns out she's really a nice girl. I spoke to her after court and ..."

"She's a criminal. Probably a prostitute too. You don't want to have anything to do with her!"

Joanne was having a hard time at work. Her company had been sold and the new owners were reorganizing, clearing out "dead wood." One of their new young men had lowered her evaluation and spoken ominously of her future. No wonder she was jumpy.

Nicole put down her fork. "I'll bet that girl is pretty."

"Why would you bet that?" Zinman said.

"Is she?"

"Yes. I've already mentioned it. Several times."

"Then I win the bet."

"Nicole ..." Joanne said.

"Yes, I know. 'Nicole, shut up.'"

Zinman held his tongue. This was between mother and daughter. He was ... well, he was only a substitute.

The next morning, as soon as he got to school, he knew one of his own substitutes had left him with a problem. There was a curious silence when he entered the office to pick up his records, and he did not fail to notice the odd looks his first period students cast his way. But it was not until he reached his Social Science class that he discovered the source.

The written assignment he had left for his substitute had not been done. "What happened here," he asked the students.

"We talked," Maria Anglaiz said.

"The whole period?"

"Yeah. Ms. Kapell ..."

"The substitute?"

"Yeah. She was talking, you know, about Mexico."

"Ah. She's Mexican?"

"No. But she's been there."

"Then that must have been interesting."

But Zinman could see that every member of the class was looking at him as if with new eyes.

"All right, Maria," he said. "Let's have it."

She was his best student, bright, pretty, and bold. He imagined her someday leading a class of her own.

"We want to know one thing," she said. "How come you teach us our ancestors were a bunch of cannibals?"

"I teach what?"

"You said, you know, that they cut the hearts out of people. Thousands of people. And you said they ate them!"

Zinman was no fool. He instantly understood.

"And Ms. Kapell said?" he asked gently.

"She said it never happened. She said if they'd have killed all those people, scientists would have found the bones by now. She said it was just a story the white men made up, so they would have an excuse to kill the Indians."

"Well now." Zinman took a deep breath. "Did she tell you where she read this?"

Now Paul Alvarez who always sat in the back row spoke up, his voice sharp and bristling with danger. "She don't have to read it. She was down there. Why do we have to believe something just because it was in some book?"

"We're talking about something that happened over five hundred years ago," Zinman said. His mind was racing ahead. The art, the culture, the glory of Aztec civilization, the Spanish Inquisition, the crusades, the witch hunts of the middle ages, the steady march toward enlightenment; he was going to have to get it all in, and how was he to find the class time?

39

He wasn't. And when the bell finally rang, he knew what it was to teach in the nineties.

Later that day, he knew even better. He was called into the assistant principal's office and told he must issue an apology to the entire Spanish-speaking student body.

"Now wait one minute," he said. "It's a known historical fact that the Aztecs practiced human sacrifice. As did, at some point in history, almost every human culture. Are we to teach the Romans did not hold those games lest we offend our Italian students? Are we to teach the Inquisition never occurred lest we offend the Catholics? What about ..."

Mrs. Cunningham interrupted here. "The point is that I don't recall you were asked to teach Mexican History at all."

Mrs. Cunningham was one of those women who wore her hair in that shade of orangish-red. "The students feel humiliated," she continued. "They feel you have depicted them to their classmates as the descendants of savages."

"They didn't feel that way until yesterday," Zinman said. "Who is this Ms. Kapell? I left a specific class plan for her to follow, and I get this instead!"

"I want you to write out a statement," Mrs. Cunningham said. "Have something for me tomorrow morning. I'm sure that when you think it over, you'll know what to say."

Zinman, angered, but not to the extent of folly, excused himself, saying he would think the matter over. This Ms. Kapell, who was she? where was she from? what was she? She had to be given her due; she had certainly stirred up the students and made them think!

At home, there was Nicole before the television, flipping channels. "Did they give you a medal?" she asked.

"For what?"

"Going to court with that girl."

Zinman laughed. He had almost forgotten the shoplifter. What an irony. Now he, the accuser, was accused himself.

40

The statement he wrote for Mrs. Cunningham admitted neither fault nor error, but nevertheless expressed regret. "It was never my intent ... to offend our students of Mexican heritage ..."

Of course, it only made matters worse. Within days, activists were on the scene with pickets and a list of demands for the school board. First among these demands was the unnegotiable call for his discharge. Entering his car after school, he was ambushed by a television crew and asked if he really believed Native Americans were cannibals. That was how the reporter put it. "Do you have a statement to make?"

"I'll make a statement," Zinman said angrily. "If you want to know about the history of Mexico, go to the library and get a book. That's what intelligent people do, instead of listening to television."

Naturally when this statement aired, the words "instead of listening to television" had been edited out. "Go to the library and get a book," he heard himself say. "That's what intelligent people do."

"They're out to get me," he told Joanne. "It's a good thing we have a union."

"They don't care at all about you. And they don't care whether the Aztecs ate their own mothers," Joanne said. "They're only thinking about what they can get for themselves. Didn't you hear their list of demands? Hire more Spanish-speaking teachers. Offer classes on Mexican culture. Et cetera. Et cetera. They'll have you eating tacos in the lunchroom."

"Well then, maybe some good will come of this," Zinman said.

"Only you would say something like that," she replied. Zinman was relieved to see her taking the whole business better than he would have expected, probably because her own fortunes had taken a sudden turn for the better. The young man who lowered her evaluation had himself been eased out of the company, and her ex-husband — according to friends — had not only been arrested for drunk driving, but sentenced to 90 days in jail for fighting with the officers.

41

That night Zinman made love to her, doing his best to ignore the heavy steps of Nicole outside the bedroom door. Joanne was a comforting partner, warm, and gently scented. Things would work out; Zinman knew they would. It would only take time.

The weeks that followed suggested they might. The mysterious Ms. Kapell may have turned his very best student, Maria Anglaiz, into his most implacable foe, but that foe now arrived in class every day bearing armloads of books arguing the case against Columbus and the five hundred year genocide his "discovery" initiated. Lively class discussions followed. Even Paul Alvarez was reading. This was what education was all about!

Then, the second court date arrived and Zinman was once again forced to trust his students to a substitute. Would it be Ms. Kapell again? He would simply have to wait and see.

Outside the courtroom Zinman was met by the assistant state's attorney, this time a heavy-set young woman with some kind of a deformity in her right foot that caused her to wear a special shoe. Behind her thick glasses, there was the look of a competitor; she had all her papers in order, had seen that the guard from Fielding's and the arresting police officer were on the scene and prepared to testify; she was ready for action.

"It's the first case on the docket," she told Zinman. "Now tell me exactly what you saw."

Zinman repeated his story which, by now, he had repeated so often to so many people he was beginning to wonder if it were still true. "I was expecting," he concluded, "that you would make some kind of an offer ..."

"I'm not bargaining on this one," the state's attorney grimly declared. "Let them plead guilty, then we'll bargain."

Across the hall, Zinman saw the shoplifter conferring with the public defender who was also a woman, dark haired and very attractive. Comparing these two young attorneys, Zinman thought of Maria Anglaiz and her armloads of books and wondered if he should encourage her to consider a career in law.

In contrast, the shoplifter seemed drab and inattentive, not at all the self-assured young woman he had seen in Fielding's. Once again Zinman wished there were some way he could undo his moment of civic righteousness. Today, at least, should see an end to this business.

He could not have been more wrong. As soon the case was called, the attractive young public defender stepped forward and asked for a continuance.

The judge, this time a genial avuncular man with a large whiskey nose, smiled indulgently. "On what grounds, my dear?"

The public defender returned his smile.

"The State had its continuance," she said. "I believe we are entitled to one as well."

Ignoring the State's obvious exasperation, the judge nodded, and the case was set back to Christmas week. This shoplifter drama, apparently, had every possibility of being an element in Zinman's life well beyond that.

Moments later he was back in the hallway with an entire open morning to spend as he pleased. It seemed as good a time as any to try the courthouse cafeteria, a clean busy place where you carried your tray to a table of your choice and sipped coffee in the company of lawyers, court officers, uniformed police, and other members of the legal profession. Zinman found an unoccupied table at the far end of the crowded room and settled in. He was peeling the plastic wrap from his sweet roll when he felt a presence standing over his table.

"Is it all right if I sit here?"

Zinman looked up and saw his shoplifter holding a tray of her own.

"No law against it," he said. "At least not that I know of."

The shoplifter slid in across from him. She had a cola drink on her tray, and a slice of pumpkin pie.

"Mary Brown," Zinman said. "Isn't it?"

"Yes, it is," Mary Brown replied.

"Emil Zinman," Zinman said, offering his hand. To his surprise she took it.

"So tell me," he said. "Is it always like this? A different judge and prosecutor every time?"

43

"I wouldn't know," Mary Brown said. "I've never been arrested before."

Zinman wondered if this were true. Then he remembered what a convincing actress this young woman had been in the store's security office. "Well," he said. "Sometimes I wish I hadn't been so diligent."

"You did what you thought you had to do," Mary Brown said. She began eating her pumpkin pie with carefully measured forkfuls. Momentarily she was the same self-assured young woman he had spotted in Fielding's. Curiously enough, he did not at all feel awkward talking to her.

"I suppose we all do that," he said. "As a matter of fact, I've been accused myself." Then he told her about the controversy instigated by the mysterious Ms. Kapell.

"Really," Mary Brown said. "They did eat people?"

"It was ceremonial," Zinman explained. He went on to speak of the Aztec civilization, and its ultimate downfall before a band of Castilian marauders.

"You must be a very good teacher," Mary Brown said.

"I try to teach the things I believe in."

"I'm sure you do. Oh, look over there."

Zinman looked in the direction she was pointing. A dozen tables away, the security guard from Fielding's and the city police officer who had made the official arrest were sitting together, drinking coffee and smoking cigarettes. Both nodded, and later, as they were leaving the cafeteria together, stopped to exchange pleasantries with Zinman and the shoplifter. Now, if we just had the attorneys, Zinman thought, we could make it a party.

That afternoon when Nicole came home from school, he was in the dining room working on his class plans. "Did they put her in jail?" she asked immediately.

"Not quite," Zinman laughed. "It's easy to see why people commit crimes. They simply never come to trial!"

"That's what my mother says," Nicole agreed. She sat down on the table, drew a crumpled package of Winstons from her jeans pocket, and clumsily lit one.

"What's this?" Zinman said.

"I just want to see if you'll tell my mother."

"I won't have to. She'll smell it for herself."

"Oh?"

"Look," Zinman said. "I realize I have no status in your eyes, but you're only going to harm your own health doing that."

"I know," Nicole said, taking a long noisy drag. "They showed us films in school. People's lungs after they died. But that doesn't happen for years."

Zinman considered snatching the cigarette from her lips. Instead, he switched the subject and began talking about the events in court, and the two female attorneys who had stood toe to toe before the judge.

"I bet he stuck up for the pretty one," Nicole said.

"Well, yes he did," Zinman conceded. "But I was impressed by the state's attorney. She was very thorough and had prepared her case well."

"A lot of good that did her."

"You know," Zinman said thoughtfully, "It wasn't too many years ago when women didn't have much opportunity to become anything but office girls or housewives."

"And now they're supposed to be lawyers," Nicole said, squashing out the half-smoked cigarette on the sole of her shoe. "Not me. I'm going to get married as soon as I'm seventeen."

"Got someone in mind?"

"I'll find someone. And when I do you won't see me around here anymore."

Zinman watched her place her half-smoked cigarette back into the package and shove it into her pocket. "Nicole," he said gently. "You mustn't blame yourself for what happened with your parents."

"Blame myself? I blame them!"

"Why blame anyone?"

45

"And I blame you too," Nicole said. "Even though you weren't there."

For a moment Zinman wondered if that was a smile playing on the corners of her lips. He hoped it was.

The next morning he checked in the office to see who had substituted his classes, especially the Social Science group. Ms. Kapell's name did not appear, but a Mr. Sanchez did. Was nothing in this world ever to be consistent again? Was it to be a new court date every month, a new prosecutor, a new judge, and a new substitute every time? He imagined an endless succession of attorneys fresh out of law school, swollen-nosed judges in their dotage, and faceless substitutes — Kapell, Sanchez, Minsky, Pellini, Brown — on and on, all because of a handful of cheap costume jewelry!

The Social Science class greeted him with sullen silence; Maria Anglaiz, especially, sat with downcast eyes. But this time the assignment had been completed, the papers collected and waiting in the proper drawer. So what had been the problem? After the bell finally ended what proved to be an exceptionally listless period, Zinman called Maria to his desk.

"Okay, what is it this time?" he said.

"Nothing."

"Mr. Sanchez?"

Maria's dark eyes flashed. She would be a pretty girl as soon as she learned not to perm her hair and paint on cheap lipstick. "He didn't do nothing. Didn't do *anything*. He's a pig."

Zinman resisted an urge to smile. "Oh, don't talk that way."

"You're all pigs," she said. "Come on now, I got to go."

Seeing the perplexed look in his eyes, she shrugged. "Don't you worry, Mr. Zinman. I'll get over it. Everything is going to be fine."

A moment later Zinman heard her laughing with her friends in the hallway. She's right, he thought, gathering his papers. We are all pigs.

There was a letter waiting for him on the dining room table when he got home, a crisp white envelope with the cleanly printed return address of an Iowa law firm. Nicole, intently gazing into the television screen, waited until he had made certain it was unopened.

"They're after you now, aren't they?" she said.

Zinman slit the envelope with his thumbnail and removed the contents. Yes, they were after him. He had been a fool to think his wife would let the matter rest.

"It's not the money," he told Nicole. "I'd gladly pay the money, but she's got to let me see my son."

"Sure it's the money," Nicole said. "You think I don't know about these things? That's all you guys think about. Money and sex."

"Don't be so sure," Zinman said. He could feel the blood rising in his face, hot and eager. How dare she speak to him this way!

"I bet you'd like to hit me," Nicole said. "Come on now, be honest. You'd like to punch me out."

"No," Zinman lied. "Someone else will do it for me someday."

"Lot of good that will do you."

"Nicole." Zinman fought to keep his temper. "I don't understand what it is you have against me. I've never mistreated you, have I?"

"Why should you?" she said. "Why should you do anything to me?"

"I try to treat you decently."

"Maybe I don't want to be treated decently. Maybe I want something better than that."

Zinman was startled. Two years ago his wife had said much the same thing. "Be more exact," he said.

"There he goes, Mr. English Teacher," Nicole said. "If you're so smart, you figure it out."

"I can't be your father," Zinman said. "I can only be your friend."

"But you don't want to be my friend," Nicole said. "Don't pretend you do. And don't be so sure that's what I want."

"I don't think you know what you want."

47

"I'll know it when I get it," Nicole said fiercely. "And I am going to get it."

"Fine." Zinman left the room, his ears burning.

The next day he sat in the school cafeteria with his friend, Mr. Kelly. Across the room, at a table occupied entirely by Mexican students, sat Maria Anglaiz, tossing her wildly permed hair. "So what went on yesterday?" he asked. "What happened with the Sanchez guy? The kids didn't say anything, but I could see they were upset."

Mr. Kelly taught Physical Education. He was young and well liked and students often confided in him. "Simple. Sanchez's a Mexican. And he turns out ... Well, let's just say he gives the assignment, he sits down, he reads a magazine, he collects his buck. What about those Aztecs? He doesn't want to talk about Indians. They got nothing to do with him."

"Too bad," Zinman said. "But I don't see why that should upset anyone."

"Well, there's your problem," Kelly laughed. "You never do!"

In spite of himself, Zinman found this amusing. He smiled. "I seem to have gotten myself mixed up in matters I know too little about."

Later, when he thought about this, it seemed less a joke. His research in the library had, in fact, been as superficial as it was well-intentioned. He was neither a historian nor an anthropologist or anything else other than a simple English teacher in a second-rate public school. No more, he decided. There was a textbook that came with this class. Now was the time for him to use it.

And a good time too, with the divorce and all its bitter memories back in his life again, with more visits to the attorney's office, and not much help there either. Zinman's attorney, Sandy Kline, had been recommended by a friend whose intentions were better than his advice. Sandy had an office in the Oak Stream shopping mall, and there were times when Zinman suspected he was the man's only client. "Let me tell you," Sandy would say, "Anything, anything is better than going to trial. If they ask for your right arm, offer them your left. In the long run, it will be cheaper." Sandy — his real name was Samuel and he hated it — was young and fun loving, but with a dark sense of humor. Unfortunately, Zinman liked him. "They got us by the nuts, Emil," he would say. "We've got to cough up, no way out of it. But she's going to have to let us have our visitation rights."

"Have to? She's already supposed to, and she's in Iowa with her mother and I can go to hell!"

"We're working on it, babe!"

"You already worked on it! We had an agreement!"

"Emil!" Sandy had a way of tapping his desk top seriously, as if he were about to say something profound. "You got to remember one thing. Your wife's a bitch!"

"I have to remember it? How could I not remember it? Anyway, maybe I don't like you calling her that."

"Sure you do. Every man likes to hear his ex-wife called a bitch."

For this, good money. They would argue back and forth for a while, then close up the office and slip down to Bennigen's for a drink. Zinman was not much of a drinker, but it felt good to sit in a bar with a lively young man who knew how to laugh. "What do you think of that one?" Sandy might say, pointing out a Chinese waitress with her hair in a long silky ponytail. "You're a single man now, you could do her. Oh, wait a minute, I forgot, you have a new lady. Leave this one for me, and you get married again. If it doesn't work out, hey, I give discounts the second time around."

The waitress's name was Sally, and she too was married. "I can fix that," Sandy told her. "Here's my card."

Sandy was fascinated by the story of the shoplifter. "You signed a what? A complaint! Emil, Emil, haven't I taught you anything? Never, never, never get mixed up with the law! Remember that guy that got shot right in the courtroom? And he was a lawyer! What are you? Some goody two-shoes, taking time off from work to nail down a lousy shoplifter. You could wind up with an ice pick in your liver."

Side Show 1995

"She seems like a nice girl," Zinman said. "I'm sorry I got involved."

"Too late for that, Emil my boy. You are involved. Next time, before you sign anything, you call me."

And to think, when the trouble with Ms. Kapell had started, Zinman had momentarily considered consulting this man.

Finally it was the week before Christmas and school was dismissed for the year. Zinman's next court appearance, to his considerable relief, was scheduled for one of these free days. No need for a substitute this time!

Joanne was less pleased. She had been hoping he would keep an eye on Nicole when the girl was not in school, it being clearly understood that part of his duties toward this woman involved babysitting her daughter. Except Nicole was far from a baby. At times, frankly, he felt uncomfortable in her presence.

"I don't like her alone in the house all day," Joanne insisted. "She's ... well, you know how moody she is."

"Yes," Zinman agreed. "But I'll only be gone the morning."

Joanne pretended to think about this for a moment before making the suggestion Zinman suspected was already on her tongue. "Why don't you," she finally said. "Why don't you take her to court with you?"

It was a suggestion he knew better than to resist. He had not forgotten what Sandy Kline had suggested in Bennigan's. Maybe he should marry this woman. And the sooner the better. A daughter like Nicole would grow up and run away in a few more years. How then would he hold the mother?

Joanne called the girl away from her television. "What about it, Nicole? Would you like to go to court with Emil?"

"Why not?" she said. "So long as he buys me lunch."

Zinman was surprised. Nicole never agreed to anything her mother suggested without a quarrel. "You can't talk while court is in session," he warned her.

"I know that," she said. "I watch Judge Wapner all the time."

"Well, this isn't quite the same as television."

"It'll be better. It'll be real."

50

That night Zinman dreamed he was about to give testimony in a courtroom presided over by Ms. Kapell — who turned out to be an attractive young woman with a dark and fragrant ponytail. He was immediately filled with a desire almost too urgent to contain. "You're accused of shoplifting," Ms. Kapell said. "How do you plead?" "Guilty," Zinman breathed. He would say anything she wanted, if only he could stand closer. "Then you must come with me," she said, grasping his hand and leading him down a corridor lined with heavy wooden doors where she dissolved, just as he was about to take her into his arms.

The next morning this dream was still clearly with him, and the empty feeling left by Ms. Kapell's sudden disappearance. But the real Ms. Kapell, he warned himself, was probably one of those stern idealists who would never lead a man anywhere.

Joanne had already left for work when Zinman and Nicole set out for court. Although a light snow was in the air, Nicole refused to cover her head. She was excited and clear eyed for a change, and did not have to be reminded to fasten her seat belt. From the first she had been fascinated with this shoplifter business. Perhaps today would leave her satisfied.

At the courthouse door, Nicole took note of the metal detector. "Most of the kids in my room would never get through. They'd have to take out their braces. After their folks spent all that money."

"Be glad you have straight teeth," Zinman said.

"What makes you think they're straight? My dentist says I have an overbite."

"Many people have an overbite," Zinman assured her, wondering what anyone overhearing this conversation would think. Fortunately, most people scheduled for court had matters more compelling than overbites to think about. There was the usual crowd gathered in the hall, poor blacks, Mexicans, tattooed whites, threadbare lawyers, uniformed police, hennaed clerks; the shoplifter was not among them. Zinman pushed through and found the schedule taped to the wall. Mary Brown was listed right at the top. He wondered if the judge would be as tolerant of a late appearance as before. When he looked up Nicole had wandered off and was talking to a tall white boy with long hair and a leather jacket.

"Come on," Zinman said, hastily taking her arm. "Let's get a seat before this thing starts."

The boy with the long hair smiled knowingly.

There were numerous seats empty in the courtroom. Zinman saw Nicole safely to one before seeking out the state's attorney who, he was relieved to see, was the same heavyset woman with the bad foot as before. "I think we've worked it out," she told him. "All we need is a guilty plea from your little friend."

"*My* little friend!" Zinman laughed. "Is she here?"

"Oh, yes. She's with the public defender now."

When court began Zinman was surprised, but not startled, to see yet another judge take the bench, this time a gray-haired woman with a thin unsmiling mouth. The first case called involved a large red-headed Polish man charged with battery; the judge promptly sentenced him to 30 days in the county jail. The next defendant, a young Mexican caught driving someone else's vehicle, was rewarded with an entire year in spite of his lawyer's plea for mercy. "This boy, judge, is the sole support of his mother!" Zinman was glad he was not a defendant today.

"What a bitch," Nicole whispered.

Immediately a uniformed woman deputy was leaning over them, ordering silence. Luckily the judge had not heard. She was busy with a young man accused of reckless driving. Apparently he had left the highway to speed around another car on the shoulder, crashed through a small grove of trees, and returned to the highway just in time to strike a State Trooper's squad car. "Your honor," he insisted. "I lost control of the wheel."

Her honor shook her head grimly, and refused to grant a continuance. This case, she noted, had been before the court three times already. Five hundred Dollars plus restitution to the state for its damaged property.

Several other requests for continuances were denied. A good sign. Perhaps, with this judge, Zinman would finally reach the end of his courtroom career.

When Mary Brown's name was called, he began to rise, but settled back on his seat when he saw the state's attorney shaking her head. She and the public defender, the same attractive young woman as before, approached the bench together. "Your honor," the public defender began. "We have reached an agreement with the state."

Her honor adjusted her eyeglasses and began reading the document they had prepared.

Nicole nudged Zinman. "Bet she don't fool *this* judge!"

Again the bailiff glared.

"Have the defendant step up," the judge said.

Until that moment, Zinman had not seen the shoplifter. Suddenly she was standing between the two attorneys, her hair short and nappy, her eyes hidden by a pair of dark glasses.

"You can take those glasses off, young lady," the judge said. "I don't see any bright sun in here."

The shoplifter muttered something about a prescription.

"What?"

"She broke her regular glasses," the public defender explained.

Again Nicole nudged Zinman. "I thought you said she was pretty."

"Do you understand, Mary," the judge was saying. "You are charged with a Class A Misdemeanor, you could be sentenced to a year in jail, regardless of what is in this agreement. I will be guided by what the attorneys recommend, but I am the one who will make the final decision. They are asking that I sentence you to a year's probation after you present a plea of guilty to this court. Is this what you want?"

The shoplifter removed her glasses and rubbed her eyes. "I don't know," she said. "I didn't do it. I didn't do anything. I bought that stuff and they're trying to say I stole it."

The judge put down her papers. "You're saying you are not pleading guilty?"

"I'm not guilty!"

"Your honor," the public defender said quickly. "Permission to talk to the defendant ..."

"I don't want to talk with her!" the shoplifter cried in a voice that must have carried into the halls. "I want a different lawyer! I'm not guilty!"

Zinman turned to Nicole. The girl's eyes were shining, her lips parted. She's really enjoying this, he thought.

A conference was going on before the judge's bench. Apparently the shoplifter had decided to take her fate into her own hands. "Why can't I be my own lawyer?" she cried. "Why do I have to have *her*?"

The public defender turned away, as if to hide a smile from the judge.

"You want to represent yourself?" the judge asked.

"And I want a jury," the shoplifter replied.

Now both attorneys were smiling — but the judge was not. "Very well," she said in a voice filled with noticeable menace. "You may represent yourself. You may have a jury. But it is my duty to warn you, without legal training you will be putting your case at risk. And should the jury find you guilty, this agreement —" She held up the document the attorneys had given her; she held it with two fingers, exactly as if she were about to drop it into the toilet, " — this agreement will have no influence upon your sentence. Do I make myself clear? Let me repeat, the penalty for a Class A Misdemeanor is one year in the county jail."

Zinman could feel Nicole squirming at his side.

The implication of this statement was not lost on the shoplifter. Shuffling her feet, she finally whispered: "Could I have a minute to think about this?"

The minute was granted, and another muted conference took place. At last the public defender turned to the judge and said: "The defendant would like to enter a plea of guilty, as agreed."

So after all of these months, and all these delays, there was no need to take the stand. Mary Brown, thoroughly defeated, whispered her plea, and stood with her head down while the judge sentenced her to a full year of probation, concluding with a stern reminder of what she might expect if she were to violate that probation. "Oh, no ma'am," the shoplifter said. "I wouldn't do that."

Zinman led Nicole out of the courtroom feeling vastly relieved. "I think it sucks," she said. "That judge came right out and said they'd put her in jail if she didn't do what they wanted." "That's not quite what she said." "That's what she meant."

It was still early, just past eleven. Zinman, led the girl directly into the cafeteria.

"Just like school," she decided with a single glance at the counter. "I thought you were going to take me to lunch. I don't eat *this* junk." She did not hesitate, however, to help herself to a large cola drink and a bag of barbecue chips. Zinman chose coffee and a sweet roll.

"I'll get you lunch," he promised. "I want to sit here and watch people for a bit."

He chose a table at the corner of the room where they could see the cafeteria line, men and women, black, white, Hispanic and Asian, some in suits and ties, some in uniforms, some in casual or working clothes, filling their trays. There were several disabled people working behind the counter — a partially blind boy, a one-armed man, a woman bent over with some kind of back deformity. They had been given their jobs precisely because they were disabled, but, of course, these jobs were not very good jobs. Sandy Kline had assured Zinman that McDonald's paid better wages.

Nicole took all this in, slowly chewing her barbecue chips. "What a mess," she finally said. "Am I supposed to learn something?"

Zinman was about to say that bringing her to court had not exactly been his idea when he saw the shoplifter approaching, carrying a tray of her own.

"I suppose I might as well sit with you," she said. "Is this young lady your daughter?"

"Please," Nicole said. "He's just my mother's boyfriend."

The shoplifter was wearing jeans and an old sweater, but when she peeled the cellophane wrapper from her sweet roll Zinman noticed that her nails were perfectly manicured. Like a whiff of secret perfume, there was again something about her to suggest that same self-assured young woman he had seen last summer at Fielding's. "Well," he said. "At last it's over."

"Over for you," the shoplifter said. "I'm on probation. Now I got a record."

"I was hoping," Nicole said with great emphasis, "that you would make them bring out that jury."

"Oh, girl! Don't even think that! Did you see the look in that judge's face? She would have put me away for sure."

"I had the same impression," Zinman said. "I'm glad I didn't have to testify. I don't know what I would have done."

"Why, you'd have done your civic duty," the shoplifter said, patting the back of his hand. She turned her attention to Nicole. "What's your name, girl?"

"Nicole."

"My name is Mary." She flashed a big smile. "But I do like Nicole. That's a pretty name."

"You can have it," Nicole said. "Who ever heard of a fat girl named Nicole?"

"Fat? That's just the baby in you! I was the same way, and now look." The shoplifter stood up, did a little spin, and sat back down again. "And," she continued, pointing at her sweet roll, "I still eat this junk."

"Looking good!" a male voice said. It was the police officer who had made the official arrest, a tall blond man with a carefully trimmed mustache. Fielding's own security guards, apparently, no longer found this case worth their attendance. Without waiting for an invitation, the officer sat down and unwrapped a jellyroll.

"Now Mary," he said. "I hope you haven't been teaching this young lady any bad habits. Is this your daughter, sir?" he asked Zinman.

"Please," Nicole said.

"She says he's her mother's boyfriend," Mary Brown said. "Her name is Nicole. Isn't that a pretty name?"

"There's five girls in my class named Nicole," Nicole said bitterly. But there was a trace of a smile on her lips.

"Uh huh," the officer said. "That's a lot of Nicoles. My name is Brian. There were a lot of them in my class too. At least seven if I remember."

"I was the only Emil," Zinman said.

"So. Mary." The officer kept his attention focused upon the shoplifter. "How do you like Judge Hansen?"

"You mean Judge Hangman," she said. "Say, that woman don't take *no* mess!"

Talking to the officer, the shoplifter allowed her voice to edge toward the accents of the streets. They could have been old schoolmates unexpectedly reunited years after graduation, immediately intimate and at ease with each other. Zinman had hoped to tell how his own little Mexican student crisis had fizzled away all on its own; suddenly the notion seemed positively ridiculous.

Now another party joined their table. It was the state's attorney with the bad foot who, out of the courtroom and her role, somehow seemed younger, and vaguely attractive. "Well, what is this," she said, dropping into a chair. "One big happy family? What an interesting trial this one would have made. But we don't try them anymore." This she said directly to Nicole. "There's so many of them, we don't have time, and if we did we still wouldn't have enough space in the jail to put them. But ..." she turned to the shoplifter, "If Mary ever comes before Judge Hansen again, we're going to have to find space for her. Even if we have to let someone else go."

"Oh, no more Judge Hangman for me!" the shoplifter laughed, and Zinman was astonished to see the stern faced state's attorney join in with her. Suddenly they were all laughing, all except Nicole who cried out:

"How can you act like you're friends? You just tried to put her in jail!"

"No, we didn't," the state's attorney laughed. "We tried to keep her out. And she almost put herself in."

"But now she's got a police record!"

The officer slapped the table. "Now? What did she tell you?"

"Don't you go talking about me!" the shoplifter laughed.

"Listen, honey," the officer said to Nicole. "When I pulled the sheet on this lady, it reached all the way to the floor."

He stood up and pantomimed the act so vividly that Zinman almost saw the computer printout unfolding before his eyes

"You are talking lies!" the shoplifter cried. "My sheet is not that long!"

Crossing the room at this moment was the pretty young public defender, carefully balancing a tray. She did not sit down but paused at the table to address her adversary. "Next time," she told the state's attorney. "Next time you get to defend her. Next time I get to prosecute."

"You better talk to your committeeman first," the officer said.

"Are you implying I have a political job?" the state's attorney laughed. They were all laughing, relaxed, and at ease with one another, all except Zinman and Nicole. Good lord, he thought. What a civics lesson this has turned out to be.

But the girl's eyes were bright and shining, and when they finally left the cafeteria there was a spring in her step. It stayed there while he took her into a nearby mall and shopped for Christmas presents. It was still there after lunch at Pizza Hut. This girl, constantly sullen, was suddenly and at last exhilarated.

Driving home, with a light snow descending upon the windshield, Zinman felt her shift in her seat, closing the space between them, and smelled the moisture in her dark hair. It had been a good day after all. He congratulated himself.

Then, just as it seemed she was about to snuggle against him, he suddenly sat straight and gripped the wheel firmly with both hands. Just as quickly, she pulled away and there was a moment of intense silence before he heard her lighting a cigarette with a match.

"I'm going to grow up," she said quite proudly. "I'm going to grow up, ain't I?" Zinman stared straight ahead. Large star-shaped snowflakes were splashing against the windshield. "Maybe, Mr. English Teacher, I should say *aren't* I," she continued. "But I *am* going to grow up. And I think I'm going to like it."

Who saw him die?
"I," said the fly
"With my little eye,
I saw him die." - Nursery Rhyme

HARRY SAYS

by Paul Perry

What pissed me off, what *really* pissed me off, was that Markey sat there on the side of that embankment for three days, three fucking days, stone-cold dead, right there in plain sight of all that traffic up on the interstate, three miles from downtown, all them people passing by and looking down at him but not *seeing* him, and he was getting bigger every day — hell, it's fucking July, sun burning down, nighty-eight, hundred degrees — his shirt buttons popping, seams of his pants splitting open, face puffing up like a ... like a balloon. And nobody fucking sees him! That's what pissed me off.

Hell, we might never have known about it, me and Ben, if this hitcher kid hadn't happened along. And you know what? *He* didn't see him. See, he'd got stuck walking along the interstate, no way somebody's going to stop to pick him up on the interstate, right? So this kid's walking along, trying to get down off the interstate to the access road so he can catch a ride to Houston, and he's walking along, glances over to where Markey's sitting, don't pay no attention, keeps on walking, thinking about how hot it is, how tired he is, how he'd like to sit down and rest some place where it's shady. Then the smell hits him, wham! So he stops and sees the flies, clouds of fucking flies, and then, finally, he sees Markey.

Okay, so the kid climbs over the railing, eases himself down to the bottom of the embankment then climbs up to where Markey is sitting, the place where Markey liked to sit and watch the traffic go by, watch all them people in their nice cars going to their nice houses, houses with roofs and bathrooms and refrigerators full of all kinds of shit — that's what Markey liked to do — and this kid skirts around him, holding his breath, thinking maybe about Markey's pockets but not about to get anywhere near close enough to check them out, just wanting to get past him and away from him, and the flies.

The kid don't even think about doing anything about Markey, just wants to get the fuck away, so he climbs up to the top of the embankment that leads up to the overpass, looks down to where the overpass leads from Highway 90 to the interstate, and he sees that there's shade under the overpass, and he decides to go down there and sit for awhile, let his stomach settle, close his eyes for a few minutes because — as he told us later — he had spent the night before in a field south of Waco, dozing on his tarp but not sleeping because the mosquitos were swarming all over him and he was sweaty and could smell his own stink, and supper had been a stick of beef jerky and a Coke.

Well, anyway, after the kid had walked a hundred yards or so, looking for a place where he could sit down, maybe stretch out for a few minutes, of course he saw down to where there was this place almost like a room with three walls underneath where the ramp left Highway 90, a nice shady place, and that place, of course, is *our* place, me and Ben's place.

We had been down on Commerce that morning, looking for a little work, standing around with some others, waiting to see what would show up. A couple of trucks had come by, looking for carpenters, but I can't do that kind of stuff and Ben has his messed-up hand, so we didn't get anything. We kind of hoped the Old Bitch would be by in her station wagon, but she had other pick-up points, up around Fredericksburg Road, down on Southwest Military, came only this way if she had trouble rounding up enough people. A couple of times me and Ben had tried to make our own signs, find our own corners, but it didn't work. The Old Bitch knew how to letter the signs, say just the right things, knew just the best places to stand. Last time she gave me a sign that said "WILL WORK FOR BEER OR FOOD," and I thought she was crazy, but damned if people didn't stop. I got over forty dollars, a couple of sandwiches — ate them right there — and a loaf of bread. "It made them think you were honest," the Old Bitch said when she picked me up that evening, so I got to keep fourteen dollars, took the bread back to the place, shared it with Ben and a couple of other people: the old lady with the suitcase, and some guy that had gotten beat up in jail, looked like shit, but ate that bread and went on his way.

The Old Bitch tried to fix Markey up once. The day after he first showed up in our place, me and Ben took him along with us. He looked in bad shape, had nothing but what he had on and what was in his pockets, slept on some folded up cardboard boxes we kept handy at our place. The Old Bitch showed up that day, looked Markey up and down. "You look sick," she said. "You got AIDS or something?" And even though Markey shook his head, she got out her black marker and a piece of cardboard and wrote, "DYING OF AIDS. HUNGRY. PLEASE HELP." But Markey just shook his head and walked away. That's the way he was.

Well, anyway, when this hitcher kid showed up and told us about seeing this dead body, this puffed-up dead body, we didn't think about it being Markey because there sure as hell wasn't anything puffed up about Markey, but when the kid said the body looked like it had shaggy brown hair, was wearing these ragged jeans and a gray-and-green checked shirt, we knew it was Markey, especially after the kid told us where he had seen him. We'd wondered about Markey, but he kind of came and went, so we figured he was off wherever it was he went now and then.

Well, as this kid was telling us all of this, while he's chewing on a baloney sandwich Ben had given him, I start getting worked up — I got this little problem with my temper — because it comes to me that Markey must have been sitting there since the last time we saw him, which was three days ago, and the more I think about it, the more pissed I get, so I start yelling some, and kicking a few things, like the garbage bag full of cans we'd picked up, and when some of the cans rolled out, I started kicking them around, and yelling some more, so this hitcher kid finally gets his ass out of there, moving kind of fast. But Ben, who knows how I am, he just sits there until I start to quieten down a little, then he says, "Harry?" and I say, "I know what you're going to say and we ain't calling no fucking cops. You know how I am about cops."

"9-1-1?" Ben asks.

"9-1-1 ain't cops?" I say to him, still a little hot.

"So what we going to do?" Ben asks me. Ben is big and black and ugly, but he's as gentle as they come, too fucking gentle for a world like this one we live in.

"I'll show you what we're going to do," I say to him, because I have just had this idea.

I get out a piece of cardboard, one we'd used before, and I get out the black marker we'd bought when we tried making our own signs, and I write: HEY, ASSHOLES! I'M DEAD!

So me and Ben wait until dark and we go up to the embankment and sure enough Markey's still there, smelling to high heaven, swarming with flies, and I hold my breath while Ben watches the traffic up on the interstate to make sure nobody pulls over, and I prop the sign in Markey's lap so that it's pointed right up toward the traffic flow, then me and Ben get the hell out of there.

Well, that was ten days ago, and we ain't seen nothing, ain't heard nothing about Markey. And we sure as hell ain't going back there to check on him. But we figure he's still there, holding that sign, facing up toward traffic on the interstate, all them cars and trucks and buses passing by, and he's still just sitting there as he slowly turns into ... nothing.

Satyrs grazing on the lawns shall with their goat feet dance the antic hay. - Christopher Marlowe

---

A LETTER

by Anne Raeff

Dear Amy,

I don't know exactly how I got here or why I'm here. I know I left during the windy season. I had been thinking about leaving for a long time, but the day I actually left was sometime in May and the wind was gusting at fifty miles an hour. As I drove out of our neighborhood towards the highway, I noticed that there were huge branches lying in almost everyone's yard. I passed by your yard, and I remember thinking that you would have to clean all that up.

That is the last impression I have of Albuquerque — broken branches lying on the ground and the wind trying to push my car off the road as I headed south on I-25. At first, I thought it was an omen — all that wind and the fallen branches. And then there was the dust, so I could hardly see. But then I remembered that I don't believe in things like omens. Sometimes I wish I did. It would simplify things, help me make decisions. This way I have nothing to gauge things by, no way of knowing whether to go here or there, left or right, stay in or go out.

If I had been a pregnant Navajo woman, for example, I would never have left the house that day because if I had, and I had run into one of those little twisters where the wind sucks the sand up into the air like a mini tornado, then I would have known that my child would have respiratory problems. So you see, it would have been easy to decide. I would have stayed home and watched television, and then, maybe by the time the wind died down, I would not have felt the need to go. But if I had been a pregnant Navajo woman, there would have been a lot of other things that would have been different too.

I don't remember how many days it took me to get here or why I decided that this was the place to stop. I could have kept going; I had not run out of money yet. But there was something I liked about this town. I liked the fact that it was humid, that you could smell the Gulf.

Even from inside you can smell the water, and the air is heavy and hot. There is nothing beautiful about Coatzacoalcos. Nothing. It is dirty and poor and it smells like a combination of sea air and rotten fruit. And the land around the town is completely uninteresting. There is a little hill, the rest is flat; the vegetation is not at all noteworthy. And even though it certainly is warm and humid enough for palm trees here, there are just a token few of them that line the promenade, if you could call it that, just south of the piers. Everyone keeps telling me that it is dangerous to walk there alone, but I always do and nothing has happened to me yet.

Maybe I stopped here because there is nothing beautiful about this place at all. There is nothing that even the most adventurous tourist would find at all intriguing, and, as far as I know, I am the only foreigner who has been here in a long time. I think that places like this comfort me somehow. Not that I was uncomfortable in New Mexico. You were the one who could never really get used to it — to the lack of good bookstores and to the proliferation of impersonal shopping centers. But that is what I always liked about Albuquerque — some nightmarish imitation of Los Angeles, filled with Pizza Huts and Burger Kings. But stuck in between all that there is always some dive with only Mexican music on the jukebox, or a bowling alley with one of the best Mexican restaurants in the city, where you have to play

65

a couple games before you get to eat because there's always a line, but it doesn't matter because the food is so good and it's fun to bowl and watch people.

I have been here for about three months. I have no idea how much longer I will stay. Who knows, I might stay here forever. I might just write to Ginny and Beth and tell them to clean out my apartment, sell what they can, keep what they want, send me the money. I have written to my friends, promised them that I am fine, that I will be returning soon. They all sign their letters with the same question, "When are you coming back? Love, so and so." Of course I had to quit my job, but that was easy, I just disappeared and then sent a letter. Unlike yours, tending bar is not a serious job. Still, there is something about my job and that place that I miss. It became my home almost, after you left. And sometimes it actually made me feel wanted, stupid as that may sound, when some poor woman spilled her guts out to me about her cheating girlfriend.

I suppose I could have written to my friends and told them that I came down here to paint, but I don't like to lie; I do it only when there is absolutely no other way. Of course, you never lie — never — you are always very honest, very blunt. I suppose I'm a coward of sorts when it comes to some things. I think about painting all the time, though. Almost every day, but I am used to that, used to thinking about painting every day. But I know I have not come down here to paint. What would be the point? No one likes my work. It's too disturbing, I don't even think my friends like it. Of course you liked it, but what does that matter anymore? That's one of the last things you said to me, do you remember? "You don't even goddamn paint anymore." As if anyone really cared. All anyone wants to see these days are beautiful colors and soft mountains and big skies. No one wants to see what I see — shadows on black or dark fires. I couldn't even sell my paintings in New York. I got tired of it, of the comments like, "Very moving and disturbing work, but not quite what we want for our gallery." You used to say to just fuck them and keep on painting, but you don't know how difficult that gets. After all, you are moderately successful, your stories do get published, even if they are only in stiff literary magazines and obscure feminist publications that no one reads. Here life is simple. No one asks me if I am going to start painting again because no one knows I can paint. No one asks me about you because no one even knows you exist. Sometimes I even pretend that I don't know Spanish. I don't tell anyone that it is really my mother tongue, that I remember going to kindergarten in New York and understanding people but not being able to speak. I don't tell anyone that my parents are Cuban Jews who are now more or less happily retired in Miami. No one has even asked me about my Caribbean Spanish, no one has made fun of the way I say *"uno, do, tre, cuatro, cinco, sei, siete, ocho, nueve, die."*

But then I don't look Cuban. You look more Cuban than I do, and you make a point of not speaking a word of Spanish.

I wonder if I should write to my parents and tell them where I am. Who knows, they might decide to call me for some reason; someone might die and they would have no way of getting in touch with me. But it would just upset them. Mexico. They would raise their eyebrows and bitch about the fact that I am always traipsing all over the world, but I've never visited them in Miami. And then they would have to ask about you. "How is Amy?" they would say, trying to be very cool, very mature about everything. And what would I tell them? No, I guess I'll just have to cross my fingers and hope that they have no reason to get in touch with me.

You probably want to know how I am making a living down here. You are always interested in practical matters. I know you'll probably think this is disgusting — cleaning and cooking for a very rich couple in this terribly poor town, filled with misery and poverty. But I like this work. I like mopping the cool, tile floors. I like shaking out the rugs. I like hanging heavy, white, linen sheets on the line to dry. And I like Marta and Rafael. I suppose you could call them my bosses, but we're very friendly. I especially like Marta. In the evenings we sit out on the balcony and drink tequila. Just because she's rich, doesn't mean she's happy. That's the one thing that you could never understand. You really believe that if you have money, you don't have any excuse to be miserable. "You don't know what it's like not to have money," you would say as if you had grown up in the South Bronx and my parents were millionaires. Remember how we used to argue about who had a more difficult childhood? And once you even said that I was just like Sylvia Plath and neither of us had the right to be so miserable. How stupid of us to argue about something like that. But we always did. And whenever I said that one of the kids in the Save the Children ads would look at your childhood and think that it was very privileged because you lived in a house and went to school and your father always had a job, you would just get even more angry at me. "That's not the point," you would say and I guess it wasn't.

But I look forward to my work here. Actually, there really isn't enough for me to do to come here every day, but Marta always finds something to keep me busy. I think she likes having me around too, because Rafael is out all day making tapes. He's a rather famous salsa musician. The whole living room is filled with photographs of Rafael and his band. Some are posed studio shots and some are just pictures that people took of them playing or just hanging out, smoking, drinking, laughing. I've never really looked at them closely. I just have a general impression of all of them together, like a big collage — trumpets shining, rounded drums, white pants, smiles, legs, hips, beards, guitars, tropical shirts, open mouths. There are a lot of open mouths, a lot of legs, tight pants. Rafael is very handsome. And Marta is very beautiful. Sometimes she is in the pictures too, looking off into the distance the way she looks at the ships on the Gulf.

Even though she never gets up until one o'clock in the afternoon, I think it comforts her to hear me moving around her house. Today she had me polish all the silverware. There were twelve boxes of it, all heirlooms from her side of the family.

I don't quite understand why Marta and Rafael stay on here in Coatzacoalcos. They have a house in Mexico City, but Marta says she feels worse there because then she has to talk to people, go out, visit her nieces and nephews. This way no one bothers her, and when Rafael isn't on tour, they don't have to meet any social obligations because there is no one here in Coatzacoalcos that they have to be polite to.

I have told Marta very little about myself. She knows I am from New York, that I live in Albuquerque. She does not ask questions. Sometimes I have this incredible desire to tell her everything, about you, about Gilbert. I can picture me telling her. There is a cool breeze on the balcony, she is smoking and looking out at the Gulf. There are three huge tankers in view, far out but visible because they are so big. We prepare to drink a shot of tequila. She puts salt on a lime, she holds up her glass, we drink, she puts the entire lime in her mouth. And that is as far as I can get, because if you start telling someone something important, you begin to expect them to understand you and that is dangerous. But we are comfortable together because we don't talk much. We listen to music, we watch the Gulf. And most of the time I am busy doing something, polishing the silver, oiling the teak furniture, folding the laundry.

I like physical work. At night, when I finally go to sleep I am actually tired. I have not felt that way in a long time, not since I was a child when I still used to be able to play tennis all day long in the blazing sun or spend hours and hours in the town pool until my lips turned purple and then even longer. Remember you used to try to get me to go on hikes, but I would always rather just wait somewhere with my sketch pad? But I have stopped drawing too. Sometimes, this past year, I would catch myself drawing a face or a hand, and I would have to stop myself, cross it out, cover it up.

At first, when I stopped painting, it was hard to find other things to occupy my time. I'm sure you must have noticed how restless I was, how, after sitting down with a book for ten minutes, I would jump up and go for a walk. I couldn't even

69

concentrate at the movies. And, remember, there was a time when I used to be able to lock myself in my studio and paint for three days straight, stopping only for meals or a short walk around the neighborhood. And then there was a big gap, I had nothing to fill my days with, neither you nor my painting. So I became more sociable. I went out to the bars, I was on the steering committee for the organization of Gay Pride Week. You kept saying it was good for me, that I had been too much of a loner, that I needed to make other friends. And then it got so bad that I couldn't be alone. So you see I had to come here, to learn to be alone again. It is not easy.

When I first told you that I was never going to paint again, you thought I was exaggerating in my usual, melodramatic fashion. You only said that you thought it would be good if I concentrated on other things for a while because painting makes me too self-absorbed, too removed from everyone and everything. I tried to explain that this was a permanent decision, but you only laughed and told me not to plan my whole future out because one never knows what is going to happen. You always loved saying things like that, like, you never know, one day you might be madly in love with one person and then the next day you might meet someone in a cafe and by evening your whole life will have changed. But I'm going out now, I can't stand sitting here much longer. I'm going to El Tambor, I'll tell you about it tomorrow, I need to rest now, stop thinking.

I have been rereading what I have written, and I don't exactly know why I have bothered to tell you all this, but I will continue because I have no one else to write to, no one who will have the patience to listen to all this. I was going to tell you about El Tambor. It's a sleazy bar where all the faggots hang out. Marta and I are usually the only women there, but we both like it that way because no one bothers us and it makes me feel a little bit at home. I know you used to hate going to the bars with me, you would always get angry about the music or start complaining that everyone was acting like a stereotype; either that, or they were depressing alcoholics, and we would always argue about that. "What do we have in common with these people?" you would always say, and I would try to explain that they made me feel comfortable, safe. But they just made you feel stupid or depressed. I guess that was something else we never resolved. Because I still like going to places like El Tambor — right away people take you in; even if you don't really have anything in common with them, you do, or I do — pardon me, I didn't mean to include you.

Anyway, it's a comforting place. I am not the only one who is comforted by it. Sometimes a traveling prostitute will find her way in there by accident, and you can tell that she is almost relieved to find that she can relax a moment, put aside her act, have a drink. A lot of the regular prostitutes that work the bars along the docks will come in for a break too. They'll have a few drinks, joke around with everyone, talk. There's one women who tried to sell me one of her children. She's got six children that she supports with no help from anyone, and once she told me that if I wanted a child — because there are a lot of American women like me (that's how she put it) who want children — but if I wanted one, I could have her youngest daughter. She's very sweet, apparently, and smart. But not tough enough. She worries about her all the time. She said it would be very cheap too, she kept saying that in English — "very cheap, very cheap" — as if I couldn't understand it fully unless she said it in English. So I thanked her politely and said that I didn't really want a child, but thank you very much anyway, or something equally absurd. Then the next day, while I was oiling Marta's bannister, I kept thinking about what it would be like to have a little girl, how I would teach her English and how to ride a bicycle and take her to visit my parents in Miami. And then I knew that I was really about to go crazy, and I forced myself to pull myself together and stop having these ridiculous fantasies. Because I cannot remember one time in my life, even when I was thirteen and all my friends ever did was talk about growing up and having children, that I wanted to have a child. I remember pretending

71

to my friends that I wanted to have eleven children, six boys and five girls, but it was just a lie. You were the one who always wanted children. And you used to say that I should adopt a child, that I am so good with children, but you were only projecting. I wouldn't be surprised if you were pregnant right now and were wishing that you could call me up to tell me the good news. You'll probably want me to be the godmother, but I don't think that would be a good idea because you know I don't believe in God even though you always tried to convince me that I really do.

But I was telling you about El Tambor. You would hate it, but it comforts me. I can get as drunk as I want to and I know I will be safe. The decor is great too. It's completely pink inside. There is not one wall, one chair, one table top that is not bright pink. Even the napkins they use are pink, and the toilet paper, when there is toilet paper, and all the lights are pink, and all the signs. The only thing about El Tambor that I don't like is Raul. He's the owner. He's about fifty, and he always wears a white linen suit and a white shirt and his stomach hangs way out over his snakeskin belt. He doesn't do much of anything, he doesn't talk much or get in anyone's way. He usually just sits in the corner smoking and drinking cuba libres. Sometimes he has close to fifteen in one night, but his mood never changes either. He's always sullen. He's even sullen when he has one of his boys with him. There's usually a different one every two weeks or so. Some nights his latest boy will sit next to him holding his hand, but Raul won't pay any attention to him unless he gets up and starts talking to someone else. Then he'll give him a dirty look and the boy will return to his table. Since I've been here, he's been through about six of these boys. And they *are* boys, between the ages of thirteen and sixteen — seventeen at the oldest. They're all thin and dark with big, Indian eyes. Right now he is with Jesus. I hate to admit this because I like to pride myself on being open-minded, but the idea of Raul touching Jesus makes me sick. I once told Marta that and she laughed. "You Americans are such Puritans," she said. But it is not that. Maybe it is because of Gilbert.

Do you know that there were times when I almost could have smashed Gilbert's face in with my boots, dug my heel into his puffy, hairy face, squooshed his nose into his skull. But, of course, I am too civilized for that kind of behavior. I was always very polite, very cool, remember? Not even a caustic phrase would cross my lips in his presence. And then I would go home and fling my books around the room and slam the doors and smash the glass on the paintings, my paintings, so that I had to spend over two hundred dollars to replace them. And then you would return from a weekend in Taos with Gilbert, and you would not even acknowledge the signs of my wrath. You would kiss me and I would cringe, thinking that your lips felt rougher, chapped, burned by Gilbert's beard stubble. And then I would leave the house in a fury, and when I returned, you would try to comfort me, tell me to be patient, that you needed both of us, that you were working things out, and I would listen and I would hold onto you like we were both drowning, and all I could see were his big hands on your breasts and his hard, hairy face, resting on your stomach, and I could not stand to be near you, so I would lock myself in my studio for hours, all night long, but I did not paint. I just lay there on the floor with the lights off. And I suppose now everything is worked out.

At first, I think I stopped painting out of spite, because I knew it was the thing you most admired about me. After all, Gilbert is not an artist. And you used to despise college professors; isn't that ironic? Don't you remember your ivory-tower harangue? But I suppose Gilbert is different, he's been out in the world, he spent a year volunteering in that Guatemalan refugee camp, and he wears colorful, handwoven shirts, not ties and jackets. But after a while I could not have painted even if I had wanted to. Once you said, "How can you be an artist and be so conventional? That's what it means to be an artist — to have strange relationships, a strange life, upheavals." But Gilbert had nothing to do with my art. And, anyway, I do not want to dwell on these

73

things. I am not here to dwell on things. I will go to El Tambor, have a few drinks, I will dance a little, I will joke with Maria and Pepa, admire their new leather skirts, let them tell me for the fiftieth time that they are leaving soon, leaving for Holland where a girl can be a girl if she wants and no one will throw rocks at them when they walk down the street swinging their hips in a brand new pair of heels. I suppose my life could be worse. I could have been born a queen in Mexico.

I haven't told you about all the aspects of my relationship with Marta and Rafael. I suppose I don't know whether to mention it at all, but I have to tell someone, and you wouldn't have the whole picture if I didn't. I don't know exactly how we started these sessions. I suppose I could stop everything, but I don't really want to. It is a sort of strange exercise for me, an exercise in what, I'm not quite sure yet, but I suppose I will figure it out at some point. All I know is that I find our sessions together strangely pleasant. It is like doing some odd form of meditation, not that I've ever even tried meditation, but I suppose it must be somewhat like this, totally mindless. But not only mindless, it clears the mind, leaves it totally blank, and that is something that I can appreciate. I sometimes get so tired of having to live with my mind and my thoughts and with this terrible anger that doesn't seem to go away. Sometimes it subsides, but it is always there, waiting for me when I am most vulnerable — just when I am falling asleep at night or when I am walking alone near the water in the hot sun. Then I will envision you and Gilbert holding hands, walking out of a dark corner, smiling, and I will feel my anger rising up in me again so that my whole body is pulsing and the only thing that will make it go away is tequila or Marta and Rafael.

How did this start? I was trying to remember. I cannot remember if there were any words spoken. I don't think so. We were all drinking tequila out on the balcony. It was dark already, quiet, but very hot still, very humid. One of Rafael's records was playing in the background, very softly so you could only hear it if you listened for it carefully. Then Rafael just got up. I don't remember if he said anything to excuse himself. Marta and I stayed on the balcony for a while longer, but after a while, I could not say how long really, she got up too, and I followed her; maybe she said something, I don't remember. I followed her upstairs and into their bedroom. Rafael was lying naked on the white sheets. He was beautiful; I remember thinking to myself that he really was beautiful, his brown body on the clean, white sheets that I myself had ironed. And so we started and this ritual has become a daily habit, in the evening after drinks on the balcony. Sometimes I stay for dinner and sometimes I don't. Sometimes I just go to El Tambor by myself afterwards. Sometimes Marta and I go together. Rafael rarely comes with us. We don't speak much. I have never even asked Marta if they had planned it, she and Rafael. Somehow it doesn't matter. If someone had told me a year ago that I would be living in Mexico and involved in a *menage à trois* with a salsa musician and his wife, I would have said something like "I have never understood what people see in that sort of thing, and anyway, I'm a lesbian, I don't sleep with men." Life is strange.

At first I thought that maybe I had to do this because it is the only way I have of understanding you. But this has very little to do with you because you are in love with Gilbert and I am not in love with either of them. I am not at all jealous of Rafael and Marta, I would not want to be them, I would not want to be with either of them alone. I am happy to leave them when I do, happy to go off to my own room even though it is unbearably hot and you can hear the noises from the cantinas all night long. I don't think I could spend a night in their house. It is so big, so clean, so empty.

I know it is clean because I clean it everyday. I have become very fastidious, very neat, I have never cleaned so much before. As you know, I have always been on the messy side. I have always waited until it really got to be too much before I would actually clean. Remember how you used to remind me subtly, politely, that the bathroom needed mopping or the stove needed

75

scrubbing? But it was never a problem, was it? It was kind of nice actually, having someone bother me about my habits. Now I can do whatever I want, no one cares.

You probably think that what I'm doing is disgusting, that I'm wallowing. But so what if I'm wallowing. Maybe that's what I need to do right now. And I don't feel terrible all the time. As a matter of fact, sometimes I feel happy almost, or energetic at least. Happiness is a word I have never understood anyway. We used to argue about it, remember? You used to say that simple things like watching your kid eat an ice cream could make you happy. But I don't really believe that, you are just fooling yourself when you say things like that. Or am I the one who is projecting now?

But I am not wallowing. I am not doing this to alienate myself. I'm sure that's what you are thinking. But you're wrong — on the contrary. When I am with them, I feel that at least I am alive, my body responds to theirs; they are both gentle and they smell beautiful — a combination of sweat and coffee. As a matter of fact, I can hear their voices coming from the driveway now. They have spent the day in the country; they were going to some village, I can't remember which one, to partake in some celebration. They are laughing, I suppose they are happy. Soon we will be sitting outside drinking, watching the water, smiling at each other. And then we will go up to their room. I could describe to you exactly what happens when we are all together, but you are probably not interested, and if you are, you would never admit it. Or you would say you were surprised with my behavior, that it is so unlike me. But I do not find it unlike me at all.

Tonight is Raul's birthday, and he is throwing a big party at El Tambor. Everyone will be there. And I mean everyone, the entire town is invited. Everything is free — free food, free tequila, free beer. I don't really want to go, but Marta and Rafael insisted and I have nothing better to do. Apparently this is the event of the year. They're roasting thirty pigs right now on spits at the pier. The smell of roasting pig combined with the Gulf's particular, watery smell that resembles rain on concrete mixed with garbage and fish is making me sick. Of course, if you were here, you would probably refuse to go. You would say that it was disgusting, patronizing. A big landlord throwing scraps at his peasants to keep them happy — bread and circuses. But so what? That is the way the world works. I'm sure there will be plenty of boys there too. Perfect, smooth boys with large eyes and small asses and tight bellies. I wonder how many of them he will take home with him tonight to help him celebrate.

But it is still too early to even begin to get ready for this event. I have hours still. What will I do? I can't read anymore. I used to be able to read all weekend. Remember? I have brought some books with me and I have read the first ten or twenty pages of all of them over and over again, but I can't get any further than that. I can't concentrate. "Why don't you draw, why don't you listen to music?" you would say. I told you, I have stopped painting and drawing, and I don't even have a radio. I suppose I could go and buy one, but I am saving my money. For what, I don't know, but I will figure it out at some point and then I will be glad to have it. And for now it is something to concentrate on. I put it all in an earthenware pot I bought at the flea market the first day I arrived. I bought it expressly for that purpose and it is almost halfway full. Maybe I will continue south in a while. Maybe I will stay here and buy myself a little cottage. I wonder how long it would take me to save up for that. Marta and Rafael pay me very little. But I am an ascetic by nature. You know that. Remember how I only had one set of dishes and two pots and a bed and desk when we first met? And now I have a houseful of furniture. Maybe you would want some of it. I know Gilbert has everything you need, but I wouldn't really know what to do with all that furniture now. I suppose I will have to sell it if you have no use for it. How about the couch? You always liked to lie on it and read. I bet you still can read. And your writing? How is your writing going? Are you still writing the greatest feminist novel of the century? Or have you graduated from the feminist phase too?

Do you still go to all those women's poetry readings you used to drag me to? You used to get annoyed at me for making fun of them, for laughing at all those women sitting on folding chairs trying to get tears in their eyes as someone with a strange name like Mira Solstice or Salad Average, even you laughed at her, filled the room with moon goddesses and Amazons and El Salvador and incest victims. You used to say that it was important for women to express themselves, that the great art would come later, once the anger had subsided, once we were free. Free from what? Does Gilbert go with you to the readings now? Does he feel proud to be there, to be part of this expression of liberation and anger? I have read and seen a lot of good art that stems from anger, there is no reason to get rid of anger, but it is self-righteous anger that inspires all that bad poetry and bad music. The only thing worse than that is self-righteous happiness. I think that is worse — I would rather listen to something negative and ugly and depressing than some uplifting, positive junk about how the most beautiful and wonderful thing in the world is women loving women. But you would probably say that is just because I have sour grapes. So what if I do?

In some ways, I wish you would come down here for a visit. You could even bring Gilbert. He might find it interesting — the poverty, the exploitation, he could write an article. I could take him into the jungle to see the Indians. But then I would have to tell Marta and Rafael who you were, and that would spoil everything because I do not want to tell them anything. You would say that that is my problem, that I do not want to tell anyone anything. But that is not true. I have told you everything, and now I am empty. I do not want to talk to anyone else. You would say that there are other people in the world besides you to talk to. Perhaps there are, but what would be the point? I guess I should take a nap, it is the only way I have to make the time pass before it is time to go to Raul's party. I will be up all night anyway, and it is so hot now; you would not be able to take this heat, it's like New York but worse.

I don't really know where to begin about last night. I am still at that piecing together stage, where I am trying to drag things out of my memory — events, words that have been buried in a mist of alcohol and then, later, sleep. I know, I shouldn't drink so much, it worries you. No, I am not becoming an alcoholic. You know I go through phases. Sometimes I just have to drink more than I should. It keeps me entertained, occupied, it helps me think. How can I think if I can't even remember everything that happens, you would ask? But I do remember, I just have to dig it out of my mind, find it, piece everything together. I like that about hangovers, about waking up in the morning with dirt under my fingernails and my hair smelling of smoke and my legs aching. It's like I have been walking for miles and miles and I have gotten all dirty and tired and I need a shower and a good breakfast. So I have already had my shower, I have already had my breakfast. I do not have to do anything today. Marta and Rafael are going to Veracruz to visit some friends for a couple days. They gave me the key to their place, but I don't think I'll use it. They said I could stay there while they're gone, enjoy myself, cool off. But I like my room. It has a few of my things — the earthenware pot, a colorful bedspread, my Francis Bacon poster which is all I brought with me from the house. Of course, it is impossibly hot in here, but that is something to keep me busy. Feeling uncomfortable is a challenge of sorts.

You would not believe the party. It spilled way out into the streets along the waterfront and onto the piers and we actually ate all the pigs. Even I had some and you know I don't like to eat pork. But it was really very good, very fresh. Raul was cutting big chunks of meat right off of the spit and handing them out to everyone as they walked by. I think the entire city attended the festivities. Even the priests were there, drunk. And the music was so loud you could probably even hear it up on the hill even though there was probably no one up there to hear it since everyone was at the party. You probably would have hated it, though. Too many people, too much drinking, too much noise. But I bet Gilbert would have loved it. It was very colorful, very festive, a perfect example of the ability that third world people have to enjoy themselves, to let go.

Of course, Raul had his usual entourage. You would think he would be happy: it was his birthday, everyone was there to celebrate, including all the young boys. But he looked even more morose than usual. After he had handed out the slabs of pork, he went back into his bar and sat at his table in the corner and just drank. He drank cuba libres one after the other, but they had no visible effect on him. None at all. You would have been amazed. Some of us spent most of the time in the bar. It was cooler in there, quieter. In fact, it was almost peaceful, funereal almost. I sat at a table with a group of men in drag. Marta and Rafael were outside dancing. You would probably think that I should have felt bad about that, but I didn't. You know I don't like dancing much anyway. I like sitting with the queens because they just chatter and you don't have to say anything. You just have to smile and laugh at their self-deprecating jokes. So that's what we were all doing, only everyone, even his boys, ignored Raul. No one gave him a birthday hug, no one even bought him a drink. I asked Ernesta, one of the queens who was wearing a fake tiara for the occasion, if he was always like that on his birthday. "Raul is always Raul," he said and laughed.

I don't know exactly how I got to talking to Raul. I guess I felt bad for him, sitting there by himself, moping. But I also remember still feeling disgusted by him, his big stomach, the wet hair on his chest. I kept thinking of him with Jesus; him lying on his back with his big stomach sticking up in the air, wobbling a little as the boy sucked on his wrinkled dick. I could see the sweat running down the slopes of his paunch and wetting the sheets underneath him. I think I was kind of fixated on him. I kept staring. I remember that Rafael and Marta came inside to try to get me to go home with them, but I didn't want to. I don't know how long I sat there thinking about Raul and Jesus and you and

Gilbert and drinking shots of tequila and making myself sick
thinking about everything. Don't even ask me how many shots
of tequila I drank. I kept thinking of Raul fucking some little kid
in the ass and your face kept replacing the kid's face and I
wanted to scream or leave, but I couldn't. And then I realized
that Raul was staring back at me, that he had been staring at
me all along, just smoking and staring. So I got up and went to
sit down with him and as soon as I sat down, all the boys who
had been sitting with him, restlessly jiggling their legs or playing
with the pink napkins, scattered like they were flies.

"You are like me," he said. He did not give me a chance to
protest. "I have been throwing this party every year on my
birthday for eight years. It was eight years ago on this day that
the only person I ever loved left me. He ran away, he went back
to his village in the jungle. He was just a boy, he missed his
mother. I told him I would bring his mother here, I would buy
her a house, but he left. I could have followed him, brought him
back. But instead I hold these parties in his honor." And there
were tears in his eyes. And they were real tears. I couldn't believe
it, this fat, sweaty man rapidly approaching old age was crying
over a village boy who was probably married by now with a
family of his own.

"Yes, I am like you." I know that's what I said. And he smiled
and called for a bottle of tequila and we drank together and
talked about insignificant things and the sun came in through a
crack in the pink curtains, and the queens went home without
saying good-bye. And then I helped Raul close up and we
walked through the town, stepping over drunken bodies, until
we came to the bottom of the hill. And he said good-bye and
started for home, and I watched him walk slowly, yet in a perfectly straight line, up the hill toward his house. And then, somehow, I made it home and fell asleep and I didn't wake up until
dusk.

I think it is time for me to move on. Perhaps I will come home,
perhaps I will continue south. Maybe I should use this opportunity to travel a little. I have saved a bit of money, I could make

a tour of Central and South America. I could even try to get into Cuba. Of course I will not send you this letter. What would be the point? I wouldn't want to upset you and you would just get upset. Instead I will send you a postcard — a picture of the market with lots of colorful fruit and fabrics. I will write, "Am in Mexico enjoying a different surrounding. Please don't worry. Love always, Ester."

LOVE IS A GYPSY CHILD

by Elisa Jenkins

I've always been alert to that sound, the click of high heels moving quickly. Smart, businesslike women with strong perfume, that's who they belong to, always.

Indeed, I smelled her perfume immediately — *Poison*. The purple kind with the look and smell of candy, one of my favorites. Whenever my mother bargain-shopped for birthday presents, I amused myself testing perfumes.

I was in my usual after-school spot that afternoon, in the Music Lobby, slipped between the Coke machine and the wall. My cave, I called it. My waiting place while my parents finished classes and lessons and rehearsals for the day. I was reading Social Studies when I heard the heels. I remember a glossy picture of Calcutta. Mother Teresa and all those terribly elongated bodies.

The heels stopped. I leaned out just far enough to see that they were black boots. So shiny they had to be new. Over them swung a soft, calf-length poncho, a purple so rich it made me taste grape. Purple was indeed her color. And black. Her hair — hip-length, I saw, leaning farther — reflected the fluorescent light into blue, like black glass. Like her boots.

Side Show 1995

She was buying coffee. I heard the thunk of the cup falling, the whir of the machine mixing it — hot and whipped, as advertised. I risked leaning farther, enough for a glimpse of her face, then snatched myself back. People finding me behind the Coke machine were always startled, and that was fun, but I didn't want to startle her. I recognized magic when I saw it, and I was superstitious enough to know that if I began wrong, I would break the spell and lose any possible wishes.

Anyway, a quick glance was all that was needed. Her face — eyes laser-cutting the miniature door where the cup was filling — left an impression. A ballet dancer's face, I thought, sharp cheekbones, sharp eyes. Red lipstick, startling as blood against her dull-colored skin. The dull, golden color of molasses taffy.

I heard her knock the little door aside. Then I heard the heels again. I leaned out just in time for a glimpse of poncho and hair, trailing softly, a beat behind the sharpness of the heels.

That was the first time I saw her.

The second was that same evening. It was thanks to the family business.

Both my parents taught in the Music Department, but the family business was the Symphony. My father conducted, my mother played in the cello section. I carried the flowers.

I'd carried flowers since I was four. Handed them to the soloist during the bows, allowed myself to be kissed and sweated over. Once, I was kissed by a very old man, a pianist, whose mouth smelled of damp earth. My mother said that was a sign of tooth decay.

This may not sound appealing, but in fact, I lived for those twenty or thirty seconds onstage. And lived, even more, for the time beforehand, backstage. It was my chance to dress up and pretend to be a diva, with real props to help me imagine. To stand with my cheek against a velvet stage curtain, clutching a dozen raspberry-smelling roses. Imagining they'd been given to me.

And then, of course, there was the attention.

My job may have originated simply as a perk for being the conductor's daughter, but it continued out of popular demand. The audience, it seemed, enjoyed my smallness and exotic look. "Awww..." I could always hear them murmuring in waves.

I was, at the time of the heels, almost fourteen years old but perhaps the size of an eight-year-old. I was born in Vietnam and apparently malnourished there. Amerasian is what I am — a G.I. leftover — and quite a combination. Almond eyes and golden hair. Born, in short, to play the child in *Madama Butterfly*. Which I did — three times, once locally, twice out of town. I got to do the out-of-town ones because my mother played in the pit orchestra. Each time, I wore earplugs. And even so, vibrated with something like pain, in the embrace of Butterfly's shattering high notes. Something like pain but enjoyable.

Something like pain was what I felt when I saw her, too, the woman of the high heels, the second time. Not that she was singing high notes. She was singing *"L'amour."* The *Habanera* from *Carmen*.

It wasn't a Symphony concert, but I sometimes carried flowers for recitals as well, if the soloist were a guest and considered special. Which she was. Catherine Klug. Visiting artist from Germany.

A Wagnerian soprano, I had envisioned, when my parents had told me my assignment — large boned, large bosomed. And sweating profusely.

We were running late — my father had a night class, so I was with my mother, at a rehearsal across town — and didn't arrive until the last number. The *Habanera*.

Hustled out of my coat and into the wings, I was breathless when I caught sight of her. Heart pounding already. So, seeing her may not have been as much of a shock as it seemed.

Still, it was a shock, finding her again, so soon. When I'd barely had time to digest my first impression. Not a ballet dancer. A mezzo. From Germany. Also, the *Habanera* was my favorite song. I'd fallen asleep to it since I was five. The dark, minor chords, the gentle, insistent pulse of the piano, automatically turned me limp.

Her voice floated over the pulse. Cautioning, "Love is a wild bird." I believed her.

Her hair was in a knot, twisted hard, like the modern sculpture in front of the Arts Building. Her lipstick was, as before, like blood. Her mouth stretched over large teeth, caressed m's and p's, spit t's. Her eyes seemed to crackle as she sang, long and pure, "*Prends garde à toi*" — "Beware."

It couldn't have been coffee, I thought suddenly, fingering the skin of the roses as the stage manager draped them across my arm. Singers didn't drink coffee, not on the day of a recital. Not hot chocolate either. Chicken soup, I decided, watching her body arch for the final note. It must have been. Hot and whipped chicken soup.

The audience erupted. Their roar buoyed me across the stage, lifted the flowers from my arms to hers.

She put her hand on my shoulder. Another perk of my job was that it allowed me several very beautiful long dresses. This one was dotted swiss, a pink cloud. She slid her fingers over the dots, lingering as if reading braille.

Then she kissed me.

With a kiss unlike any other. Not tense or puckered. She brushed her lips across my cheek the way I brushed mine across an ice cream cone.

And she looked at me.

Not as other adults did, not patronizing, not amused. Not uneasy. Interested.

Not in me personally, I could see that. Interested generally. She would look at anyone that way. I knew, because in her eyes, I recognized my own eyes, my own way of looking. Eyes that seemed to tip forward. I'd gotten in trouble for them, often.

As I left the stage, I imagined her eyes following me, seemed to feel their warmth, like a blush. I turned to look and nearly jumped out of my skin. She was watching me. I hurried off.

It was only then, safe backstage, that I realized I could smell her perfume. Purple candy again. As if smell would have been one sense too many.

We dashed away while the applause was still going on. Usually, after concerts, I hung around to meet the soloists, got their autographs if they were famous. But my mother had exams to grade.

This was fine with me. Every Easter, my grandmother, the impractical one, sent me a basket overflowing with chocolate bunnies. Every Easter, I hid it, deep in my closet, for at least a week, terrified to take the first bite. Afraid I might not stop until the last bunny was gone. I'd done that one year. After the first few bites, it had all tasted of rubber. But I'd been unable to stop.

The thought of meeting Catherine — I'd already begun to think of her — gave me the same fear. I wanted to savor the impressions she'd given me, keep their flavor, unspoiled. Also, I had the hiccups — not a fortuitous sign. As I said, I knew to tread carefully where magic was concerned.

Instead, I pumped my parents for information, over pizza. We hadn't had time for a proper dinner that evening.

Yes, my mother said, she'd met her — briefly, she said — in a faculty meeting. She had sat beside her. "Very quiet," she said. "Except for her eyes."

I smiled.

I'd been doing that, on and off, since the recital.

"A visiting artist, yes," my father said. He'd missed the faculty meeting but had met her, he said, the previous spring, when she'd interviewed for the position.

"Here for a year," he said.

"From Germany, yes," he said. "Not German, though. American. American Indian, I believe, somewhere in her background."

"Which would account for the extraordinary hair," my mother said, between red pen strokes. She'd brought her exams to the restaurant.

"'Appropriate for gentleness or madness,'" my father quoted.

87

I smiled. He loved her.

"Luxurious," my mother agreed, sucking her pen.

I smiled. She loved her too. My parents loved everyone. Similar to the way I was interested in everyone. Not the same but similar.

"She was apparently something of a prodigy," my father said, mouth full of pizza. "Went to Germany right out of school. Had success in provincial opera houses. Intended to come back. Then married a German husband."

"But she's divorced," my mother said earnestly. "Now. So I hear. Regrouping."

"She is. Which is why we were darned lucky to catch her at this point. Next year, she'll be off to bigger and better..."

She was divorced. I smiled.

She must be sad, I thought. Especially if the divorce was recent. Sad and lonely.

I felt strangely elated. Relieved. Perhaps she was in need of magic too. I reminded myself to eat pizza, thought this over. Perhaps we could exchange magics.

"Yes, a promising young woman," my father was saying. "She'll be soloing with the Symphony, we start rehearsals in a few weeks."

I swallowed pizza painfully.

"And she's doing *Carmen* in the spring."

So, I would see her again. I would hand her flowers again.

And I would be in the children's chorus of *Carmen*. I was always in the children's chorus.

I smiled. Even if she never bought chicken soup again, I would see her.

I would draw a picture for her, I decided. Slightly abstract. Fanciful. And very colorful. Like the Chagall paintings at the Metropolitan Opera. I would present it to her on Symphony night, along with the flowers. "Here's to the day you'll sing where the real Chagalls are, at the Met." Something like that. Nothing childish. Not for those scrutinizing eyes.

That fantasy lasted a week. Until I saw her again. Again, from behind the Coke machine.

She was leaving the building. She had a boy with her. A boy about my size, maybe taller. So, about nine. Very thin, serious looking. Dark hair to his shoulders. Like the Spanish prince on my mother's *Don Carlo* poster. My mother saved posters from all the operas she'd played for, papered her studio with them. I often stared at that prince. He had such dignity. As if there were an invisible armor holding his back straight.

They were talking in German, Catherine and the boy. They didn't see me when I leaned out of my cave to watch them pass. He was showing her something, explaining it, a painting on construction paper. A splash of bright colors.

She had a son.

For a while I comforted myself with the idea that she had always wanted a daughter, had always felt an ache, an unfulfilled need. But then I remembered the dark-eyed intensity, the exclusivity, of their German.

I almost gave up. I almost decided to think of her as, say, Marilyn Horne or Maria Callas. A bodiless voice. An angel. Someone who could sense my love without needing to know that it came from me — as, I believed, those ladies could, even Maria Callas, who was dead. Someone to love like God.

But she was not a bodiless voice.

Already, she was Catherine. She was a body, a hand. A mouth. A swish of black hair. She smelled of purple candy.

And she had looked at me.

I wanted her magic. I recognized her magic; surely, I reasoned, that alone qualified it as a right desire. And I knew God granted all right desires, my parents had told me so, repeatedly.

By the time I saw her again — again with her son — an idea was forming.

When I saw them, it crystallized.

They were in the grocery store. We nearly ran into them, my mother and I, as we swung into the candy aisle. They didn't even notice. They were in front of the gourmet candy display.

My mother started to say hello. Then she thought better of it. They were arguing. In German. Catherine's mouth stretched over her large teeth, just as when she had sung, forming words with precision. Her eyes crackled.

The boy was waving three packages of licorice. Three colors. Black, red and purple. The thin, worm-like kind that disgusted me. She, it seemed, would only allow him one. One or none. Anyway, that was my guess. In the end, he put them all back.

It was then that my idea crystallized.

Symphony rehearsals were scheduled to begin the next week, my father had told me. The first was to be a piano rehearsal. Just my father and Catherine. And Dr. Andreas, at the piano.

And I would be there. My mother had a night class, so I would be there. Catherine's son would be there too. I was sure of it. She would not leave him with a babysitter.

I would make my move then.

The difficult part would be obtaining the licorice.

I had no pocket money. None. Aside from a cache of pennies found on sidewalks. Every quarter of birthday money, Christmas money, grandmother money, went into the bank. It had always been that way.

And I got no allowance.

My one set of grandparents, the practical ones, thought this was disgraceful, they said I would never learn responsibility. My mother, their daughter, said, on the contrary, I would learn a far greater responsibility than a monetary one. I would learn moral responsibility. I would learn Divine Providence.

If your desire for something is a right desire, she told me, you'll find you already have the means for getting it. Automatically. No matter what it is.

"Don't give a thought to the means," she told me. "Give a thought to the desire."

The courts do it too, my father told me. Examine motive and opportunity.

"But if your motive is good," he told me, "Divine Providence hands you the opportunity."

Of course, Divine Providence was usually my parents. There were a few moments of revelation — a quarter found on the floor just when I needed to make a phone call; a *Best of Callas* album protruding from a trash can, one week after I'd learned it was out of print — but usually, I found myself examining my desires before an earthly court.

I'd never minded. I'd never wanted to buy anything in secret. Not that my parents objected to candy. Particularly if they could share it. But they knew I hated licorice. And even if they'd forgotten, I would run into the same problem the boy had. They would only buy one kind. Unless I told them my plan. They were always eager to buy gifts for other people, especially ones who were new in town.

But this was my adventure. Somehow, I didn't want to share it. Didn't want them watching it.

I'd never realized I was so helpless. I couldn't even save money by going without lunch. I hadn't eaten lunch since I'd started junior high, I practiced my violin instead. My orchestra teacher had given me permission. This, too, was Divine Providence. It got me away from the cafeteria.

Not that I disliked the other students. On the contrary, I saw them as extremely interesting alien beings and thoroughly enjoyed watching them. Interacting was more difficult; then, I watched myself and missed a lot. My small size made me self-conscious. As did my interests. No one else went into convulsions over *Carmen*. So, I confined my watching to the classroom and made do with granola bars in my cave after school.

But even if I told my parents I was eating lunch again, I realized, I would only have time to accumulate $2.75 before the rehearsal. Fifty-five cents a day. The licorice cost $2.75 a bag. Plus tax.

I decided the licorice must not be a right desire.

I would have to accept an alternate plan.

My grandmother, the impractical one, had come for a visit a couple of weeks earlier. She had given me a candy bar. Fifty break-apart squares of chocolate.

I knew this because she had described it to me. I hadn't opened it yet. She had wrapped it in sequined paper and tied a metallic bow around it. I had told her it was too pretty to unwrap, and she, proud of her wrapping, had been pleased. But it was really the Easter basket dilemma all over again.

I decided it would have to do. It was imported from Germany, she'd said. Maybe it would make him feel at home. Then again, maybe he was allergic to chocolate. I would have to trust Divine Providence.

I unwrapped the candy bar. And was greeted by the intoxicating smell of chocolate in glossy paper. A picture of smooth, brown squares, gleaming. And something else.

Intersecting the picture, wrapped neatly around it, was a ten dollar bill.

Divine Providence.

The actual buying of the licorice was tiresome. My only time alone was after school, but I couldn't go straight to the store from there. I had to go to campus first, miles in the opposite direction, to assure my mother I hadn't been kidnaped between school and the Music Lobby. Being late would cause an incident.

I ended up with blisters on both heels. But I got the licorice. Red and purple and black. And more than a dollar in change. I would put the dollar in the bank, I decided. I would tell my parents that my grandmother had given me a dollar with the candy bar, and in my thank-you note, I would say, "Thank you for the money," unspecific.

Better, I would ask my mother to send the dollar to Covenant House with her next donation. I owed Divine Providence.

When Catherine arrived for the rehearsal, I was waiting, hidden in the auditorium. Huddled in the back row with my flashlight, reading *Great Expectations* to keep calm. I heard her heels thumping the carpet. And with them, a shuffling. Her son, trying to match her stride.

I covered my flashlight. They didn't see me. The auditorium was dark except for a yellow light onstage, a halo framing my father and Dr. Andreas as they leaned against the piano, making each other laugh.

My backpack was on the floor. I touched it with my toe, gratified to hear a crackling. Inside it were the three packages of licorice.

She settled her son in an aisle seat at the other end of the auditorium. He had a backpack too. He pulled a book out of it. Then he pulled out a flashlight.

I was startled. But, of course, I realized, he'd been at dozens of rehearsals, just as I had. Rehearsals in Germany. An ocean away. I found the idea strangely exciting.

She was speaking to him quietly, giving him instructions, it seemed. Then she kissed him. And launched herself down the aisle, waving to my father and Dr. Andreas.

She was wearing her purple poncho again. Her hair was loose.

She flashed a smile as she mounted the stage, kissed Dr. Andreas, kissed my father. The same way she had kissed me, lips brushing his cheek like ice cream. I saw him blush — my father was ruddy complexioned and blushed easily — then try to pretend he wasn't affected. I giggled behind my hand. Poor Daddy, I thought.

"So," he said heartily, clapping his hands. "What shall we begin with? Any preference?"

"The *Agnus Dei*," she said immediately.

"Ah, yes, " he said, still hearty. "Religion first, flirtation and tragedy later. Very wise."

"Very," she said, fixing him with her tip-forward eyes. "Offer first fruits to the Lamb of God, and rehearsal will go well, I assure you." There was a pause. Then she smiled.

I saw Dr. Andreas' eyes dart sideways to meet my father's. I smiled too. I'd provoked that look myself — in teachers, Girl Scout leaders, my practical grandparents — though never so deliberately. I'd never been able to control it, my penchant for making people uncomfortable.

I waited until they were absorbed in the music, then eased my backpack onto my shoulder. And crept along the row of seats to the aisle. The haunting waves of Rossini's *Agnus Dei* crept along with me. I held myself stiff so the packages of licorice would not make any noise.

I allowed myself one glance at Catherine. Her face was stretched long, in an "Ah." A mask of holiness. But fiery holiness. Carmen in church. I waited long enough to see her mouth luxuriate around "*Miserere nobis.*" Then I crouched in the carpeted aisle. And inched myself along. Until I was behind the boy's seat.

His hair had fallen forward, as he bent over his book. It hid his face.

"Hi," I whispered.

He turned to look at me.

His eyes didn't crackle like his mother's. But they were as steady.

I took a deep breath, didn't allow myself to hesitate.

"I have licorice," I said. "Red and black and purple. Do you want some?"

He studied me calmly.

He doesn't speak English, I thought. For some reason, I hadn't anticipated that.

But he did. He was considering. After a moment, he said, "Sure."

"Except we're not allowed to have food in here," I added quickly. "We have to go out to the lobby."

He glanced up at the stage. "I'm not supposed to leave."

His words seemed softened around the edges, as if the letters had been blurred with an eraser. Not exactly a German accent, I thought. Not like the pianist's, the one with decayed teeth. Individual.

I glanced at the stage too. Catherine was leaning over Dr. Andreas' shoulder to study the music, hair dripping onto the piano keys.

"A single line," my father was saying, "your voice emerging from the orchestra, bleeding in, like a ... like ..."

"A vein of silver," Catherine said.

94

I allowed myself a small shiver. Then I turned back to the boy. "They're not thinking about us," I said. "And they can't see us. It's too dark. As long as we don't stay too long, they'll never know."

The boy thought this over.

"All right," he said. He got up quietly, eased the seat up. He set his book on the floor. I saw it was *Alice in Wonderland*.

This, too, was strangely exciting.

Alice in Wonderland had been my bible when I'd started junior high. I'd found it a great comfort to think I'd fallen down a rabbit hole and shouldn't be amazed at anything I saw. I wondered if the boy was comforted too, living in a new country.

I cast a last glance at Catherine. Said a prayer to Divine Providence. Then I opened the auditorium door, slowly, just wide enough for the boy to pass through.

We collapsed onto a bench in the Music Lobby. We had tiptoed the whole way.

The lobby was deserted. The vending machines glowed, like nighttime shop windows. Everyone was in class or rehearsal. I was glad. I tended to act strangely when I thought I was being overheard. And I felt strange enough already.

I pulled the packages of licorice out of my backpack and lined them up on the bench between us. I studied them for a moment, unsure what to do. I hadn't been able to envision beyond this point. It had no precedent. Eavesdropping had always been my *forte*, not friendly conversation.

"What kind do you want?" I said finally.

He shrugged. "What kind are you going to have?"

"Oh, I don't want any," I nearly said, but caught myself in time. He would obviously suspect something then. Though he didn't seem suspicious, oddly, didn't even seem surprised to find the exact candy his mother had refused him turning up one week later. I wondered if he believed in Divine Providence too.

"I've never had purple," I said. "Have you?"

He nodded.

"What does it taste like?"

95

"Grape."

"Oh! That's what I'm going to have. But you can have whatever you want. I'll open them all."

"Actually," he said, "they're good mixed."

"Mixed?"

"Mmm hmm. All three."

I wondered if he was serious. Or if he was like his mother and me, saying strange things just for the sake of it. I peeled the plastic apart. "Okay," I said. "Go ahead."

"Thanks." He disentangled a rope from each package, then lined them up in stripes. He looped them into a knot, pulled it tight. He bit off the ends luxuriously.

"You should try it," he said.

I decided I might as well. It would give me time, perhaps, to think of something to say.

Not that he seemed to care whether I said anything. He was too absorbed in the licorice. So absorbed, he was almost like a statue, an art exhibit. Completely unself-conscious. I felt a stab of envy. Unself-conscious was something I'd never been.

I lined up the ropes carefully, took a long time over the knot.

Then, for a moment, I forgot him. He was right. The sweetness of cherry and grape softened the impact of the licorice flavor. And, at the same time, heightened it. Like alcohol mixed with Coke. I'd discovered that when I'd picked up someone else's drink by mistake at a Music Department party. The mixture improved the licorice.

And the texture was tender. Not hard — not like dried worms, as licorice had always seemed to me. It was worth $2.75 a package.

"It's good," I said. "It's actually good!"

He nodded, grinning. "I know. I used to live on it. For free."

"For free?"

"Mmm hmm." He popped the knot into his mouth, disentangled three more strands from the packages. "There was a man who liked my mother, he came to see her every time she sang, and he always brought her flowers. And he brought licorice for

96

me, all flavors." He giggled. "He thought if he was nice to me, she'd fall in love with him."

I stopped chewing. I swallowed. "Did it work?"

He snorted. "Are you kidding? He was old and fat."

"But," I said, barely breathing, "if he hadn't been old and fat ...?"

The boy didn't answer. He was too busy tying a knot in the three new ropes. He may not have heard me, I'd spoken very softly.

I jumped up. "Downstairs, there's a hallway that looks like a long, red tongue. Have you seen it?"

He shook his head.

"Do you want to?"

He shrugged. "Sure."

"It's like walking into a monster's mouth," I called over my shoulder, as I swung the licorice into my backpack.

The licorice wasn't enough, I could see that. If I wanted our association to last beyond that night, I'd have to impress him further. Particularly if he was following the *Alice in Wonderland* approach to life. The one I'd perfected in seventh grade. That is, enjoying the strange creature — me, in this case — as long as it was there and friendly. But not expecting to see it again or expecting it to be friendly again.

I tried not to panic.

The red hallway was, in my opinion, one of the wonders of campus. Surely, I thought, it would impress him.

And walking gave me an excuse not to talk, as we tiptoed past classrooms. A chance to think what my parents might say. They'd always been good at what they called drawing people out. And they'd sponsored several foreign students.

"Do you like school better here or in Germany?" I said, as we started down the stairs. Then I realized that was a mistake. He hadn't told me he was from Germany.

But nothing seemed to surprise him. I felt another stab of envy. He was better at the *Alice in Wonderland* approach than I was.

97

He shrugged. "Germany, I guess. Because I never went much there. I was always going away with my mother, wherever she was singing. Here, I've gone every day so far. But she's going to be auditioning all over the country. So, I can miss some then."

My life, I thought, the life I wanted. Even when I'd been in shows, when dress rehearsals had lasted past midnight, I'd gone to school the next day. "Take me with you," I wanted to say, "all over the country." Since I couldn't say that, we fell silent.

Then I realized I hadn't asked his name. Or told him mine. But it seemed too late for introductions. Maybe it didn't matter, I thought. Names were an adult idea, anyway.

"You speak English so well," I said.

He nodded. "I always have. My mother and I spoke English all the time in Germany. It was fun when other people couldn't understand us."

"But here you speak German, right?"

He grinned. "Yes."

"I'm going to learn German," I said. I would, somehow. We would speak German, the three of us. We would eat in restaurants, like expatriates, and no one would understand our conversations. We would dress in bright colors and revel in our separateness, our unusualness. Some people are born expatriates, my parents said. No matter where they live.

"Do you go out to restaurants a lot?" I said. "Or does your mother cook?"

"She never cooks. We eat at The Olive Garden."

"The Olive Garden!"

"Mmm hmm. Every night since we moved here. One of her grandmothers was Italian. She says the food's as good as hers."

My parents considered The Olive Garden appropriate for special occasions only. They liked to savor things, as I did, not wear them out with excess.

At that moment, though, I was ready for excess. I imagined the three of us, Catherine, the boy and me, dark-eyed in candlelight, stuffing ourselves. Swirling breadsticks in mounds of pasta, scooping up melted cheese and sauce. Brushing our lips across the coolness of spumoni ice cream.

"Does your mother let you get dessert?" I said.

He nodded. "I always get spumoni."

I couldn't help it, I grabbed his shoulders. "You're so *lucky!*" Now he looked surprised. And a little frightened. It was my tip-forward eyes, I knew. I'd learned, very young, to curb my excitement, but I couldn't always do it.

Fortunately, we'd reached the red hallway. I flung out an arm. "Here it is."

It had the desired effect. His mouth dropped open. He walked in, hand caressing the smooth, red wall, and seemed to forget my wild eyes. I closed them for a moment. Listened to our footsteps. They echoed like notes on a piano, buzzing with overtones, overlapping.

"Wait till you get around the curve," I said. "Then you can't see anything but red."

He took it all in, red walls, floor, ceiling. Red elevator at the end. Its doors like giant tonsils. All of it shiny as wet paint. He turned slowly, a full circle. I did the same. It was the best way to enjoy the deliciously disorienting effect.

"This is brilliant," he said. "It really is like a monster's mouth. What's it for?"

"It goes to Recital Hall," I said, grateful to find I could speak calmly, if a little quickly. "It joins the two buildings together. We're underneath the sidewalk now. They use it for moving pianos and harps and things. Choirs too. So they don't have to go outside. They go up in the elevator and come out backstage. My father thinks it looks like a mouth because it's supposed to be good luck. In Italy, they don't say 'good luck' or 'break a leg' before a performance. They say '*In bocca al lupo.*' That means —"

"'Into the wolf's mouth.'" He smiled. "I saw the elevator there, backstage. I didn't know where it went."

That caught me off guard. "You mean — when your mother sang? You were there?"

It shouldn't have surprised me. I simply hadn't thought of it before. That night seemed to exist in a vacuum. Just Catherine and me and the impersonal roar of the audience.

Then I realized. "Did you see me?"

"Of course." He shrugged. "I saw you. Onstage, I mean. You smelled of curry. That's what my mother said."

"Curry?" I thought back. Yes, I'd been at Mrs. Gupta's house, we'd rushed to the recital from there. And, yes, she had been making curry. She played viola in my mother's quartet. Supermom, my mother called her. Able to cook dinner and rehearse at the same time.

"Curry." I realized I was blushing. "Your mother told you that?"

He nodded. "She loves curry. Are you going to have some more licorice?"

I felt as if I'd turned transparent, one of those cellophane, fortune-telling fish, curling up at the edges.

The boy was watching me calmly, waiting for an answer. I suddenly, irrationally, wanted to hug him.

Instead, I handed him the packages of licorice. "You have it," I said. "All you like."

He slid down the wall to the floor, gave the licorice his full attention. I watched him loop the knot, again envying his unselfconsciousness. His businesslike, thin fingers.

I wondered if he'd been malnourished too. My parents said eating too much rich food was the same as being malnourished. We both had the bones of street urchins.

"Hey," I said, "are you going to be in *Carmen*?" The children in *Carmen* were street urchins.

He shrugged. "I usually am."

"You mean — with your mother?"

"Mmm hmm."

I suddenly wanted licorice. I tore three strands from the packages.

"I'm going to be in it too," I said, hearing my voice jump. I kept my back to him. I knew how my eyes must look. "I'm always in the children's chorus. And I already know the song."

I began to sing the children's march, softly, as I twisted the strands. Singing in the red hallway was wonderful. It turned one voice into a choir. I often sneaked down after school to do it but usually lost my nerve; there were generally people passing by. At this hour, though, it seemed safe, it felt as if the boy and I were the only ones in the building. Even the boy seemed safe, his concentration on the licorice seemed to insulate him, insulate me from him. I let my voice rise to meet a cascade of overtones.

Then I fell silent. He was singing too. In a clear boy soprano, shimmery as an overtone. "*Nous marchons la tête haute, comme de petits soldats...*"

We stared at each other, wide-eyed.

It seemed miraculous, for some reason, that we both should know the words. In this unreal, red world.

He seized my arm. His voice a whisper of controlled excitement. "I bet you can't sing *Carmen* from beginning to end, everybody's part."

"I bet you can."

"I can."

"I can too."

We'd gotten pretty far — we were launching into "*L'amour*," her song, and not being too careful of the volume — when we heard the heels. Echoing like typewriter keys in the long, red tongue of a hallway.

We'd lost complete track of time.

She rounded the bend, hair switching. She stopped short when she saw us. The two of us, curled against the wall, packages of licorice strewn around us. Her eyes took it all in, her eyes that seemed to tip forward. The purple of her poncho seemed too rich, unbearable, against the red.

Then she started toward us, mouth twitching, covering and uncovering her oversized teeth.

101

The boy hadn't moved. His shoulder was warm and solid against mine. She pulled him to his feet and slapped him across the face.

He didn't cry.

I was already on my feet when she turned to me. Her hair seemed to ripple with anger. The entire hallway seemed to ripple with it, to expand and contract around us. Red and purple and black. She studied me for a moment. Then she slapped me too.

I cried.

I reached for the boy, grasped his narrow shoulders. I pressed my burning cheek to his. The skin tingled, seemed to crackle, like silver paper between us.

Then I smiled. It was like an opera.

I smiled. Already, I was included.

"*Prends garde à toi*," she'd sung. Beware. Love is a Gypsy child. Love is a wild bird. But was it? Wasn't love a right desire? Hadn't Divine Providence made this possible?

I realized she was watching me. Eyes wide. Angry. But interested. The hallway had stopped rippling.

I felt I should say something.

"*Die Götter selbsten schützen sie.*"

The gods themselves protect you. It was the only German I knew with certainty. I had once auditioned for *The Magic Flute*.

She didn't reply, only stared.

I felt the boy slip away from me, heard him gathering the bags of licorice. He pressed them into my hands.

"You can keep them," I whispered, "if you want." He did. He handed me my backpack.

We started back, in silence. She had not stopped watching me. Finally, she shook her head.

"*Ach, mein Kind,*" she said.

This was my cue. I was sure of it. I stretched out my hand toward her. Not hesitating, not trembling. Not taking my eyes from hers. I reached up to touch her hair.

I was amazed at its heaviness. It was like putting my hand under a stream of water. I stroked it once, twice.

She nodded, as if this were what she had expected. *"Die Götter,"* she said, "indeed."
Our footsteps turned dull as we emerged from the red mouth. It was going to be quite a year.

FATHERBIRTH

by Martha Kent

He was fed up with sitting around. He was wondering whether this child was going to be on the way forever, but he did his best to conceal his boredom from Amy.

They sat on the porch in the heat, waiting for his mother and father to arrive. Amy lay back in the big chair he had to drag out from the living room. Her feet, resting on the hassock, were splayed out as though she didn't care how she looked.

He couldn't get over the changes in her. Her face had coarsened, her lips, still delicious and pink, but broadened over her teeth. Her beautiful, glowing color was still there: the rich dark gold of her hair, now plastered against her forehead in the heat, and the rose-like blush of her skin, a color wash which covered all of her, down to her toes. But she was like a mountain, her belly and breasts huge, her whole body bloated. He could see the veins standing out in her legs and somehow her feet had gotten longer, awkward looking in her sensible shoes. He missed her sexy high heels.

She smiled at him calmly and then flinched and a strange expression crossed her face. "The baby just got up! You have no idea how odd it feels ..."

He responded with a sigh. Out of his sense of duty to his love for Amy, to the relationship, he tried to enter into her feelings and said, "He'll be out soon."

"Sometimes I feel like I've been possessed. There's a demon inside me. It pushes so hard on my insides that sometimes, for a second, I can't feel anything, and then when I can feel again, it's so queer, like electricity, a wobbling kind of a shock." She drew a labored breath and continued her inward canvassing.

"I'd love to have some iced tea — I think I'll go make some." She heaved herself up and started to walk away, flat-footed and swaying.

He jumped up, "I'll get it for you!" and he turned her around and forced her to sit down again.

While he was getting the ice and slicing a lemon, he was thinking, wistfully, of when they had first lived together and he couldn't get enough of her. When she had whispered to him, "Aren't we crazy-happy?" and blew her warm breath in his ear, it had made him lunge at her with instant desire. When she soothed him and held him lovingly in her arms after a quarrel, he marveled at her unselfishness. Most of all, though, he loved her physicality, because she was tall and broad shouldered, had long legs and beautiful brown hands and could play tennis nearly as well as he could. And yet in bed, she was soft and pliant, with skin like silk. And he loved to hear her laugh, her attractive, husky laugh — oh, Amy, he thought, come back!

Now she seemed immense, embarrassing, endless, with her motherhood. He sometimes thought of the baby growing inside of her and wished it away, pictured someone or something relieving her of her burden. He had even dreamed once that he was extracting something from her under a white tent. It had ended in some dim place that had frightened him, but which he couldn't remember.

"I wish my Dad would get here," he said fretfully, when he came back with the tea. "And Mother. You'll need Mother soon."

"I'll need the hospital soon and you'll have to entertain your parents." She laughed, but added, "It's nice of them to come ... I have no idea what they'll do with themselves though."

He felt that she hadn't faced up to the fact yet that there was going to be an actual baby to take care of. She seemed satisfied with her bulk and her dreaminess as though the whole thing ended there. "Don't forget two of you are going to come back and you'll need Mother then," he reminded her.

Without responding to his cautioning, she sighed to herself, "Oh, how uncomfortable I am," and he felt sorry for her and for lack of anything else to do to make it easier for her, he kissed her on top of her head.

At that moment they saw the car draw up and his mother get out and wave from the curb. She came hurrying up the walk and his father brought two suitcases into the house and everybody talked at once. Then his mother looked Amy over quite frankly.

"Soon," she said.

"Hope so," Amy responded.

"Are you afraid?" his mother blurted out.

Amy gave her a half resentful look, but then her face relaxed and she pushed her head back against her chair. "Sometimes I wonder what it's going to be like ..."

"You have a good doctor." His mother made this a statement. "I thought you might insist on having it at home. Did your doctor talk you out of it?"

"I thought of it," Amy said vaguely, "but Tim here didn't want to," and she gave him a faintly mocking look. "He's the one that's scared to death."

His mother ignored the comment. Tim knew his mother had never been entirely reconciled to his marriage. There was a block of coldness between her and Amy which he wished would melt. Maybe they'll get friendly over the baby.

There was a great deal of maneuvering over dinner. The parents wanted to take them both out and Tim said there was plenty to eat in the house.

"You wouldn't have to do anything," he assured Amy hurriedly, "I'll heat up the stuff..." But finally he saw her lose her
patience. She shut her eyes and said, "Go, all of you. Leave me
alone."
When she saw their offended faces, she laughed, uncaring.
"You all look identical. You sure are one family," then, unwilling
to give it any more effort at all, "You can bring me some ice
cream — I'll be all right here...Please!"
"O.K.," Tim agreed, "We'll get you a hot fudge sundae — you
used to love them."
She turned away from him impatiently, but the anger faded
immediately from her face because she was too tired to keep it
with her.
Her mother-in-law turned around then, patted her arm and
gave her a gentle, sympathetic smile.
"Rest a while Amy. Maybe we can find something to tempt
you. We'll come right back. Don't worry yourself."
In the car Tim took the chance to complain, "I don't ask for
much, but, it hasn't been easy ... she's so full of herself ..."
"She's full of you," his father chuckled.
His wife tartly inserted, "She's full of her baby."
"That's what I meant, Ma," protested Tim's father, "Tim's son-
to-be," he grinned at his son.
"Son *or* daughter, she's the one that has to do it."
Both men, although they did not look now at one another, drew
together by means of a glum, disapproving silence.
"I hope for her sake, it's over soon." Male silence.
"A first baby isn't easy." More silence.
"No baby is easy." That shut them all up until they were half
way through their meal, when Tim's mother began to relent and
placate them with some cheerful chatter about Nora, Tim's oldest
sister, who had already "dropped two babies," as she put it.
Quoting Nora and the casual way she refers to the process is
supposed to cheer me up, but it doesn't Tim thought gloomily.
When they arrived back at the house, Amy was nowhere to be
seen. Tim leapt up the stairs to their bedroom, saw the open

bathroom door, began to call her, "Amy? Amy? Where are you ...?"

Her voice came from the little spare room where the parents were to sleep, until the newborn baby supplanted them. He looked in at her. She had opened the couch into its double bed status and was spreading sheets on the mattress. When she bent low to straighten and smooth the sheet, her unwieldiness and the mal-distribution of her weight almost toppled her. For a moment she struggled, then straightened herself, got up off of her knees and pressed her hands into the small of her back, throwing her head back to ease her burden. She had looked up at him with such a completely unselfconscious look of patience, willingness, sweetness, that his heart went out to her. He wanted to embrace her, stroke her hair, make her comfortable and easy. A wave of love for her, and pity, swept over him and he had to leave her to conceal his emotion. He shut himself in the bathroom and some unexpectedly hot tears ran down his face. He filled the basin with cold water and plunged his whole face into it to wash away the evidence of weakness. Then they went downstairs to give Amy her treat. She thanked them nicely but didn't eat it. "I think I'll go up to bed," she said and toiled back up the stairs.

During the night the light suddenly woke Tim up, his heart beating with apprehension. She was sitting up in her bed looking wan and big-eyed.

"Has it started?"

"No, I don't think so, I'm just so uncomfortable and I have a pain ... I guess it's just a gas pain ..." she sighed and wearily picked up her book. "Go back to sleep ..."

And that is what he did although he fully meant to stay awake beside her. He saw how she was looking at him with a tremor of hurt tightening her face, saw her shrug and rub her sides, heard her whisper, "Oh, never mind, I'll ..." and even so he was asleep before she had finished whatever she was saying. And he didn't wake up until after she was up and gone from their room in the morning, and he felt remorse for that.

His parents waited at the breakfast table. Tim's mother, alert, quizzed Amy about her pains in the night, but no one knew what, if anything, there was to do.

"Oh, just wait, I guess," Amy murmured vaguely.

But then, at precisely half past two that afternoon, Amy appeared from her room and there was a subtle change in her face. She said hesitantly, "I think ..." she looked at her watch, "Yes, I'm sure I'm having real pains. I've timed them."

Tim leapt to his feet, wild-eyed. She laughed. "It's all right Tim — they're not bad, but would you call the doctor for me and ask him?"

Tim, hands shaking, dialed, misdialed, redialed, finally had the doctor's office on the phone.

"This is Tim Willis," he announced in a cracked voice like an adolescent. "The wife of Amy Willis."

His mother stifled a snort of laughter and Amy smiled. But her smile faded quickly for her attention was turned abruptly to an inward signal. She began to look flushed, wary, hostile. Something in her had suddenly activated quite without her will and Tim felt she was accusing him of being to blame for it. Tim was afraid of that expression on her face.

When the doctor finally came to his phone, again Tim quavered "This is Tim Willis. I'm the wife of Amy Willis ... she ... yes ... how often? How often, Amy?"

"Fifteen minutes apart."

He repeated that and listened to the doctor. He put down the phone and told his staring audience. "He says I can bring you into the hospital, but there's no hurry ..." he looked at them like a dog, waiting to be told what to do.

"All right, Tim. You might as well. I'm all packed and I took my shower."

He left his parents sitting in the living room and took her away in the car. Like a somnambulist he was, beside his changed and terrifying wife. He was thinking, how'll we get through this ... maybe she'll die ... he couldn't swallow properly with his dry throat.

She put her hand in the crook of his arm. He thought she wanted to ask him to stay with her in the labor room if they would let him, but she didn't. Anyway soon it would be out of their hands.

I should have learned how to go through the thing with her, he confessed to himself as they passed through the familiar streets. Only they no longer looked familiar and ordinary, but strange. Again he was afraid of losing his self control. But then she drew her breath in sharply. "That was a real one," she even gasped this time. It riveted all his attention.

He put his foot down hard on the accelerator. They shot past the hospital entrance and he had to make a U-turn to get back.

The nurse put Amy in a wheelchair, wheeled her into the office behind the reception area and nearly barred Tim from following, but he glared at her and she left them together there, indifferently. Finally, a small self-important woman appeared and began to rap out intrusive questions like, "What was your mother's maiden name?" and to write down the answers on forms. Amy looked more and more strained. Tim wanted to say something sarcastic to the registrar, like, "Do we have to pay the bill *before* we have the baby?"

Finally it was over but the bossy little woman took her own sweet time calling the nurse back. Tim hated the nurse even more than the receptionist, as he followed Amy's chair down the hall.

The nurse said to him, he thought, condescendingly, "You can wait in the sunroom over there, while we get this young lady ready for action." She smiled down at Amy, but Amy only gazed miserably around at Tim. She looked scared and abandoned and not at all like herself. They disappeared, and the hospital door squunched shut with a little squeal.

Tim waited and waited and smoked and waited. The nurse finally came to warn him: "Nothing much is going to happen yet awhile ... you might as well go home."

"I want to see my wife," he insisted stubbornly.

"Okay, okay," she grinned at him lewdly, he thought, and opened Amy's door. "Just a few minutes now ..."

110

Amy was propped up in her hospital bed; she clutched Tim's
hand gratefully.
"She shaved me and gave me an enema — it was awful." Then
she produced a little, normal giggle. "The water broke, I think.
The plug plopped out."
"What?" he asked stupidly.
"The plug in the cervix, *you* know. It popped out just like a
champagne cork!" she laughed again.
Then suddenly he saw that wary and hostile look on her face
again.
"Whew," she whispered. Her face looked ugly with strain, "...
Not too bad." She was still determined to be jaunty, but he,
frightened, felt awkward and ungainly and was beginning to
wonder desperately if he was going to have to stand there all
night.
The nurse tugged open the heavy, sluggish hospital door again
and gave him a quizzical look. He hated her big white shoes
and strong legs. "Doctor'll be here soon."
"Tim, go home. No use your waiting here. They'll call you
when ... won't they, Nurse?"
She nodded and planted her foot firmly, forcing the door to
stay open.
"Are you sure, Amy?" he wavered, hoping she would insist.
She gave him a childish — perhaps pleading? — smile. But
before he knew it, he was outside, starting the car, and feeling
guilty, hideously guilty, and relieved, although he had half a
mind to rush back in.
At home, his mother wanted to know everything. He couldn't
tell her what Amy had said. "She's okay" was all he muttered.
"I need a drink," he decided, and hurried to the kitchen. He
made a tall, strong scotch-and-soda, gulped it down, and mixed
another. His mother began to harangue him about drinking at
such a time.
Tim's father came into the kitchen. "Leave him alone, Ma. Let
him unlax," and patted his son awkwardly on the shoulder. Tim

finished the second drink and started on a third. He suddenly felt a little drunk and a little hilarious. He wanted more whiskey. His mother was mad.

"Never mind, I'll do any driving that needs to be done, Ma. You know a first baby is hard on everybody." Tim's father was placating her and grinning privately at Tim. "Eat something," he said.

When the phone rang, deep in the night, Tim woke with a terrible taste in his mouth. He answered thickly. It was the doctor, brisk and cheerful as though it were eight o'clock of a sunny morning. It seemed everything was fine. Amy was fine, sleeping, no need to come in immediately. Baby fine ... Tim interrupted, babbling gratitude. "Doc, I really want to thank you." His cracked high voice again made him feel foolish.

"Don't you want to know what you've got?"

"What? What?" He'd forgotten about the baby.

"A beautiful little girl. Eight pounds two ounces."

There were plenty more marvels to come, set off by the event in the night.

The first was that Amy, the next morning, looked radiantly happy and beautiful as she motioned to her considerably flatter stomach.

"How was it?" he asked, putting his roses down on her bedside tray.

"It was ... there were some bad parts." She looked at him, smiled at the flowers, but he could see she wasn't thinking about him. "I'll tell you about it later." And right after saying that, she began an eager recital: pain like a boa constrictor twisting around her insides; how they left her alone for so long; how the nurse had lectured her for complaining about the pain and told her she'd gotten herself into this fix; how she'd been afraid and then had stopped being afraid; and in the delivery room they made her lie on her stomach. She said it was like trying to balance on a big bowling ball. The caudal block was taking forever to work, and how another doctor had come in and taken her hands in his and comforted her, meanwhile gossiping with her own doctor cheerfully, about another delivery. She said this unknown man's hands were so warm and pumped such care and kindness into her and his voice was so resonant and beautiful, that she fell in love with him, there on the delivery table, even though she never saw him. And Amy had the effrontery (quite innocently, he had to admit) to expect Tim to sympathize with her sudden crush on this hero!

He had immediately turned wooden with jealousy: "Holding hands with you? On the delivery table? Weird way to get your kicks." And he knew himself how foolish he sounded.

"Tim, are you crazy?" Amy laughed into his disapproving face. "After all, I didn't have you to hang onto, did I? And besides this love affair, it only lasted 'til they turned me over. Then I had other things to think about. The caudal block wasn't working and finally they put a mask over my face and knocked me out. And that's all I know. But not all I want to know," she added slowly.

Even though he still didn't like what she had confessed about that upstart doctor, common sense told him it had to be put aside.

"Here's your breakfast," he hastened to say. "You can tell me the rest later."

She pulled herself up. "Tim, I'm so happy! I didn't think I'd be so happy! And so hungry!"

"Eat, sweetheart," he said and kissed her soft cheek.

Then a different, nicer, prettier nurse presented the baby to him out in the hall and he was startled at how strange-looking it was, really awful, even though his parents were cooing and murmuring, "Beautiful" and "Lovely" and using some terrible baby talk.

The baby didn't look like a baby, nor like a girl. It was red, it had no hair — just some black fuzz, and when it opened those puffy eyelids, he saw big, very dark, opaque blue eyes. They reminded him of the ocean depths you look down into when you're doing blue-water sailing far out of sight of land. He liked best the small, firm, three-cornered mouth. This little, round-headed, ever so faintly snuffling and creaking thing looked like it had been asleep for a thousand years and knew things he'd never know. He felt a strange pang before the mystery of that closed, far-off face, until he saw the little fist and felt the tiny, velvety, pink fingers. He wanted to say something, but could think of nothing, and turned away quickly because he felt unable to rise to the occasion, to feel whatever it was he was supposed to feel.

The baby was taken to Amy.

"How do you like her?" It was Amy demanding praise. She was holding the little tightly wrapped bundle now, and when the baby let out a tiny wail, he responded to the sound with a suddenly sentimental, inane moo.

"Do you think she's pretty?" pursued Amy.

"Oh, fine ... What'll you call her?"

"Don't you care what she's named?"

"Sure. How about Amantha?" he had never precisely thought of that name before in his life, but it seemed to fit.

Amy was very pleased with him. "Amantha," she said and he saw that thin teary film that made her eyes glisten. "Amantha Willis ..."

During the next few hard-pressed weeks, he got to know that baby voice by heart. He and Amy quarreled about which of them was the more tired. He said disgustedly, "The kid doesn't like being here ... at all."

The pediatrician said she'd soon settle down and Amy, reassured, contentedly observed to him that same day, "You know, Tim, the most miraculous thing is that now the baby's here I can't remember what it was like without her. It seems like she's always been here. As though the world without Amantha had never really existed at all. I can't imagine life without the baby!"

He didn't understand the feelings she was trying to give expression to, but he liked to sit nearby while Amy suckled the baby, who was quiet and contented then. The curves of breast, of the two heads, of Amy's soft closed face, were beautiful, and the sweet, warm milky smell gave him pleasure and peace. But if someone had demanded of him, "Are you a father?" he would

have felt unable to apply such a label to himself. He was a ...
man, a boy (secretly to himself), a husband, a son ... all of that
... he was an engineer — that's what he *was*, that's what he *did*
— but a father? He hadn't made the connection yet.

It was easy enough for Amy — she was automatically con-
nected. But he had no part in it — in that system of rosy curves
and warmth and private satisfactions there before his eyes.

Very soon, however, he was taking the whole thing for granted,
going grumpily to work, wishing for freedom, and doing what
Amy asked him to do without much enthusiasm, as the baby
grew.

One Sunday afternoon he found himself posted to watch beside
Amantha. She was lying naked except for her diaper on a fleecy
puff of blanket on the grass, waving arms and legs in the air,
like a cherub on a cloud. She was absorbed in the quiver of green
leaves overhead, and Tim gradually became absorbed too, in his
book.

When a small sound from her broke his concentration, he
looked over at the baby to find her staring roguishly, expectantly,
at him. She had stuffed one fat pink foot entirely into her mouth.

He was caught by laughter, scooped his daughter up and hurried into the house to find his wife. He had suddenly understood
what Amy meant about not being able to remember what life
was like without the baby. It was true, she was right, Amantha
had changed the world.

"Amy! Amy!" he proclaimed with amazement and delight.
"The kid's got a sense of humor." And he danced the crowing
baby around the room, around the mother, and out into the sunshine again.

The lost heart stiffens and rejoices ... - T.S. Eliot

AWFUL DARING

by Colleen Crangle

As Lilian opened the double-swing doors into the lobby, Isaac was on his way out, coming toward her with a mop in one hand, a bucket in the other. At the same time, Mrs. Theron, a brown leather handbag looped over her forearm, her cable-stitch cardigan buttoned all the way up her chest, descended the stairs to the lobby. Uncertain where to go, Lilian hesitated and, as if out of step in a dance of strangers, bumped into Isaac as he strode by her to the doors still swinging gently from her entry. Mrs. Theron, at Lilian's side in a second, took her arm, explaining that the cleaner, a black man (she called him "the cleaning boy"), was inclined to insolence. "You've come to see the empty flat?" she asked. "I can show it to you." Lilian glanced at the handbag still over Mrs. Theron's arm. "My shopping?" said Mrs. Theron. "I'll do it tomorrow. No hurry. No hurry at all."

Two days later, Lilian moved in. It was a sharp, biting late winter day in Pretoria. She plugged in her heater and, sitting close to it to soak up warmth from its two gleaming elements, began a letter to her sister in Cape Town, a Sunday evening ritual. "I have found a wonderful place to stay," she wrote. "It's sparkling clean, the rent is low, and a magnolia tree grows right outside my bedroom window. To top it all, there's an elderly widow, a Mrs. Theron, who lives alone downstairs and keeps an eye on things. I think I'll like it here."

That Friday Lilian came home from work to find Isaac waiting for her. He stood in the middle of her living room, next to the clotheshorse she had set out that morning. His khaki shorts, too big for him, hung just above the polish pads strapped to each knee. He held a tin of floor polish in his hand.

"The water drips," he said, pointing with the tin to the parquet tiles at his feet. "Water on wood, it makes tiles loose." He tapped a loose tile with his foot. "You must not hang your washing here." His black canvas shoes had thick rubber soles and his slowly thudding foot was the only sound in the room.

Lilian looked at the clothes draped over the wooden frame — on the top rung a grey mohair cardigan and a black pleated skirt, both almost dry, and lower down on an inner rung, her stockings, the toes still dark with dampness. Nothing had really dripped badly, though, she thought. Who was he to tell her what to do in her own home, she a senior accounts clerk and certainly no longer a child at 32? His job was to clean the floors, hers to use them. She looked back at him, taking in his stocky build and noticing, despite herself, that his legs were far too short for his body, just as hers were. She looked around, hesitating. The room was spotless, red swirls of polish glinting off the veranda floor behind him, above, the windows clear and shimmering in the late sunlight. Still, it would not do to tolerate this arrogance. She told him she would hang her clothes wherever she chose. In silence, Isaac walked out, leaving the door wide open.

"I hope he hasn't been bothering you," said Mrs. Theron from the passageway, approaching the open door with a plate of scones and jam in her outstretched arms. "Be careful or he'll ask for money. He drinks, you know, and has a tendency to thieve."

"Everything's fine," said Lilian, embarrassed by Isaac's reprimand. "You'll stay for tea?" she asked. Mrs. Theron, already inside, accepted the invitation.

Side Show 1995

Lilian soon fell into the quiet rhythm of the place. By the time she left for work each morning, Isaac had already raked the gravel yard behind the flats, leaving long, perfectly even indentations in his wake. He had already scrubbed the concrete walkway that skirted the rear of the building, and she would pass him, bucket in hand, waiting to clean the flats. On Lilian's return from work, she would join Mrs. Theron for a cup of tea. They began to have dinner together Friday evenings, once venturing out to the theater, to a performance of *Othello*. Lilian made sure she mentioned this excursion at work on Monday morning, casually referring also to the Athol Fugard play soon to be staged in town, anxious to give the impression that the theater was her true milieu. The three women who shared her office, all younger than she was and all three married, had sons in nursery school. They never tired of talking about their husbands and their sons. Lilian tried hard not to be boring.

At weekends, quietness gathered like the shirring of a cloth and covered the lives of Isaac, Lilian, and Mrs. Theron. Isaac had Saturday morning off and he used this time to clean his own room, a corrugated iron structure out in the back yard next to a peach tree. Lilian once peeped inside the door, having found it ajar on her return from an early morning stroll. There she saw an iron bedstead with two blankets folded on top of a bare coir mattress. Elsewhere on the concrete floor were two straight-backed chairs, a wooden crate with clothes stacked inside, and a wooden crate turned upside down for a table, on it a jar of sugar and a small sack of meal. Next to the bed was a transistor radio with a wire coat hanger jammed into the aerial socket. Inside a shallow blue plastic basin at the foot of the bed was a large, smooth bar of Sunshine soap.

Later that morning, on her way out again, Lilian glanced down from the walkway outside her door and saw Isaac as he turned from under the peach tree, a bundle of clothes piled high in the blue basin. She stopped for just a moment, wondering where he did his washing and if the water ever ran warm. He looked up and saw her watching. She turned away ashamed, as if she had caught him naked.

Coming home unexpectedly early one afternoon, Lilian surprised Isaac reaching up into her kitchen cupboard, filling a glass jar with sugar. They looked directly at each other for just a moment, then looked away.

"A mouse. I saw one in your kitchen," he said. "I am here to catch it."

"Thank you. Please. Catch it for me," said Lilian, instantly entering into the conspiracy.

The next day she brought extra sugar home from the grocery store. The following week she added coffee to her shopping list. The canister, she noticed, must have been empty for some time. She also bought a large jar of apricot jam. These three items, she learned, needed to be kept in good supply.

A sudden thunderstorm one day early in the summer caught Lilian without umbrella or raincoat, and she arrived home shivering, trailing water up the stairs and into her flat. Still feverish two days later, she called Mrs. Theron, who came immediately with aspirin and hot tea. "Don't worry about a thing. I'll just make a little extra for you each meal and bring it up."

Lilian was in bed for a week, and each day Isaac cleaned her floors with quiet concentration, sweeping and polishing without a word around the clotheshorse on which Mrs. Theron had hung the rained-on clothes to dry. Three times a day, Mrs. Theron arrived at Lilian's bed, a tray of food in her arms.

The last tray she brought carried a sheet of paper. It was a petition to the owner of the building, objecting to a proposed salary increase for Isaac on the grounds that he was "lazy, cheeky, and prone to drunkenness." Lilian read it in silence. She wanted to do something courageous: to be fair. So she began, "I think he works very well. He's not cheeky, just proud of his work ..." But Mrs. Theron interrupted, saying that, never having married and run her own household, Lilian didn't know what

119

she was talking about, didn't know how to manage servants. The increase, Mrs. Theron argued as she stood over Lilian's bed with the tray of hot vegetable soup and buttered bread still in her hands, would surely mean an increase in their rent and Lilian must know how little she, Mrs. Theron, could afford an increase on a widow's pension, struggling to make ends meet and still care for friends and neighbors in their time of need.

Feeling inconsequential and in her debt, Lilian took the pen and signed. She told Mrs. Theron that she really needed to rest then. But once alone again, she sat hunched on the edge of the bed, not moving until the sun had dropped well behind the branches of the magnolia tree, showing in sharp relief against the sky its large solitary flowers.

Lilian announced her decision to move the next day. Mrs. Theron said, "I really thought you liked it here." Her sister wrote the following week, "What a pity. You seemed so happy at last." By the end of the month, Lilian had moved out.

She came back the first night for a fern she had forgotten on her doorstep. Going up the stairs, she encountered Isaac coming down. He was drunk, but managing to stay almost upright by holding tightly onto the handrail. Then leaning for a moment against the bannister for balance, he looked at her directly and said, "Please come back and visit me sometime." Embarrassed, she asked "Why? I don't live here anymore" — as if that were the fact that needed explaining. He said, "Just because. We have been friends," and stumbling down the stairs, he repeated, "Because we have been friends." He turned then to her, steady for just a moment. "That piece of paper. It means nothing."

Lilian drove home with the fern on her lap all the way, not noticing the brown, soggy stain that was spreading across her pleated skirt. She could not forget what she had done. Years of prudence, of doing what was expected, had led her to that act. Now the memory lay like a crab in a tidal pool, its shape distorted by the moving water, scuttling to hide under a rock but never quite getting both its claws under cover at the same time.

She took a week off work and flew to Cape Town to visit her sister, going for long walks on the beach while her sister was at work. The last day was wild and blustery, with clouds that lay in streaks across the sky as if tugged and stretched to breaking. The wind blew hard at her back, wrapping her hair around her face so that as she walked she could see only intermittent patches of white sand and blue-green sea. Turning around and beginning to walk backwards, she took the full force of the wind in her face. Her wandering steps led her to the wet lip of the water's edge where each squelching step sucked her deeper in the sand. She marvelled at her willingness to walk backward, even on a wide empty beach, not knowing what she might back into. It was, she thought, perhaps quite daring. She tried out other words that might apply to her, 'kind', 'quiet' — and 'lonely.' It came to her just like that, 'lonely,' without her having first to use another word for what she felt, 'independent' or 'single' or solitary.'

Just hours before her flight back to Pretoria, the postcard came. It was old, slightly yellowed, and bent at one corner. On the front next to the address was a picture of a wild flower, the *Erica Ventricosa*, its pink tubular blossoms jutting out from a long green stalk. On the back, in printing that was a mixture of small and capital letters, she found this message:

It is my pleasure and opportunity to write this
postcard to you. Mrs. Theron gives me the address
of your sister. Everything here is still going very good.
I would much enjoy to hear from you. My compliments
for your holiday and for your new life. It is a sorrow
that I have missed you. I know mountains don't meet
but they sometimes can meet by their shadows.
 In anticipation.
                  Yours full of faith.
                  Isaac Masango, Pretoria

Side Show 1995

Returning from the airport late that night, Lilian drove past Isaac's block of flats, a small detour. She stopped the car just beyond a pool of light from the street lamp. She looked up at the windows of her old flat behind the branches of the magnolia. She tugged at her skirt, loosening the button at the band where it dug too tightly into her waist. She rubbed her hand down the side of her face, over her temple and cheek and along the jawbone. In a moment's surrender, she stepped out, opened the double-swing doors into the lobby, and walked through to the back of the building. A sliver of light showed under Isaac's door. She knocked quietly and, calling his name, pushed the door open slowly, an act of daring that not even a lifetime of prudence would ever retract.

Scratch a lover, and find a foe. - Dorothy Parker

MON DESIR

by Laurell Swails

Under wisteria hanging purple and sweet, a brown peahen walks, gawky-gaited, pecking in the dull gravel. Water whirls from the lawn sprinklers.

"Where's its colored tail?" Clayton asks.

"Only males have colored tails, Love," I say.

"I wonder where he is," he murmurs and looks around.

"Maybe his colors didn't please her and she left him."

Parched hills howl for water. Smug amid hand-watered foliage and broad lawns, I take Clayton's arm, cross the porch of Mon Desir in the aura of my perfume—*Ondine*.

"Whew." He blots his forehead with a white handkerchief. "This restaurant's an oasis."

"Or a mirage." Fuschias hang from baskets, hearts on plumb lines.

"'Ash-land' is a town properly named. I hope tonight's play isn't so aptly named."

"*Much Ado About Nothing*?" We cross the threshold into the dim interior.

"Where's the head waiter? Did I tell you I joined the Lakeside Club?"

"You did? I should get to know you."

"Know me? You're going to marry me." With an absent look he strokes his short pointed beard.

123

Side Show 1995

In that niche high above the slate-green sea, sturdy salal strung with blue berries and a wind-torn cypress sealed us in. Corn roasted in green sheaths on an Indian kitchen midden of broken shells and sand. Leaving the silver logs and a fire ringed with stones, we descended to an empty beach where anemones in quiet tidal pools beckoned with pale arms; skipped across worn rocks, chased the waves at surf's edge out to sea, until they calmly chased us back. We ran so fast the wind seemed to lift us as it carries sand. On the other side of Devil's Churn, which was with the outgone tide nothing more than damp fault in the cliff rocks, we stopped. You touched my cheek with one finger, quickly, as if you thought I would burn.

"I've been enchanted."

"Isn't it nice?"

We sang of ourselves, patterned the future in damp sand, like a star chart or concerto score, which vanished in the next high tide. Dry on a high, warm outskirt of sand, sheltered by a sea-borne log and caught in place by cliff rocks, incoming tide, Devil's Churn, dark, and waiting for the moon to light our way, we were wed. I heard nothing, only felt the constant beat of the sea, a crash upon rocks that spun me to nothing. Whipped, dazed, we spent the night in silence, watched the moon fall into the sea.

"... lonely. It won't be much longer. Now that I've a foothold in psychology I'll take you away from it all."

Yes, that's what I'm thinking.

"Imagine. It's been two years since we decided."

Remember.

"... this place is full. Maybe we should've made reservations. Things like this don't happen at the Club. It isn't even air conditioned in here."

"Did you ever wind up a tin man and watch him beat his drums? Rat-a-tat-tat—woodpecker rhythm over and over. A person almost hopes for a stroke of thought."

"Does that have something to do with what I was saying?"

"What do you think?"

"You've changed. It's probably the heat."

Strange account. "When you're on a train going south do you suppose it's the land that's moving north?" Water runs down my back, as if I had stepped from a hot river.

"What do you mean? You need a drink. Like a drink?"

"White wine. I'm parched." Fragrance of *Ondine* comes to me, is gone.

"Good evening," the proprietress in black says. We echo her words.

"Can you seat us?"

"This way, please."

Clouds have teased the land all day, holding water out of reach. Where is the man who went away? Clayton wears his face. I shall return to the sea, chant to the white waves until the waters toss him as I thought he was from the deep.

"What?" He has spoken and I have not heard.

"I shot nine under par last week, I said. Go on—follow the lady." He gives me a push toward the black receding form. I follow.

Candles on the table give his beard a sensuous sheen, but his jaw and chin are small, like Trotsky's.

"Veal Prince Orlov for us both and the best white wine you have."

"Pouilly-Fuissé, sir?"

"That will be fine."

A small figure in black moves away from us, the backside of a domino disjointed at the middle.

"A rosé is better with veal ordinarily," Clayton says.

"Must we be ordinary?"

"You should've seen the look on Stan's face—"

"Who's Stan?"

"One of my colleagues. He was with me when I shot nine under par."

"Oh."

"You said this was a French inn. There wasn't a French dish on the menu." His eyes go blind-blank.

125

"Someone told me it was." Long black tapers burn in clusters throughout the dim room. Subdued voices hum monotonously, embellished now and then by a stray laugh. Through a far window I watch the sun in its decline above clouds moving inland. Why doesn't she bring the wine?

"Don't you want to go up river and float down?"

He is California golden, aided by a squeeze tube that advertises Your Money Back If Not Fully Satisfied.

"What'll you be teaching next fall?" I rub guaranteed gold on his back.

"Put more on my shoulders. Look—my legs are peeling."

"'Tis the season to shed skin."

"You think you're smart. Get my neck, would you?"

"What're you going to—"

"—Abnormal Psychology—to a bunch of idiots."

The Rogue River, swift and fifty body-lengths across, rushes around a bend, green and silver through the dry earth.

"What're you doin'?" yells a bald man with hair on a belly overhanging tight green trunks. "Get back here where you belong."

"But, Daddy—" answers a five-year-old sopping water sprite, shoulder high in yellow weeds, tan and bleached, hair tied in two wet bunches.

"No buts—you heard me. What're you doin'?"

"Picking flowers for my lizard."

"Your lizard's for the birds. Buzzards. Ha! Ha! Ha!" The man's great belly quakes. "That jaundiced toad!"

"Lizards don't care about flowers," Clayton says.

"Hers does."

"Anybody as fanciful as that will never get along in the world."

"That's your opinion."

"Doubt it?"

"Let's go in the water." I rush away from Clayton, who follows, slip neck high in the cold river and paddle.

"You look like a duck." Clayton cuts into the water.

O, sing me a song of the sea. "Let's go upstream and float back with the current." Sing me a song of the sea.

"*All right.*"

"*I'll be Ophelia ... but I should have garlands—yellow flowers and purple thistles.*"

"*Don't overdo it.*"

"*Do you know why she drowned?*"

"*Let's go.*"

I suck'd the honey of his music vows ... o! woe is me, to have seen what I have seen, see what I see.

Rocky banks rush past, cool and swift we ride the current. His head is a buoy. The minutes of his soul tick away; I hear them counterpart to mine. Any ding-dong song of the sea will do.

"*I'm a swan in Lithia park,*" *he claims, and slides away through the green water.*

Back on the towel: "*Rub this on my shoulders, will you? God, my legs are peeling.*"

Butterflies and bumblebees, white and black, flit and buzz among the yellow lizard flowers.

"*I'm sweating like a pig,*" *he says.*

O, we know not what we are, nor what we may become.

"Pouilly-Fuissé, sir." She pours a mouthful into Clayton's glass.

"Very good," he says, placing the glass to one side. It reflects the tapers, seems to hold shivering fire.

"Pour me a glassful—"

"—of the wrong kind of wine at the wrong time?" He folds his arms.

"Pretend the entrée is mis-timed fish."

"They shouldn't have brought it now."

"Some people think-of-themselves-as. Have you noticed? Listen to a person who does it, and soon you'll think, 'He's thinking-of-himself-as'."

"You make sense about three-fourths of the time. God, it's hot."

Three-quarter time is good measure. "It's cold as hell."

"What's the matter with you?"

"I was referring to the room in the motel. Pour the wine."

Last night the air-conditioner hissed cold air as I lay on the sheet I wished were foam. You did not touch me although you held me. You

hovered for a moment, then left me withering. I touched you in your
sleep, and you moved—away. I fell into dream:
"When shall we be married? Aren't you anxious to start keeping
house?"
"No! No! No! No! No!" You jarred me awake to empty coldness,
turned to let me fall again...
"If we aren't served in a hurry, we'll miss the play," Clayton
says.
"Let's miss the play. You can take me to the bus tonight and
leave immediately for California."
"You're out of your mind—"
Too much in it.
"—I paid for the tickets. I want my money's worth."
His money's worth, he says he wants his money's worth. He
paid for my return bus ticket, too.
"Please pour the wine." Let me drown out the frenzied crea-
tures a table away who expel Shakespearean soliloquies while
devouring veal cutlets. I do not want to hear those words. No!
"... marvelous—
To-morrow, and to-morrow, and to-morrow,
Creeps in this petty pace from day to day
To the last syllable of recorded time,
And all our yesterdays have lighted fools
The way to dusty death.
Marvelous. Simply marvelous! ..."
O, cure her of that. "Did you say something, Clayton?"
"In San Francisco you can buy almost anything you want, any
time you want it."
"Convenient. Is everything you want for sale?"
"I can't think of anything that isn't. That isn't to say I can afford
everything that has a price. I have a list of things I can't afford
just yet. But eventually—"
"Did you say something, Clayton?"
"Don't you listen when I'm talking? Where are you?"
"We have to talk—before it's too late—" I reach for his hand,
but he moves it.

"I've been talking all evening." He looks puzzled, strokes his beard. "What shall we talk about?"

What use to press the issue? "Oh ... you won't pour the wine even though I'm turning to dust!"

"It goes with the main course."

No! No! No! No! "As money goes with banks, and love with marriage?" I ask quietly.

"Well..."

"What did you say while I was 'gone'?"

"How should I know? But while it's on my mind, why did you bring me rose petal preserves?"

"You used to like such things."

"Where did you get that idea?"

Lizards do not like flowers.

The domino brings, "Pasta, sir."

"Where Neptune can be seen in the foam. On the coast, near Devil's Churn. Don't you remember?"

"No. Cigars would have been nicer. I brought you *Ondine* because..."

"Yes?"

"No reason."

"I didn't know you'd taken up smoking." We partake of pasta.

"Nothing but miniature White Owls. Don't forget to tuck a few ashtrays in your hope chest."

I fall, freezing. Shall I give over to wrong action? Give over to inaction, wrong too? In what direction shall I go?

"What are you thinking about?" Clayton asks, detached. His eyes focus for a moment.

Words, words, words. I reach for his hand. Look; come back with me. I will show you what was.

In that cypress-sealed niche above the slate-green sea, before we descended to the sand, you said you didn't trust women.

"Why not?" I stirred the coals and tossed bits of shell at the trunk of a tree.

"Betrayal isn't easily forgotten."

"You mean ignorance is bliss?"

129

"I don't follow."

"You haven't lost anything but your misconception, painful as that might be."

You said I should be a psychologist, then came and sat beside me, turned from stone to flesh, having lost your reticence as if it were your virginity.

"Some say mermaids sing. Can you hear them?"

"I hear them. Listen ..."

"I don't hear anything. What should I listen for?"

"Voices in song. I can teach you to listen. They sing only to those who listen."

You heard them, we both did, when finally we reached the other side of the Churn, where we stayed the night out. Some would say we heard the song of wind, sand, sea. Some would not allow even that. We went then beyond mermaids, beyond the sky, far, far beyond ourselves, where nothing at all is known.

"Veal Prince Orlov, sir."

"... Out, out, brief candle! ... I make all my students memorize Macbeth's renunciation."

Canst thou not minister to a mind diseased, quiet this raving woman?

"Strange how he blundered to the end," Clayton says, alluding to the woman's spiel.

"Yes, strange." *If chance will have me king, why, chance may crown me, without my stir.* For desire's fool, the hoax of prophesy lay in wishful thinking.

"Please will you—"

"I poured the wine."

"—listen to me ..." He draws his hand back at my gesture toward it. The wine stands before me, white, clear; moisture condenses on the glass; a tongue of water slides over the curved crystal. Stuff me into a contractual relationship and refuse my touch? I look at Clayton. His neck grows long and feathered. He glides serenely through smooth green water, the mirror image of his sleek white body beneath him, rises on powerful wings

130

which beat the air around me, trumpets a grim prophesy. I fall into a blazing knowledge of the future.

Macbeth knew, finally, as Leda knew in the white rush of feathers and shudder in the loins; as I knew in a blast of cold air, emptiness, outcries; knew but denied; knew and thought to resolve by acceptance, letting happen what would, a Leda ripe with chaos, progenitor of death. Give over to wrong action? Give over to inaction, wrong too? An ashtray holding a burned out cigar is my compass. Action by inaction and back into the Sea of Chance, sure of what is not, rather than miserable in an ash-certainty from which I could not rise, burning to know who has found the song and keeps it.

"You haven't finished and we're going to miss the play."

"I feel sick." Through time, the sand shifted. Take your scar and go. "I can't breathe."

"The heat must have got to you."

He lays three new salal green bills on a silver tray.

"What is it worth?" I ponder.

"These bills?" he asks.

"A sea-song."

"I don't understand."

He lifts the glass and drinks the wine which stood before me. The room, infused with *Ondine*, circles around me.

From having been closed, the car is stuffy, holding the heat of the past day, and the smell of new upholstery and cigars.

"Don't put your heel through the floor mat. Are you all right?"

"I needed air."

The highway to the outdoor theater in Ashland lies before us, black and endless. Clouds press so close I can almost touch them through the open window. If only I could fly, into the night, off to the sea.

"Look at that—rain. The play is cancelled. All this fuss over nothing."

Great drops splash against the windshield and, pressed by the wind, take amoebic forms, blur the world. I extend my hand through the window, withdraw it wet, rub my face. The wind cools my damp cheeks.

"If you take me to the bus station, I'll catch the 9:30 express. I'm sure the motel will refund tomorrow's rent. You can head for California tonight while it's cool and there's no traffic."

"That's not a bad idea. It'll cut our visit short, but I'll see you in a couple of months once and for all. Sure you don't mind?"

"No, I don't mind."

He puts me on the bus, stands outside near the front seat I have taken, talking through the open door of furniture. Our life is arranged.

"... and all sanitary fixtures will be yellow. I've already ordered them." He blows a quick short sequence of yellowish cigar smoke, watches as each puff dissipates. "The kitchen appliances and bathroom cupboards will be black."

"Black? Yellow? Black and yellow. Like a great lizard."

"I knew you'd like it. Here comes the driver. You're ready to pull out."

"Yes, I'm ready to pull out."

"What do you mean by that?"

"I mean I'm about to pull out, as you said."

"But we don't seem to be speaking the same language."

"You're right."

"It's time we had a talk. Get off." Clayton steps aside to let the driver on.

"It's too late, Clayton. I don't understand your language. Good-bye." The driver reaches for the steel handle, pulls it toward him. Through the glass I see Clayton's lips form the words "Get off." I hear a *thump thump* on the tightly closed door.

"That man out there has been bothering me all evening. Please don't open the door."

"Gotcha."

As the bus rolls away, I return to my seat, observe Clayton's surprise. He yells "GET OFF!" as though in a voiceless rage. He stamps his foot and points at the cement. I look away.

In the seaward distance someone is singing.

The meaning of our cheerfulness. — Nietzsche

DARCY

by Susan Welch

She scanned the bus as she was lifted on, her eyes feverish and alert, her crushed body stuffed scarecrow-like into awkwardly-hanging cowboy clothes, gleaming with spangles and sequins. Her chair folded up the way a rain bonnet does, compact and flat, and was put under the bus with the luggage. She seemed to be as light as a hatbox as she was carried down the aisle, a life-sized doll. When she saw Nora try to look away, it was decided. "Put me by the babe," she said in a throaty, narcotized voice, and the driver set her down.

Nora's nostrils flared as she moved her bag for the new passenger, who smelled musky, like a slightly soiled child. Nora watched as the little woman stuck her cheap, decorated cowboy boots of cracking lavender plastic onto the top of the seat ahead at impossible angles, a closed drawbridge.

She inclined her head coyly at Nora's fancy outfit, velvet skirt and silk blouse, silly for a bus trip.

"Say, what's your name?" Darcy said to a small boy who stood in the aisle, sucking on his finger with lips the color of plum skin. "I'll bet I can guess your name. It's Zippy the Pinhead, isn't it?"

Darcy laughed. The kid gaped at her. His mother, across the aisle, looked benignly on, leafing through the book in her lap. "Do you know what my name is? I'll bet you can't guess, can

133

you? It's Darcy. See, I could guess your name but you couldn't guess mine. Aren't you Zippy?"

The little boy gave her an enraptured look. "Is that your car, Zippy?" Darcy asked. "I think it's *my* car ..." She made a feint for his toy and he squealed. "Say, how old are you?" The child drew closer. "Come on, Zippy, tell me how old you are."

"Talk to the nice lady, tell her how old you are," prodded his mother, her gnawed lips compressed into a thin little grin.

Just behind Nora sat an old man whose left eye never stopped crying. She heard him murmur approvingly. Darcy surveyed the passengers on both sides, who watched the scene between her and the boy with doting smiles.

"I won't say how old I am until you say how old you are," she said. The bus was rumbling out of the station. Lights erupted overhead, crackling along tired old circuits.

The child held up his fist and blurted out, "Two yis old," which Darcy apparently misheard.

"Too old?" She turned to Nora to verify his words and when she got no response she said, to everyone in general, "Too old. He thinks he's too old. Well, Zippo, if you're too old then you're older than me because I'm not too old. Can you get over that kid?" she exclaimed to Nora. "He thinks he's too old." She leaned over and tried to catch the child in her frail, outstretched arms, but he ran down the aisle. "That's all right, go ahead, try to escape, I'm still going to get you."

She relaxed in the seat, passing on a conspirator's smirk — wasn't the child adorable?

"My name's Darcy, what's yours?"

"Nora."

Darcy pressed her upper arms and spine against the seat, thrust her head back, a stretching exercise. "Well, at least you talk. I thought I was going to get the silent treatment. Some people think they're too cool for Darcy."

After humming awhile she turned to Nora again and said, "Where are you going?"

"Cleveland."

"You from there?"

"No." Her reply hung blunt in the silence.

"That's all right, you don't have to be specific," Darcy said, laughing deep in her throat, hundreds of tiny pieces of glass tinkling, her eyes never leaving Nora. Darcy groomed herself, stroking her blouse — it was yoked, it had deep ruffles, there were red roses embroidered on the snap pockets, outlined by sequins. "Where are you from?"

"Minneapolis."

"No kidding. Minneapolis." She let out a long, deep breath. "I stayed there once, in an apartment with my mother. I had three brain operations in five months. Ha, ha, ha. Now I live in Black Duck Falls ... dumpy town, dead little town, but I go back to Minneapolis all the time. Say, you don't mind if I take off my boots, do you? My feet are killing me."

Darcy removed her gaudy doll boots with the smooth, unmarked soles, weathered though they had never been walked on. Her feet curled coquettishly on the top of the seat before her, the toes crossed like fingers, chicken feet boiling in a pot.

"Let me tell you about my boyfriend," Darcy said. "He's twenty years older, a Vietnam vet. We met in a rehab center. He can walk now but his ears got messed up real bad over there. He was attacked by sea snakes, these weird snakes that are only poisonous part of the year. Ever hear of them? He's hearing-impaired, not totally deaf, though." Darcy squinted at her. "He has a job. He's getting along. There're all kinds of programs these days for the differently-abled." Darcy moved closer, peering. "You don't know what I'm talking about, do you?" she said with satisfaction. "Formerly deaf and dumb. Formerly 'Hire the Handicapped.' Nobody uses those old rubber stamps anymore. I bet you'd call me a cripple, wouldn't you?"

Nora winced. "I wouldn't call you anything," she said, but she sounded sorry. Her long white fingers trailed upward in Darcy's direction. "That's a beautiful necklace," Nora said. "What kind of stone is it?"

Darcy's eyes crackled into focus. "A sandstone agate," she said. "It's very rare. Want to buy it?" She eagerly turned.

"No, that's all right."

Darcy bent nearer. "Look, what this really is is a bolo tie," she said, swiveling to give Nora a better look. "You fit the strings around your collar, see? They're genuine leatherette." Darcy tightened the cords till it looked as if she might choke herself. "Adjustable, see? Check out the scene on the agate. It's a dune."

"I really wouldn't have anyplace to wear it," Nora said miserably.

"Well, think about it," Darcy said, the turn-down sliding right off, and she massaged her pockets. She was leaning over so far that Nora was pressed up against the window. As Nora squirmed, something fell out of her purse. "What's that?" Darcy asked, instantly alert.

"Vitamins," Nora muttered, scrambling to pick the bottle up.

"Ha, ha, ha, that's funny. Darcy needs more than vitamins to make her feel good. Are you a health nut?"

Nora shifted in her seat. "I don't think so."

"Not me, either, are you kidding? Look at me, I'm a disease nut. Ha, ha, ha." Darcy grabbed Nora's bottle, inspected it, looked at her shrewdly. "Prenatal ... Aw."

Nora couldn't stop her own pleased smile. "Yes," she whispered.

"I was pregnant once," Darcy said. "Didn't think I could get pregnant, did you? Thought I was a roller skate. But I was, sure as can be. They said it was in the tubes, never would have been born. But it was in there." She looked at Nora through blank brown eyes. "The guy ran out on me anyway, the slime." She pushed Nora with a tiny elbow like a chicken wishbone. "Not like my boyfriend now. He's so crazy about me. It's about time I got one who really wanted me. I've told the guy to get lost lots of times, but he just keeps crawling back." Darcy stroked back her lank mousy hair. She turned to Nora as if something had just occurred to her and demanded, "Are you married?"

"No," Nora said. "Well, almost."

"Does he know about this?" Nora shook her head. "Boyfriend doesn't know?" Darcy started to laugh.

"He'll be happy," Nora said, and it was as if the words swarmed around her like gnats. "He'll be happy," she said again. "That's why I'm going to Cleveland. You see, my fiancé works in a K-Mart in Parma. Pretty soon he'll be promoted to assistant manager. And then I'm going to be married." Nora fumbled to find her wallet. She handed Darcy a picture of a very white young man in a very white shirt and black tie.

Darcy handed the picture back. "Lots of luck," she said. "You'll need it."

"We've been planning this for a long time," Nora began again, but it seemed that Darcy had already forgotten her and was looking for the little boy. Outside the window were lilacs, everywhere lilacs, blossoming on a hill in the countryside; they passed a ramshackle red building in some little town, what town? The bus driver didn't even call it out. They saw a decaying, shambling barn with the paint peeling off, rotten boards, and, all around, lilacs, just hanging, shivering there.

"Zippy the Pinhead, I've got you," Darcy squealed, voice piercing and oblivious. She pulled the boy to her and sank her fingers into his shiny, taffy-colored hair, covering him with kisses. Oh, the ardor of those kisses, and the heated, fervent look she flashed back at Nora when she felt her stare.

"Say, do you know what sign I am?" Darcy bent her head inward, nodding to Nora to do the same. Then, looking wickedly around, she unsnapped her blouse at the chest, pushing toward Nora a round milky breast with a pink nipple being attacked by a purple and magenta tattoo crab. "Oh, Nora," said Darcy, "isn't that pretty? Isn't that pretty, honey? Hey, you like me, don't you?" she said with a cackle and Nora, desperately, nervously, started to laugh. "Oh, I'm funny, am I?" said Darcy, starting to button herself up. "So just how do I amuse you?"

"No, no, it's nothing," Nora said, and when Darcy kept looking at her, she said she was sorry, she was just so tired, she'd been on the bus for hours.

While Nora pretended to sleep, Darcy drummed her fingers on the armrest, looked out the window, took out a pack of cards. Then she roused Nora, tapping her on the shoulder. "Look, we're coming to a rest stop," she said. "It's about time." The smitten little boy bobbed into view. "Hey, Zippy, look, it's Booger King. Don't you want a booger from Booger King?" The boy's mother smiled, a pained smile. As the bus stopped, Darcy stirred. She gripped the tops of the seats and hoisted herself up, then traveled crabwise along the headrests to the front of the bus, as adept as any trapeze artist.

"Will you get my chair?" she asked the driver, then came back to Nora. "You can take me around Booger King, all right?" she said.

Nora did seem proprietary and pleased as she wheeled Darcy into the restaurant. "Excuse me, excuse me," she said, trying to get in line, but she was blocked by two young men from the bus, one black and one white. The black man was handsome, with a glorious head of succulent-looking, sausage-like dreadlocks. He took off his sunglasses and turned to look at Nora, staring at her as if to ignite her.

"Don't rush so, baby," he said. Nora tried to push past. "You are so fearful," he said. "Why won't you speak to me?"

Nora stared back. "Because I don't know you," she said, standing there lovely and proud.

"I think you're prejudiced."

Nora's mouth trembled. "That's ridiculous. I'm not."

"I think you should talk to me a little about this ugly prejudice you have," he said insistently.

"You're really wrong," Nora said. "You have no right to say that."

"Then why are you running so fast to get away?" He peered at her intently.

"We've got stuff to do," said Nora.

"Look, she's your friend, isn't she?" he said, nodding at Darcy. "Well, how did she get to be your friend? You didn't always

138

know her, right? You stopped and talked to her, that's how you got to be friends with her, right?"

"I'll be friends with you, honey," said Darcy, and the white guy started to laugh.

"Looks like you got a live one, Wilson," he said. "Way to go, Killer Joe."

With elaborate politeness, Wilson leaned over and took Darcy's hand. "Pleased to meet you, Miz ...?"

"Anything you want to call me, you hot thing," said Darcy and she wouldn't let go of his hand. "Just keep talking, sweetheart."

"We'd better get our burgers or it'll be too late," squeaked Nora, plowing Darcy past the men. Darcy looked back, licking her lips. They got into line and waited for whoppers and chocolate shakes.

"You should be more friendly," said Darcy as they sat down. "In my profession, you learn to be open. You learn to connect with other people, find out what they're all about. You learn about your place in the world."

"What is your profession?"

Darcy wiped her mouth with a piece of ketchup-smeared waxed paper. "Switchboard operator," she said. "I lost my job, took a tough bounce, but I always hit the ground running ... ha, ha, ha."

At the Burger King door, the driver barked, "We leave in five minutes."

"You've hardly eaten a bite," Darcy said, sucking her fingers and gulping down the last of her milkshake. When Nora didn't answer, Darcy began to primp in the napkin holder, gazing approvingly at herself, combing her lank brown hair with a tortoiseshell comb right there at the table.

"Hey, Nora." She snapped her fingers. "Say, Nora, would you get me some cigarettes?"

Nora bit her lip. "Sure."

"Some Marlboros," Darcy said. "Make it the hard pack."

139

Nora wheeled her back to the bus. The driver hadn't reappeared, so she held out her arms to Nora, sweetly. Gravely, Nora lifted Darcy up.

The bus pulled onto the road. Nestled next to Nora in their seat, Darcy once again took off her boots with their elaborate stitchery ... leaves, arrows, ran up the sides of each, surrounding a plumed bird. The toes were capped with imitation lizard tips, Darcy informed Nora.

Then, rubbing her hands, she said: "I need a cigarette bad. Want one?"

"You can't smoke here."

"Ah, chill out. The driver don't care. Anyway, they're smoking in back." Both of them turned to look at the area around the chemical toilet. No females were anywhere near, but Darcy saw Wilson and waved. "I guess I'm gone for awhile then." Darcy shrugged apologetically. "I got an awful habit." She hoisted herself up and, using the headrests, began traveling to the back of the bus.

"Mind if I sit here?" she asked in her sleepy voice.

"Sure, go ahead," said Wilson's friend, a freckle-faced redhead wearing a leather vest over his bare chest.

"Got to have a cigarette," she said, and she laughed her merry laugh. "Sure you can have one," she said to her new seatmate; he took the pack and pulled out two, three. "What the fuck are you doing?" she said. "Give me back my smokes."

"Watcha gonna give me for 'em?" he asked.

"No fuckin' way," she said. "I got more to sell than you think. Come on, give 'em to me."

The front of the bus was silent, with Nora, Zippy's mother and the other, older passengers seeming to listen intently to what was going on behind them. The back of the bus was a clubhouse, smoke-filled, and sprawled around were several young men and Darcy, who now sat on the edge of a seat like a child-sized puppet, her useless legs folded to the side like wings discarded after the Christmas play.

140

"Thanks, Wilson. Thanks for getting my cigs back from that creep. What's his name? A.K.? That's a weird name. Hey, Wilson." She blew smoke at him. "How old are you, eighteen?" She inhaled deeply. "I'm twenty-three. You're practically jailbait, the way I see it. What sign are you, Taurus? Oh, Libra. Libras are off the wall. Want to see something? Oh, forget it. You're too immature. Why are you looking at me like that?"

Wilson teased her. "Why are you so suspicious?"

"Because I hate men, that's why, what do you think?" Darcy said, not missing a beat. "Look at that Casanova, that A.K. I give him my cigarettes and what does he do? Just blows me off. I've never been so insulted." No one said anything. Darcy, inevitably, filled the silence. "Hey, you moron in the orange shirt and stupid-looking hat."

Across the aisle from Nora, the little boy's mother slammed her book with a sound like a pistol shot. The noise was so loud they could hear it in the back. Darcy looked forward. Amazing how ominous and overloaded the atmosphere had suddenly become. People were nervous, glancing around. The boy's mother sat with a look of stunned fury, back straight up.

"Why don't you go back to your seat?" said the guy in the orange shirt. His cap had a preserved sunfish on the front of it.

"You're supposed to be asleep," Darcy chirped, but something caught in her voice.

"I was, but it's kind of difficult," he said. "You're sitting across the aisle, not across the bus."

"What's your problem? Hard up?" She wouldn't take no for an answer. "Give your hand a break. I bet I know somebody who'd get you off. For free, too. Hey, Wilson, go over and do that guy. You need the experience."

"If you weren't a woman, or whatever you are, I'd smash your face in," he said.

"Just try it, dirtball. I've got upper body strength."

Wilson said, "Hey, baby, I think you should leave. Go on, git."

"Who pissed on your Wheaties this morning? What's the matter, Wilson? I give you a rush, don't I? Oh, no, I can tell. You

141

don't want tuna with good taste, you want tuna that tastes good."

"Oh, so that's what the smell was — tuna," said A.K. The young men's laughter echoed from the back of the bus as from a dark cave, dangerous and private. They were whistling, stomping their feet. The filthier Darcy's language got, the louder they whooped.

Voices drifted to the back: "They ought to kick her off the bus."

"The Lord hates people like her," croaked the man with the weeping eye. "He'll shut her down early, may His will be done."

The young men in the back laughed uproariously. "Thanks, preacher man." Zippy's mother stared straight ahead. And Darcy sat there with a small smile, as if she knew they wanted to pull her apart — the job was started, after all. In the haze of smoke she wiggled the toes of her snow-white feet.

Nora looked startled when she saw Darcy peering tentatively around the side of their seat.

"Hi, it's me, I'm back," Darcy said with an inquiring look, as if she weren't quite sure that Nora would welcome her. She continued brightly, in a stage whisper, "They've got rum and pot back there," and she slid in. Nora gave her wide berth.

The little boy scooted forward and tossed his car into Darcy's lap.

"Hey, lady, isn't this your kid's toy?" Darcy leaned to pass the car across to the boy's mother who turned to look at her and pointedly did not say anything. Darcy tried again. "Look, I don't want him to forget it."

"He hardly needs that toy anymore, things being what they are. In fact, I wouldn't let him touch it," the woman said. Darcy received the slight with all the antagonism intended. Her face seemed to swell as if she'd been slapped on that side, her arms crossed in front of her like objects she had just found, they had nothing to do with her. Her bravado was flagging. The whole bus sat silent.

"Hey, Darcy!" The young men in back were calling her now. "Come on back here. I've got something for you to do since

142

you're out of cigs." They pounded their feet. They had put their mark on her. "You don't need no cigs," A.K. chided. "I've got something that will keep your mouth full."

"Why don't you just shut up?" Darcy squeaked over her shoulder, but she was smiling. "They're getting fresh," she said to Nora, who gave her a terrified gaze. "It gets old fast, don't it?" But anyone could see it. Deep satisfaction stained Darcy's flushed face as they stamped their feet in unison. She was preening. "Do you think I should go? Just to shut them up?"

"Wanna give me a try, Darcy? Once black, never back."

Darcy elbowed Nora in the ribs. She called loudly to the back of the bus, "I been there and I came back. Eat your heart out, Wilson."

"Hey, Darcy, watcha gonna give me to eat?"

In an instant she had scuttled back and was sitting next to Wilson. "Start on these," Darcy said, wiggling her bare toes in front of his face.

"Shut your mouth, there's a little kid," someone said.

"Well, pardon me, I'm sorry, I didn't see him." Darcy spoke in a gentler tone. "Hey, Zippy, want your car?" She tossed it. He was too little to catch, so the car hit his chest, ricocheted, then landed under a seat. "Whatsamatter, why didn't you get it?" The boy began to whimper.

"Billy, don't touch that. Come back here." The mother craned her neck, looking at her son, but he was already running back toward her.

"I didn't mean to hit him," Darcy said half-heartedly. The boy's mother was shaking with rage. She seemed barely able to contain herself.

"We're getting near my stop, Wilson," Darcy said. "If you're ever in Black Duck Falls, give me a call."

"What do you mean, if I'm ever in Black Duck Falls? I'm in Black Duck Falls right now."

"You want to get out with me?"

"I sure do. The place is named after me, I might as well get out here. What do you say, everybody?" Wilson and his friends laughed.

The bus pulled onto a cloverleaf, past a sign that said "Black Duck Falls, Home of WCOW Radio: Five Miles."

"Come on, Wilson, get me a smoke from A.K. Thattaboy, thanks. I'm leaving soon. You gonna miss me?"

"I don't know whether I'll miss you, but I'll miss your mouth." Darcy made kissing noises. "Yum, yum, yum."

"Hey, what did I tell you. There's a little kid."

He was back beside her, gazing at her out of the corner of his eye. "Hey, Zippy the Pinhead, do you forgive me? Come on, get on my lap, give me a kiss." It was awkward for her, she had to lean over as the bus bounced on the badly-paved road. She nearly toppled, pulling him up to her. "Come on, little sweetheart," she said, "Talk to Darcy," and she began to hug the boy and kiss his cheeks passionately.

The boy's mother jerked to her feet, all gangly arms and legs, and rushed down the aisle. She grabbed her son by the arm, yanking so hard that he started screaming. Darcy wouldn't let go. "He'd rather be with me and you know it."

The mother flushed a horrible prickly red. "If I was you I'd jump out of the bus right now and let it run me over."

"I'm sure you would, as stupid as you are."

The woman lunged with all her might, pulling her son away and sending Darcy sprawling in the aisle.

For a moment she lay there, unable to right herself. She thrashed and squirmed, shuddering as the bus shuddered, but no one made a move. And then, all at once, Nora, who had been craning her neck to watch, got up and ran, hurtling herself toward the boy's mother, stopping just short. "Can't you see she hasn't got anybody in the world?"

The mother looked at Nora in astonishment, Nora in her silk blouse, keeping her balance by holding onto the headrests.

The bus bumped down the interminable night-time roads. From somewhere came the smell of sweat curdling, sweetish, sticky.

Finally Wilson lifted Darcy up and together he and Nora took her back to her seat.

Nora kept her arm around Darcy's small jellyfish frame. "You know what you are? You're just like a little baby," Nora whispered haltingly.

"I'm no baby, you stupid sap, and don't you forget it," Darcy hissed, twisting away from the arm, and then she sat there limply. It wasn't hard to crumple her, she was crumpled anyway, after all, wadded up on the seat. How aggressively she came on, how easily she gave in. The bus's brakes wheezed. They were nearing the station.

For awhile Darcy and Nora sat in silence. Then Darcy began crooning in a peculiar singsong. "Under the bus, is that right? Shut down? If you weren't a woman or whatever you are ... what could that possibly mean? What do you think I am?" She was in a trance, muttering, shaking her head, as if she were used to speaking in whispers to herself.

All at once she looked over at Nora, and said, "Thanks for getting that fucking bitch off my back." Then, with a sly look, she said: "Now how about the bolo tie. Are you ready to make a deal?"

"Well, I really hadn't thought ..." began Nora.

"You're showing good taste," Darcy said cheerfully. "This puppy is my pride and joy." She began unhooking it from around her neck. "That'll be twenty dollars. Don't look so surprised. You've got to pay for quality, Nora." Nora hesitated. "Well, if you don't want it, I can always put it back on." Sadly, she began refastening it.

"Oh, no. That's all right. I'll take it." Nora dug into her bag, found a bill.

"There. Now you'll always have something to remember Darcy by." Darcy smiled tenderly at her, putting the cash into a lavender leatherette pouch that matched her boots, swirling with arrows, cactus designs, fancy stitchery.

After that she snapped to, jabbering to Nora as before. "Well, it looks like this is goodbye. You're a nice person. Maybe I'll see you in Minneapolis sometime." She leaned past Nora, getting a view of the station. "Say, I don't see my boyfriend. I wonder where he is, the shithead." She swung herself into the aisle. "My bags are all under the bus. You think the driver will get my stuff now?"

"Of course he will, he has to," Nora said, and, sure enough, the driver was already coming down the aisle to get her, a scornful expression on his face.

"You can name it after me if you want," Darcy said to Nora with a wink, looking over the driver's shoulder, and that was the last Nora heard from her.

Darcy looked sunken and very small, plastered to her chair when the driver put her in it, as if she had been soaked and stuck on it, her body as insubstantial as a spider web.

Nora tapped the glass and waved her hand. Darcy peered at the bus but couldn't seem to make out where the noise was coming from; she scanned the length of it, gaping. Then she rolled alone into the terminal and began trailing back and forth.

"It's lucky she left when she did," said Zippy's mother to everyone in general. "If she hadn't, I've have thrown her out with my bare hands."

"She's gone, the Lord be praised," said the teary-eyed man. "Satan's got ahold of her. She won't be around long."

Nora took her vitamins out of her purse, tried to remember if she'd taken any. Why had Darcy said she needed luck? It seemed an obvious question, but when Darcy sat at her side, she hadn't dreamed of bringing it up. She wished Darcy would come back, so she could ask her now. She watched Darcy wheel from one end of the storefront terminal to another, her bags in her lap, scanning all horizons. Her glitter reflected brilliantly on the sheet of plate glass; soon her speed set the spangles in motion till they seemed to leap and fade like fireworks.

Act One of a two-act play in progress about the great French philosopher, Simone Weil...

THE PANEL

A Play in Two Acts

by Dorothy Bryant

CHARACTERS

Marsha Lee. The moderator of the panel. In her mid-twenties, with the touchiness of an intelligent, aware woman who grew up with the contradictions of the years of resurgent feminism. An ambitious graduate student in Women's Studies, she, like her field of study, occupies an ambiguous and tenuous position in the university. Her style of dress reflects the contradictions between her academic ambitions, her rebellion against traditional "femininity," and her temptation to make use of the youthful female attractiveness she still possesses. Hence she wears something like a very tailored jacket with a very short, tight skirt and high heels. It is professionally important to her to call attention to herself by arranging and moderating programs like this, yet, because of her youth and insecure position, she lacks the smooth control and experience a panel moderator needs.

William Bettencourt. In his middle to late forties, political activist, grassroots organizer, and writer. His clothing is clean but casual, even shabby, lumberjack shirt and jeans. His appearance and gestures make clear his wish to declare himself not part of academia, though he is very intelligent and well-educated. He is a sincere, intense, accomplished activist and organizer who lives in voluntary poverty, sees daily the effects of poverty and injustice, and works very hard.

Nathan Schneider. In his late fifties or early sixties. A psychologist-historian with a mission: Holocaust Studies. He wears tweedy (not too formal) suit and tie. Both contentious and emotional, abrasive and affectionate, he sees himself as a debunker of the "Simone Cult." A prolific writer and lecturer, much in demand, has taught as a guest lecturer at many universities, now a visiting professor at this university, sponsored by a Jewish endowment.

Sister Cecilia Vero. Any age over fifty, wears a simple blouse and skirt, no habit, no make-up, perhaps a nun's headdress. A bland, gentle, patient demeanor, not easily roused to the anger she shows in Act II. Guarded, aware that the nun's identity that was once protective is now, in this century and especially among intellectuals, is an identity that invites condescension if not contempt. She is far from comfortable within her church as well.

Ghost of Simone Weil (pronounced Veil). Just over thirty, thin, aquiline nose, dark hair, parted and carelessly combed. Huge, dark-rimmed glasses. She wears a shabby, shapeless skirt and sweater. Flat, clumpy sandals on bare feet. She is a victim of almost constant migraine. She looks not quite put together, rumpled, fragile, vague yet intense looking, a bit awkward in her movements. Yet there should never be any doubt that this unkempt figure is a member of France's World War II intellectual elite. She is childlike, yet a deep thinker, a mystic, yet an activist, with unshakable faith in the potential of all human beings. French accent desirable but must not muddy her perfectly clear diction. We must hear every word of hers. She is a benign ghost but a disturbing one, like a conscientious, but unrelenting teacher. She haunts each panelist by giving close attention to what each says, then challenging with a contradiction that is as much a part of her as what the panelist prefers to identify with as SW's opinions and identity. The audience, of course, hears everything SW says, but each panelist hears SW only when SW speaks directly to him or her. Other panelists remain frozen, unhearing, during the timeless moments when a single panelist argues with her. Characters often interrupt or cut off each other. The interrupter should start speaking on the second to last word of the speech he or she is interrupting.

(SCHNEIDER and SIMONE should look like European Jews, but the other characters may be of any ethnic or racial mix.)

Side Show 1995

Act One

(Stage is bare except for four stools and a podium to one side. Completely dark. We hear the voice of SIMONE beginning before a single spot gradually lights her, standing center stage.)

SIMONE

Two prisoners in adjoining cells communicate by knocking on the wall between. The wall separates them but is also their means of contact. Everything that separates us from God is a link to God.

(during her next speech the lights gradually go up, showing the stools and podium)

God is always present in authentic beauty. Therefore, good art is essentially religious. But good art rises out of the community, and since we have lost all our roots of community, there can be no good art.

(SIMONE becomes aware of the audience, speaks pointedly to audience.)

Yet we could not have been born at a better time than this, when we have lost—everything. *(Looking around)* Where am I this time? *(She recognizes the setup—chairs, podium, audience. Smiles ironically and nods to audience, moves about as she talks)* A panel discussion? *(sighs)* Another one. Fifty years of talk. *(amused, then more serious)* Still, it is always possible that someone will say something real. How will we know it is real? If it is real, it will be hard and rough. In this hard reality you will find joy. Not in pleasure. Pleasure leaves only a void. I prefer a real hell to an imaginary paradise. *(looks at the stools again, hopefully)* Yes, in the midst of all the talk, someone might really use his intelligence. The closest thing to true humility is intelligence. When you are really exercising all your intelligence, *(smiles)* you cannot feel proud of it. *(becoming serious, confiding an important key to understanding her)*

When I was fourteen, I fell into a bottomless despair. I had begun to realize how brilliant my brother was, a mathematical genius. Compared to him, I was less than mediocre. I had no talent. Oh, I didn't envy his talent. I cared about only one thing.

150

I knew he would grow up to be one of the great minds, one of those who can enter the kingdom of *(reverently)* truth. If I could never make that ascent to truth — I wanted to die. Then, after months of deep inner darkness, I had a revelation. I knew, without any doubt, that if I longed for truth, if I gave all my attention—complete, whole attention—to truth—and waited in patient longing, then I too could be admitted to that transcendent kingdom where truth dwells.

(LEE enters, carrying pitcher of water and paper cups, not seeing SIMONE, goes to podium, puts pitcher and cups on shelf below, fusses with papers, looks at her watch, smiles nervously at audience. The pitcher and cups will give other actors something to fuss with, taking a drink when it seems necessary to pause between lines.)

SIMONE
(watches LEE, then raises hand to her head as if the sight of her causes a headache)
The headaches began later, and I have never been entirely free of the pain, even when I sleep. The pain is seated at the central point of my nervous system, the meeting place of body and soul. What was I trying to say? *(gathers her strength to rise above the pain)* Attention. Yes! Attention would bring me to truth and to all that it contains—beauty, goodness, love, meaning, joy. Furthermore I knew—without any doubt—I knew that what is true for me is true for all human beings.

(As SIMONE goes on, SISTER and SCHNEIDER enter separately through audience, come up to stage, are greeted by LEE, shown to stools, introduced to each other.)

(to audience) True for all of you. We can all enter that kingdom of genius, that place of truth. No matter how limited we are, we can partake of genius. Aristotle had talent *(shrugs to show she doesn't think much of Aristotle)* but a simple-minded beggar on the street might love truth more than Aristotle did. So Aristotle has talent, but that beggar, if he loves truth with all his heart, is a genius. Of course, if we have no talent, our genius will be invisible from the outside. But within—we hold the secret of

genius. And this secret, the key that opens the gates of truth—is attention.

LEE
(looking at watch as she goes to podium, speaks to audience) We're going to begin in just a minute. One of our panelists was held up in traffic. As soon as he arrives we'll start. *(turns back to chat with SISTER and SCHNEIDER)*

SIMONE
(to audience) Attention. Unswerving, devoted, longing, patient attention. *(laughs gently and shakes her head)* No, no. You are just like my students. When I tell them to pay attention they stiffen and frown. That's not attention. That's just tensing muscles. Attention is—attending. Waiting. Open yourselves. Let go of all thoughts. Give yourselves, in quiet, patient attention. Not active, not searching. Quietly alert, open to the truth that lies within this moment, this task, this event.

(BETTENCOURT hurries through the audience to stage. LEE greets him, introduces him to other panelists, moves to podium.)

If you spend all your time here today trying to open yourselves, patiently attentive, seeking nothing, not even seeking to understand—and if you leave here understanding nothing—you will have moved closer to that kingdom of truth. And if during only five minutes of your time here you achieve true attention, *(her face opens into a smile of satisfaction)* then you will have achieved five minutes of genius—truth—Reality.

LEE
(stepping on the last two words of SIMONE, who moves aside, listening to LEE)
Good evening. I'm Marsha Lee, your moderator for today's panel. I'm a graduate student in Women's Studies here at the university. I also work as Assistant Coordinator of Programs for the Women's Center, which sponsors our series of panels on Outstanding Twentieth Century Women. It is my pleasure to welcome you to the fourth and final program in this series, a panel on the life and work of Simone Weil. *(clears her throat and begins formal introduction)* Virtually unknown during her short lifetime,

Simone Weil is now, fifty years after her death, the subject of many books and panels.

SIMONE
(to audience, amused) Too many? *(LEE and panelists don't hear.)*

LEE
Albert Camus called her "the only great spirit of our time." She has often been called "the saint of outsiders." *(SIMONE shakes her head.)*

SCHNEIDER
(not quite under his breath) Too often!

BETTENCOURT
Amen! *(SISTER is not amused.)*

LEE
(nervous, disconcerted by SCHNEIDER'S comment, determined not to show it) You probably know that because of recent funding cuts, we nearly had to cancel this program. Only the generosity of the panelists in volunteering their time made it possible for us to proceed. *(leads applause for panel)* Our format will be our usual one. Each of the panelists, including myself, will speak for *(emphasis)* no more than ten minutes. The—uh—enthusiasm of panelists has made some of them run overtime in our previous programs so ... *(to panelists)* I've been asked to be very strict about time. After each of us has spoken for ten minutes, we'll take a break and then return for the question period. *(to audience)* As you came in, you received blue cards? *(waves a stack of cards in her hand to show them)* I'd like you to write your questions on these cards. I'll collect them during the break. Then during the second part of the program, the panelists will discuss your questions—as many as time allows. So please, hold your questions for now, write them down, and we'll deal with them after the break. Proceeding then, in alphabetical order, our first speaker will be William Bettencourt. *(reading notes)* Mr. Bettencourt took his BA in history here at the university. For the past twenty-five years he has devoted himself to political organizing and writing. I won't read the long list of labor unions, peace and justice organizations, and political campaigns he has worked with. His

153

latest project is a community-based literacy program. He is the author of many articles on grassroots organizing and is now working on a beginning reader for adults. Mr. William Bettencourt.

BETTENCOURT

(begins talking as he gets up to go to podium, then stands to one side of it, not wanting to place a piece of academic furniture between him and his audience) That's a very flattering introduction, but it's not quite true.

SIMONE

(to LEE)
The truth is essential. *(LEE hears, glimpses SIMONE, turns away, pays attention to BETTENCOURT.)*

BETTENCOURT

(amused at LEE, at his even being here) Ms. Lee just gave me an honorary BA. Actually I left the university two units short of my BA, during the well-known Strike for Truth in nineteen— *(ruefully)* well, no, I guess it's not well known anymore. People forget. Anyway, I left without a degree, and I never came back—until today. Oh, I've spoken here before, but outside that door, not in here. In demonstrations, but never invited—until today.

SIMONE

Good! *(also amused, a little proud. To BETTENCOURT, waving a straight arm, closed fist)* I demonstrated with the workers.

BETTENCOURT

(smiles and nods approvingly at SIMONE, then goes on, mischievously, determined to deflate academic pretensions) My inside sources tell me a philosophy professor from Harvard canceled when your funds were cut. *(LEE is squirming, BETTENCOURT enjoying himself.)* So you tried the Philosophy Department here. But no one from that gang would touch anything sponsored by "Women's Studies." Then you ran across that old article I wrote on Simone Weil the worker, so in desperation—I hope you don't end up regretting it. *(LEE's strained smile shows she is already regretting it.)*

SIMONE
(to the audience) Isn't the truth fascinating!

BETTENCOURT
I agree with Dr. Schneider that there's been a lot of silly stuff written about "Saint Simone." There's a kind of morbid interest in her last years when she began to lose contact with reality.

SIMONE
(to BETTENCOURT, not contentious, but serious) No, I began to find reality!

BETTENCOURT
(hears SIMONE but chooses to ignore her, perhaps shaking his head in pity) A lot of her writing was—well, to put to mildly—pretty haywire, but her actions were solid. Forget what she said. Look at what she did. I'm glad my name is at the front of the alphabet, glad that for once, a program about Simone will start off with a list of the real things she did instead of all that ... mysticism. *(SISTER looks disturbed at his contemptuous distaste for the word. SIMONE is sober, but lets him have his say.)* But first, to appreciate what she did, you have to know where she came from. The Parisian upper-middle class—comfort, security, culture, privilege. She and her brother were sent to the best schools. They were headed for a secure place among the intellectual elite of France.

SCHNEIDER
Secure! *(BETTENCOURT stiffens, bristles at the interruption.)* You could hardly call a family of—

LEE
Please, Dr. Schneider. Your turn will come.

BETTENCOURT
So, what did this privileged, protected girl do? Once, when she was a child, she disappeared. Her frantic parents found her—two hours later—marching in a workers' demonstration. When she was in school, she was so active with petitions, pacifist demonstrations, that the director of the college named her "the red virgin."

SIMONE
(to BETTENCOURT, who listens to her, amused) He sent me to the most remote teaching post he could find. On a hill in the center of the town, there was an old statue, all rusty. The townspeople called it the Red Virgin. *(gaily defiant)* So I sent a picture postcard of it to Monsieur Director!

BETTENCOURT
(laughs with SIMONE, nods, then speaks to audience) She taught at a girls' school. But at night, on weekends, in every spare minute she had, she went out to teach the workers, to help them with union organizing.

SIMONE
Oh, but those communists running the unions. *(a headache coming on)* They wouldn't listen to anyone, not even to each other.

BETTENCOURT
(doesn't want to listen to that. To audience) In 1932 intellectuals just didn't do such things.

SIMONE
(to BETTENCOURT) A union bureaucracy is just like a capitalist bureaucracy! *(frown of pain, perhaps hand to head)*

BETTENCOURT
(to SIMONE) But people have to organize. Then we become strong. Then we have a voice to tell what we believe, what we know is real, the hard reality you prize so much.

SIMONE
(to BETTENCOURT) "We have a voice"? "We believe"? There is no such thing as *we* believe, or *we* think. One person has thoughts. A group, never. Collective thought is not thought at all. The collective kills thought.

BETTENCOURT
Only the strength of collective action can lead to change.

SIMONE
And to another totalitarian bureaucracy.

BETTENCOURT
Not necessarily.

SIMONE
Yes, necessarily. It is a dream to think otherwise. Revolution, not religion, is the opiate of the people.

BETTENCOURT
(waving her away, refusing to listen, speaking to audience) But teaching and organizing wasn't enough for her. She took the next step—step? Really a giant leap for those days. *(emphasis)* In 1934, in the depths of the Depression, at the age of twenty-five, she left teaching and went to work in a factory, living on a factory worker's wages.

(SIMONE begins to go through assembly-line motions, awkwardly, repetitive motions, her headache obviously getting worse.)

In 1934, Sartre and that gang were sitting in the cafes, talking about the depression. But not one of them, not for one minute, considered even *talking* to a worker, let alone going to work in a factory.

SIMONE
(continuing repetitive motions, in pain) I must not think. If I think, my work slows down. I must become a part of the machine. I must stop thinking. I can't! I must. I can't. I will.

BETTENCOURT
She had to learn, first hand. To know the whole truth.

SIMONE
(stops motion. To BETTENCOURT) So exhausted I forgot why I had come to the factory.

BETTENCOURT
(trying to ignore her) No one knew who she was. She was just one of the workers. They accepted her, in solidarity, as one of them.

SIMONE
There was no solidarity. The workers cared nothing for each other. And the women! The men treated them like dumb beasts.

BETTENCOURT
(ignoring her) Her factory journals tell how carefully she documented the conditions that had to be changed.

SIMONE
Yes, but tell them what else my journals documented. About
the workers. There was no fight in them. The work made us
mindless, docile. That was the real horror. Never once did I hear
anyone talking about the realities, the social issues, the demean-
ing nature of our labor. All was petty gossip or cheap romance.

BETTENCOURT
(to SIMONE) You shouldn't have written that. Are you trying
to destroy our faith in progress?

SIMONE
Progress! You believe in progress? That is very dangerous.

BETTENCOURT
I must believe in progress. If I didn't—

SIMONE
People who believe in progress are cruel. They dismiss the suffering of those who came before, because it was "part of progress
toward where we are today." And the suffering of today becomes part of "progress" toward a utopian tomorrow.

BETTENCOURT
I don't do that!

SIMONE
Good.

BETTENCOURT
I try to help the poor to get power—now, today. Power to get
just rewards for their work.

SIMONE
Rewards? More money.

BETTENCOURT
Right.

SIMONE
That's not enough. Nothing will change until we can change
the work itself, make the work fit for human beings to perform.

BETTENCOURT
That's all well and good, but the workers need more money
now.

SIMONE
There will never be enough money to restore the humanity this work destroys.

BETTENCOURT
(brushing her aside again. To audience) So read her factory journals. Read *The Need For Roots*. That's where you'll find her real writing, not the masochistic piety of her later notebooks.

SIMONE
No, listen! What I learned about suffering—

BETTENCOURT
(ignoring her with distaste, drowning her out) In 1936 she went to Spain to fight against Franco. Yes, this girl, who had been a pacifist, saw that fascism must be stopped. She joined a commando brigade of anarchists. Again, she needed to be there, to see—

SIMONE
—the horrible atrocities on both sides.

BETTENCOURT
(to SIMONE) That's beside the point.

SIMONE
What is the point?

BETTENCOURT
The point is that it's not words but actions that make a difference.

SIMONE
Actions come out of words. In war people are taught hateful words about the enemy, and they know they will not be held accountable. *(shudders)* Do you know what we are all capable of when we are free of normal constraints?

BETTENCOURT
(waving her away again) But an accident disabled her—sent her home. When she and her family fled the nazis in 1940, they went to southern France where she worked in the vineyards—yes, field labor.

SIMONE
Hell must be a place where you eternally pick grapes.

159

BETTENCOURT
(to SIMONE, impatiently) That's what I'm trying to make these people see, so they'll do something.

SIMONE
You should never do anything, no matter how good you think it is, unless you cannot stop yourself from doing it. But if you give perfect attention, longer and longer moments of perfect attention, there will be more and more good actions you cannot resist doing.

BETTENCOURT
Saying things like that only gives people an excuse for doing nothing!

SIMONE
Therefore, one moment of perfect attention is worth all the good works in the world.

BETTENCOURT
Well, most of us aren't capable of your perfect "attention." We just have to do whatever we can—we have to, for God's sake, do—something!

SIMONE
(understands how well intentioned he is) Oh, my poor friend. I understand. Idealists like you believe that goodness will conquer force. *(sadly)* It is not true. And that makes you suffer. But listen. You can go through that suffering to—

BETTENCOURT
Don't give me any more of that crap about suffering. I'm doing my best to create respect for you, to extract the sense from all the nonsense you wrote. *(LEE is looking at her watch.)*

SIMONE
(shrugging, turning away, giving up on BETTENCOURT)
God save me from my rescuers.

LEE
Mr. Bettencourt, time.

BETTENCOURT
Already? Okay, I have just one more point to make. While France was being invaded, and Simone was trying to save her

160

family, and others, from the Nazis, she didn't forget the faults of her own country. She protested France's imperialism in Indochina. She actually wrote to the American Ambassador to France, Admiral Leahy, telling him to cut off aid unless France gave Indochina its freedom.

SIMONE
(to audience, shrugging) He never answered.

BETTENCOURT
That may seem like an act of wild idealism—

LEE
Mr. Bettencourt—

BETTENCOURT
—but ask yourselves, would this country have made such a mess in Vietnam if Admiral Leahy had paid attention to this letter from an unknown French intellectual? *(LEE is at the podium nudging him)* Okay, okay. I just want you all to remember, whatever else is said here about Simone Weil, remember that her extraordinary political action set a model for the college activists of the sixties. Judge her, not by what she said, but by what she did!

LEE
Thank you, Mr. Bettencourt. *(an edge to her voice, not quite gracious in her thanks)* I'm sure you'll have more time during the question period to explore the political life of Simone Weil. *(takes a breath)* Our second speaker was to have been Dr. Marjorie Fisher, professor of history at Stanford University. But Dr. Fisher was called to Washington, D.C., to speak at the opening of a new exhibit at the Women's History Museum. She asked me to speak in her place, to discuss Simone Weil as a woman. *(SIMONE clutches her head and groans as if the subject gives her a giant headache.)* We have to remind ourselves of what it meant to be a woman in her day. For instance, we have to remind ourselves that Simone never voted. Women in France were given the vote at the end of the war, in 1945, two years after her death.

SIMONE
(gesture of dismissal) The vote is meaningless. In a world dominated by nationalism, there is no true choice.

LEE
(hears but tries to ignores Simone) When Simone was admitted to the elite Ecole Normale, only three other women were there. *(emphasis)* Women had not even been allowed to apply until the year before she entered. She passed first on the entrance exam.

SIMONE
Meaning what?

LEE
First among all applicants, male and female.

SIMONE
Meaning nothing! Passing exams is not learning. Studying for exams will destroy attention. *(to audience)* Never allow your children to study for exams!

LEE
As a student, she hung out in workers' cafes, smoking, arguing union strategy, at a time when the only unescorted women in such places—and smoking in public—were prostitutes. After graduation, she was assigned to teach at a provincial school for girls. But her teaching didn't stop there. At night, she traveled all over, teaching workers, attending meetings. She would miss the last train, then curl up on the floor of a bar or some worker's room, catching an hour of sleep before the morning train took her back to the classroom.

SIMONE
(trying to reach out to LEE) Must you go over and over—

LEE
(hearing SIMONE but resolutely ignoring her) Now, how did she, a woman in her society in the 1930s—and a pacifist at that—how did she avoid scandal, disgrace, rape?

SIMONE
(firmly) Pacifism ends where rape begins.

162

LEE

She chose an extreme solution to the problem. She refused to be in any way a sex object—refused to be the attractive woman she could have been. Nearly all her contemporaries describe her as unwomanly. They were talking, of course, about her appearance, the surface she presented to the world. *(SIMONE is standing in half-amused presentation of herself as awkward exhibit.)* What was that surface? In the age of the marcelled, painted flapper, Simone wore her hair plain and natural. Her face clean. Big glasses. She wore a loose sweater and skirt, sandals on her bare feet. Like a beatnik of the fifties? Yes, but a generation earlier, when such a costume did not say, "I am a rebel." It said, "I'm odd. I'm ugly." What she meant for it to say was, "Don't make a pass at me; talk to me. Be my friend, not my lover." Why not both? We all know why. Women were—and are—caught in a double bind. Sexually attractive, "womanly women" are not taken seriously. And those who refuse to attract sexual attention are despised. Some people understood what she was saying. Most did not. They were repelled, both men and women. People also described her as awkward, clumsy. Her students said she would show up to class with her sweater on inside out. She couldn't keep up on the assembly line. The accident that sent her home from Spain happened because she didn't look where she was going. She stepped into a pot of hot oil. Clumsy, awkward, ugly, unwomanly. I ask you, if she were Einstein with his sweater on backwards and his hair uncombed, what would people have said? Unmanly? Ugly? No. Absentminded genius. Brain occupied in more important things than what he wore or where he stepped or how well he performed mindless motions on an assembly line.

SIMONE

(shrugs) Maybe God enjoys pushing truth out through defective material.

LEE

(to SIMONE) You were not "defective material." You were strong. You skied. You hiked. You leaped over class lines! *(to*

audience) She stepped across class lines with unprecedented grace. The poor people she taught and worked with adored her, respected her. *(pause)* I'm tempted to stop here—

BETTENCOURT

(muttering) Especially since you're just about out of time?

LEE

—and leave you with a portrait of a rational feminist ahead of her time. But that would be, unfortunately, less than the whole truth.

SIMONE

Yes, the truth! *(Listens intently but soon shows headachy disappointment.)*

LEE

The whole truth is that Simone went to fanatical, fatal extremes in her denial of her woman's body. We all know, of course, the terrible words of the coroner's report in the London hospital where she died so young: "Self-starvation whilst the balance of her mind was disturbed."

SIMONE

(impatiently) I simply refused to eat any more than the rations of the people of France under the Nazi occupation!

LEE

Her anorexia had begun years before.

SIMONE

What does that word mean?

LEE

(to SIMONE, surprised that she needs a definition) It means a psychological eating disorder in which—

SIMONE

(impatient gesture) No, no, let's not play dictionary. What does it mean to you? A convenient label to put on something you don't understand? Take care. Don't put a word between yourself and truth.

LEE

(refuses to listen, drowns SIMONE out) Her eating disorder began in childhood.

164

SIMONE
(to LEE, insistently) I devour books!
LEE
It was a denial that went beyond clothes and make-up—
SIMONE
I am ravenous for truth!
LEE
—denial of the body beneath the clothes, a starving out of the
female within—
SIMONE
I desire reality!
LEE
—a starving out of her sexual drive, which was probably as
formidable as her mind.
SIMONE
(an erotic cry) I crave ... beauty!
LEE
Apparently she had no sexual experience at all.
SIMONE
You don't know that.
LEE
(to SIMONE) Well, did you?
SIMONE
And you don't need to know that.
LEE
(determined to ignore her) Her friends described her as cold.
SIMONE
When someone says, "I love you" he usually means, "I want
to eat you." Isn't that true? Come, why don't you admit it's true?
The lover you have now has half devoured you, and you know
you must escape before it is too late.
LEE
How do you know that? *(SIMONE smiles ironically.)* That's none
of your business—
SIMONE
Exactly.

LEE
(shaken, to audience) She had an aversion to being touched—or was it a fear of arousal?

SIMONE
Fear? Never. Listen to me. Lust is a hunger that grips the soul. Lust is a great energy that can be transformed into—

LEE
So she tried to destroy her sexuality with starvation and inhibition.

SIMONE
(exasperated at being so misunderstood)
Destroy it? Sooner die than destroy that power.

LEE
(determined to ignore SIMONE) It was inevitable that her strong sexual drive became sublimated—

SIMONE
Oh, not that old Freudian sublimation again!

LEE
(snaps at SIMONE) I am not a Freudian.

SIMONE
Good. You know how the Freudians hate sex, how they reduce the grand power of lust to simple physical craving.

LEE
(to audience) But her sexual drive, probably as strong as her intellect—

SIMONE
Of course—they are one and the same—

LEE
(desperately ignoring her) Her thwarted sexual drive burst through all efforts to repress it, and exploded in the classic way, in mysticism.

SCHNEIDER
Right, she was a very sick girl—

BETTENCOURT
(pointing to his watch) Look, you're running way over—

SIMONE

(to LEE)
You have it all wrong. Listen to me, pay attention. Yes, every longing is sexual. God gives us this precious energy. We can release it in sensual pleasure or *(emphasis)* we can feed it back into our souls, transform it, transform ourselves into that divine energy—

LEE

(stopped for a moment by SIMONE's insistence, but refusing to think about it) I'm sorry, I did go over my time.

SIMONE

(to everyone, with a gesture of giving up on LEE) Read Plato! *(sits down on the floor crosslegged. Will remain on the floor.)*

BETTENCOURT

(to LEE) You certainly did.

SCHNEIDER

I believe it's my turn now. Finally.

LEE

Yes. *(to audience, reading notes)* Our next speaker is Professor Nathan Schneider. Dr. Schneider needs no introduction. A prominent theorist in both psychology and history, he has written many books, the best known of which are *Daughters of the Holocaust* and *Genocide Within*. He lectures frequently at universities in this country and abroad on the psychic effects of the vast uprooting of peoples in the twentieth century. Throughout this year he has been a guest lecturer in Holocaust Studies here at the university. Dr. Schneider.

SCHNEIDER

(goes to podium with a brisk, impatient air. Uses no notes. Clearly he has given this talk many times.) Thank you. *(slight portentous pause as he makes eye contact with audience)* I am appalled. *(shorter pause)* I am appalled that we have gone this far into the program without stating the central fact about Simone Weil. *(slowly for effect)* Simone Weil was a Jew.

167

SIMONE

What is a Jew? *(starts as if she is going to tick off all the old questions about culture, religion, ethnicity.)*

SCHNEIDER

(snapping at SIMONE) A person who is forever asking that very question! *(to audience)* She was born in the same year as my mother, 1909. She fled the Nazis in 1940, the same year that my parents did, almost too late. Both her parents were Jews.

SIMONE

Freethinkers.

SCHNEIDER

Russian Jews on her father's side, Franco-German Jews on her mother's.

SIMONE

When I was a child, someone asked me if I was a Jew. I didn't know what he meant.

SCHNEIDER

(to SIMONE) You can admit that so casually? You, who always wanted to know the truth!

SIMONE

(skeptically) Some tribe in Palestine two thousand years ago?

SCHNEIDER

(to audience) She looked "Jewish," so Jewish that her ludicrous scheme to fight in the French Underground would have endangered everyone she contacted.

SIMONE

(gets on her knees, as if to get up and argue with him) I have always held the Christian ideal of love—

SCHNEIDER

(to SIMONE, impatiently) When you were telling that priest you were a Christian at heart, you spoke exactly as a Jew would—

SIMONE

That Christian ideal I summed up in one word, justice.

SCHNEIDER

Justice! You used the word justice over and over again, like a Jew. You argued interminably with those priests who wanted to baptize you. Like a Jew.

SIMONE

(serious, intense) The cruel god of the Old Testament is not the god of the gospels, not the god of love.

SCHNEIDER

(to audience, dismissing SIMONE, who is showing signs of a bad headache, sitting back on her heels) She was a Jew who knew nothing of her tradition but the stereotypes and cliches of the so-called Christian world. These she quite rightly rejected, but they are not the rich traditions of Judaism. Like the classic victim of oppression, she took on the values of the oppressor and condemned herself. *(SIMONE is shaking her head)* If you want to look for reasons behind her abuse of her body, her self-starvation, I suggest that you look for them in her self-hatred, the self-hatred of the victim, the anti-Semitic Jew! *(He is getting very angry, voice rising, so he stops to get control. He pours a glass of water, drinks, and composes himself during SIMONE's next speech, which he is determined not to hear.)*

SIMONE

(to audience, rising to her knees, pleading her case) The god of the Old Testament punishes the Hebrews for breaking his law. *(with horror)* Then suffering is deserved?—earthquakes, plagues, floods, all are punishment for—what? Sin? How cruel! To punish the victim! In this world we all must suffer pain and grief and death. Suffering is— *(As he interrupts she keeps trying to go on, repeats the word suffering several times while he is talking, but is always drowned out. She begins to hold her head in pain and to slowly crumple and sink to the floor.)*

SCHNEIDER

(composed again) Quite frankly, I am sick and tired of the sentimental veneration of a brilliant neurotic who had lost her roots. Yes, isn't it ironic that her most complete writing, her one book, was titled *The Need for Roots*? She wrote that a rootless life was

169

the worse suffering inflicted on modern man. True. But even worse is to live in ignorance that anything has been lost!

SIMONE

(clutching her head, sinking, weakly tries to argue with him) Suffering turns us away from our distractions. Toward God—

SCHNEIDER

She hated herself for being and not being a Jew. She punished herself for her loss. She wallowed in suffering—

SIMONE

—and in turning us to God, suffering becomes a blessing.

SCHNEIDER

(speaking right over her last three words) —from her headaches to her starving herself. She slept on the floor, refused to heat her room, worked herself into exhaustion and more headaches. But all these measures did not work quickly enough for her self-hating suicide. Her body was too strong even in its frailty. So she found self-annihilation in mysticism. The destruction of rationality, of her brilliant intellect. She chose this passive, mindless, self-torturing path and called it the way to God. She turned away from all that is good in life, from beauty, love, friendship.

SIMONE

(holding her head) No, no, beauty is a bridge to God. Love is a bridge to Reality.

SCHNEIDER

She turned away from her people. While her fellow Jews were being driven to the death camps, she was numbing her mind in trances of ecstasy.

SISTER

(who has been getting more and more disturbed during his speech) You cannot simply dismiss her religious development as— (as everyone turns to look at her, and SCHNEIDER slowly turns to glare) Oh. I'm sorry.

SCHNEIDER

If I may continue.

LEE

Yes, please, Dr. Schneider. (to SISTER) You'll be next, Sister.

SCHNEIDER

Simone was no worse than any other Western European Jew of the nineteen thirties. In fact she was an archetypal Jew of her class and generation, of my parents' class and generation. Secular. "Enlightened." Assimilated. Ignorant of her own tradition. Uprooted.

SIMONE

(her head bursting with pain, raises her head in one last effort) Tear the tree out by the roots, make it into a cross, and carry it!

SCHNEIDER

(to SIMONE, furiously) All your talk of taking up your cross! But that was your cross! To be a Jew in 1940 was your cross. And you refused it. *(SIMONE falls prostrate, still) (to audience)* Simone was what we call a catastrophe Jew—a Jew who never knows he is one until they come to take him to the death camp. No, she was not even that, for she managed to die in ignorance of who she was. It would have been better for her if she had not escaped to England. If the nazis had swept her up and pushed her into a cattle car with other Jews headed for a concentration camp. If she had been reunited with her people, yes, had been given the suffering she so valued, but suffering that mattered. Then, in that horror, the great woman she might have been—with all her reckless devotion to others, her fearless indifference to her own life, her absurd gallantry—all the beautiful intensity of her rare spirit *(pause)* would have finally made some sense. I know, I've shocked some of you. Don't misunderstand me. I don't wish for yet another dead Jew in the Holocaust. If she could have lived—but she didn't live. She starved herself to death in that London hospital, feeling alone, betrayed—

BETTENCOURT
She was betrayed, dammit.

SISTER
You're dismissing her most productive—

SCHNEIDER

A useless death. If she had to die, let it at least have been a death that meant something. *(He abruptly leaves the podium, sits down.)*

Side Show 1995

LEE

(like everyone else, she is shaken as she goes to the podium) Our fourth panelist is Sister Cecilia Vero. Sister Cecilia is a teacher of biology at the Sacred Heart Girls' Academy. She has published science books which are used in public as well as parochial schools, and also a series of children's books on Catholic saints. Her recent article in the *Catholic Worker*, titled "Saints Outside the Church," includes a discussion of Simone Weil. Sister Cecilia.

SISTER

(uses notes, starts out as a soft-spoken, hesitant, methodical speaker, resigned to having her view of SIMONE disdained by the majority secular society) I suppose my role here is to give a different view of Simone's religious experiences. But first, I think we should review what we know about these experiences. Experiences that came to a young intellectual who did not seek mystical experience, who, until these experiences came to her, had called herself an atheist. *(SIMONE raises her head to look at SISTER. During SISTER's description of her religious experiences, she will gradually rise.)* There were three religious experiences that she described to Father Perrin, a priest who became her friend. The first was an insight that came to her after her year of work in the factory. That was in 1935, when she was twenty-six years old. She was ill, exhausted, feeling—as she put it—permanently marked as a slave by her year of factory work. Her parents took her on vacation to Portugal. There, in a little fishing village, she saw a candlelight religious procession, heard women singing an old hymn. It came to her, she wrote, that Christianity was the religion of slaves. *(SIMONE is sitting up)* The second—uh—incident came two years later during a trip she took alone to Italy. *(aside from notes)* By the way, no one has mentioned those six months, probably the happiest period of her life. People who describe her as masochistic, turning her back on the joys of life *(clearly she means SCHNEIDER)* forget her response to the beauties of art and music she found there, especially the frescoes of Giotto in the cathedral at Assisi. While she was in Assisi, she went into Santa Maria degli Angeli—the tiny old chapel where

172

Saint Francis had prayed. There, suddenly, for the first time in her life, she felt compelled to go down on her knees. I would not call this a "religious experience." It is a response many people have in a setting that appeals to spiritual needs, *(gently, tentatively insistent)* needs that are universal.

(SIMONE has risen to her knees, arms hanging at her sides. Her aching head is hanging, but slowly begins to rise.)

SISTER

(checks her notes again) Then in 1938, when she was twenty-nine, came the actual "religious experience." She went to Solesmes during Easter week to hear the Gregorian chants. There she met a young Englishman who introduced her to the English metaphysical poets. Her headaches were very severe at that time, and she tried to soothe them by reciting a poem by George Herbert. I'd like to read that poem to you, so that we'll all hear the words, just as she recited them—in English.

(Picks up a small paperback book and reads from it. During the reading of the poem both speak outward toward audience. SIMONE gradually rises, gets to her feet at "Love took my hand," and "sees" something with her inner perception. From there to the end of the poem she takes on beauty, peace, not a release from pain but a rising to a reality beyond it. Something of this should echo in SISTER's voice and demeanor as she reads.)

Love bade me welcome
But my soul drew back
Guilty of dust and sin
But quick-eyed Love, observing me grow slack
From my first entrance in,
Drew nearer to me, sweetly questioning
If I lacked any thing. *(As SIMONE begins to recite, SISTER is quite aware of her, pleased and moved by their dual reading.)*

SIMONE

A guest, I answered, worthy to be here

SISTER

Love said, You shall be he.

SIMONE

I the unkind, ungrateful? Ah my dear *(meaning love, God, Christ)*
I cannot look on thee. *(rises during SISTER's next line.)*

SISTER

Love took my hand, and smiling did reply,
Who made the eyes but I?

SIMONE

Truth, Lord, but I have marred them: let my shame
Go where it doth deserve.

SISTER

And know you not, says Love, who bore the blame?

SIMONE

My dear, then I will serve.

SISTER

You must sit down, says Love, and taste my meat:

SIMONE

(infusing the six simple words with passion and peace)
So I did sit and eat.

(SISTER takes a beat or two to bring herself back into everyday mode, clearing her throat, sip of water)

(wryly) Another eating metaphor for the psychologists to work on. *(clearly she looks differently on SIMONE's "anorexia")* It was during her recitation of this poem that, as Simone wrote to Father Perrin, "Christ himself came down and took possession of me." What did she mean? Did this brilliant young intellectual have orgasmic visions from bad religious art? No. Again, let me quote Simone. "Neither my senses nor my imagination had any part. I only felt, in the midst of my suffering, the presence of a love like that which one reads in the smile on a beloved face."

(SIMONE continues to stand at beatific peace.)

(aside from notes) This is the religious experience you have heard dismissed today as *(referring to LEE)* an expression of repressed sexuality, *(to BETTENCOURT)* of mental illness, *(to SCHNEIDER)* and as a masochistic flight from life. Most of us will never understand her experience. So how can we judge it? I think the only way is to judge its effects on her, on her behavior during

the five years of life left to her. Did she go around telling people she had "seen God?" No. She never mentioned this experience to anyone. She wrote about it to Father Perrin when she left France, convinced that she would never see him again. In her notebooks, she wrote hundreds of pages on the spiritual insights that came to her with her continuing experiences. But she never showed a page of that writing to anyone. She gave the notebooks to another Catholic friend when she left France—again, correctly guessing that she would not live to see him again.

(BETTENCOURT is poking LEE and pointing to his watch because LEE forgot time while listening to the poem. LEE now begins to try to signal SISTER.)

SISTER

What did she do during the five years left to her? Were those years a flight from reality? Hardly. They were an amazing burst of energy, an outpouring of writing of political and social essays that make up her best work. Even her style changed, gaining clarity and conviction. In the four month period in England before her death she wrote *The Need for Roots*, the book that made T.S. Eliot call her "a woman of genius." Was all this work the product of a sick mind that had retreated into religious delusion? I do think her mind was under great strain. Besides the horror of the war, she was forced, in a sense, to split her mind in half. She could not talk to her friends of the French political left or the intelligentsia about her new spiritual insights. They would have responded just as the other members of this panel have. She could not accept the baptism Father Perrin offered her, and that she longed for *(SIMONE loses her beatific look and turns her head sharply to look at SISTER, listening suspiciously)* because she was still working through the many questions and doubts that are natural in a sincere, intelligent convert. The saddest thing about her early death may be that she did not have enough time to resolve these doubts—

SIMONE

(shaking her head) **Wait.**

SISTER
—and allow Father Perrin to baptize her.

SIMONE
(didactically, pointing her finger at SISTER, who looks very conflicted, unwilling to listen) The Catholic Church became the second Roman Empire. It is one thing to see into the truth of the gospels. It is another thing to see into the cruel history of that institution.

SISTER
(to SIMONE) But you hungered for the eucharist.

SIMONE
Yes, and I loved the liturgy, the ritual. But I did not love the church.

SISTER
Not to be able to receive communion was a greater starvation than any other you suffered.

SIMONE
(agonized) But I could not. Not if others can't. I belong to all those people outside the church, now and throughout all history, outside.

LEE
Sister, time.

SIMONE
The man who prays to Krishna, to Buddha, is answered by Christ too.

SISTER
Yes, and the church has learned from you. It has become much more ecumenical.

SIMONE
(impatiently) No! That's all wrong. To dilute, to weaken a tradition. Any spiritual path leads to God, but you must give yourself wholly to that path.

SISTER
(to audience, trying to ignore SIMONE) In time she would have put aside her doubts.

SIMONE

Not about the church. Not unless the church acknowledged its crimes before the world and began—

SISTER

(to SIMONE, brushing her aside) I have read all that—your indictment of the church. There have been many changes since then. And even then—you could have—if you could only have swallowed your pride.

SIMONE

(serious, not angry) It was not pride.

SISTER

You might have helped make more changes, faster, from inside the church. If you could have been a little less insistent on your opinions, your ideas.

SIMONE

But they are not *my* ideas. They come into me, settle for a moment, and then demand to be let out.

SISTER

Nothing can be as pure and perfect as you demand. If you had been able to bend a little—

SIMONE

As you did?

SISTER

(very disturbed) We're talking about you, not me!

SIMONE

I wonder.

LEE

Sister, time.

SIMONE

(to SISTER, who ignores her) I could not be baptized into the church because God did not order it. If my eternal salvation were right there *(puts out her hand)* within my grasp, and God did not order me to take it, I could not reach out to it, could not touch it.

177

Side Show 1995

SISTER
(looking at her watch) I know I'm out of time, but I want to say just one thing. Regardless of the technicality of not being baptized—

SIMONE
(not angry, just impatient) Technicality? No! My place must be at the intersection of Christianity with everything that is not Christian. Why won't you listen to me? You are just like the others. All of you take one little bite out of me and spit out the rest. You will never know me unless you swallow me whole.

SISTER
(to SIMONE) Stop tormenting me! *(desperately)* Leave me alone. *(SIMONE makes a gesture of giving up on the whole panel, and exits.)*

SISTER
(to audience, composing herself with some difficulty) Though technically not a Catholic, Simone anticipated a new spirit, an important new Catholic movement known as Liberation Theology—social activism as an expression of faith. Grounded in service to God. She still inspires that spirit. I want to close by mentioning a dear friend of mine, a nun who was murdered while working among the poor of El Salvador. My friend kept the books of Simone Weil beside her bed. In her last letter to me she told me that she prayed every day to Saint Simone. *(leaves the podium and sits down.)*

LEE
Thank you. *(to audience)* I'm sure the panelists have raised many questions in our minds. Please be sure to write them down and give them to me during the break. Now, to conclude the first part of our program, I'd like to read a statement by Simone Weil's brother, Andre Weil, distinguished mathematician at the Institute for Policy Studies at Princeton University. Speaking on a panel at Princeton in 1978, he said, *(all panelists look unhappy with the following statement, but all for different reasons)* "My sister has been called a saint. I believe it was her vocation to be a saint. By vocation, I mean that which one is called to do. It is my vocation to be a mathematician. From my earliest childhood, that

178

was the work I was called to do. No one had to tell me. I always knew it. Gauguin was meant to be a painter, and he found that he had to give up many human values to do that work. Some men are meant to be carpenters, and—by the way— my sister believed that their vocation was as important, as sacred, if you will, as that of any artist or intellectual. To have a vocation does not mean necessarily to have great talent, just the call to that work. I have a friend who is a writer. She will never write a great book. But she must write. It is her purpose in life, her vocation. It was my sister's vocation to be a saint. Whether she became a good saint or a mediocre one, a first-class saint or a third-class saint, is quite another question, and one you must judge for yourself." Well, maybe that's one of the questions we'll go into after we take *(looks at watch)* a ten-minute break. *(Panelists exit, stage and house lights left up.)*

(End of Act One)

For Jane Austen lovers ....

THE CRAWFORDS AT NEWBURY:

EPILOGUE TO *MANSFIELD PARK*

by Lee Vining

In a private room of the Tongue and Lyre Inn in Newbury, Miss Mary Crawford waited for the soon expected arrival of her brother, Henry. Her anticipation at seeing her brother was tinged with more excitement than usual and just a touch of dread to add piquancy. She moved around the room, unable to sit down anywhere, staring out the windows at the changeable sky above the town. She had been driven to Newbury by the friends whose house at Bath she was leaving after an extended visit. Henry, returning from Wales where he had been shooting at a friend's estate, was to accompany her from Newbury to their London house.

Having known that she was to meet him so soon and that the likelihood of a letter reaching him before he left Wales was problematical, she was still the possessor of a momentous piece of news she had learned less than three days ago and had been carrying locked away in her breast in the expectation of sharing it with the person next to herself most directly affected.

Yet it was an hour and a half after they met that the first words were uttered on a subject she had been preoccupied with every waking hour since receiving the news. But she could not break the habit of years in her relations with her brother in order to throw everything into confusion by an ill-timed and dramatic announcement. Henry would have been annoyed. They were so alike that she could anticipate his feelings on most matters and this put a strong restraint on any stray impulse. She used him as a mirror and a guide to her own feelings. Whenever uncertain on any point, she had only to glance at Henry to clarify her own reaction.

Of course, since he was a man, there was a whole side of his life that was mysterious to her. He must do as all young men of fortune do. That is, to behave like boys for as long as possible before marrying precipitously in order to break the enervating cycle of bachelorhood. Henry, who was making his youth serve him as long as possible, was still putting off this inevitable moment. As for herself, she had recently all but made up her mind that her lot would not include a husband. With this more or less decided, Mary's main care was to keep her interest in life stirred up enough so that she need not turn into a pillar of salt from looking too long at her lack of scope.

Mary had a lively intellect, a great deal of imagination and curiosity chiefly directed at the interesting, many faceted complexities of human intercourse which she viewed from the perspective of an enlightened outsider. Since her study of mankind was entirely particularized and personal to herself, it was only with Henry that she had a common language in which to communicate her observations and conclusions. Never having felt bound by the constraints women voluntarily undertook in order to show themselves inoffensive and eminently marriageable, this gave her point of view a detachment which might have been almost too free if she had not known herself to be the very model of unswerving virtue — though for motives more pragmatic than conventional. Endowed with intelligence of a particularly discerning kind, and being pretty enough to have experienced most of what she might encounter in the way of male admiration, she felt neither the usual temptations that girls faced with the inescapability of marriage must, nor any of the imperatives either. Mary believed that all old women look alike because they had never come into a realization of themselves, having been drafted into the ranks of the married before they had a chance to become anyone. Her feeling of being cut from a different cloth led to the necessity of dissimulating the degree of freedom she permitted herself in her thoughts and made her more than usually deliberate in her behavior.

While Mary owed her independence to the fact that she was the possessor of an ample income, she owed much of her mental latitude to her aunt and to an unconventional upbringing. Orphaned at an early age, she and Henry had been brought to live with this aunt and her husband the admiral. Mary's aunt, aware that, though her philosophy was irreproachable, her application of it in her own case had been particularly disastrous, had decided to train Mary to follow in her footsteps but without falling down the same precipice.

Mary's aunt as a young girl had been headstrong. Depreciating and scorning a woman's lot, she determined that she was cast of a metal less malleable than the majority of her sex. Following her vow not to marry for any socially approved reason, she had met the admiral (then a captain) and found him to be utterly unlike any other man she had ever seen. While this was enough to cause him to be shunned by most of the women he might have hoped to marry (if he could ever be accused of having had such a hope), it had been the foundation of Mary's aunt's regard for him. Curiously, they had been brought together initially by the similarity in their low opinion of the gentler sex. The captain, seeing that she was blindly self-willed enough to think herself a match for him, took up her challenge. His response to her had been everything she could desire in the way of brutally eschewing conventional hypocrisy. Mary's aunt had been warned against him on every side, but this had merely reinforced her determination to follow her own course. It was only after the wedding day that the scales fell and by then it was much too late as she had burned all her bridges by quarreling with the very friends who might have made a rescue possible.

Alone with the captain, she now discovered that a similarity of opinion could still result in conflict. She found herself married to a man who saw in marriage an arena for single combat carried out entirely on his own terms and without the slightest regard for fair play. She had had to relinquish all hopes then, in order to devote herself entirely to the study of this predator until she knew him so thoroughly she could parry every blow he aimed at her. Not that the admiral was a wife beater. It would have been a symptom of defeat to descend to that level, though he might sometime let himself go by threatening to turn her out of his house by force.

Mary and her younger brother had entered the arena *in media res*. They had quickly been enlisted as the aides-de-camp of the two combatants. The admiral had fastened himself on Henry while the aunt was left to the possibly weaker part in Mary. Mary's aunt had done everything she could to insure that Mary profit from her mistake and that she be well armored against any tendency to sentimentalize the enemy.

Henry meanwhile had grown up listening to the admiral aggrandize himself by diminishing women — all women in general and his wife in particular. The admiral fancying that he was an elegant and urbane man did nothing rude or boorish to alienate Henry's goodwill; he expressed himself with the blandness of a philosopher. "Henry, my boy. I was taught to suspect them of anything and that teaching has never failed me. The serpent seduced Eve because of all the creatures in Eden, she was possessed of a nature closest to his own."

The brother and sister remained committed to their original filial bond but in secret, each finding a shelter in the other against the marital storm going on over their heads. The two antagonists treated each other's favorites with the greatest forbearance so that Mary and Henry had never developed a personal reason to dislike their uncle or aunt. Mary always fancied that her uncle, though cruel and violent enough in manner, became rather frightened of her as soon as she grew tall and pretty enough to stare him in the face. And on her side, Mary's aunt treated Henry with the utmost civility, pretending that his closeness to the admiral was only the result of coercion.

If outliving one's adversary is winning the war, the admiral had won. The aunt was worn down at last. The spider that waited tensely for the slightest vibration of its web felt her involuntary tug and rushed to take her to her rest.

To mark his triumph on this occasion, the admiral had installed his mistress in his house, thus driving Mary out of it.

Mary's musings were interrupted when her brother re-entered the room. He had been out making arrangements for a postchaise, and his mud-spattered boots, reddened face, and dripping cloak brought into the room a feeling of wildness and vigorous life.

"They shall have the horses no sooner than three. It is just as well, my dear Mary. We will be more comfortable sitting out this downpour. Meanwhile, I shall order our dinner to be brought."

Mary nodded, waiting until every source of distraction was out of the way. She stood up and walked to the window. It was indeed raining very hard. The town was sodden and dispirited under the onslaught of foul weather as though nature herself had determined to be as nasty and discomforting as possible. Behind her a fire crackled in the grate, dispensing its own sort of counterbalancing cheer. The room was threadbare and plainly furnished, an ordinary inn room, meant only to house those in transit.

She held her mittened hands toward the fire and was standing there when her brother returned and threw himself into an armchair. "We have nothing to do now but wait," said Henry. "How was your stay at Bath?"

"The same as always. The usual mixture of coxcombs and unprincipled scoundrels leavened with minxes and bold flirts and not a single thinking being in the lot. Sometimes my life reminds me of those crude images of a *danse macabre* with death as a grinning gentleman leading us on a round of pleasure that leaves us dissatisfied but insatiable until we wake up one morning no longer young."

"My goodness, Mary, that does paint a vivid picture."

"Perhaps it is different for men. For you, at least. You balance sport and idle pursuits very well and manage to keep your looks and your health without spoiling your pleasure."

"I am not admitted a pretty man."

"Handsomeness would only detract from your charm," said Mary. "In any case, it is only in girls that prettiness is a necessity."

"As you certainly are, Mary."

"Yes, but pretty and twenty-seven are not the same thing as pretty and eighteen."

"What, are you feeling your age?"

"Not so much that, I fear, as a creeping sense that I have done everything there is for me to do, and yet so much time remains. So much blank time. If I am happy now, and I am not, how much less reason will I have to be in the future?"

"You sound in low spirits, Mary. Has something happened?"

Mary hesitated, looking meditatively at her brother who had gotten up to stand with his back to the fire.

"Perhaps we might have some tea?" she said. The innkeeper was sent for and the order duly given.

When they were sitting at the table and she had poured for him, Mary said gently:

"Yes, something has happened. It is very surprising and very shocking and yet one can't help but think that it is exactly right as if once at least life has come out as it should."

"Do not keep me lingering in suspense," said Henry concentrating on his tea. His sister looked at him shrewdly. How much his life depended, she thought, on not making occasions for the receipt of bad news.

"I am afraid you will not like this news. It comes from Mansfield Park."

There was an involuntary start and a quick recovery on his part.

185

"Ah, yes. Mansfield Park, where we were both almost un-horsed."

"I am sure you gave as good as you got," said Mary.

"Be just. I only reaped what had been sown."

"Yes," said Mary. "You have a weakness for that."

"Call it rather a talent," said Henry. "And so what news do you hear from Mansfield Park?"

"It is only this: Mrs. Grant writes that Edmund Bertram and Fanny Price are married. To each other."

Henry's first impulse was to laugh, which he did. After a moment, Mary joined him. They laughed merrily with perfect satisfaction, which restored Mary's spirits wonderfully.

"Now that is what I would call poetic justice," said Henry. "They were created for and by each other. It is quite amazing that you and I should have betrayed ourselves so wholly for such a pair of prigs. Can you fancy yourself now as a country parson's wife? Even if he had conceded you winters in London, think how little pleasure he would have brought to the removal. It would have been a marriage of forbearance on his side and unconquerable irritation on yours to be always the recipient of principled generosity."

"Very likely, but I have always considered that I had the strength of resolution to rise to an occasion. I might have made a very nice country parson's wife as long as Edmund Bertram were there to sustain me in the role."

"Perhaps, but think of me now, living in Norfolk, the productive country squire, the name of every tenant's child at the tip of my tongue, a small scale Solomon engaged in perpetual good works for the improvement of everyone within reach. For that is what I would have had to become in order to earn Fanny Price's unconditional approval."

"Yes, we are neither one of us of quite such a tight compass to fit into either life."

"And that is to your credit, Mary," said Henry. "As Fanny Price is my moral pattern, you are certainly my model of unyielding independence of spirit. You have seen more clearly than any woman I have ever known that a young woman with an independent income has nothing to gain by a marriage, no matter how seemingly advantageous. I admire you for it."

"Perhaps you admire me only because you do not see the paucity of my choice in the matter. It seems very hard to me that the only man I ever loved, I could not imagine myself living with; while the men I could bear to live with, I cannot imagine loving. But it is as you say. With Edmund Bertram, I should have been perpetually chafing at the restraints that a good man in the fullest exercise of every virtue must impose on a woman like myself, endowed with intelligence. No, in Fanny Price, he has made the perfect choice. She will always admire his rectitude without ever finding it a burden. She is a limited creature."

"Now there I think you wrong her, though I agree in general with what you say. It is a perfect match for both of them and this piece of news you bring me drops the single missing element into the puzzle that makes its solution clear."

Henry stood up and then sat down again restlessly before continuing:

"So little Fanny had already made her heart's selection, unencouraged by anyone, mightily discouraged in most quarters, and had clung to it though it held only the slenderest hope. Unlike the majority of her sex, particularly one in her dependent circumstances, she had not been merely holding out her heart as though it were an empty receptacle which might be filled by any man who happened by with the minimum requisite qualifications for a lover and husband."

"I sometimes almost suspected it," said Mary. "Her interest in Edmund was what drew me to her, and his regard for her made her a perfect go-between for us. Yet, I never thought her to have the spirit required to passionately attach herself where there was no certainty of return. She concealed it so well behind the facade of kinship and family affection that I am sure that Edmund himself never suspected it. If he had, I should have known it also."

"Tell me, Henry," said Mary after a pause in which Henry's merriment had by degrees turned to somberness. He fiddled with his tobacco pouch, stuffed a clay pipe, and then set it down again without lighting it. "What was it that made you yield your heart to Fanny Price? You who were so used to cutting a swath of wholesale destruction — like Mars in the service of Cupid — among feminine hearts without ever feeling a pang in your own? In that at least you were our uncle's apt pupil — and his equal — since he exercised his destructive spirit over but a single woman while you mow down an entire generation. In that respect, you men may have it both ways. You may retain your character while debauching yourselves, while we women must fall forever when we fall once — unless we are duchesses or the sisters of poets. Even to admit to a desire is tantamount to admitting ourselves unfeminine."

"A woman with desires is not a lady to be sure," said Henry. "At least if she forgets even for a moment that she is the bearer of all sanctity and morality in human life."

"You deny us our humanity while deifying our sex. Oh, Henry, I should have thought you were wiser than that."

"I only assert what all the world acts by. If not these rules, there must be others, and why not ones as odious and reprehensibly unjust as these? You are none the worse for them and it is sheer hypocrisy on your part to mourn the weaker members of your sex who throw their only value away."

"They throw away their womanhood in gaining it and for this sin are exiled by society where they must prove their ultimate worth by either dying of the shame or living despite it. However, a man may dip his beak anywhere and has only to change his location in order to shake off the pollution."

"It may seem to you that our latitude is greater, but the moral burden is no less exigent upon us than it is upon you. I do not escape unpolluted and I envy you the social strictures which so clearly delineate the boundaries of your conduct. Our freedom merely tempts us to go too far in a wilderness full of unmentionable dangers. You have little idea of the unwelcome curiosity, the uninvited intimacies I have let myself in for by persons who would never have dared thrust themselves upon my notice had

I not classed myself among them by my behavior. I have involuntarily been enlisted into the brotherhood of scapegraces and reprobates. It matters not that I feel myself their superior, they do not consider me so and all the most unanswerable evidence is on their side."

"Shall you marry, Henry?"

"I suppose I must, if only to mark the passage of time. I only hope to yoke myself in a deliberative spirit with a partner who will not prove another example of egregious delusion."

"As Fanny Price might so easily have been?"

"No. With her, I should have had to make up my mind to live entirely according to her lights."

"I hope your chances are better than the majority of mankind. Whether they marry in haste or not, they usually repent at leisure. And even the strictest adhesion to every canon of virtue and goodwill cannot guarantee a happy married life."

"I will settle for concord and understanding."

"One has to wonder at times why morality must be paid in such very small coin."

"Virtue must be its own reward," said Henry. "Otherwise it is not virtue."

"Even if purchased at the expense of every other human quality which sometimes comes into conflict with its iron rule?"

"One stores up virtue as one does grain against the promised seven years of famine. You and I, dear sister, are not convinced that there will be a famine, or that we would be affected by it. We are cynical optimists, my dear, and our rudder through this trying time of youth and plenty is merely self-interest. This will scarcely guide us during a time of famine."

"I sometimes long for famines," said Mary. "I long for protracted wars and epidemics. Anything to break this chain of circumstance I wear around me. I know that it will take something out of the ordinary; no mere skirmishes or cholera outbreaks in Irish villages will do."

"That, my dear, is because you still have your beauty. But when that is gone and virtue becomes more than theoretical, or less,

189

where will you be? I am afraid among the first precipitate victims of whatever calamity elects itself to save you from ennui and too much reflection."

"And what about you, Henry?" asked Mary. "Where will you be?"

"Why, I am a man and will be wherever the men are. I have a reputation to maintain, and though it has little virtue in it, it binds me just as jealously."

Mary shivered slightly, moving her shoulders under the merino of her travelling dress, and shaking out her skirts as though she had been brought to mind of herself.

"Well, we have wandered far astray of the subject of the newest Mr. and Mrs. Bertram."

"I do not like to think of them, so proof against the wayward-ness of human inclination, so very vulnerable in their happiness because it reposes in each other alone. They have forsaken every possible road for a footpath only wide enough for two. It pains me for Fanny Price's sake. Her gratitude in finding herself so blessed will shackle her. She had a grateful nature. It was her one point of attachment to me."

"Tell me, Henry. How do you explain your lack of success with her?"

"What is more amazing is that I came so close to succeeding. Do you think, my dear sister, that if you had married Edmund, she would have long withstood my impassioned pleas?"

"Why then did you destroy your prospects if you were so certain of success?"

"Perhaps that is why I did. I feared my dearest wish being granted. Only those in a state of grace can take that chance."

"Then why with Mrs. Rushworth?"

"Why, I imagine, is because I like a certain symmetry in my designs. But if you would like a short accounting of my feelings at that time, I will be glad to tell you."

"Oh, yes, do."

"I had just left Fanny at Portsmouth where I had burst in on her family home, playing to the hilt my role of unaccepted but

undeflected and ardent suitor. I was met there by the smell of
boiling starch and cabbage and something like sausage gone off.
The narrow hallway and staircase were aswarm with noisy
children. Her mother is a slattern; except for her age, one cannot
tell her apart from her maid."

"Poor Fanny," said Mary.

"Yes, it would have distressed you to see her embarrassment.
But I retrieved the situation with all the finesse at my command.
I managed to turn her mother into a lady and her tippler father
into, if not a gentleman, at least a jovial honest fellow."

"Surely you exaggerate."

"Well, you know my poor opinion of the human race at its
pinnacle so you can imagine how I feel about those below that."

"What? And do you really consider yourself at a pinnacle?"

"The pinnacle of being unanswerable to anyone, and as independent as air."

"Rather heavy inert air."

"It is difficult to make oneself ferment without yeast, yet I
would do nothing to disturb the equal tenor of my life for all
the fermentation in the world."

"And so you cornered her in the place where she would find
your arrival most discountenancing and most desirable. And
how did you press this advantage?"

"I was a fool in that matter. I thought she could be handled
like other females — I had no good opinion of women at that
time and I thought it impossible for any woman, no matter how
committed to Christian sacrifice, to withstand such a chance as
I represented."

"If we are weak in that regard, Henry, and earn your contempt,
remember please that that is how *men* have desired it to be since
time immemorial."

"I except both you and Fanny Price from this indictment," he
said. "You are both in a category which draws a special strength
from some secret source in order to escape the low fates of the
largest part of your sex."

191

"In any other man, Henry, this must sound like the rankest sexual prejudice. First you sink us to the status of domestic animals, and then you discern from among the casualties the few fortunate survivors and single them out for commendation for having risen above their fates."

"You are not understanding me, Mary. Our sexes merely give us the clothes we wear, the pursuits we elect, our privileges. I derive no power from your lack of it."

"What sort of a man would Fanny Price have made?"

He laughed. "You have put your finger on the weak spot of my tolerant discrimination. It was because she was so very unlike me that I began to love her. She dominated without saying a word, silently watching everything with a self-forgetfulness so free of egoism that her sympathy could penetrate all pretense and hypocrisy. She was indispensable to all without being noticed by any. She created our moral atmosphere. Do you recollect the play?"

"And how delicious was my gratification when Edmund — so pious and disapproving — could not bear the prospect of anyone else playing my lover? As soon as he could find an unexceptional excuse for doing something that went so completely against his grain, he succumbed to his baser instinct. First, to keep his own countenance, he consulted with Fanny and gave her all his reasons, winning her reluctant sanction. That was when I knew I had him and could reel him in at any time. But I delayed, and made him miserable, counting on bending him not merely to my will but to my view of life."

"You have no idea of the rigid strength in a full scale prig."

"Yes, but I'd hoped to find inside the prig the man who sat behind me one summery morning while I played my harp in front of an open window, with the breeze sometimes blowing a curl or stirring the sash of my white lawn dress. I played him my favorite tunes, and I felt him overflow like molten lava which scorched me. I have never encountered such a burning hot sensibility in a man and it was coupled with a pleasing exterior and excellent manners. One thing I am sure of is that he will never

192

experience an answering warmth in Fanny Price. I alone had that."

"Well, I found him agreeable myself, but like Fanny, he only tolerated me because it would have been ungenerous not to give any man who tried to please him the benefit of the doubt. Though I know what you mean about his heat, Mary. I sometimes felt it myself. He is a man who is almost everywhere glacial, but when something burns through the ice, one is met by a jet of heat."

"But you were telling me about Portsmouth," said Mary after a pause.

"Yes, well, I saw her there. I talked with great volubility and high spirits about the reforms I was bringing about on my Norfolk property, showing her by a multiplication of detail that I was deep into my subject, and she listened, but I could feel her shrinking and becoming faint-hearted again, and I had to warm her up by reminding her of the service I had done her brother. That was my greatest mistake. I tried to give her too many conflicting reasons for finding me irresistible, when there should only have been one. In my self-defeating cynicism, I expected her to capitulate as much from an unwilling attraction to me as by the most cold-blooded self-interest. I am much afraid that my uncle's monomania has made its inroads on my heart in spite of my reason, for I very often find myself treating women in a way he would approve. I should never have approached her in such a meretricious fashion. I rated her far too low and cheapened myself, staining my every act and word, and throwing into relief time and time again the man I should have been against the posturing fellow I was. I maneuvered and manipulated, and played a Sheridan or Congreve hero in what I considered the finest style. Only *I* was fooled by it. She was never imposed upon. I thought it was because of her innate discernment, but it was only her unconfessed and hopeless love for Edmund Bertram which protected her from such as I. I thought she was virtuous for virtue's sake in shunning me, but she has

193

proved it pays after all to be ruled by an iron conscience in achieving every honorable estate at no expense of spirit."

"No, I cannot think you are sincere in that. Your cynicism is a mask."

"You are right. I have a curious faith in her. I have developed a regard for her strength and would not like to have this golden image shattered. When we were all giddy with the play, do you know what gave our pleasure such an intense hue? After all, the occasion was not unique. You and I, in our perambulations, have run into many amateur theatricals, but never was any of them fraught with so much pleasure as that. Do you know why that was so?"

"Because we were both in love: I with Edmund and you with the charming and vivid Miss Bertram, while at the same time you were breaking Julia Bertram's heart. Don't tell me it was because you were all the time conscious of Fanny Price, who — if I remember correctly — was not even particularly pretty, at least not in comparison with the Bertram sisters."

"She was much more than that. She was the root of our pleasure. She suffered so intensely when Edmund broke faith with himself in order to play Anhalt, and she was so painfully conscious of the vanity and indulgence of our pastime, the viciousness underlying our frivolity. The play was merely our vehicle for striking attitudes, and the cover for illicit lovemaking, devoid of true feeling..."

"Speak for yourself, Henry."

"I was much more aware of her moral pain, touched with heart-soreness, than I was of her. It gave me all my zest for an amusement which otherwise might have been stale."

"You paid her not the slightest attention beside what civility demanded."

"That is quite right. Not knowing that I loved her, I had no ground on which to approach her. But this in no way lessened my need of her. When we lost our cottager's wife and everyone entreated Fanny to read the part for our rehearsal, I think I was alone in feeling her distress. Even the fatuous Edmund pressed her. It was then I marked Maria down for an insensitive, small-spirited woman because she felt no incongruity in the idea of her cousin being forced to take a part simply to oblige our whim. She was a callous woman, Maria, hardened around her own vanity. I could no more have approached their cousin while those two vivid girls were thrusting themselves upon me than one can pick a single out-of-reach wild rose, when two large garden roses are plucked and offered to one."

"Listening to this expression of your regard for Maria Rushworth, perhaps it was mere vengeance that made you single her out for ruin? Perhaps vengeance against me as well since it was this rash deed that destroyed my prospects with Edmund. What made you do something that could bring you only universal censure?"

"I don't know. I believe I was somewhat beside myself. I remember coming back from Portsmouth with the highest hopes. I asked you to write Fanny with an offer I was convinced would be the *pièce de résistance*: to rescue her from the misery and degradation of her family and to return her to Mansfield Park and to the afflicted Bertrams. That was the time when Tom Bertram was lying near death."

"Not near enough," said Mary. "I had hopes that his older brother's death would provide Edmund with the impetus I could not give him. It might have at least snatched him away from the clergy. But I might have known that he was a younger son to the core."

"At any rate, I was so certain that Fanny would succumb at last — that my reformation, the proofs of sincerity I had offered, not only in suing for a woman without fortune, but in persisting despite all rebuff, would win her — that my disappointment when she wrote back, saying piously that she awaited her uncle Bertram's escort in order to return to Mansfield Park, made me realize quite suddenly — though I didn't recognize to what extent — that even if she married me at last, I would only get the residue that survived going so violently against every inclination, every right feeling, hope and desire. I was ripe for the picking when I met Maria Rushworth, who after a most tantalizing coldness, made it quite clear that she was warmer in my favor than before, having had six months to find out in how many ways a husband like Rushworth could fail his wife. Her desperate desire to enjoy what she had thought eternally out of reach overpowered her every instinct of prudence. Her making herself so scandalously mine was her proof of love."

"But what did you find in this commonplace situation attractive enough to stain your reputation, making you not only the greatest enemy of the Bertram family but a reproach to your own family and dearest friends? I could not reconcile myself to the folly of it. It was so contrary to everything I knew of your character."

"Perhaps my keen nose for danger had made me long for a sudden plunge into the very thing that I had always skirted so scrupulously. And Maria loved me precisely for those qualities that Fanny distrusted and deplored. In one woman I was aware of a negative view of myself that was intoxicating because it argued a real interest, a fine appreciation of character, a rare discernment and a keen moral sense, all at my expense; while in the other, there was simply intoxication, a passion for me created by the friction between Maria's self-love and her frustration at not attaining to what she had aspired to with such confidence. With Maria there was no imperative for the deep reformation that Fanny would have made necessary. I have always had an unconquerable fear of change."

"Well, I couldn't shake off my surprise, and it was exactly this which alienated Edmund forever and made me assume the character of a vicious woman in his eyes. I kept dwelling on the *folly* of the flight, knowing that you, Henry, who are too fastidious for public scandal, was behaving in a manner too deeply out of character to be considered evil. But Edmund, blind to motives that he was incapable of sharing himself, saw nothing but the act itself, which must be condemned, which separates once and forever the sheep from the goats, and he could not bear to find me as morally obtuse as I appeared to be when I talked merely of your 'folly'. And I found that I could not lend myself to his view."

"He was a fairly humorless man."

"Though I was very wretched, desperate in fact," said Mary. "I felt a certain relief too. It was good to relax once again into a less narrowly bound universe. I even thought for awhile of doing something: perhaps traveling to India and 'adventuring on a shore unknown.'"

"While I, in losing Fanny, gained Maria and spent the next year trying to disencumber myself without appearing more caddish than necessary."

They relapsed into a long silence. Henry stood at the window and Mary lay on the sofa with a volume in her hand which she did not read. So much of what she was expected to take an interest in was insipid and divorced from the vividness of reality.

After awhile, Henry said without turning, "It is clearing. In a moment the sun will be out." His sister joined him at the window.

"It must be time for our departure," he said. "I shall go see about the horses."

When he came back, he announced that the horses could not be brought before five o'clock. They debated whether to take rooms for the night, and decided instead to go on to London, neither finding the prospect of a night at that inn in any way appealing.

"Perhaps we might take a walk around the town, Mary," said Henry. "Some fresh air may throw off this miasma we have talked ourselves into."

They strolled around, conscious of and taking pleasure in their extreme compatibility. When they took places in the post chaise, they spent the journey, while the rain fell intermittently, sitting in their respective corners in the dark, sharing a warm and luxurious silence. As they reached the outskirts of London, Mary roused herself to tell Henry of some new acquaintances she had made shortly before leaving Bath.

197

"I shall introduce you to the house, Henry. It is a brother and sister. They each have eight thousand pounds a year, sterling, from a father who made a fortune in bootblack. Can you imagine a world in which it is possible to accumulate a great fortune in bootblack?"

"Are they ill-bred?"

"Not at all. They have the prettiest manners imaginable and unfettered minds. Their mother is French and though she now has the air of a countess, I believe she began life as a governess and might have remained one had she not met her Hephaestus of bootblacking. I think you will find them piquant, Henry. The sister is very pretty, raven-haired with a bisque complexion, and she is almost as good a musician as I am myself, and where her skill falters, her feeling remains pure. And the brother is a great traveler who has been all over the Levant and can tell you a great many stories — fit only for the ears of men, I'm afraid — about the practices of Turks. The sister is already kindled to meet you, Henry, certain that a brother of mine must be charming."

"Her brother has undoubtedly already discovered the converse to his cost," said Henry. "I shall be glad to be introduced. Your recommendation is always enough for me."

FIRST PRIZE STORY
Feel the strange heart beating where it lies... - W.B. Yeats

THE TURTLE

by Carol Ann Parikh

It turned out that Nina didn't get down for Manuel's birth, but the following August she wrote that she was coming "at last" and Elizabeth spun into a frenzy of preparation. She cleaned off the tiny back porch to make room — threw away the odd wood, frayed nets, cracked jars and broken toys, neatly lined the ledges with pots of flowers, and bought two new sheets and some yards of mosquito netting to protect the bed she'd borrowed from Antonio's aunt.

Propped against the cool adobe wall nursing Manuel in the darkness, she was haunted by flashes of the way Nina held a match to her cigarette or hunched her shoulders over late night coffee. She saw Nina lecture to a class the way she herself had done, and slip beneath the sheets with strange attractive men. She imagined Nina leaning against a threadbare arm of their old blue sofa reading Elizabeth's favorite poets — Herbert, or maybe it was Hopkins.

During that week Elizabeth quarreled almost every day with Antonio — about grocery money, about the coffee, about keeping Manuel while she went to market on yet another errand.

Afterwards she would feel guilty, and over dinner, while spotted moths slammed into the lantern, she would hold her feelings out for both of them to look at. She would confess that last night she'd fallen asleep remembering the pink dogwood in the courtyard of the Radcliffe Library or that this morning she'd been thinking of snow on the bare boughs outside the window of the apartment she had shared with Nina.

Although it was clear from the way he tapped his foot or thrummed his fingers that Antonio didn't find her recollections nearly as interesting as she did, he would keep his elbows expectantly on the table long after he had finished eating.

It was only when she wept that his face clouded over. Pushing his chair back, he would attack whatever, at that moment, seemed most dear to her. Sometimes his jealousy would turn her grief to rage; other times, overwhelmed by pity for all the sorrows of his life, she would find consolation in comforting him. Pressing his face into her breasts, she would see Nina's commitment to Thomas Hardy and the late Victorians as a plank thrown down across the chasm in which she whirled with Antonio toward the mysterious heart of life.

"Shall I come home early?" Antonio shouted from the bedroom.

"Of course. She'll be dying to meet you." Elizabeth spooned another mouthful of oatmeal into Manuel, holding the bowl away from his flailing fists. "Anyway, we'll have the whole afternoon to ourselves."

"Will you take her up to Tia's?" He sat down at the table, his face shining from soap, his short hair still flat and wet from combing. In the morning sunshine his eyes sparkled like river pebbles.

She smiled at his ignorance. "I think we'll have too much to talk about."

"But what makes you think she'll be just the same? You've changed."

"Yes. I've got fatter."

"More healthy." He stirred his coffee and watched her at the stove. "I hate to say it, but the coffee tastes burnt again."

She carried the frying pan to the table and bumped an omelet onto his plate. "Why not just make it yourself?"

He smiled down at his eggs. "And nurse the baby?"

"No. Just make the coffee."

"Earning our living is not enough?"

"I earned my own living for nearly ten years." She managed to slide another spoonful of oatmeal into Manuel's mouth. "There, darling," she whispered, smoothing the jagged edge of her voice.

"Anyway, I don't know how to use the new pot."

Her head was throbbing. "I'll teach you," she said, stabbing the little spoon back into the oatmeal.

"No, that's all right." He pushed his empty plate away.

"All right for whom?" She remembered Nina hunched over a crossword puzzle to avoid the ungraded papers in her bag. With burning eyes, she raced into the bathroom.

Over the rush of the tap she heard Antonio calling through the door. "Eliza?" She wiped at a damp spot on the tiled floor; she rolled the toilet paper back up neatly. "Tomorrow you'll show me how you do it."

"Mmm," she sniffled, straightening a towel, thinking that all her preparations for Nina's visit — the new sheets, the pots of flowers, even the chicken *mole* she'd labored over all day yesterday — were futile, worse than nothing, no different from ordinary lies.

When she heard Antonio's retreating footsteps, she opened the door and hurried across to Manuel.

"Come, darling," she said, unstrapping him from his chair. "We've got to get ready for Nina." His face was as red and puffy as hers; oatmeal ringed his mouth and a few lumps had dried on his forehead.

Antonio was in the bedroom buttoning on the pale green shirt she'd bought for him last week. She stood in the doorway watching him, the apology that rose in her throat checked by a sudden jealous sense of his separateness. Although she knew he didn't like her to change Manuel on their bed, she laid him down and unpinned his diaper.

"Why not use his table?"

201

"Why should I?" Although he had spoken in English, she used her own coarsest Spanish.

"Eliza?" As he reached his arms around her she felt the hardness of the outside already in him. "What are you so nervous about?" Crying softly into his shoulder, she was comforted by the ghostly presence of generations of women with long gleaming braids who set down food and lifted away empty plates and cried softly into their husbands' shoulders.

"Shall I drive you to the airport?"

"No, no, I'm fine," she said. She turned away to blow her nose and laughed for no reason. Manuel looked bewildered. "Poor baby. Such a silly mother." She lifted him onto his table and gave him his furry mouse before reaching over to kiss Antonio. "See you tonight, darling."

Two years ago Antonio had slipped into the empty chair beside her in the cafe on La Condessa. "You are a teacher?" he'd asked. She'd nodded without looking up from *To the Lighthouse*, which she'd propped against the sugar pot so she would have her hands free for the taco. It was a technique that had worked before.

"Ah, Virginia Woolf," he said, and something in the wistful tone of his voice or in the way he said "Ver-heen-ia" made her look at him, forced her to see the slant of his eyes and the elaborate cut of his lips. His cheekbones were high but narrower than those she'd grown used to after a week in Tikal. His skin was dark bronze, almost black. Although he wore his hair dipped over his forehead and long in back like the other beachboys, his body had thickened into manhood and his eyes no longer smiled with his mouth.

That night over dinner she was content with their silences and with the meager shaping of their conversation — her questions about his childhood in the green hills behind them and his answers, brief, harsh, and joyless, rougher than perhaps he'd intended, offered to her with the rolling r's and guttural vowels of the English he'd learned from other young men like himself

202

who sold themselves at night to randy tourists. As if they were children playing dominoes, she searched her own experience to match his answers. In the moonlight he held all the lively promise of a stranger, of someone else's handsome husband.

Oh, she felt rich and gifted in those first few weeks, a peach, a melon, a cornucopia tumbling down from the North into her lover's dry dark arms. She admired the curious imposition of the curl of his mouth on the coarse muslin sheets, and the straight line of his back when they danced at La Condessa. When they swam, he took her far beyond the high September waves to where the sea was calm and green and bottomless. The swimming out was like the beginning of an airplane journey, cigarettes snuffed, engines humming, only the sense of danger then. Afterwards, diving through the ten-foot waves, rocked in green troughs, sucked so far out that shapes on shore blurred into color, herself blurred into the immensity, she wouldn't know if she was breathing air or water, and she wouldn't care.

She cast off the veil of other people's words and felt as vulnerable as a child. With Antonio stroking her hand along an embroidered tablecloth in the steady glow of a glass-bound candle, the air heavy with garlic and chilies and newly cut papayas, their voices blending with the lapping of waves and the occasional high note from a far-off mariachi band, she relinquished her intimacy with Mrs. Ramsay. She wrote a brief letter of resignation to the English Department, a note to Sol, and a picture postcard to Nina with just three words: "*Lo encontraba. Adios.*"

When they married, Antonio built them an adobe house in the hills beyond the last hotel and cut his hair and found a job in his uncle's plant nursery. He would come home for lunch, avocado salad or scrambled eggs with sausage, and leaf through an old seed catalogue while she washed the plates. Through the heat of the afternoon they would lie together, and she might dream that she was the sloe-eyed Indian girl who sold mangoes in the market.

On Saturday mornings they went shopping or took the long
bus ride into the hills to Tia's house; in the evenings they walked
down to dance and drink rum punch at La Condessa. It wasn't
until December, when tourists came to crowd the beaches and
beachboys flocked down from the hills, that the bitter taste of
his jealousy displaced the sweetness of the punch. It was a potent
brew, a heady distillation of his ragged childhood and the nights
he'd sold himself to women older than her grandmother. Sometimes when they got home she raged in self-defense; other times,
sick with the degradation of his accusations, she would press
herself against him till she felt his body soften: drunk with pity,
she would immerse herself in that furious river where life rushed
beyond the reach of words.

She never suspected she was pregnant until late in the third
month when her waist began to thicken. Trying to rid herself of
disbelief, she wrote to Nina and to her father and his new wife.
She spent her weekends in the hills with Tia, eating special cereal
concoctions and drinking goat's milk. She wore a charm of cotton
flannel on her neck and an auspicious silver ring. It was only
when Nina wrote to say that she was coming down "at last"
that she felt like an impostor. Lying in old Tia's hammock, ad-
miring the deep green leaves of coconut palms and the deeper
blue of sky, she began to dread the meeting of what she'd been
and what she had become.

She cried when she saw Nina climbing down the steps from
the little plane. Nina had cut and curled her hair, she wore a
long flowered skirt instead of jeans, but the two years hadn't
changed the way she hunched her shoulders or took her glasses
off to have a better look. As they waited for the suitcase,
Elizabeth tried to keep Manuel from throwing down the teddy
bear that she'd brought "all the way from Cambridge," and Nina
kept on laughing at how stubborn he was, "just like his mother."
Rattling down the road in the old taxi — such a ride a rare
thing in itself these past two years — Elizabeth felt her spirit
lighten. She gave herself up to Nina's energy, to her fantastic

flow of words, to that way of naming everything that in just two years she had forgotten. The stretch of scrubby jungle looked more vivid than it had on the way out — the sky seemed bluer and more empty, the occasional shack of a small ranch more dilapidated; goats and donkeys poked along the dirt with an amusing aimlessness.

Nina talked mostly about the university, who'd got tenure and who hadn't, and about Sol's new wife, a historian Elizabeth had met once at a party. When Elizabeth asked her about Frank, she admitted that she was still seeing him "sort of." They fell so easily into their old way of talking — "You know how I get, I was so nervous that I said I just loved Crashaw and it was only afterwards..." — that it was hard to believe that so many months and so few letters had passed between them.

Carried away by the pleasure of Nina's company, Elizabeth found herself amusing her by making fun of the things she was most fond of. She imitated the wide smiles of the beachboys and the nasal voice of the blind peddler who recognized her footsteps; she listed the pretensions of the restaurant with the glassbound candles; she laughed at the gaudiness of her new dress from the market, although she loved its reds and blues and yellows hurled onto cloth as stiff as paper. Even kind old Tia lay absurdly before them in her tattered hammock, sucking fly-ridden mangoes from the basket on her swollen knees.

But after lunch, when she went to sit on Nina's borrowed bed hoping to talk about herself and Antonio, the outpourings of doubt and reassurance she'd envisioned in the taxi didn't come. The shifting sun and shadows across the bougainvillaea, her awareness of Manuel sleeping in the next room, the occasional distant crowing of a cock, made her feel drowsy but not relaxed. As she listened to Nina's meticulous analysis of Frank's ambivalence toward his female students, she shuddered to think that she had once viewed men through the same fine lens. The very subtlety of Nina's perceptions seemed like a distortion; she felt reluctant to talk about Antonio with someone as committed as she herself used to be to what now seemed rather arbitrary notions of personal freedom and the rights of women.

In the relative cool of early evening, Elizabeth put the chicken *mole* on to warm and stirred the rice and beans. "Smells wonderful," Nina said.

"Took me all day yesterday." Elizabeth passed her a thin green glass of rum with lime. "It's chocolate chicken."

"With garlic?"

She nodded, smiling down at Manuel, who rocked between her legs mashing a banana through his sandy toes.

"Did Antonio really build this place himself?" Nina lay in the kitchen hammock looking toward the center of the house, where striped rugs lay along the bright glaze of the floor tiles. Beyond the new straw chairs, a basket of mangoes glowed amber on the low stone wall.

"He had some help running the water pipes." Elizabeth took her favorite dishes from a cabinet carved with curling vines, and spread the table with a handloomed cloth.

"What pretty plates!"

"The potter lives just up the hill." She slid Manuel onto her lap and opened the top of her dress. "We can go see him tomorrow, if you want to."

"Start my Christmas shopping." Nina took her glasses off and peered around the edge of the hammock. "Doesn't he, you know, eat by himself?"

"Of course he does, don't you, honey?" She smiled into his bright round eyes. "But down here women go on nursing until they have another child. It's not unusual to see a four or five year old taking out its mother's breast."

"But you won't..."

Elizabeth smiled. "Who knows?" she said, patting Manuel's chubby thigh.

In the silence between them, she was relieved to hear Antonio rounding the path. He paused uncertainly in the narrow doorway while she fastened her dress and Nina struggled out of the hammock. "I've never been in one before," Nina said, hurrying forward to take his hand, "as you can see." Hoisting Manuel to his shoulder, he smiled across the kitchen at Elizabeth.

There were a few minutes of scattered conversation while Elizabeth served the food. Nina said how charming she thought their house was and how wonderful it felt to be inside and outside at the same time. She asked Antonio about his work at the plant nursery, and he spoke briefly about his uncle's plans to landscape a new hotel that was being built up near the river. When he fell silent, she began a long and, Elizabeth thought, charming, story about trying to find a home for her potted Christmas tree. Although she alluded to Sol only in passing, in the middle of her story Antonio disappeared into the bedroom.

When he came back with Manuel's wind-up bear, Elizabeth was amused to hear Nina ask him what he thought of the most recent Mayan excavations, since it was what she herself might have asked two years ago. From where she stood at the stove, warming more tortillas and sipping her rum, she watched the bobbing of their heads, one fair, one dark. Nina's lively curiosity seemed to epitomize what was best about the past, and Antonio, with his intense inwardness, suggested all the mystery that lay beyond the reach of words. She could see that Nina had no more interest in the chicken *mole* than Antonio had in the Maya, and she was touched that they were making an effort for her sake.

The moon had risen, tracing a milky path across the floor tiles and shadowing the trees beyond the low stone wall. They were talking now about deciphering the glyphs at Dos Pilas, and Nina was saying that epigraphers need just as much luck as farmers do. Antonio was nodding, occasionally leaning over to wind up the bear or jiggle Manuel on his knees, but as Nina grew more animated, his silences lengthened. In spite of his occasional remarks, he seemed bored by the conversation, and by the time Elizabeth served the coffee she couldn't help noticing certain things — the imperfection of his accent, the way he ordered her about the kitchen, the way he kept his elbows on the table and

207

waved his spoon. Why wasn't he asking Nina more about herself? After all, she was the guest.

When he leaned forward, his brow furrowed, to consider
Nina's question about the Spanish word for jade — she said the
Aztecs had used a word like "quetzalitztli" to refer to the most
beautiful stones because they were the same iridescent green as
the bird — Elizabeth got up to scrape the dishes and put water
on to boil for the washing up. Hunched over the sink she felt a
kind of despair. It didn't seem possible that Nina would see his
inability to enter into that kind of conversation as a mark of his
connection to a deeper sense of life; she probably found him
stupid. Peering back at the candlelit table, Elizabeth thought she
could see pity in the tilt of Nina's head: her smile seemed to say
that Elizabeth was not the first woman who'd been carried away
by a dark-skinned man and a tropical moon.

One morning Elizabeth took Nina to La Condessa. They spread
their towels in the shade of a straw umbrella and settled Manuel
down to fill his pail with sand.

"Maybe I'll ask the athletic department to buy a wave machine
for the pool," Nina said, taking out her sunblock. "I've got completely addicted to the sound."

"Me, too," Elizabeth said.

"I guess you don't need this." Nina held out the tube. "You're
so dark — you must spend every day here."

"Lately we've been coming down at night," she said, afraid
that Nina would laugh if she tried to describe the way she held
to Antonio in the pitch-dark tossing water, sure that she'd start
laughing, too, that soon they'd both be rolling in the sand, their
stomachs aching, her meltings in the moonlight as dull as incan-
descence in the sunlight.

"Was it hard to get used to all this ... beauty?" Nina rested on
her elbows staring out to sea.

"Not really." Elizabeth trickled a fistful of sand into Manuel's
tiny pail. "I just woke up and here it was."

"You said something like that in your postcard. The Spanish one that said you'd found 'it'." Nina turned her head away. "The one that made me cry."

"Oh Nina, why?"

"Well, why wouldn't it? It was my idea that you needed a holiday. I just thought you'd got depressed by success. Your book got such good reviews. They were talking about giving you tenure in the spring." She rummaged in her bag for a tissue and blew her nose.

"I never told you," Elizabeth said, "but they wrote back to offer me leave." Heavy with the weight of those days, she stumbled over to rescue Manuel from the water's edge. "I burned the letter," she said, dropping back into the sand with him fussing on her lap. "It was incredibly patronizing; it even mentioned the ticking of my 'biological clock'."

Nina laughed. "I thought of that, too. I mean things had got so bad with Sol it seemed like a good idea to trade in James for Lawrence. But only temporarily. I never dreamed you'd decide to get married. And..."

"To a beachboy? Well, neither did I!" She helped Manuel turn his pail over. "But it wasn't actually a decision. It wasn't like we went on about it like Sol and I used to. It just happened."

"Happened how?"

"Out there." She gestured toward the horizon. "I just stopped making choices."

"Out there with the sharks?"

Elizabeth nodded, reaching to tilt the umbrella across Manuel's shoulders. "They were indispensable. I'd feel something brush my leg and get this burst of terror, like an electric shock. It was only when we got out past the waves, when it was too late to save myself, that I'd feel this sweet delight. I'd turn on my back and open my eyes and it was like I was part of the sea and the sky and the sharks, too, and if I was going to be eaten up, well, so what?"

"And from that you concluded that you should marry him?"

Elizabeth adjusted the waistband of Manuel's little bathing trunks and felt his crotch. Standing him up against Nina's shoulder, she pulled his suit down with little jerks. "Do you realize that I'd never been out of school? I was thirty-four years old, I'd just spent nine years with Henry James, the skin around my eyes was crinkling like paper." She sat him down bare-bottomed with his shovel. "It was like I'd forgotten there was a world those words referred to."

"But we all go through periods when everything seems remote and arbitrary."

"Nina, I used to dream in words. Words instead of images." She rolled the suit into a newspaper and tucked it into her big straw bag. "What really scared me," she said, "was seeing that I'd chosen that."

"Of course you chose it. You loved Henry James. You loved teaching, too. You used to bore me to death talking about your students." She turned over on her stomach. "But I guess I'm with Marlowe. I mean, I think words are there for a reason. I don't want to know about the heart of darkness."

Elizabeth laughed. "Well, I'm not crawling through the bushes yet."

"Of course I always was a coward compared to you. I could never have spent nine years on one book." Nina tilted her face up toward the water. "I stick along with Frank even though I always feel like I'm making him up."

"I know." Elizabeth noticed the fine lines patterning her forehead, the thickening beneath her eyes. "Nina? I'm sorry that I, you know..."

"That you what?" She put her glasses back on. "Left me alone in the endless forest? Of course, you might have written. It was as if you'd gone out for a drive and died in a car crash."

"I guess I couldn't — or maybe didn't want to — put into words what was happening." She passed a biscuit over to Manuel, who dropped it in his pail.

"I guess that's what hurt me."

"But it wasn't you I was abandoning, it was the arbitrariness. I felt like I'd been trapped in a supermarket. Temperature controlled, Muzak from the speakers, fluorescent lights bouncing off the canned goods." She flung out her arms. "Hey look!" she called, then lowered her voice when Manuel's tiny face puckered in alarm. "Here's a nice thesis on Henry James. And down this aisle's a nice new job. We'll just toss this nice new lover in the basket with a week's supply of colored condoms. Oh, great, over here you can trade in your old baby for credit toward a nice new one."

Nina was laughing. "Here you've just got those crummy little stalls."

"Here we've got triple digit inflation. We don't need Voltaire to teach us to tend our own gardens."

She scooped up Manuel and stepped across the wet sand to the water. Pressing her lips into his hair, she smelled the soft sea-smell and heard the burbling at her knees. Everywhere she looked was blue and green.

One afternoon Antonio took them for lunch to a tiny village down the coast — a collection of straw huts, really; chickens and pigs and naked babies huddled around sandy front yards. On the side of the narrow road nearest the water were a wooden shack, some unpainted tables under a thatched roof, and a row of hammocks. Trumpets blared from a radio turned up too loud. As they settled themselves at a table, the burnt smell of tortillas wafted toward them on the salty air. No one else seemed to have considered such an early lunch.

Antonio took a paper napkin from the little plastic holder and wiped his hands and mouth. He pointed up the coast: "If you watch closely you'll see dolphins diving from that place." The jungle behind them had melted into a dull green where the water was shaded by clouds, a translucent green where the sun shone. "When we come this far to fish, they swim out and follow us."

He spoke to the small girl who came to take their orders. "She says they brought a turtle in last night. There's turtle soup, bar-

becued turtle, turtle steak. What shall we have?" Vultures tame
as chickens pecked around the sand beneath the empty tables.
The women agreed that he should order for them.

A shrill voice sang of Carta Blanca over the rushing waves.
Nina gave Manuel her glasses to hold and Elizabeth tried to take
them away from him. "Really, he'll just break them." Nina
shrugged. So like her, Elizabeth thought, the rest of her trip
spoiled, she'd laugh about it when she got home. "Do you have
another pair?"

"Can't afford it." Nina smiled.

"Oh Nina, I'm going to miss you."

"Me, too. I keep a journal of things that I can only say to you."
Manuel was fussing on Elizabeth's lap. "Here," Nina reached
to take him up. "Let me walk him around a little. After all, I'm
almost his aunt."

"Look Manuel. There's a bird. See? Bird." They passed along
behind the compound and then Nina came running back.

"Oh my god, there's a turtle in that yard as big as a boat! He's
just flailing around on his back! Why don't they turn him over?"

"Because he'd crawl back to the water. That fence wouldn't
hold him."

"But they should let him go!" Antonio just looked at her. "You
mean, this is *that* turtle?"

"Yes, of course."

"But it can't be. It's not dead."

"They can't kill it because they have no refrigeration. Like this,
it will last for several days."

"You mean they eat it alive? Just hack off a leg and eat it?"

Antonio shrugged. "They've always done it like this."

The girl brought out two bowls of turtle soup and went back
inside for one more. Then she brought a cloth-covered plate of
tortillas and one dish of salad. She was very serious and very
careful, as if she felt her mother watching.

"I can't eat this," Nina said. She set Manuel down on
Elizabeth's lap and grabbed her glasses from the table. "That
poor creature writhing about over there!"

"We'll order something else for you." Antonio raised his hand for the girl, who stood a few yards away on the unshaded sand. Her oiled braids glistened in the sun.
"No. I won't have anything, thank you."
"Something to drink? Coca-Cola?"
"I'm sorry to be making such a fuss," she said, already standing, her hands resting lightly on the chair back.
"It's okay," Elizabeth said. "I still can't look at images of Huitzilopochtli. The Aztecs used to sacrifice prisoners to him by the tens of thousands."
"Tens of thousands? What did they do with the bodies?"
Elizabeth shrugged and kept her eyes on the banana she was peeling for Manuel. "Maybe I'll just wait in the car," Nina said, turning toward the road.
Antonio smiled, his lips stiff, his head tensed squarely on his neck. "The turtle will be here no matter where she goes."
Elizabeth bent dumbly over her soup, a terrible nausea rising from the pit of her stomach. The soup was as green as the sea; small bits of white floated at the top: his thighs, his belly, a piece of tail? She thought how easy it would be to slip in beside Nina and drive away. Better yet, she and Manuel could hitchhike down the coast, or inland to Oaxaca and the deeper jungle. Her spoon circled the bowl like the fin of a shark.
"Shall I order something else for you? What about chorizo?"
"Tonio?" she said, watching him tilt his glass up to the dark mouth of the beer bottle. "Why did you bring us here?"
"Your friend wanted to see how 'the people' live."
"And what did you want?"
The way he shrugged, the very brightness of his eyes beneath his lifted brows, filled her with rage. She leaned toward him, breathless with fury. "To spoil things? Just like you always do! My god, remember that night at La Condessa...?"
"But Eliza," he broke in, his voice as steady as if he were speaking to a lunatic, "your friend loves to talk about the days when kings pierced their penises and queens ran barbed wire through the center of their tongues. Why should she mind what we eat?"

"*We?*" She stood up, hoisting Manuel, who was crying as hard as she was, to her hip. With her free hand, she flung her soup into the sand.

"You knew about the turtle," he persisted.

"No, no, I didn't!"

"You like the soup."

"I loathe the soup!"

"You ate the soup."

Although she did her best not to look at him, something in the tone of his voice, something hapless and forlorn in his insistence, curled her spine back into the chair. "Shh," she said to Manuel, tucking a piece of tortilla into his sticky fist and struggling to bring the planes of Antonio's face back to their familiar lines. It was clear that it wasn't merriment that had clenched his teeth and drawn his lips back into the semblance of a smile.

He leaned toward her. "Tonight when I'm asleep, my belly full of turtle soup, you can come back to him, and pry him over, and coax him back into the water. If what you really care about is him, you can take this knife right now and cut his throat. There's a place just before the shell begins..." In the low rough roll of his voice she heard feelings so old and so terrible that their names had been forgotten.

Handing him Manuel, she got up and walked round the little shack to a makeshift pen of driftwood and broken glass. With her arms folded across her chest, she forced herself to watch the thick stumps of its flippers brush the air, the trembling of its spotted neck where flies had gathered. Its huge ribbed under-shell was obscenely exposed, like the stela of a Mayan king uncovered by a plow. Herself the epigrapher, she watched its heavy eyelids moving up and down, up and down.

The discovery that the universe is expanding was one of the great intellectual revolutions of the Twentieth Century. - Stephen Hawking

HIROHITO, THE FAT AUNT, AND

THE UNIFIED FIELD THEORY

by Kal Rosenberg

Outside the tall, narrow leaded windows of Shepherd Hall, silent snow starts a swirly dance in the hazy glow of city street lamps. Soon it will line the stark tree limbs, sift into the brown stubby grass of the park, layer the cars parked end to end on Convent Avenue. They predict ten inches; it could take me three hours to get back to Yonkers.

My lecture is on epistemology and quantum physics. A soldier in the army of Descartes, Newton, and Einstein, I hold forth on the essential nature of things. My students and I quantify the universe; continually search for that undiscovered Unified Field Theory: the one brief, elegant equation expressing all that is or can be. I discuss Spinoza, Brownian Motion, and the Gödel theorem. I cannot concern myself with snow.

But when I glance offhandedly at my lecture notes and notice the date in the corner, everything changes: December 7. A flood surges around me; at once it is 1941 — another life, one epoch removed. A deluge from a vanished, equation-less ether.

Now I am six.

On my own, I learn how to eat a Mallowmar properly: I shear off the bottom cracker with my flat front teeth and coax the white stuff out from the bottom up, until there is only a soft squooshed chocolate shell. I have contests with fruit cocktail: the grapes against the pineapples — I count them up and the grapes always win.

Mom helps me pack up old baby toys; I go to school now and am not supposed to like kid stuff anymore. I make her promise not to give my yellow tricycle to my sister. School changed me a lot: starched white shirts, ink stained lips, too-tight ties, new friends. No homework on weekends.

Mother and I live at Aunt Ricka and Uncle Abe's. My little sister lives there too. Early one Sunday morning Mom takes my sister someplace. I am napping in Aunt Ricka's enormous bed. I dream of tricycle days — my youth.

In sleep, I hear soft music from the big wooden cabinet radio in the living room, and into my dream comes the ray-like glow from the tubes in back. I am half-aware of the scrubbed clean fragrance of drippy laundry on the pull down dryer suspended from the bathroom ceiling. In my nap I hear plink-plink drops on the spread-out newspaper under the dryer. I know some of the water will run onto the tiny white octagonal floor tiles.

I am happy, in my dream, when I hear the Italian fiddle player. We call him Caruso. He only comes around on weekend mornings, but not regularly. You know he is coming, you just can't say when — only it would be in plenty of time to disturb a lot of sleepy working people in the four six-story buildings surrounding the alley. I love to hear him.

Caruso, in baggy, soiled pants and jaunty peaked wool cap, sports a three-day stubble. He strides brazenly through the maze of apartment building back alleys, right into ours. He cradles his instrument as if it is his child, then hunches over and plays — loud and sad — accompanying himself in strident Italian.

Every time Caruso starts his concert, irritated tenants fling their windows open. Some toss coins — quickly, so he'll leave sooner. Some of them are not tossed near him, but at him, aimed at his head. He probably wears that taxi driver's hat so the pennies won't hurt. Some neighbors greet him with Yiddish epithets,

216

such as 'I hope you get cholera, you toad,' and, 'may you live a long life, but one day shorter than your worst enemy's.' Caruso blithely ignores abuse, fiddles away, intent on his music while estimating the sum of coins on the ground about him. When he feels satisfied with the haul, he stops, sometimes in mid-note, and, scoop, scoop — he's gone!

Then — talk, static, the front door slams shut, the sputter of speech, a shriek. The dream ends.

Aunt Ricka shakes me like a malted. She screams in panic, "Wake up! Quick! Crawl under the bed. Right now!"

I'm scared so I scoot under. Now she is on her hands and knees, peering at me.

"Japan bombed Pearl Harbor. There's a war now." My mouth pops open and my eyes bulge.

Suddenly she lowers her voice to nearly a whisper and I think maybe it's because someone in Japan might overhear. One hand clutches and unclutches the lacy collar of her housecoat. I hear the screech of the C trolley along the wide cobblestone road by the corner I'm not allowed to cross, and two faraway *oogahs*. I ask her to please speak a little louder.

"Hirohito bombed Pearl Harbor," she says. "There's a war. Do not come out from under the bed. Do you understand?" I nod yes. "If you do," she cautions with her metronome finger, "I will write to Aunt Rose and tell her." This is a serious war! A letter to Aunt Rose only contains really good reports or really bad ones. No in-betweens. My cousin Herb told me that Aunt Rose keeps the books for God. On Yom Kippur she opens them up for Him to check, and all the stuff kids did is in there. He says you sink or swim on-acounna what Aunt Rose writes down on your page.

Then I think how that story is like the sick lady downstairs. Once we lived someplace and Mom kept saying we have to stop all that noise because there was a sick lady downstairs. Then we moved to some other place and there was still a sick lady. I didn't know if it was the same one or not. Herb says as long as we keep making noise, the sick lady will live downstairs. He knows a lot about stuff like that, he tells me.

So then Aunt Ricka grabs me with two hands and gives me a hug.

"I'm going downstairs to talk to John-The-Super. Then maybe I'll join up. Be a nurse. Or something. You must stay under the bed and not come out."

"Don't worry, Aunt Ricka. I'm a-scared of Aunt Rose," I say.

"That's good, dear," and off she goes.

I feel pretty bad for the soldiers if Aunt Ricka is the nurse. All she does is shmear Vicks on you and say "Boy, are you lucky," then recites even worse things which could have happened to you but didn't. But that's just for when you're sick. If you have a cut, and maybe it's even bleeding, then she swabs red acid on it while she tells you about your wonderful luck.

Alone, I whisper, "Pearl Harbor, Pearl Harbor." But I still don't know who she is. I already heard about Japan and Hirohito — everybody has. But who the heck is Pearl Harbor? Meanwhile, I am counting dust balls, and it smells like I'm breathing them, too. There's the red truck I lost, next to that old slipper with the pom-pom. I grab it. Even though it only has three wheels now, it might come in handy if Pearl needs to use under the bed for a magic escape tunnel.

Pearl Harbor, Pearl Harbor. Then I remember the Fat Aunt. I don't know the Uncle. The grownups mostly talked about her, not him. She had umpteen kids, like Mother Goose.

Once I heard Aunt Bea say, "Howdaya like that! The whole tribe ups and moves to Sommerville, New Jersey. To buy a laundry!"

Uncle Moe helped: "Just like that," snapping his fingers, "poof!"

Then Aunt Molly and Uncle Carl said they went out there to see.

"They're a pack of brats," she said. "Freckled. They run barefoot, full tilt down a gravel path to the lake. Like wild things."

218

"Hooved!" chimed in Uncle Carl. "Very eccentric."

"Carl," said Aunt Molly, "Not eccentric. It's crazy! My God, New Jersey is bad enough, but whoever heard of Sommerville? It has to be further than the moon."

"Poof," put in Uncle Moe again. He liked to say 'poof.' "Might as well be Poopik, Missouri."

Uncle Abe just listened. He never said much. Just listened and shook his head. I didn't know if the shake was for the Fat Aunt or if it was for the other aunts and uncles, whom he often calls 'Ladies and Yentalmen.' Every time Uncle Moe said 'poof,' Uncle Abe looked up at the ceiling and bit down on his cigar. Uncle Abe and Uncle Moe had a lot of arguments when they played gin-rummy.

Some of the aunts and uncles were usually mad at the Fat Aunt. I don't know why. Once I asked Mom how many kids the Fat Aunt had, and she said twelve, and started to name them. Some had funny names. There was a Zelda, a Manfred, a Reginald and a Lulu in there. And I thought there was a Merle. Or an Earl. Or a Burl. But now I think it could be a Pearl! Omygosh, the Fat Aunt's daughter, Pearl, must have got bombed by Japan!

Why would the Empire of Japan send Hirohito over to Sommerville, New Jersey, to drop a bomb on my freckled, hooved cousin, Miss Pearl Harbor? Maybe he was mad at the Fat Aunt too.

What exactly is a war anyway? Will it be over soon so I can come out for lunch? I look around. There are no bathrooms in wars. I picture piles of poop and puddles of pee, and decide, when the time comes, to do them under Aunt Ricka's side — not Uncle Abe's. I wonder if Japanese children are under their beds too, having this very same problem.

But what nerve! Hirohito just marches right over here — how do you do? — and plops one on cousin Pearl! I know Uncle Abe is coming home pretty soon. He'll really be sore about this bomb business — he'll take it personally. Sure, he's not crazy about the Fat Aunt and all, but Aunt Ricka says he thinks "Family is family is family." Once he gets mad, there'll be trouble.

Side Show 1995

Uncle Abe is scary. He has big red hands and soft blue eyes that seem like someone else's, and they stick out. He doesn't talk. He wears a tie when he eats supper. Aunt Ricka puts a whole raw onion on his plate; he bites it like a peach. I can't sit close. After supper he goes into the dark living room and sinks into his private chair. But first he turns on the big Philco radio — children are not allowed to touch the dials. He listens to *The Lone Ranger*. Herb sneaks out of the house so I have to help my cousin Sylvia wash and put away the dishes. No one speaks until eight.

Wonder what's for lunch? I'm not worried about the war any more — nothing much seems to be happening. The main reason I'm not worried is because, between John-The-Super and Uncle Abe (who it just so happens is a very close friend of the Lone Ranger), Hirohito doesn't stand much of a chance: Japan, you are doomed.

I find more lost stuff under the bed. Pencil, matchbook, scrap paper, *Collier's Magazine*, a Marvel comic. I start to build a fort, when in walks this pair of saddle shoes with legs in them. The legs look exactly like my cousin Sylvia's, right down to that scratch on the right shin. She doesn't know I'm doing war under the bed. In a voice that sounds just like Sylvia's, she calls out for me — like I don't know she's a spy! What a dope. This is tricycle stuff! I stay still until she leaves to report to her commander.

My eyes are closed and I play pretend. There is the Japanese Emperor on a large ferry. There are no other passengers. It's pulling up to a wharf someplace, maybe California. The water between the pilings is foamy and goes whoosh; the salt spray smells like Lanoff's Fish market. I hear the bump-bump before they fasten the metal ramp with chains. Hirohito carries a bomb under his arm. It says "Pearl" on it. His other hand is a clenched fist as he walks east. He looks real mad and wears a sword on his wide sash belt. The road is deserted. The sun starts to set. It begins to rain, but drops never fall on the Emperor's glasses.

220

Hirohito walks for many days without food or water, until he comes to a small town called Poopik, Missouri. There's a dingy old gas station. The pumps used to be red, but the paint is all chipped, and they're rusty. A guy in greasy dungarees fixes the engine of a dust-covered old truck. The Emperor asks him where Pearl Harbor is, but the guy shrugs. This makes Hirohito mad, and his fist clenches and unclenches.

"Pearl Harbor," shouts the Emperor, "Pearl Harbor! She belongs to the Fat Aunt!" At the sound of that name, a mangy bloodhound asleep by the screen door jumps awake and looks across the Mississippi, I guess in the direction of New Jersey. The dog raises his muzzle, trying to sniff the cold wind. A blotchy-faced man with a straw hat puts down his bottle of Spur and whispers, "... the Fat Aunt." Suddenly the station, the street, the whole town, fills with people — more people than live in St. Louis and Kansas City put together, all waving, shouting, pointing. "The Fat Aunt ... Sommerville, New Jersey ... that way ... over there ... the big laundry ... wild things."

This is only my first war, but I think I figured it out pretty good. The family strategy is to get Uncle Abe and John-The-Super over to Sommerville. Uncle Abe will eat an onion in front of the Emperor while John-The-Super yells: "Get off the stoop, you lousy kid!" Blinded and afraid, Hirohito will run to California and catch the next ferry to Japan. And that will be that. I am to stay here in case Pearl evacuates and needs my truck, or if that girl spy comes back. So long as I can hold the pee in, it will go according to plan. Soon Aunt Ricka will return; Mom will come home with my stupid sister. We'll eat lunch and everything will be fine.

* * *

I continue to probe for the Unified Field equation. This inattentive slip, this reverie of mine, has only taken a moment. Neither Hirohito nor Aunt Ricka must cloud my thoughts. I lock the shadows of memory back into their distant chamber: a wispy, ephemeral plane, so as not to touch or pollute my Unified Field. From the worried faces of my students as they glance out the window, I deduce the snow has deepened. I continue. We approach the outer limit. It is where symbolic logic and mathematics break down and become unreliable. It happens, in the "macro" sense, in deep space; in the "micro" sense, with the indeterminate behavior within the atom. Some sharp students understand the implications of this, at least insofar as our quest for a Unified Field Theory is concerned. For their benefit I offer them what I have come to call the 'Spinoza Band-Aid.' "Our universe is like a crossword puzzle in which both the questions and the answers are all around us. Except that we are missing the crossword grid itself: the diagram which tells us what goes where. We have only our brains to use, along with the often irritating compulsion to use them; we have to make the best of it with out the grid." Some are satisfied with this evasion. Others not.

As apology I add, "That's why we keep doing science and philosophy. As of right now, we quantify. But there exist attributes — *qualities*, which scientific method is unable to define. We haven't found the bridge, if there is one, so most of us just choose one side of the river or the other."

"Sir, then don't we miss a lot?" someone asks.

"I don't know."

The bell rings and soon I am alone. I do not notice the distant chamber door ajar, the one prompted open by wistful thoughts, nor the clouds of quality which have already drifted in and mingled with stark quantity. I catch myself staring at a magnificent, fitful blizzard, and cannot determine exactly when my stare began. I suspect there are some quanta which may be quite wretched or simply wonderful. I won't tell the class.

Am I enchanted by a storm? A Cosmic insignificance? I feel strangely unfulfilled with the charmless realm of Atoms and Plastic. The storm draws me in, I can feel the pull of the wind, the frenzy of crystal flakes, as if they strike my cheek through the frosted panes.

The strains of *Vesti la Giubba* fill the room in the baritone of my back alley Caruso. I see the family from long ago here in this room with me. They have cut deep paths for me. I wonder if they have always been there, haunting my treatises and corridors. Did I lack the grid to know what went where?

I ponder the "date which will live in infamy." Those years ended with nothing the same as it was. Like a spiked iron wheel it spun everything viciously counter-clockwise, in one certainly wretched continuum. Did my soul flow through a watershed and divide: this to the left and that to the right?

At this moment my ideas cloud but my feelings clarify. I think a wicked, audacious thought — that the Unified Field might be gobbledy-gook, but I hastily bury it.

As I head for the car an icy whip slices me. It hits me so cruelly that it makes my eyes hurt. That happened to me once on my yellow tricycle. I remember.

THIRD PRIZE STORY
Her lips suck forth my soul; see, where it flies! - Marlowe

YOU ARE HERE

by Susan Segal

She looks nothing like the women you are used to, the kind you like to have seen on your arm. It's not that she's ugly, it's simply that she has the sort of looks that have never interested you, that often have, in fact, repelled you. The darkness that encases her seems to go beyond her wood-tone skin, her eyes are so black there is almost no differentiation between pupil and iris, the sleek sheet of hair falling to her shoulders encircles her like an emanation. You have always preferred women who look like they come from California — women with their hair slightly uncombed, as if they'd just stepped in from surfing or from sex, women with deep, vivid color to their eyes and skin that feels as if they've been soaking in cream all day, who have airless laughs that at once arouse and leave you mildly indifferent. But women like this one, who look as if they harbor poetry, you steer clear of. Women like this do not look like fun; they look like work, like anguish.

So you are surprised when you feel compelled to elbow your way through a group of bare-armed women to tell her what an interesting scarf she's wearing. Her dress is loose and parsley green; the scarf is tied intricately. She's small, the top of her head coming perfectly to the middle of your neck, but you can't really tell what her body looks like. The woman you came with, whose every taut muscle is intimately known to you, is still here; you

224

can occasionally discern her suggestive laugh over the hills and valleys of party chatter. The woman with the complicated scarf tells you her name is Amber and you say of course it is, and you tell her yours and something important happens, a curtain parts or comes down, but something, something vital has already changed.

When she tells you she is a stewardess ("We prefer, 'flight attendant'") you begin to relax. You're on familiar ground here. You tell her you're a writer. She says she has a Masters degree in English. And although she lifts the corners of her mouth and shakes her head no, you insist she must write poetry, thinking of thick sticky love sonnets flowing from a fountain pen that requires bottled ink. Come on, you tell her, I know there's a dog-eared notebook hidden in the bottom drawer of your nightstand. There's a Whitman quotation in calligraphy on your bathroom wall.

"No," she says, sharply. "There's nothing on my bathroom walls."

Something about the penetration of her gaze causes you to amend your self-description. What you actually get paid for is account work at an advertising agency and you feel an unexpected twinge of guilt at what is ordinarily one of your standard minor deceptions. Under her probing eyes you laugh nervously and admit that at home you have piles of notes for a novel bursting out of drawers and closets, carpeting your floor. Her hand touches your arm lightly and briefly and her eyes won't let yours go. You are about to say something extravagantly flattering, but sinking into her gaze, you feel a tightening in your chest that melts almost immediately, pleasantly, the feeling of a child whose mother has just bandaged a painful wound. You are understood.

You ask to see her again.

She says that would be lovely, then she sees a friend across the room and excuses herself.

You spend the rest of the night trying to make your way back to her. When you do, you are absurdly happy, as if you'd been crossing deserts on her behalf. Her face lights up at the sight of you and she turns away from a man with a pipe who's been standing too close and she writes her number on a piece of paper torn from a spiral notebook in her purse.

She says goodbye and holds out her hand.

You accept it, feeling its delicate bones, its terribly thin skin.

"Darling," says the woman who came here with you, breathing damply into your ear. "Where have you been? The party's over."

When you talk Amber seems to listen not just to your voice but to your soul. You can see her pupils expand and contract with every word you speak. No remark — down to pass the butter — is boring to her. Nothing is meaningless.

Your friend Frank, the Senior Account Executive, is skeptical. "It's true," he says, "This gal sounds a bit different from your usual, a bit more exotic perhaps, but I know you, friend, in a few weeks you'll be bored again."

You don't contradict him. You half hope he's right. You're not entirely comfortable with the sensations Amber arouses in you, the feeling, when you're with her, of being overfed.

She asks something about your childhood and you tell her about how after your mother moved out you used to write her letters in which you claimed to have been thrown out of the sixth grade, or arrested for arson. Amber's eyes fill up, right there over the lemon chicken. She doesn't let you stop. She wants to know more. You can tell by the way she leans her torso across the table, as if she's afraid of missing a syllable of your thoughts, that she wants to know everything.

You start to laugh. It's just a silly story from my childhood, it's meant to amuse, you are about to say, but the brilliance of her eyes, the utter stillness of her gaze seems to reach into some place you have not known about and you feel, suddenly, not a bit like laughing.

This is what she does to you. If you describe something painful you feel the pain enter and overtake her, if you ask her opinion she gives you the answer you wanted without your even knowing that's what you wanted. She is not a sounding board, she is a vessel. You end up telling her everything. Night after night. You keep thinking you'll run out of things to say, you always do with women. But not this time. You say things you've never said to anyone. You stop seeing the Other Woman and begin to avoid conversations with Frank. No one can hear what Amber can hear. Eventually you wonder if it is worthwhile talking to anyone else at all.

So when she starts disappearing for days at a time, it is worse than betrayal, it is like a series of little deaths. You feel yourself put on hold and begin to store up your experiences and thoughts and feelings for her return. People look at you oddly in the office, and occasionally ask if you are feeling quite well, you look so blank and sunken. You mutter something about the latest diet fad and they go away, nodding in sympathy. You go about your life, but there is always the sense of anticipation, as if you were in the intermission of a riveting play and the clock is moving at half-time, carrying you too imperceptibly toward the beginning of the second act.

The longer you know her, the longer the absences. You call her machine and get her annoyingly perky message. The regret, the dismay rings in her voice when she apologizes for not being there to receive your call. And at the same time there is the manic gaiety, the sense, as she speaks, that in her head she is hearing some wild, frenzied music. And you leave your message and hang up and wait. After a few days you call again. And leave another, sadder message, this time tinged with worry — has she gotten your first message? Is everything all right?

You try to work up some anger at her. You try to distract yourself. You follow the receptionist with the amazing eye shadow to the xerox room but once there you can't think of a thing to say. In the middle of the second week of silence, the longest

ever, you make one more call, this time all concern and apology
— you don't mean to exert any pressure, but you're really worried now, is she ill, is there something you can do? And every
night when you come home from work and the red light on
your own machine is lit, your head goes light; you leave your
keys in the door and your coat and hat and muffler on and rush
to rerun the tape. Your brother in California. Frank changing the
time of next week's tennis game, the *Times* with a special one
month offer. And for the rest of that night you watch television
or read or go out to dinner, or work, anything but think, anything but focus on the hole she has carved out in your chest.

At first she has the excuse that she's been flying. Three days
in St. Louis, two in Dallas, then off to Miami she tells you breath-
lessly when finally, two weeks since you last heard her voice,
she calls you.
"I'm so sorry," she says, and there is genuine pain in her voice.
"I long to see you. Can we have dinner soon, tomorrow, please
say you'll see me, I understand if you won't because I'm awful
but I've missed you so."
You have barely been breathing since she left. You say, what
about tonight? But she laughs and tells you how she just came
in and how exhausted she is and you wouldn't think you could
get jet lag on her runs but she does and oh, she doesn't want
you to see her like this, please, let's make it tomorrow, and so
of course you say, whatever you say.
And then there's the dinner and wine and baskets of bread and
she eats as if during her disappearance she fasted — cleans a
huge plate of eggplant Parmigiana and half the carafe of wine
and listens and asks and listens some more, with such intensity
that it crosses your mind that she is trying to distract you from
something.
After dinner she leaves the table and is gone for a long time
and your heart begins to pound and you imagine for the
hundredth time the nightmare of her gone forever. You drain
your wine glass and tell yourself that you are being silly; she's

real, she has substance, look, there is her purse slung over her chair, she isn't going anywhere without you.

It suddenly occurs to you that you have never seen her apartment. It's always a mess, she says, or being painted or just been sprayed. You've never pushed the issue because you so like her in your own home. You like to see her move around your bathroom with easy familiarity, go without asking to the kitchen for a glass of soda water. You imagine that her own refrigerator is bare, or full of inadequately wrapped airline leftovers that are inexorably mutating in various, deepening shades of green.

Your hand snakes around the side of the dinner table and into her purse, burrowing until it closes on the spiral notebook which it lifts and places in your lap. You glance in the direction of the bathroom. Hurriedly you leaf through the notebook, searching for the important parts, sure that everything is important. The book is three quarters filled with her large thick handwriting. Her touch is heavy; where she has dotted her i's the paper is often punched through, and everywhere the pages are bumpy and crinkled from the pressure of her hand. It appears to be a diary, there are dates throughout, but the sentences you read here and there don't make sense: "I sing the tiles to sleep" appears on January 15, "The six Mark Twain books have been disposed of by flame," on February 7, and in June, what seems to be a lengthy meditation on the toxicity of airplane fumes. You flip closer to the end of the year, to December when you first met, and what you see makes you shiver. It appears that from December up to yesterday, the latest entry, the notebook has become a sort of to-do list. Each page has a new date, and on each page is a numbered list that grows longer week by week. The first few weeks there are five or six items, then eight, ten, and yesterday's entry has 22. You bring the book closer to your face, as if studying the letters might reveal the meaning of the words. The entry for the morning after the party that you met reads:

1. Wash
2. One chapter, Dickens

3. Dishes
4. Clean up mess from this morning. DO THIS! !
5. If you know who calls answer the phone.
The entry from yesterday reads in part:
14. Three miles three times
15. Re-roll coins
16. Wash
17. Clean up mess. NO EXCUSES!!
18. Check the locks
19. Wash
20. Throw away the l's. EVERY SINGLE ONE!!
21. Call you know who
22. Market — MILK ONLY

You slam the book shut, dig your fingers into its cardboard cover and wonder how to ask her what seems to be the only important question, although there must be others even if you can't think of any: just who, exactly, is "you know who"?

But then there she is, gliding back to the table with one hand against her mouth, her hair tousled, wrapped in a huge pink sweater and long skirt and still looking fragile, and you have the feeling that if you say anything at all right now, she will shatter into a thousand pink, brittle pieces. At the table you reach for her hand which is ice cold and her fingernails look newly chewed and the black of her eyes make the whites look so perfect it's as if she'd gone over them with white-out. As you watch, tears gather and drip beautifully out of the corners, down the sides of her cheeks. I'm just so happy to see you, she says.

And as you sit beside her in the taxi home and watch the colored lights from the store signs on the streets ripple like speeded up film across her face, you think of how you might write her, capture her essence. You think of touching her skin, or her weight pressing into you, and let your questions fall away like clothing that is getting in the way. Soon now, you think, soon she's all mine.

In your bed she sips wine as you turn down the lights. She asks you to turn them all the way off and you do, though you want so badly to feast on the sight of her.

"Wait," you say, as she begins to draw you down onto the bed. "I want to ask you a question."

"Fire away." She runs her hands up your arms, pressing herself against you so that you feel her nipples graze your chest.

You close your eyes. "Well," you say, as you both descend. "What I want to know is."

"Yes?" She moves expertly.

Her hip bones scrape against yours, the hollows between each of her ribs smell like oregano. You feel her effort to relax beneath you. You say her name and touch her face and press with your right hand the stiff fingers of her left until they are spread out flat. As soon as you remove your hand they spring back into a claw. She holds you tightly and kisses your mouth and says your name and the lines you want to write about her form and dissolve and reform rhythmically in your head, matching the rocking of your body as you press yourself blindly into her.

In the middle of the night you wake up and the place where she was lying is still damp. You start to call out, then you see the light under the bathroom door and say nothing. When you open your eyes again it is barely morning — the traffic on First Avenue is not yet in full swing — and find the two-word note on her pillow torn out of the spiral notebook. "Thank you." In the kitchen the wine glasses are washed and put away. A pot of coffee sits on the warmer and an English muffin rises expectantly from the toaster.

Your head fills with last night's unasked questions. You call her when you get to work and get the machine. At the sound of her voice your throat closes. Thanks for the breakfast, you manage.

Her job ends abruptly and you think things will be different. Over cappuccino on a sidewalk on Columbus Avenue she shimmers in the cold spring sunlight and talks.

231

"I don't know what happened exactly," she carefully spoons the whipped cream from the top of her coffee onto her saucer. "It was a regular run, no special problems, everything the way it usually is." Flicking away the last of the whipped cream, she wipes her clean spoon with her napkin, then stirs her coffee. She peers up at you from under her lashes. Her pupils are pinpricks. "I was pushing the drink cart down the aisle. Business class, that's usually the best. The passengers are working and preoccupied, they don't usually give you much grief."

"All those travelling businessmen?" you say, daring her to lie. "You mean to tell me they don't—"

"Sweetie, these days there are as many women as men. You have nothing to worry about." She pats your hand and pouts at you until you laugh.

"So what happened."

"Well, it sounds silly, really. I was walking down the aisle and this man in 12B stopped me. A perfectly ordinary man with lovely hands, I remember. Very smooth and dark, like chocolate. Anyway, he asked me for a Diet Coke." She lifts her coffee cup and puts it down again without drinking. "I opened a can, I got a cup, and I was digging for the ice when it happened."

"It?"

"I couldn't do it. I just couldn't. I realized I could not pour one more Diet Coke, not now, not ever. If the plane was going down and I had to pour a Diet Coke to save us, I wouldn't be able to do it. Not that I wouldn't be willing to you understand." She leans very close so that you can smell the cinnamon on her breath. "I simply am incapable of it. My body will not perform that function any more."

She sits back in her chair and taps her fingers on the saucer. For one moment it seems that all the muscles in her face have sagged. Then she smiles enchantingly. "And how was your week?" she asks.

* * *

She is on sick leave now. She says the airline views her abandoned drink cart and locking herself in the lavatory for the remainder of the flight as a form of nervous exhaustion. You advise her to look upon it as an opportunity, a chance to get out of a job that is beneath her, that she hates, and use her prodigious talents to do something satisfying. You could write too, you tell her, painting verbal pictures of both of you at matching desks, word processors whirring, suckling inspiration from each other. You could do anything you want, you say, and she nods enthusiastically, her eyes shining, oh, you're so right, this is such an opportunity for me. And what you're secretly thinking is, now she will stay home, now she will answer her phone and I will have her. You never have to worry, you tell her, about money or anything. I'll always be here for you. You stop just short of saying I'll always take care of you, because although of course you would, saying so right now might frighten her. She needs time to get used to the idea of being entirely yours.

She presses her face into your neck until all you can breathe is her and she tells you that you are too good, too good for her. And you feel your heart swell with gratitude to the Coca Cola company. You want to write them a letter thanking them for existing, for making your own life begin at last.

When you call the next morning her machine answers. She's at the store, most likely, buying typing paper. You leave a message. You call again at five, at eight, at midnight. You hang up when there's no answer at eight the next morning. You hang up before the machine even picks up when you call from work. You find yourself crying onto a client's can of cut green beans, loosening the label as you grope to wipe it dry.

On the third day of silence you walk to Tudor City, where she lives. It is a mock high-rise village, the buildings dotted with turrets and crenelated balconies and it's not difficult to think of her as a princess captive in a tower in these surroundings. You

233

lean over the long gleaming desk and announce yourself to the doorman, your mouth so dry you can barely form the words.

"She's gone away," he says, his heavy-lidded eyes flickering at you.

"What? Where?"

"Flying," he says, beginning to turn away.

You reach over the desk and grab his shoulder harder than you meant to, but once you have him you hold him fast.

"She can't be flying," you say. "Where is she?"

He tries to shrug his shoulders but the weight of your hand stops him. "We don't give out information about our tenants," he says, low.

"Tell me," you say. "It's an emergency, you idiot." Your fingers plunge through his flesh.

"Look Mister," his voice is so soft now the hairs on your arms stand up. "I got my finger on a button right here where you can't see. You got four, maybe five minutes before the cops come."

The strength leaves your hand. Your arm drops to your side. You look at your reflection in the speckled mirror behind the desk and it looks mottled, leprous.

"Did she leave a forwarding address?" you say, feeling as if your bones won't support you much longer.

"What forwarding address? She left me next month's rent. She said she'd be back in three or four weeks. Hey Mister, you okay? Maybe you better sit down over here for a minute. You don't look so hot."

"Oh no," you say, barely able to speak through your laughter. "I'm fine, really. I'm happier than you could possibly know."

Instead of sleeping you lie with the air conditioning off, sweating even between your toes. It's achingly clear now that you haven't shown her sufficiently how you cherish her. When she returns you will make a concerted effort to be less selfish, to listen avidly to her. Although she doesn't like questions you will demonstrate as passionate an interest in her as she always does

234

in you. You lie damp and wide-eyed, gorging yourself on sweaty images of her skin, her hair, the apartment you've never seen but which you envision as empty and cave-like. And savor your sudden inability to breathe, as one willingly suffers the pain that accompanies the act of tearing away a scab and reexamining an old, gratifying wound.

Four weeks and six days later Amber calls and says she went home to Cleveland to visit her parents. Can I come over now, you say, but she puts you off till tomorrow. The hollow in your chest echoes; you ache to fill yourself up with her.

At dinner the next night she looks thinner though she eats and talks with her usual gusto. There are faint shadows under eyes like newsprint smudges, and fine lines you never noticed before above her top lip. You adore each of them. She makes lots of Cleveland jokes. She swivels her head around the half-empty restaurant, as if she were trying to make herself dizzy.

"Are you looking for someone?" you say.

"What?" She circles her eyes back to you while keeping her head twisted over her left shoulder.

"Who are you expecting?" You say, between clenched teeth.

"What?" She swings her head forward and peers at your right ear. "No one, Sweetie. I'm just interested. Did I tell you about the book I read in Cleveland? It's supposed to help you pick a career. It has you take all kinds of tests and draw charts and trees with branches and things, covering every interest you ever had." She smiles the most innocent of her smiles. "I'd completely forgotten I used to do needlepoint. My mother's house is filled with cushions I made when I was 10 or 11. One of my rugs is on the floor of the guest bathroom."

She picks up half of her torn open french roll and holds it in the palm of her left hand. With the fingers of her right she scoops out its contents and places them on top of the fragile fish bones on her plate. Her nails, still short almost to bluntness, are dotted with patches of chipped red polish. The tips of her fingers become dusty. You examine her face as the crumbs pile up and

235

see for the first time the effort it takes to hold her smile, as if her cheeks were being held back by taut, painful strings.

You lean forward and put your hand lightly on hers. "Tell me what you're thinking," you say.

Her mouth drops a little, as if she were surprised, or even frightened. But she recovers quickly and speaks almost wistfully. "I'm thinking how much I don't deserve you. I cause you too much pain. I should probably leave you for your own good." She lowers her head and you are at a loss to figure out how you arrived so suddenly at the very edge of disaster.

"For God's sake, don't say that. Don't you know how happy you make me?" You fight to keep the panic from your voice.

She looks up shyly. "I have hurt you though, haven't I?"

"Never. No. I love you. I love you." Immediately you want to hit yourself, sure that now you've lost her forever. Instead she settles more firmly in her chair and tosses back her hair. She looks suddenly like a sinewy animal who has just enjoyed a satisfying meal.

"You're not going to go on like that though, are you?" she says, smiling slowly. "You're not going to get crazy on me? We can't have you getting crazy."

Now it's not in her absences but in her presence that you seem to be losing her. She pulls out her notebook many times in an evening, sometimes not even writing in it, just holding it in her lap, carving grooves in her palms with its spiral edge. She still embraces your every thought but her eyes travel often to other faces, to bathrooms, to exit doors.

The last night she lies in your bed with her back curled into your chest, facing the bedroom window. The light from the construction project across the street pours in and throws slanted shadows onto her cheek. You run your palm down the staircase of her spine, wondering if everyone's bones feel so sharp when you get this close to them.

"Never leave me," you say, before you can stop yourself.

236

She slides gracefully out from under your hand to her underwear on the floor.

"Where are you —"

"I'm sorry, I have to go now. My phone machine breaks down so often, it makes me want to cry," she says.

"Wait," you say, "I want some answers."

She stops with both hands behind her back fastening her bra. Her elbows form sharp isosceles triangles. "What were the questions?" she says. Her breathing is audible.

"I know none of your secrets," you say, "you know all of mine." Her arms fall to her sides. "I have none," she says gaily, but you sit up into the light and make sure she sees your grim expression. You reach out and grab her hand, crushing it, longing to feel it collapse completely in yours. She says that you're hurting her. You don't let go.

"What about that notebook of yours," you say. "And where you go. And who you are with when you're not with me." You are trying to sound gentle and yet intractable.

For a moment she stands cold and hard as marble, then with a sudden movement, she wrenches her hand free. "I have to go now. Honestly, I do." There's something new in her voice. She scrambles into the rest of her clothes.

"Wait," you say. "Jesus, wait. I'm sorry. Okay? I'm sorry, sorry, just stay, just stay here for now, okay? I won't ask. I swear, I won't ask any more questions."

She leans over the bed and kisses you hard on the cheek. "It's all right," she whispers. "I promise you, it will be all right."

At the sound of the door closing you are finally able to rouse yourself. Throwing a coat over your nakedness you go after her but she's not in the hall; you miss her in the elevator. In the lobby, your doorman, studiously ignoring your appearance, says he's not sure which way she went. Outside the night air is thick and wet; your bare feet stick to the pavement. Even at this hour there are people moving languidly up and down the street. Amber is nowhere in sight.

237

* * *

You haven't heard from her in three and a half weeks. Frank took you off the whiskey account because you have been unprepared for the last two meetings with the client. You're not oblivious, it's not as if you're going around in a fog; you spend your time productively but nothing registers fully — sales figures and marketing campaigns are like impenetrable passages of prose. You feel as if all the thoughts and stories and longings you've been saving for her are backing up inside you, clogging your brain. You're basically a reasonable person, not given to rash action, but you find yourself staring at flow charts and consumer surveys and thinking about weapons — guns and knives, about roofs and the long plunge down, about murder. You think that now you know the meaning of the expression, *I can't live without you,* because it's true that the life you have known, the life you imagine you have been living is dissolving as rapidly as bones in acid.

You go back to Tudor City. It needs a drawbridge and a moat, you think, something for you to storm. You show the doorman, who looks like he's trying to remember you, the manila envelope you have ready and explain its private nature and how she told you to slip it under her door if she wasn't home. And when he draws in his lips and folds his arms across his chest, you produce three 20 dollar bills you also have ready and he turns his back and you take the elevator to the eleventh floor. 11M. It is a door like all the others, canned bean green, a small peephole curved like a suspicious eye. You ring three times. Press your ear against the door. You think you can hear water running, then silence. You ring again. Nothing. You stay like that, with your cheek against the door and presently a chill runs down your face and into your fingertips. You are sure that someone is leaning on the other side, ear pressed against yours, cheek to cheek with only the slab of green wood between you. You hold your breath and though you hear nothing, you can feel someone breathing — rapid and staccato, as if she's been running.

"I hear you," you say. "I hear you."

In the manila envelope is a four-page letter that you were going to leave, but as you stand there and match your breathing to hers you realize that its sentiments are all wrong. You should have spoken of her needs, not yours, but what you realize as you listen to her silence is that you don't know her needs, not one of them.

"I know what's going on in there," you say with bravado, pressing your lips against the door, tasting mold. What you are thinking is that if only you did know what was going on in there, you would be able to make yourself leave.

You slide down the door until you are sitting with your knees pressed in your chest, close your eyes, and breathe with her for what seems like hours. Eventually it begins to sink in that she is mortally alone in there, with her imagined bare walls and famished rooms. No one is in there with her, no one was ever in there with her; you believe this at last because of the way she breathes on the other side of the door, the silent words her lungs are shouting to you. Her betrayal, you realize now, was never that she was moving away from you toward someone else, it was that she refused to move at all, that something — some pain or secret pleasure you will never understand — seduced her into disappearing altogether — slowly and relentlessly becoming thin air — practically right before your eyes.

"Are you there?" you say. "Is it over?" you say.

She breathes her voiceless response. You stand up, slowly, creakily, like an old man, and make your reluctant progress to the elevator.

On the way down it hits you that you feel absolutely nothing. Carved out like her french rolls, empty of either pain or joy. You try your usual trick of imagining her moving about her apartment, her dark skin blending into darker walls and find it produces nothing, no pleasant ache in your limbs, no inclination to moan, just dumb hollowness. The heat slams against you as you leave the building; your eyes water. I'm fine, you inform yourself, I'm back on earth. I've finally accepted reality. Walking up First Avenue with your eyes on the cracks in the paving

Side Show 1995

stones, you savor the screaming car horns, the jolts of wet, un-
seen bodies that make your teeth rattle. Watch it Jerk, people
snarl, and you feel like one of those hysterically smiling Mylar
balloons; as long as nothing pierces the skin, you tell yourself,
you can float intact forever.

And months later, when you have accepted a transfer to the
Los Angeles office in recognition of the sudden spurt in your
business efforts, when you have settled into an apartment on the
Westside and bought a car and have begun to be able to focus
on women with dark eyes again without feeling your stomach
drop, there will be a night when you are studying a marketing
report and thinking of how successfully you are not thinking of
her, and of the opening in the art department for a copywriter,
and how your writing talent might finally blossom in that setting. And a sudden feeling will come over you, like oil oozing
over your scalp. It will be a heaviness that is tinged with horror
— a dreamlike alarm that will momentarily immobilize you.
Something horrible has happened, is what you will think. She
is ill or injured, she is lying on her bathroom floor and her heart
is stopped and no one knows. You will force yourself out of
your chair and to the phone. You will the dial the number as
you did quite often your first months in California (just to hear
the machine, to know she had not moved), the number you have
almost managed to forget. The phone will ring twice and then
a strange buzzing noise will follow and then silence. No voice,
not even music. You will move in slow motion to your desk and
pull out a sheet of paper and write these words: "I don't want
anything. I just want to know you're all right. I feel like something awful has happened."

You will mail it the next morning and after having done so
something magical will happen. You will forget the note, forget
the phone number, and when you try to think of her face you
will see instead the round pink cheeks of your own secretary.
And you will feel light again but in a new way. Unburdened of
something so familiar you'd forgotten it was a burden. You will

240

stop telling colleagues how much you miss Fall in the east. California will look beautiful. You will give up your novelistic pretensions when your supervisor tells you you are in line for a promotion in your own department. You will take out one of your female clients for dinner three times in a week and a half. You will have your car detailed.

And one night, when you stop at home to change before another dinner with the woman whom you have started to tenuously refer to as your girlfriend, the red light on your answering machine will be lit, and before you listen, you will know. You will reach out to erase the message without hearing it, but will press the wrong button and Amber's voice will come out, cheerful, regretful, passionate. "Sweetheart," it will say, "I just got your note. I'm so sorry it's taken me so long to reply but the thing is I've moved. I'm back in Cleveland. I'm terribly, terribly happy. I long to talk to you and tell you all my news. I miss you so much. Am I running out of time? Did I say I'm in Cleveland? Here's the number."

There will be a long silence and then the time on the message will have run out; a protracted buzz will sound. You will let the tape run on, waiting for her to have called back with her number. You will listen to the low rustle of the blank tape until the ringing phone startles you.

"Darling," your girlfriend will say. "It's eight thirty. Where are you?"

If one would like to see our European morality for once as it looks from a distance... - Nietzsche

BIG PURPLE WRAP

by Colleen Crangle

I

Come, look here, Mbulelo. See this gate. I can open it, no problem. They think this little gate will keep us out. You stay there, behind that big plant. There. Just me and the baby will knock at the door. Baby on the back, they always like that. Is he still asleep? Look. Is he still asleep? What did you say? You are tired, cold? So what do you think? You think I've got money for the train? We must have money. Do you want to walk home? I will knock and ask. Maybe they've got a place for us to stay.

Sh! Here they come.

Hear that? "Wait" she says. I say we've got no money. Need to catch the train. Need a place to sleep. She says "Wait" and she locks the door. You all right? What do you complain about now? I too have sore feet. What is this in my shoe? A stone, another stone.

Quiet. Here she comes. Go back. Back. Behind the bush.

242

Did you hear that? "Wait" again. I show her the baby. She closes the door. This time I saw right into the house. Very nice. What? You heard a laugh? Yes, inside they can laugh. Quick. The door, it's opening. Hide.

Come. We're going. Hurry. Think we've got all night? Out the gate. Oh, you will close it for them? Very good. So no one can come in their nice garden. Well, if you're so good with locks and things, go see there on the garage door. You can open that one you think? Wait, there's your Uncle Ayanda. What did you say, Ayanda? What did we get? Only eighty-seven cents. I will try the next house. Mbulelo, you wait here with your Uncle Ayanda and you stop whining.

II

The address is 54 Zambezi Lane, Pretoria. A gate, midway along a high brick wall, opens to a stone-paved path that curves to the front door. There a Strelitzia bearing long, spiky, upright leaves grows against the house. The air is cold. The sky is clear, the moon high and misshapen.

Numsisi opens the gate, points Mbulelo to the Strelitzia, and shuffles up the path. The baby asleep on Numsisi's back is secured by a large purple cloth that is wrapped around her body. Up and down the street sit dark, silent houses. Two cats break into a fight. There is a howl then a whimper. A dog barks from deep inside a far-off house. Another yaps, nearby. Numsisi knocks. Her breath is short and sharp.

A light snaps on. The door opens a crack and a woman peeps out above a safety chain. Numsisi talks. The woman says "Wait," closes the door and locks it. Numsisi bends down to slippers of black matted fur, overtrodden at the heels. She removes a stone from between her toes. Mbulelo fidgets, rustling the elongated leaves of the Strelitzia. Beyond the gate, outside the wall, Ayanda stands under a street light, the bright tip of a cigarette between

243

his fingers. The road curves and its semi-circle of light nestles inside another arc of light, then another and another. Beyond lies darkness.

At 54 Zambezi Lane, the front door opens, this time wide. The woman of the house peers out at the baby. Numsisi shifts her weight to her right leg and stretches her neck to see into the house. Laughter trickles from an inner room, leaks out the front door, and dissipates along the dimly lighted path. The woman says "Wait," and as she closes the door, it pushes out a pillow of warm air. Numsisi turns to Mbulelo. They talk softly. Somewhere beyond the street, a car starts up and, revving, roars away. An airplane overhead cuts through the night, dropping a low drone on the streets below. Mbulelo rubs his hands and the movement releases soft swishes into the air.

The door opens again and the woman steps out, clutching a cardigan across her chest. Numsisi cups her hands, just in time to catch coins that the woman drops. Numsisi counts, looks up to speak, then half turns suddenly on her slippered feet, jerking the baby and bringing it face to face with the woman. The baby wakes up, wide-eyed, and cries. The woman says, "Sorry. Maybe next time," and closes the door. The light goes out.

III

My wife, Sandra, is a soft touch. If I weren't around to look after her, she'd be taken in by every Tom, Dick, and Harry, especially if they're black. She has this guilt problem, acts like she's responsible for the plight of every non-white in South Africa.

Last night is a good example. Around ten-thirty there's a knock on the door. I'm working in my study so I tell her to see who it is. She comes back two minutes later and tells me there's a woman at the door, with a baby on her back, who wants train fare home or a place to sleep for the night. She says, "What do you think? It's cold tonight. Could be frost. And you know what, I think there's another child with her, hiding in the dark."

"Where will we put a native girl?" I ask. "And her brood? We don't have a servant's room."

Sandra asks, "What about the garage?"

"Oh no," I say, "my new tools are in there, not to mention the cars. As soon as we're asleep, she'll call in a couple of boyfriends and they'll clean us out. Tell her maybe next time."

So I think, that should be the end of that, lucky I nipped this little escapade in the bud. But Sandra comes back and stands at my desk. She's shivering so I say at least put on something warm if you're determined to do charity work in the middle of the night. She's a skinny one, no resistance to the cold. Anyway, Sandra stands there and reports, "The woman says she will sleep anywhere. She's afraid for the baby." Sandra is hooked, I can tell. "Doesn't the garage lock from the outside?" she asks. "We could lock them in then."

That was a silly idea and I told her so. So she thinks for a tick and then asks me how much small change I have. I empty my pocket, but Sandra complains, "That's not enough for the train."

"Sandra dear," I explain, "the last train left at ten. Your friend's not catching any train. She's probably got a boyfriend skulking in the bushes outside who's escorting her around the neighborhood. On a cold night like this they could net fifteen rand, all from the same story, even with the last train gone. Tell her maybe next time." Sandra likes to say that — maybe next time. She thinks it's nicer than no. As though she's holding out hope or something.

Anyway, I think that should settle the matter, but she comes back again with this worried expression on her face and says, "The baby looks sick. It's starting to cry."

I make a suggestion.

"There's the guest cottage. How about accommodating your visitors there?"

I am enjoying this now, leading my liberal-leaning wife into a corner. It's that English-speaking background of hers. Can't get her ideas straight. The way I always look at it, you got to take

245

the consequences of your politics. If you can't, change your politics — simple as that. No guilt, no problem.

Sandra begins to look really worried now.

"But the cottage is newly carpeted and she's rather dirty. She was cleaning her toes when I opened the door just now. What if the baby, you know, throws up or something?"

Like I said, that should have settled the matter. But she just stands there looking forlorn.

I have a further suggestion.

"Your sewing room has a bed in it. You can put them in there."

"You're not serious," she says, looking at me with wide eyes. "Inside the house. You said yourself she could be up to anything."

I shouldn't have laughed at that point. She's still angry with me. Before going to bed, she blurted out that next time somebody came around to the door she wouldn't ask for my advice. She was going to find an organization to refer such people to for shelter.

I told her good luck with that.

IV

Sandra phones her sister the next day. "What? You got no frost last night? Our lawn was sheet white when I woke up. Sheet white." Sandra fingers the telephone wire that coils and trails along the kitchen counter, down the wall, and into the baseboard where it disappears. She fiddles with a tangle that has formed a knot. "Dieter? I'm not talking to him right now. Had a fight last night. Do you know what happened?" She picks up the telephone, tucks it under her arm, and wanders down the passageway, the wire dragging behind her, unravelling slowly.

"There's this knock at the door, really late, loud and insistent. Urgent, I thought. Dieter's in his study — working again, you know how he is — and I go see who it is. Yes, of course I used the safety chain. Anyway, there's this woman, I swear she has nothing more than one thin jersey on, and she's huddled there with a baby on her back. She's well padded, mind you, buxom type, but not exactly cheerful. One thing I notice is this: her hands, they're enormous with long slender fingers. Anyway, at the same time, I hear the rustle of little feet in the bushes nearby and I think, oh no, another child somewhere out in this cold." Sandra stops and, turning in the passageway, flicks the wire to release a twisted loop.

"No, I didn't see anyone else. Just this woman and her baby and the sound of another child. Sis, my heart sank to my shoes. You know, suffer the little children, when you saw Me naked and hungry, and all that. So I rush back to Dieter to share this with him. Yes, of course I closed the door. Well, I ask Dieter, what should we do. Practical as always, he points out the possible complications of having a black woman and her family on our premises for the night. I mean, I don't even know what the law is these days about such things. As Dieter always says, there has to be slow ev-o-lution in this country, not rev-o-lution." Sandra straightens a picture on the passage wall, a pastoral print of huge overhanging trees beside a dirt path, with oxen standing in a group, heads turned all one way. "You remember his big lecture that day at lunch when we had that visitor from America. Here's this chappie, been in our country only two weeks and he says, 'Folks it's 1980, when're you going to wake up and smell the coffee?'

"Anyway, I still feel terrible so I give the woman some money. With a heavy heart, I tell you. But what would you have done? You just can't tell. Know what I'm saying?

"But here's the strange thing, sis." Sandra has reached the sewing room. She looks it up and down and all around. Curtains of tiny purple pansies hang from the ceiling to the floor. Morning sun seeps through, casting shadow blotches on the rug. The rounded wooden top of a Singer sewing machine is on the floor. The machine itself, black with gold lettering along the shaft, rests in its stand, a converted wrought-iron treadle. Dress-pattern pieces and snippets of cut cloth cover a yellowwood table pushed against the wall.

"Strange, sis. Yes, I said strange. Something strange is going on." Sandra turns and walks back down the passageway. The wire curls round and creeps behind her.

"This morning after Dieter's gone to work, I go out to the cottage. Want to air it, get rid of that new carpet smell. What do you know but one of the windows is open already. The one in the kitchen. Yes, it's really small but a child could get through. No, nothing was missing, nothing messed up, but there's this feeling I get like someone's been there. I look closely and I can just make out footprints. Faint footprints all over the carpet. All different sizes, not just little ones. No. Clean footprints. Just sort of like, indentations. I inspect the bedroom, look everywhere. Then I check the bathroom. Not a spot. Isn't it funny? You'd think if they got in, they'd have done something, used the place."

Sandra enters the kitchen, the wire still snaking down the passageway behind her.

"But that's not the end of it. I go back in the house and get on with the cleaning. I open the kitchen door to throw something in the dirt bin outside and something tells me, go look in the garage. Dieter's car's gone by now of course, but mine's still there. And in the back seat, I find it. That woman had a big purple wrap around her to hold the baby on her back and it's lying there. Just lying there with some old dirty slippers underneath. First thing I think is, how'd she carry the baby after they left. Funny thing to think, huh? Then I get to worrying. I check the glove box. Nothing gone. I check under the front seat where I keep that ostrich-skin purse with change in it. It's still there. Then it hits me. I jump out that car. They know how to get in. They got in the cottage, they got in the garage. What else do they know? Are they coming back?"

Sandra's through the kitchen door, outside now, and she pauses, whispering into the mouthpiece, "Tell you one thing, though. I'm not telling Dieter. He'd probably overreact. Or worse, tell me I imagined it." She crooks the telephone between her ear and shoulder and opens the door into the garage. The telephone wire pulls her up short.

"The funny thing, as I said before, is that they almost left no traces. As if they walk but do not tread. Know what I mean?" Sandra stands quite still inside the doorway.

"What do you think, sis? Think they'll come back? What do I do?" She looks around her. A curl of garden hose dangles from a hook, next to it hangs a new green spade, then a hoe, then a rake. Pushed against the back wall to the left of where Sandra stands is a metal cabinet. On top sits a stack of transparent plastic drawers filled with — from the bottom up — nuts, bolts, screws, and nails. A silver grey sedan with white upholstery is parked directly in front of Sandra, a purple cloth spread on its back seat. Sandra turns and steps outside, the telephone wire now coiled, once, around her legs.

V

My mother says, we're going to stay here tonight, they can like it or not. So we search and we find a little house in the back with a window that's open just a little. I climb in, mama pushing me from behind, and I go and open the door for them. I'm ten already but I'm small. We all walk around with our shoes off. Nice soft carpet. But my mother says this is too fine, we'll make a mess and then there'll be trouble. Uncle Ayanda's mad because he likes the big bed he sees in the bedroom, but he's been following my mama around ever since my daddy left and he knows she's the one who gets him money so he does exactly what she says. They go out, I lock the door behind them, and I climb out the window again. Back out the front gate we go. Then, all of a sudden, I see on the garage the padlock is not closed all the way. It just looks like it's closed but somebody forgot to snap it. Very quietly, we open the door a little and we crawl under. We settle in the cars, me in the little red one with no roof all by myself — a treat because I saw the trick with the lock. Uncle Ayanda, mama and the baby lie in the grey car. We sleep so well, it's a very warm garage, that in the morning I almost jump out my skin when I hear a noise and a knocking in the house. Someone

Side Show 1995

in the kitchen it sounds like, and we're out of that place so quick my mama grabs the baby and we're down the street already before she sees she's got no cloth and no shoes, and all the way to the house where our cousin works mama has to walk barefoot carrying the baby in her arms. She says those shoes they're old, no matter, and the cloth it's gone now. But I don't know. It was a very nice cloth. One night, soon, I will go back and see if I can find it. I know the trick with the lock now. I will learn other things.

OPPRESSORS AND OPPRESSED

by Charles Fenno

He jumped her from behind, grabbing her tightly around her throat with one hand and shoving something hard in her back with the other. "One false move and I'll kill you," he hissed, pushing her off the sidewalk toward some bushes.

She thought, irrelevantly, "No, he's wrong, it's 'one false move and you're dead,'" but her body grabbed itself loose from his grip and she fled to the center of the road, then spun around and faced him. She noticed a car pull over and park on the hill to Stow Lake, two faces looking out, watching. He began to move toward her. She put her fists up and danced a jig of frightened rage in the middle of the road. He began moving sideways, across the street muttering, "I ain't doin' nothin'. I ain't doin' nothin' to you." She watched him cross and get into a battered VW bug. He drove off and she dropped her fists and turned to run. A big car was creeping hesitantly, slowly toward her. She ran waving and shouting, "Hey! Hey, stop!!" A terrified young man stopped for her. He sat, clutching the wheel and staring straight ahead. When she saw he was alone she backed away, getting ready to fight again. There was a sick, old dog on the front seat beside him. "I— I was just taking my dog for a ride. I saw— I...."

She nodded severely and said, "Will you give me a lift?" He nodded, clutching the wheel more tightly and shrinking down. "I'll get in back. Thank you. But listen— go slow— I'm still panicky." He nodded again, slouched down behind the wheel, miserable. "If you go straight we'll come to the Concourse— there are always police there."

When they got to the road leading to the Concourse there was a squad car. She began shouting and he honked and stopped. "Thanks," she said, getting out of the car.

"I'm sorry, I couldn't do anything. I saw..." he looked around, helpless, then he waved at the dog. "My dog— she's very sick— I couldn't do anything."

"Yeah," she said, shrugging. "At least you didn't just pull over and watch, like those others."

She climbed into the back of the squad car and realized she'd gotten into a small, close cage— there weren't even handles on the back doors— but she felt safe there, almost comfortable. She began talking in a rush of words. The officer driving reached for his radio and began speaking but she couldn't hear what he said. They cruised slowly through the park. The other one asked, "Can you give us a description of him?"

"Well, he was about six feet, two hundred pounds. He was wearing a three-quarters length khaki army coat— you know the kind? with great big pockets?— and dark pants."

"Colored? Any distinguishing marks?"

"He was just ordinary looking, clean shaven, round features— not a sharp angle on his face. Boy, that's a startling experience, you know? I've never been a victim before."

"Well, you are now I guess." The driver spoke in his radio again.

"No, but listen, I want you to understand. I mean I was just walking along, you know?, sort of depressed— well, really depressed, actually, I was in a real oppression of the spirits, burdened with misery, you know?, and everything around me, the park and all, just seemed dreary and little and insignificant when Wham!! somebody grabs me and Wham!! I'm out in the middle of the street and everything was just sort of illuminated— I mean, the park was suddenly huge and absolutely motionless and crystal clear and I was about as big as a microbe and avid to be alive— you know what I mean?, like it was all important and beautiful and I wanted to be part of it. All I could think, out there in the street with my fists up was, 'Why this is no burden. This is ME!'" The two cops glanced at each other. One of them shrugged, but she didn't care, she had to talk.

"Uh huh. Did he hurt you?"

"No. Well, he grabbed me by the throat." She could still feel where his fingers had dug into her neck, nearly strangling her.

"By the throat?" The officer turned. She showed him her neck. His face changed, startled, and he gave a low whistle. "You all right?"

"Yeah— it hurts a little, but that's all."

"Well, we'll have to get a picture of that. Evidence." He gave his partner, who tried to see her throat in the rearview mirror, a sharp, serious glance.

She laughed. "Is it that bad?"

"You got some bruises there. What happened then?"

"I don't remember too clearly— it's just one minute he had me and the next thing I was in the middle of the street with my fists up and thinking, "But this is no burden. This is ME!"

"All right. And then?"

"Well he walked across the street with his hands out, palms up and then got into the VW and drove away."

"A VW?" The driver reached for his radio again.

"Yeah, a battered grey bug."

She'd run out of steam and started staring out the window as they drove slowly through the park. "Are we going anywhere?" she asked.

"Just waiting to see if we get our man."

"What, you've already got all that out?"

There was a soft blur of talk from the radio. The driver picked up the microphone, spoke quietly, put it back. "All right— we've got him." The car picked up speed and headed toward Kezar stadium.

"So quick?!" she said, and thought, "But what if it's the wrong person? What if they've arrested the wrong person? What do I do?"

They pulled up in a parking lot. There were three other squad cars, six cops and two men in street clothes standing around. It was him— she recognized him with relief. He was in the back of one of the cars, locked in a little cage like the one she'd been riding around in. She could tell he was handcuffed. As soon as he saw her he began shaking his head, shouting, "Hey, not me. Not me."

She got out of the squad car. One of the plainclothes men came over to her. "Now don't be frightened."

"Frightened?" She looked at him incredulously. "Of him? With all of you around? I don't think so."

He gave her a sour look and walked away.

They went to the station in the park, a great big room with no furniture full of cops and duffle bags and chatter. She stood by the door next to a sullen, silent detective. He was brought in, through another door across the room from her. He stood, hands behind his back, feet apart, head up, looking insolently at her. The detective moved to open the door. "We better wait outside or they'll claim you intimidated him."

"Intimidate *him*? Me? How? More likely he's trying to intimidate me."

The detective shrugged and said bitterly, "That's how it's done. That's how they play the game."

"Some game!"

For a long time— weeks— nothing happened, then one day she was told there was going to be a line up. There would be five women altogether— five women who'd been attacked in the park. There were two new detectives driving her. One of them turned on her, snarling, "You remember what he looks like? Describe him."

"Well no," she said cautiously, "I'm not going to describe him— I've been careful not to do that ever since it happened." "Oh? You haven't been remembering what he looks like?" His hatred was palpable. "You afraid?" he sneered.

"No," she was hesitant, she wanted to make him understand. "But if I'd been describing him all this time, I'd believe the description, and maybe I wouldn't be able to recognize him. Sometimes when you describe things it just blinds you. This way, I'll know him as soon as I see him."

"Well you better."

After the line up the five women huddled together. "Well, was yours in there? I didn't see anybody," a tall officious woman asked.

Two of the others shook their heads, "No, wasn't any of them," but she said "Yeah, number 3." The one with blazing red hair who hadn't said anything came over to her, staring at her steadily. "You said it was him? I didn't. I was afraid— he looked right at me. I was afraid. I said it was 7." She hesitated. "Do you think they'll know?"

She shrugged. "How can they?" She felt sorry for the woman with her awful red hair. "Listen, you don't have to worry about him— he couldn't see anything, those lights are too bright to see anything."

"Yeah," the redhead said sullenly, eyeing her distrustfully. "That's what *they* said, too."

The same detectives gave her a ride home. The car was filled with hatred. The radio was turned up so loud even its silence was a blaring staccato buzz and when it clicked to life with some short burst, the volume made it physically numbing and totally incomprehensible. The detectives began talking between them, under the radio. She strained to listen. "Anything?" the driver asked.

"Yeah, this one held," his partner said, jerking a thumb at her, "but the other one lied."

She was startled and blurted out, "How do you know she lied?"

They glanced at each other. Then the partner turned around and glared at her with contemptuous anger. "You think we're dumb, don't you?"

"No— that's not right. I just want to know how you know she lied. I mean, I know because she told me— but she certainly didn't tell you. So how'd you know?"

He snorted. "Hell, I knew she was going to lie as soon as she walked in with that dyed hair and eyeglasses and all. And I let her know that we knew. I let her know she was lying. And you know what she told me? She said she thought we were oppressors. Is that right? Is that what you think," he snarled, "you think we're oppressors?" His hatred was venomous.

"I don't know," she responded mildly, quietly. "The only thing that's made sense to me is something an Indian brujo— don Juan, you ever hear of him?— said." She spoke carefully, slowly, enunciating each word: "'Oppressors and oppressed meet at the end and the only thing that prevails is that life was altogether too short for both.'"

There was a sudden startled stillness in the car. The detective's face softened. He grunted, turned back to the front. The driver reached over and turned down the radio so it became a soothing undercurrent of sound. When they reached her house the partner jumped out of the car and opened the door for her. "You have a nice Thanksgiving now," he said, not looking at her. The driver nodded.

Just before trial a very young, very nervous city attorney tried to coach her. "I'll tell the truth," she said angrily, "I don't have anything else to tell."

"Well, you should be ready— they may ask you personal questions— questions about your sex life, you know?"

"What for? I haven't done anything. Anyway, my life's my business."

He shrugged, hopeless. "If you don't answer they won't believe you."

"I don't care— I haven't got anything to hide." But still, she rummaged around anxiously in her mind, wondering if there was something slimy in her past, something they could use against her.

There was some confusion about his name at trial— apparently he'd given five or six at various times during his questioning. The public defender— he was just as ineffectual as her city attorney— tried to explain to the judge who waved him aside impatiently and addressed the defendant directly. "Well, which name are you using in this court?"

He considered for a while. "Brown," he said finally, with conviction, "James Brown."

The judge glared at him. "I'm not putting up with any nonsense now. That's the name you're using?"

"Yeah." He was proud, confident, critical. He approved entirely of the testimony given by the man whose VW he'd stolen— it was very accurate, detailed testimony and he nodded agreement, interjecting an occasional "Yeah, that's right." He found her testimony ridiculously inadequate. After she'd described his clothes, to the best of her memory, the public defender asked, "Was he wearing a hat?"

"I don't remember," she answered hesitantly, "but I don't think so."

In a loud stage whisper he announced, sneering, "I wore a hat the whole time!" The judge glowered a warning look at him and he looked back haughty, confident, blooming with satisfaction.

Even with his announcement, she couldn't remember if he'd had a hat on or not, unless maybe he was wearing one of those tight woolen seaman's caps.

Several days later she was told that the assault and attempted rape charges would be dropped. He'd agreed to cop a plea to auto grand theft. "That's a longer sentence," the officer told her with satisfaction. "Three years without parole."

"But why would he cop a plea when that gets him a longer sentence?"

He looked at her with contempt. "We don't look for them in jail."

The idea startled her and she thought about it for a moment. "You mean you think he's done something worse? Murdered somebody?"

He looked away from her and shrugged. "We don't look for 'em in jail," he said again. "He knows that."

"No." She was sure. She remembered his easy confidence in court, his comfortable assurance when he was being taken, hand-cuffed, back to his cell and she compared that with his immense unease when he attacked her, and shuffled away at her show of fight, muttering, "I ain't doing nothing." "No. He just wants to be in jail— he knows that world, and how to get around in it, he's comfortable there. That's all— he just wanted to get back to the world he knew."

The officer gave her a surly, knowing look. "Maybe. He's spent most of his life in there."

To have died once is enough. - Virgil

NIGHT TRICK

by Gary Earl Ross

1.

His name was Molyneaux, and before compact disks redefined recording standards and the rise of rap music finally pushed him into a weekend slot at a National Public Radio affiliate in Rhode Island, he had hosted the all-night jazz show on WSOL-FM in Buffalo. He was a tall, nimble man with smooth umber skin and long tapered fingers. His face was thinner then and faintly equine, his eyes wide and engaging, and his beard neatly trimmed. Despite his thirty-five years, the tight nap of his hair had more than a sprinkling of gray. Whether clad in a three-piece suit or a pullover and wrinkled cords, he would likely have been called distinguished-looking. But on the street few of his listeners would have recognized him. It was his voice they knew, that soothing baritone. It was his voice in which they believed.

Hello, brothers and sisters, friends and lovers. This is Al Molyneaux bringing you the mellow side of midnight on WSOL, 97.5 on your FM dial. It's ten past twelve on a cold and rainy night here in the Big Nickel, and I hope you're in the mood for a little Bessie Smith...

Molyneaux had come to Buffalo after a bitter divorce and nine years on the Northeast AM circuit. Having worked Top 40 and soul stations from New York to Philadelphia to Cleveland, he had watched half a dozen AM outlets die, only to be resurrected as sports, business, or religious stations. Relieved to have moved to FM, he was comfortable at WSOL and felt no urgency to move on. He liked the midnight-to-six slot because he engineered his own broadcast and was free to ignore the charts, free to concentrate on the music he had loved since his Louisiana childhood. And he felt a deep affinity for his listeners. They too were night people: watchmen, nurses, desk clerks, truckers—all caught in their own night tricks—as well as poets, insomniacs, unsatisfied lovers, and solitary drinkers. Like Molyneaux, they understood the night and its silences, the darkness and its echoes. Between album tracks he read them poetry and told them stories about the selections he played. On the request line he listened to their opinions of music and politics and current events, regularly putting their calls on the air. But most of all he gave them music, the music of struggle and survival, of passion and salvation. Night music. Blues. Jazz.

2.

WSOL was housed in a remodeled brick duplex on Franklin Street, in the heart of a shop- and tree-lined section called Allentown. The station owners had had the wall between the apartments knocked out so that the first floor was highlighted by an unusually large reception area, the walls of which displayed various broadcasting and civic service awards, autographed photos of a couple of dozen recording stars, and a gilt-framed oil portrait of the station's late founder. The remainder of the first floor was occupied by austere business offices and an elegantly papered conference room. Most of the second held broadcast and recording studios. From the oversized glass-knobbed vestibule doors to the winding balustrade to the intricately carved fireplace in the reception area, the wood had been restored at great expense and was kept immaculate and smelling of lemon oil. But the leaded windows of an earlier age had been replaced on both floors by tinted plate glass, even in the studios, where windows were a concession to architectural integrity. It was from the window of Studio B, a circular corner room nicknamed the Tower, that Molyneaux first saw the girl.

3.

It was a brisk night in October, a few minutes past twelve, and Molyneaux was cuing Fats Waller's "Mama's Got the Blues." He had purposely dimmed the studio lights and raised the black-louvered venetian blinds so that he could gaze outside. An occasional car cruised up Franklin, the bounce of its headlight beams betraying every bump and hole in its path. Naked trees, their shadows long and foreboding, swayed in the wind. Waller's piano tinkled, and then Molyneaux saw her, stepping into the glow of the street lamp on the corner opposite the station.

She was young, certainly no more than eighteen and probably less. But it was not her age, or lack of it, that caught his eye; it was her beauty. Even from the second floor, even though she stood in such poor light, he could see that she was striking: huge saucer eyes, high cheekbones, cherry lips set in a copper face framed by the tinted elasticurls that were popular then. The collar of her nylon jacket was upturned against the chill of the night. Visibly cold in her short denim skirt and white designer boots, she kept her hands jammed inside her jacket pockets and shifted from foot to foot.

At the end of the Waller number, Molyneaux swiveled back to his control board to read an announcement about an up-and-coming jazz trumpeter booked into the Tralf three nights next week. Then he punched up a long Brubeck track and spun back to the window.

He watched her close to twenty minutes before deciding she was a hooker instead of a fresh runaway. A runaway would have had a duffel bag or backpack; this girl wasn't even carrying a purse. Something deep inside Molyneaux withered at the thought that such an exquisite sliver of creation might be tainted by whoredom. Yet he had to accept the obvious. Several years back, subway construction and diligent vice cops had forced the working girls off Chippewa Street and out of downtown altogether. Some had gone east, to parts of Genesee and Broadway, deep into the poorly policed black community. Others had moved a few blocks north and filtered into Allentown, raising the ire of residents and shopkeepers alike. Of course this girl was on the hook, he told himself. Why would she be on a corner at this hour, apparently waiting for no one in particular?

"Because she's too young to work the bars," he whispered, shaking his head sadly. Still, he could not help wondering why she had elected to stand on a dark one-way street like Franklin when prospects for business were certain to be better one block west on brighter, busier Delaware Avenue. Her illogical choice of streets sparked in him a hope that he was wrong.

Half an hour passed before Molyneaux saw a rusty yellow Pontiac slide to a stop alongside the curb near which the girl stood. She approached the passenger side with deliberate hesitation. After a few seconds of conversation with the driver, who had leaned over to roll down the window, she climbed inside.

"Damn," Molyneaux said softly, cuing Louis Armstrong.

4.

Three nights later she was back, standing under the same street lamp as if it were her timeclock. This time she wore faded jeans and jogging sneakers and did indeed carry a sizeable blue knapsack slung over one shoulder. For a moment Molyneaux told himself he had been mistaken about her the other night, that she was either a runaway or a student with a night job somewhere nearby. Despite her coed look, however, something in her pose— perhaps the hip cocked to one side or the head tilted at a provocative angle—advertised a commodity for sale. Her jaws worked feverishly on a piece of gum.

As he watched her, Molyneaux felt an iciness spread between his shoulder blades. It was not surprise that chilled him, for he had expected to find her on the street again, however impractical this particular corner. It was the gum-chewing that unsettled him. It made her look even younger than she had the first night. He wished he could throw open the window to say something to her. And what, he asked himself, would he say? That life held countless alternatives? That she didn't have to sell herself to survive? That she was risking a catalogue of diseases—the newest of them fatal, the press was beginning to report—to feed and clothe some child-raping-son-of-a-bitch pimp? Molyneaux's hands shook with frustration. More than anything, he wanted to rage at the night that she was too damn beautiful to be a piece-for-hire.

In the end he was vaguely relieved that the plate glass window could not be opened, relieved that he would not have to embarrass himself by shouting to her. But he dialed up the lights in the studio—even though it meant he could see her less clearly—so that if she happened to gaze up she could see him watching, could wonder at his interest. He wanted her to know that he was there, that he cared.

For some reason.

The car that night was a Lincoln with a silver-gray body and matching vinyl top. Just before she sank into the passenger seat, she glanced toward the WSOL building, leaving Molyneaux to ponder whether she had noticed him and if she had, what she had seen in his face.

5.

When next she stationed herself on the corner, a week before Halloween, she wore the headphones to a Walkman. *Radio or tape player?* Molyneaux wondered. *Is she listening to me?* His heart began to race.

During the fadeout of a John Coltrane tune, Molyneaux began to speak in his gentlest poetic rhythm: "Come on in out of the cold, baby. Come sit by my fire and let it melt your troubles. You're much too beautiful, much too precious to walk the wicked side of night alone. Just give me your hand..." Punching the green GO button on his control board, he started a remastered recording of Ellington's "Mood Indigo" and turned back to the window just in time to see her cross the street to a Volkswagen Jetta.

As the door was thrown open for her, she looked up at the studio window and waved.

6.

She returned to the corner—*her* corner, Molyneaux had begun to think—only four times in the next few weeks. The nights she failed to appear were hard for Molyneaux to bear. Not seeing her left him feeling incomplete, anxious, susceptible to uninvited imaginings. He pictured her in squalid surroundings, eating out of cans as she sat on a verminous floor, or hospitalized with tertiary syphilis, though she was much too young to have reached stage three. Each third or fourth successive absence was the worst, for by then he had begun to believe she was dead, beaten and strangled by a psychotic john or razored to ribbons by her pimp as punishment for some small offense.

But the next night, or the night after, she would step into the glow of her street lamp, headphones in place, and smile up at him as he worked. Upon seeing her, Molyneaux was helpless to check the note of joy that crept into his voice. Often he found himself talking directly to her: "Count Basie's 'Nails.' If you liked it, smile. Yes, that's it. Your smile is infectious. It gives off just enough light for the weary soul to find his way in the dark." But the joy was always temporary, because sooner or later she would get into somebody's car, and Molyneaux's stomach would clench so tightly he almost doubled over.

On weekends, when he was off, he cruised surrounding streets to see if she had staked claims on other corners. He never found her and always worked his way back to Franklin, where he parked under her street lamp and waited, sometimes until dawn. On such nights he thought that if he could meet her, talk to her, hear her side, maybe he would understand. If he understood, maybe he could save her.

7.

5:15 a.m. The first Friday in December. Molyneaux sat at the control board, sleeves rolled up, sipping black coffee from a styrofoam cup and leafing through program sheets for tomorrow's show. He was glad to be in the home stretch. However tired he was, however unflagging his backache, however sore his feet were in his stiff leather shoes, he never had difficulty getting through the last hour of his broadcast. There were fewer calls, fewer requests, which meant fewer people were listening. To compensate for the reduction in on-air conversation, he played longer tracks, sometimes the entire side of an LP, sometimes even a complete LP if he had it on tape. When sign-off came, he would turn everything over to Rockin' Rick Slick, the kid who did the morning show. Then Molyneaux would break for the parking lot and drive to Morgana's Kitchen for breakfast. Afterward, he would head home to bed and sleep till late afternoon. When he rose he would have a large dinner and then maybe take in a movie or catch the early show at the Tralf. By 10:30 or so he would be back at the station, verifying that production assistants had pulled the records and tapes he wanted for that night's show. At midnight he'd be back on the air.

5:18 a.m. Wild Bill Davis was "Jumpin' at the Woodside" when the request line jangled. Molyneaux pressed the answer key on his board.

"WSOL. Al Molyneaux on the mellow side."

"I need your help."

The voice was female, young. Molyneaux felt his shoulders tense.

"What?"

"I need your help. Please."

"Who is this?" It amazed him that a voice asking for help was so steady, so free of urgency.

"C.C.," came the reply. "The girl outside your window."

At 9:30 that morning, Molyneaux appeared in City Court and put up three hundred dollars to bail a stranger out of jail.

8.

"Why me?"

Her name was Cecily Styles and she was seated opposite him at the table in his kitchenette. The plate before her bore the greasy residue of the two Egg McMuffins she had nearly swallowed whole. She was on her second cigarette. Smoke curled in the air between her face and his, and Molyneaux stared at her as if seeing her for the first time. Proximity, he reflected, in no way diminished her. Even without makeup she was astonishingly beautiful. Her lips were full and looked soft. Behind them were even white teeth. Her huge round eyes danced with a luminescence that Molyneaux would not have expected to find in a whore. Her skin glistened, unblemished, unwrinkled. He realized that she had not been in the life that long. She was not yet past hope, redemption... Molyneaux kept his hands under the table; he did not want her to see them trembling. He felt something gelatinous and indefinite in his throat and swallowed to clear it.

"Why me?" he asked again. "Why not your pimp?"

"Ain't got a pimp," she said.

"Sure." Waiting to post bail, he had imagined her on the skids with some overdressed clown named Bubbles or Silky—which was why she needed someone else to get her out of jail—and he had pictured a wildly customized Cadillac squealing to a stop in front of the radio station and the pimp skipping up the walkway with his gun hand sliding inside his suit jacket.

"I don't," she said, neither emphatically nor angrily, but easily, almost sounding amused. "It's my decision to go out or stay in, to work or not work, to be what I am. Every day I gotta choose to live or die, and every time I make the choice, it means I'm in charge of me. I make all the choices, not no pimp."

Her voice had a musical quality that sent a shiver through Molyneaux. He shrugged it off, smiled faintly, nervously. He knew that she knew that he did not believe her, but his disbelief seemed not to matter to her. She returned his smile, and he couldn't help feeling grateful that she had not been smoking long enough to damage her teeth. *What a puzzling, fascinating child,* he thought. *Yes, a child.* And the lump re-formed in his throat. This time he did not swallow; he let it sit there, let it grow.

"How old are you?" he asked, catching his breath after several seconds.

"It ain't important," she said.

"It is to me."

"Why? You tryin' to figure out if I'm statutory?"

Molyneaux shook his head.

"Eighteen."

"Eighteen," Molyneaux said thoughtfully. "You look younger than that."

"I be what I be." She shrugged. "You gonna tell me I should be cheerleadin' and gettin' ready for the prom?" Her smile was fixed, almost dreamy. There was the faintest hint of a challenge in her tone.

"No," Molyneaux said. "I was just thinkin' about what it was like when I was eighteen." He remembered a summer back home in New Orleans. He remembered the heat and the music and the great reefer. Mostly, though, he remembered a long-legged girl with dark brown nipples and skin the color of glazed sand. He wanted to tell C.C. about that summer, about Lucienne. For

267

some reason he thought she ought to know. He paused to let her ask him about what it was like when he was eighteen. She did not. Instead, she left her cigarette to die in the ashtray and got to her feet. She stepped out of the kitchenette and into the combination living and dining room. She examined the African and Caribbean hangings and carvings and plucked a few notes on the large thumb piano which rested on a metal stand on an end table. Then she ran a hand over the back of the black leather sofa that served as a room divider, pausing briefly and tilting her head slightly to read titles on book spines on the shelves built into the wall perpendicular to the couch. In denim skirt and pale blue Danskin top, she moved without restlessness, without agitation. Her rhythm was indefinable yet almost ghostly in its precision. He watched her drift toward the French doors that led to his balcony, which overlooked Lake Erie.

"Where are you from?" he asked.

"No place special," she said. Her back toward him, she gazed out at the gray, ice-laden water. "But I suppose you'll tell me it's important to you."

Molyneaux said nothing.

"Albany," she said finally. "Now there's a city that never wakes."

"Do you have family there?"

"Yes and no."

"What brought you to Buffalo?"

She was quiet for a moment, then said, "Guess you think puttin' up bail gives you the right to interrogate me."

"I'm sorry," he said. "Really."

Back still toward him, she laughed. "It's okay. I'm just waitin' for you to ask me the big one."

"The big one?"

"The one every man wants to know." She shifted her weight from one foot to the other. "Why I do what I do."

"Maybe," he said. "The question had occurred to me." He stood and set the plate and coffee cups in the sink.

"Why do you do what you do?" she asked.

"I like it and I'm good at it." He leaned back, buttocks against the counter, and folded his arms. "Is that why you turn tricks? You like it and you're good at it?"

Leaving the question unanswered, she pivoted to face him. She smiled a dazzling smile.

And he felt his groin tighten.

"Why me?" he asked again, almost hoarsely.

"You're a nice man," she said. "I could tell by your voice."

9.

That afternoon Molyneaux slept.

And dreamed.

He stood in a clearing at the edge of a forest, in the fragmented light of a dying day. Ahead of him was a brown-skinned woman in a diaphanous white gown. She might have been Lucienne, or his ex-wife Sandra, or C.C. Because her back was to him he could not tell. As the dream crystallized, he realized that whoever she was, she was running away from him and toward the gathering shadows of the forest. Without seeing, he understood what lay in wait for her. Somewhere ahead crouched something cool and reptilian, its yellow eyes focused on the path on which the woman would pass. When she reached the thing, it would spring and hold her firmly in one ancient claw, while the talons of the other began stripping away great swaths of skin. It would peel her until it found what it sought, and when it spied its prize, it would lift the glowing, quivering mass of her soul out of the center of her and take the first bite...

Molyneaux understood that he must stop her at any cost. No matter how fast he ran, though, he could not catch her. Perhaps if he called to her, called her by name, she would hesitate long enough for him to reach her, wrestle her to the grass, shield her from the disappointed thing that would stalk out of its hiding place. Uncertain what name he would shout, Molyneaux opened his mouth to scream. But he had no voice.

He lurched into a sitting position, his heart pounding and forehead damp. He made an effort to control his breathing, and gradually his heartbeat slowed. Then he lay back, struggled back into sleep, but failed in his attempt to return to the forest.

10.

At half past four he stirred to find C.C. naked beside him in bed, her tongue darting over his hardening right nipple, a thumb and forefinger lightly pinching the left. She smelled of cigarettes and perfume and the apple juice he had left in the fridge. Her tongue followed the line of hair down the center of his abdomen and she blew a teasing stream of air into his crinkly pubic hair. Then her lips, warm and moist and every bit as soft as he had imagined, closed around him and gently pulled. "Baby," he murmured, fully awake now, heart thudding in his ears. When he was erect, she straddled him and wriggled about, eyes closed and breaths deepening. Alone for over a year, he came quickly and muttered something apologetic. But she pressed her finger to his lips, slid off him, and buried her head in his lap once more. When he was firm enough, she straddled him again, and he pulled her face down to his. Her tongue scraped his lips, making them, him, tingle. Then she sat up. And moved. And groaned. And shook. And he thought she was like good jazz, electrifying but smooth and unpredictable, hitting unexpected highs and lows. He felt his hands on her body, moving up her sides, his fingers on the magic keyboard that was her rib cage. His hands climbed higher, held onto her small breasts as if without them he would fall backward through the mattress, through the floor, into the apartment below. Next his hands found her face, his fingertips marveling at the delicacy of her skin, the liquid warmth of her breathing, the curve of her jaw. And then his fingers were on her neck, gently, the thumbs near her windpipe. Somewhere in his head a voice screamed, *Save her!* And he thought that he could, that it was in his power to do so. *Save her!* Yes, and he began, ever so slowly, to squeeze, to save. He closed his eyes and listened to the small gasping sound that she made. *Save h—*

Abruptly, she stiffened and shuddered, her contractions pulling him, and he followed her into orgasm, his hands going slack and his eyes widening at the realization of what he had almost done. Afterward, she placed her head on his chest and clung to him. Molyneaux lay still, feeling the sweat between them turn to ice.

11.

When he woke the third time, alone, it was dark outside and he was cold. The digital clock on his nightstand read 7:43. He lay still in the dark for several minutes, listening. There were voices and footsteps overhead, and someone was grinding a starter out in the parking lot. But there were no sounds from elsewhere inside Molyneaux's apartment. He was sure C.C was gone, that she had been swallowed by the night. His momentary intervention had done nothing to change the course of her life. *And my hands on her throat...* Swallowing involuntarily, he slid out of bed and turned on his bedside lamp. Then he stuck his feet into his slippers and pulled his robe off the hook behind the door.

Molyneaux stepped into the darkened living room and saw the tip of a cigarette brighten as oxygen was drawn through. He hit the wall switch. In yesterday's denim skirt and a wrinkled black translucent blouse that must have come from her backpack, C.C. sat on the open sofa bed, caught in the crossfire of the track lighting. Looking only momentarily surprised, she exhaled a lungful of smoke.

For a moment neither of them spoke. Then Molyneaux said, "I didn't hear you get up."

"Didn't want to wake you."

"I thought you'd be gone by now."

271

C.C. smiled and crushed out her cigarette in the ashtray on the coffee table. Then she got to her feet and crossed the room to him. As if in answer to the uncertainty in his voice, she slid her arms around his waist and stood on tiptoe to kiss him, hard.

"I gotta get ready for work," Molyneaux said when the kiss ended. Embracing her only lightly, he bit his lower lip and shut his eyes and waited for her to say, *Me too.* When she did not, he disengaged himself and opened his eyes but shifted them to avoid meeting her gaze. "Let me grab a quick shower," he said, "and maybe we can go get something to eat." *And then what?* He was helpless to check his thoughts. *Am I supposed to sit in the dark in that goddamn studio and watch her get into another man's car?*

"Sorry I got your towels all wet," she said. "I don't know where you keep the clean ones."

"That's okay," he said, kissing her again, briefly this time, as if he needed permission to linger. Feeling awkward, he backed away from her and pivoted on his heel to head toward the bathroom. Then he stopped, hesitated before facing her. "I have to tell you I'm sorry," he said.

"For what?"

"I'm sorry if I hurt you..."

"What?"

"Or almost hurt you. I mean..." Molyneaux fell silent, unsure of anything except the irony that a professional talker should find himself speechless. He had no idea why he'd involved himself with this not-quite-woman or why he'd squeezed her throat or where his involvement might lead. But the longer he stared at her, the more he wanted her—and the more he hated himself for wanting her.

"You didn't hurt me," she said finally. "You never even came close."

12.

In the bathroom Molyneaux hung his robe on the back of the door and fingered his face in the mirror. It had been three or four days since he had last trimmed his beard and cleared the stubble from his throat and the hollows of his cheeks. One of the benefits of working in radio, especially late night radio, was that he could let his appearance slip without jeopardizing his job. If C.C. had not been there, he might just have showered and gone to work. Tonight, however, he found himself wanting to look his best. Maybe he could take C.C. to the station with him, give her some idea of the business. Maybe what she needed was to see alternatives. In any event, she'd be safe there while he worked, and if she grew tired she could sack out on the couch in the reception area. In the morning, after sign-off, they could go out to breakfast and spend all of Saturday together since he would not have to work tomorrow night. And maybe Sunday too.

He opened the medicine cabinet, splashed on lime pre-shave lotion, and plugged his Norelco shaver into the outlet beside the mirror. Then he leaned over the sink to get a closer look at himself and thumbed the ON switch. He had lifted his chin and was poised to apply the humming shaver to the left side of his Adam's apple when, in the mirror, he saw the razor blade. He switched off the Norelco and turned around.

The razor blade rested on the edge of the bathtub, on the unfolded waxed wrapper in which it had come. Molyneaux picked it up carefully, pinching the sides with the waxed paper. He had not used blades in over fifteen years and wondered why C.C. would leave an old one, not even stainless steel, on the edge of the tub. Maybe she had shaved her legs, though there were easier and cleaner ways than using an old-style safety razor. But then he remembered the smoothness of her legs against his skin, beneath his fingertips, and knew she'd had no need to shave. Had she cut some drug on the rim of the tub? He examined the blade closely, saw no trace of hair or powder. But a thin line of blood—fresh blood—clung to one edge.

Every day I gotta choose to live or die.

Molyneaux stopped breathing. For an instant he envisioned what he might have found if C.C. had chosen differently: her body languishing in rusty water, wrists laid open and hair matted against porcelain, sightless eyes fixed on the ceiling. He shut his own eyes and inhaled deeply, almost smelling the blood on the razor blade. Somewhere on that child's body was a razor cut, and suddenly Molyneaux wanted to know where. Was it on her wrist? Arm? Leg? Was there a single cut or a series? Perhaps she was a self-mutilator whose body carried a barely visible notch for each man she slept with. Molyneaux opened his eyes. His notch would be the freshest, would have no scab to seal in her blood.

You didn't hurt me. You never even came close.

Molyneaux shrugged into his robe and opened the door.

C.C. wasn't in the living room or the kitchenette. Heading toward the rear of the apartment, Molyneaux opened his mouth to call to her but stopped himself, afraid there would be no reply. When he stepped into the empty glow of his bedside lamp, he did not notice that his wallet and car keys were missing from his nightstand. Nor did he imagine that his Toyota would later be found abandoned on the lakeshore twenty miles south of town. He knew only that C.C. was gone, out of his life, and her absence deepened inside him like an afternoon shadow on unbroken snow.

Long before he would glimpse her face inside passing cars or beneath the glaze of frozen ponds or outside every station window from Buffalo to Providence, Molyneaux shuddered at the memory of her body against his. He sat on the edge of his bed and opened his robe to look at himself, arms and belly and legs. Then he held up the razor still pinched in his fingers and wondered, for only an instant, where he should make the first cut.

What passing-bells for these who die as cattle? - Wilfred Owen

SOUTH WIND

by Margot C. Kadesch

In 1981 when Joanna spent a year teaching American literature at the University of Sarajevo, it was the south wind that preoccupied her colleagues on the English faculty. "Oh, how I hate that wind," Yasna had said as they sat in the sunny third floor office Joanna shared with four other members of the English faculty. "It gives me migraine."

Joanna smiled, unbelieving.

"You laugh," Selma said, "but you will see. Soon the wind will turn, and you will see. You won't be able to concentrate. Your kidneys will ache."

"Everyone is so very irritable and depressed," Gordana added. "They drive like idiots. You must know, Joanna, that when the south wind blows we have to excuse all kinds of behavior. "

"Yes, even murder," Yasna said. "If someone commits murder when the south wind blows, he receives not so great a punishment."

Joanna never quite believed in the south wind. It was one of those things which seemed to have a vivid reality for the Yugoslavs but simply didn't exist for her — rather like the laundry they told her was right by the old cathedral. "Just around the corner from it," Yasna said. "By the yogurt shop. You can't miss it." But of course she could miss it, and, in time she gave up and assumed it was no longer there. It was rather the same with ethnicity. She had read Rebecca West and heard about the atrocities of the Second World War, but those ancient, bitter rivalries — like the laundry — eluded her. "We are all Yugoslavs now," her students said primly when she questioned them about their backgrounds.

"Yes, we are all Yugoslavs these days," echoed Professor Mladic who came over from Belgrade in October to examine the third year students and took her out for coffee during his break. "My mother is Serb, and she ought to hate Croats, but my wife is Croat, and my mother loves her. Our children are both Serb and Croat, and my mother loves them even more dearly than she loves my wife. It's all a bit of a muddle, you see." He laughed, and Joanna was shocked to see that a front incisor was missing.

"So it's not really an issue any more?" she asked.

"An issue? Why should it be?" he answered, lighting a second cigarette from the burning stub of the first one. "We're all Yugoslavs now." He waved his hand, dissipating her questions with the blue curl of smoke from his cigarette.

Yet even though Joanna denied its reality, she now wonders if the south wind was blowing the day Yasna introduced her to Branko. "Here is your tutor," Yasna had said, throwing her arms wide as though to embrace them both. "He will teach you to speak Serbo-Croatian like an angel."

Joanna had been too busy before she left — those final days with David had been too strained and stressful — to think about learning the language. They had told her she would lecture in English, and she gave the matter no more thought. Besides, she reasoned, Yugoslavia is European, and everyone in Europe speaks English. So she was dismayed, when she got off the plane in Sarajevo's tiny airport, to find that neither the woman at the information desk nor any of the cab drivers spoke English. How was she going to get along?

"Use German," Yasna told her. "It's the lingua franca here. Our men, you see, go as guest workers to the factories of West Germany. You do speak German?"

"No," Joanna said sadly. "Only a little French."

"Then we must get you a tutor." Yasna was decisive. "I will arrange it. You will see."

Yasna was the first member of the English faculty to befriend her. She drove Joanna to the airport to get her belongings out of customs. She took Joanna to the large open market across from the town hall where strong-boned peasant women crocheted under umbrellas behind tables anchored at both ends by pyramids of scarlet peppers. She led Joanna through the cobbled maze of the old town to a bakery where loaves of flatbread, big as dinner plates, came hot from a roaring wood fire. When Joanna bought a fancifully embroidered cloth from one of the peasants who displayed their wares in the old Turkish market place, Yasna looked at it critically. "How much did you pay?" she demanded.

"It was cheap," Joanna said. "Three hundred dinars — only ten dollars."

"You were cheated," Yasna snapped. "Next time, I will go with you."

Yasna's husband was a journalist — one of the best in Yugoslavia Joanna was told. He was always away on assignment, leaving Yasna to manage their house and their daughter Mirjela by herself. Yasna was small and waif-like, with thin ash brown hair that clung in wisps to her neck. There were deep circles under her eyes, and the downward droop of her lips gave her a look of perpetual patient sorrow. Later Joanna remarked on Yasna's sadness to Selma. "What can you expect?" Selma said. "She married a Hercegovinian. Her mother-in-law lives in Mostar, but even from there she makes Yasna's life miserable."

Because of Yasna's sadness Joanna felt guilty about accepting her help. "I can manage for myself, Yasna, really," she said on the day Yasna insisted on taking her to the police station to register as an alien.

277

"No, no. Serbo-Croatian is really so very difficult that you are like a baby here," Yasna said. "We always help our foreign lecturers. Besides, this is our famed Yugoslav hospitality."

"Speaking of Serbo-Croatian," Joanna said. "What about my tutor? Have you found someone?"

"I am vorking on it," Yasna said. Yasna's English was fluent. She phrased each statement precisely, with careful British pronunciation, but now and then something darker, richer, more Slavic crept in when she was distracted or annoyed. Now she changed the subject. "You must carry your alien card always," she said, looking sternly at Joanna. "Even when you go to the market for eggs or walk in the evenings, even then you must carry it. Think that you are married to it." She smiled, revealing crooked, tobacco-stained teeth. "It will be your husband in Yugoslavia."

Did Yasna's metaphor conceal a question? Joanna assumed that her arrival here — a married woman choosing to spend a year alone in a foreign country — must arouse curiosity. Still, she decided not to answer. "I can't thank you enough for helping me, Yasna," she said, adding slyly, "Once I learn more Serbo-Croatian I'll be able to manage for myself. When do you think you'll have a tutor for me?"

"Soon, soon," Yasna said vaguely, stopping to consider a blouse displayed behind the wavy glass of a dress shop tucked between a hairdresser and a candle shop. "I vill find you someone soon. I promise."

And of course she found Branko. His office was in the Philosophy Faculty, where the English Department was housed. He taught French. "Branko spent years in Paris," Yasna explained as she led Joanna to his office. "He earned his master's degree from the Sorbonne and then taught the Slavic languages. He is a good teacher, an excellent teacher. You will see." They found him sitting behind his desk in a pool of light. A lock of dark hair had fallen over his brow, and the cigarette left burning in an ashtray by his elbow wreathed him in rings of smoke.

At Yasna's greeting, Branko jumped up and came from behind his desk, smiling. He had a wonderful smile. He kissed Yasna on both cheeks and extended his hand to Joanna. As she reached out her hand in response, he bent over it slightly so that for a moment, just a moment, Joanna thought he was going to kiss it. *"Enchanté,"* he murmured. And it was then Joanna learned that he did not speak English.

"But that is the point," Yasna said when Joanna questioned the practicality of the arrangement. "You will teach him English and he will teach you Serbo-Croatian. It will be a trade, you see. That way you won't have to spend your salary on lessons. You do speak French, don't you?" she asked.

"Well, yes, but only a little," Joanna stammered. "I..."

"Good. Then it's settled." Yasna beamed. "I will leave you now to your lessons."

Joanna and Branko stood there, alone in his office. They looked mutely at each other.

"Vous parlez français, madame?" he asked at last.

"Oui. Un peu," Joanna said.

"Bon." He smiled and rubbed his hands together. *"Allons-nous commencer."*

Yes, the south wind was definitely blowing that day.

Determined to make the most of her year, Joanna embraced every gesture of friendship from colleagues and neighbors, though she was normally fastidious in choosing friends. When Gordana, with her husky voice and Melina Mercouri looks, invited her out for coffee after their classes she accepted eagerly. Gordana warned her about other members of the faculty.

"Watch out for Slobodan," she said, restlessly rolling the burning tip of her cigarette in the ashtray. "He lives with his mother because he's unmarried and does not qualify for housing. When he learns you have a whole flat to yourself, he will try to start an affair with you so he can move in."

"Did he move in with the other American lecturers?" Joanna asked.

"The last one was married," Gordana said, "and the one before that was a man.

"Then what makes you think he'll try with me?" Gordana looked up from her cigarette and regarded Joanna with knowing, hooded eyes. "But it's quite obvious," she said. "What else would you expect him to do?"

Ivana, too, took Joanna up. Her friendship came in the form of endless thimbles of Turkish coffee which she brought up on a copper tray from the coffee shop on the main floor and kept warm on the hot water radiator in their office. Ivana warned her about Gordana. "She will befriend you only to find out if you are sleeping with her husband," Ivana said. "He's an important hydraulics engineer here. He travels, and Gordana is obsessed with his fidelity. At least once a month she comes to the office hysterical because she thinks he's found a new mistress. She will certainly think you are a threat."

Joanna, still sad and bruised from the long, intimate war with David didn't feel much like a threat to anyone. Not to Gordana, not to Ivana, not even to Yasna, whose husband had flirted with her openly when Yasna introduced them during one of his rare visits home. Of course, everyone agreed that Yasna's marriage was only a sham. "We told her not to marry him," Ivana said. "But she wouldn't listen. And now all they have is their misery — and Mirjela, of course, with her aspirations to be an actress. They spend millions of dinars on that child — her make up, her clothes, her acting lessons. Yasna's obsessed with Mirjela's talent, and Mirjela's obsessed with herself."

"Poor Yasna," Gordana added. "She is married but not married to that journalist of hers. She should take a lover, but she's too timid." Gordana smiled significantly, and later, much later, Joanna learned that Gordana had taken her own advice.

"With Pjetar," Selma confided. "Can you imagine? He's only a kid." Selma had earned her master's degree in Michigan and spoke English with an American flair. "I only tell you because everyone knows about it." And, indeed, once alerted, Joanna could not help intercepting the long, searching looks between the pair during faculty meetings or noticing them sitting in the dark back corner of a coffee house, utterly silent, their hands not quite touching on the table top.

In those days, it seemed to Joanna, Sarajevo fairly pulsed with love and desire. Certainly her students were bewitched by love. They were all girls; the young men were away, fulfilling a mandatory two-year service in the army. Every one of the girls in her class, apparently, had a boyfriend in uniform. Shyly, after class, they confided their loneliness to her, especially Dijana, Dzenana, and Biljana — "my trio," Joanna thought, feeling like Miss Jean Brodie. They waited for Joanna after classes and walked her part way home. They asked her out for coffee and questioned her about American boys. They talked about their boyfriends and sighed, looking mournfully into their tiny Turkish coffee cups, eyes lowered, lashes beaded with mascara and tears. They counted off the days their boys had been gone and thought about the days until they got leave.

Dzenana, poetic and beautiful with huge black eyes and a halo of golden hair, showed Joanna a crumpled, tear-stained letter from her boyfriend. She read it aloud in Serbo-Croatian, then interpreted. It spoke of his love for her, his yearning, she said. He quoted love poems and said he thought of her constantly. He wept into his pillow. "He is a very beautiful person, my Ivo," Dzenana said. She spread her arms and threw back her golden hair. "They are all beautiful, these boys in uniforms, the flower of our manhood learning to defend our country. Surely you have seen them on their way to maneuvers?"

Joanna had. In fact, she saw them often, those young trainees, packed in the backs of battered dark green trucks. They smoked and looked out at the civilians with hungry, homesick eyes. Some hung over the high wooden sides, waving and calling to every pretty girl who passed. Recalling them now, Joanna can't equate those fresh-faced boys with the tight-lipped men she watches nightly on TV, aiming mortar shells at women with babies, who only months before had gossiped at the corner with their wives and mothers.

What drove Sarajevo in 1981 was desire, not hate. All Joanna's acquaintances — the students, Gordana, Yasna — were consumed, each in his or her own way, by desire. Every day as she faced her classes of love-sick girls, each afternoon as she sat in her office sipping coffee and gossiping with Ivana or Selma or Gordana, it was this hot pulse she felt. Desire was epidemic, and it passed from person to person like a fever.

So it was no wonder that, as her lessons with Branko progressed, Joanna found herself sometimes preoccupied with the dark hairs on the backs of his strong fingers as he wrote out a dialogue for her to memorize or unable to remember the lesson because his front forelock had tumbled into his eyes again. Now, they often fell silent. Was it because they had no common language? Or was it in an all too common language they communicated during those long silences? Branko smoked endless cigarettes which enclosed them in a charmed, smoky circle. Joanna sat on the other side of his desk, eyes downcast, playing with the clasp of her wristwatch.

In November Yasna told Joanna about the faculty excursion to the coast for Narodna Dana, the Yugoslav independence day. "The university makes a special train and gives us a low price, you see," Yasna said. "So you can afford to come. You will come? With Mirjela and me?"

She did. With Mirjela and Yasna. And Branko. He tapped on the glass of their compartment just as the train for the coast pulled out of the station. He was grinning, his dark lock fanned over his forehead. Yasna leapt up and opened the compartment door. She spoke quickly to Branko in Serbo-Croatian while Mirjela looked from them to Joanna with eyes too wise and world-weary for a child. In a minute Branko was inside, stowing his suitcase on the rack overhead with an easy swing and wedging himself in between Mirjela and Joanna. Yasna sat opposite. She looked at Joanna and threw out her hands, blowing a little puff of air between pursed lips — the universal Bosnian response to the vagaries of fate.

For the first time Joanna wondered why Yasna had paired her with Branko. The arrangement was totally impractical. Was she matchmaking — lonely American woman, handsome Yugoslav man? Was that still another of the services she would perform so willingly for Joanna? Or for Branko? Joanna wanted to get off the train, to go back to Sarajevo and hide in her flat, never seeing Branko or Yasna again. Instead, she remained on the red plush first class seat, her eyes fixed on the floor where a cigarette stub rocked to the rhythm of the train.

Branko seemed completely at ease. He stretched out his long legs and nudged Yasna with the toe of his shoe, saying something in Serbo-Croatian. Yasna laughed. "Branko says why don't we sing Yugoslav songs to you? He pretends it's because I don't speak French and you don't speak Serbo-Croatian and conversation's impossible. But really it's because he wants to show off his nice voice for you. He is really so vain, you know. Aren't you, Branko?" she asked him in English. "Aren't you so very vain about your singing?"

Branko looked at her quizzically. Yasna translated, and he shrugged in his acquired French way. Instead of answering he began to sing. Branko did have a nice voice. It was warm and deep. He looked to Joanna for her reaction, but she refused to respond. He shrugged again and pulled a little face, but he went on singing. In a minute, Mirjela joined in. Their voices blended — Mirjela's clear and sweet, Branko's rich and throbbing — in the close Balkan harmony Joanna heard so often spiralling from the coffee houses in the old town. The music was sinuous and slightly oriental. It spoke of joy and sorrow and, yes, desire. Like Sarajevo, like all of Yugoslavia. When Branko and Mirjela finished the song, Yasna applauded.

"That was from our own Bosnia," she said. She conferred with Branko and Mirjela. "Now they will sing you something from each republic. First, from Macedonia."

Then, as the train rocked down the Neretva River valley to the coast and to the bus that would carry them to their hotel, Joanna relented. She looked at Yasna, who was smiling, though the shadow of her sadness still lingered in her dark-ringed eyes. Joanna accepted that smile and the sadness and trusted Yasna. How could she suspect her of anything but trying to help? She closed her eyes and let the voices of Branko and Mirjela bear her through all the regions of Yugoslavia. Branko's side was pressed to hers. Through her tweed jacket she could feel the vibration of his singing, and his warmth crept along her arm and into her resisting heart. His hand lay on his thigh, only inches from hers. From time to time the fingers twitched, as though his hand, of itself, were struggling to engulf hers.

It was cold and rainy when they climbed from the bus under the wide canopy at the entrance to the hotel.

"Oh God!" Yasna cried. "The south wind is blowing. How it makes my head ache." The others echoed her dismay. As they collected their luggage from the belly of the bus and straggled into reception for their keys, they kept up a litany of complaint. The clerk at the desk, too, seemed victim to the south wind. Unsmiling, without welcome, he dealt out guest cards and room keys to the cluster of vacationers as though conferring enormous favors on them. The guests snatched them from him and hurried to their rooms, pressing the backs of their hands to their foreheads and complaining about the wind.

When she had unpacked, Joanna wandered out into the deserted guest lounge. The rain outside came in a steady drizzle, and the famed view from the terrace was cloaked in low hanging clouds. Forlornly she settled in a deep chair and ordered coffee. It was there Branko found her.

"*Ah, bon,*" he said, rubbing his hands together and smiling with pleasure. "*Café. Quelle bonne idée!*" He signalled the bored waiter and ordered a double espresso. He alone was unaffected by the weather.

That night, Joanna lay next to her new lover in the deep Adriatic night and smiled, while the waves hissed on the shingle below her open window. For more than a year, ever since her marriage had erupted into open warfare, she had been sexless and empty of desire. Now, in a rush, desire came back. It was like spring in her body. Little rivulets of pleasure ran along her spine and down her thighs. The long darkness of her ruined marriage had lifted.

Branko left sometime in the night. He did not come down to breakfast, and Joanna did not see him again that day. The rain continued. Yasna and Mirjela moped in the hotel lounge, listlessly exchanging gossip with other faculty members. Left to her own devices, Joanna went out and splashed along the esplanade. The tiny shops and restaurants that lined the harbor were shut tight against the weather. The outdoor tables and chairs, which spilled out to the water's edge in fine weather, were stacked under awnings, the umbrellas furled and beaded with dark drops. No one else was about; she was alone with the sea. She hugged her raincoat to her and thought how different it would be if Branko were there. Then they would cherish the solitude of the lonely esplanade. They would walk — arms laced, pressed against each other — in the daze of new desire, oblivious of the rain and the chill, every sense tuned only to the other.

Branko came to her room again that night. "Where have you been?" she cried when she answered his knock, long after midnight.

Branko smiled and put his finger to his lips, shutting the door and pulling her to him. "We must be discreet, chérie," he murmured into the hollow of her neck. "We have the nights for love." He drew back and searched her face, tracing the contours with tender fingers. "It will be enough," he whispered. "I promise." And it was.

Next day the sun shone. The wind turned, and the little coastal village came to life. The restaurants flung open their doors, the gay umbrellas dotted the esplanade, and the tidy harbor, round as a moon, sparkled under the deep blue sky. Yasna and Mirjela, their headaches gone, dedicated themselves to Joanna. They prowled the cobbled alleys and climbed to the hilltop mausoleum designed by Mestrovic. By afternoon it was warm enough to sunbathe, topless, in a hidden cove on the other side of the small peninsula that protected the village from the open sea.

It was snowing in Sarajevo when they returned. On the broad pavement fronting the station, the taxis were drawn up in a circle awaiting their fares. They were outlined in snow, hoods steaming in the cold, headlights boring golden channels through the drifting flakes. Snow sifted down on the muffled passengers as they fanned out, gesturing and calling to the drivers. Joanna stopped to sniff the pure, cold air before she threw herself into the melee to get a taxi. Three days ago she had boarded the train in the smoky gloom of autumn. She returned to the pristine white of winter.

"My season has changed, too," she thought later, examining herself in the bathroom mirror. She pressed her face close to the glass. Did her changed state show in her eyes? In her smile? The mirror answered by distorting her face: Branko's new lover had an enormous nose and pinched temples with tiny, crowded eyes.

Now that Joanna and Branko were lovers, the language lessons ceased. Branko made excuses. He was too busy. He was doing some research. Instead, he came to her flat, tapping softly on her door late at night. Some nights, without explanation, he stayed away, and Joanna paced, listening fruitlessly for the quick tattoo of his feet on the cobbles. They didn't talk. It was too difficult; there were too many languages between them. Joanna tried to get Branko to make love to her in Serbo-Croatian. "Tell me the word for love," she begged. "How do I say 'I love you' in Serbo-Croatian?"

"My language has no word for love," he said in French.

"But ..."

"Shhh."

"In French, then," she cried, her head thrown back to receive his kisses on her neck. "Make love to me in French."

"Non, chérie," he murmured. "Silence is better."

He would trace her ears, her hairline, the curves of her belly with his lips. She would tug playfully on his dark forelock or mimic his Gallic shrug. They would smile and look deep into each other's eyes. Yet somehow, even while Joanna clung to his kisses with her arms locked around his back, she could not quite reach Branko. There was some gulf she could not breach — a disjunction in their rhythms, a lack of communication more impenetrable and yet less tangible than their lack of a common language — that separated them.

"I should break it off," she told herself. "Next time he comes, I'll send him away." But when night came she lost her resolve and paced in her flat alone, while outside the snow fell softly in the dark, uncaring night. She went again and again to the window, pulling aside the thin gauze curtain to look into the street though all she could see through the screen of sifting snow was the empty cone of light from the streetlight. If at last she heard Branko's furtive tap, she rushed to open the door. Finally she decided to have it out with him. "Why don't we ever go out together?" she burst out in her stumbling French as soon as she shut the door behind him.

"*Comment?* "

"I want you to take me to dinner ... to a movie. Out. Somewhere ... out, not here," she faltered.

Branko was still in his coat, with a bright muffler wrapped around his neck and snow glistening in his dark hair. He didn't reply, but his brow wrinkled and he pursed his lips, cocking his head to consider her. Then he pulled her to him. "Joanna, Joanna," he murmured into her hair.

"No!" She pulled back, stiffening her arms against his chest. "We have to talk. What's going on?"

"Going on?" he echoed, and he seemed so genuinely puzzled that Joanna wondered if he understood what she had said.

"*Je pense...*" she began, "*je veux...*" But whatever it was she wanted to say — and she wasn't sure quite what that would be — she couldn't begin to express in French. Or in Serbo-Croatian. Certainly not in Serbo-Croatian. In her frustration she began to cry. "Shit," she wailed in English, unable even in her own language to articulate what she wanted. "Oh, shit, shit, shit!"

Side Show 1995

Branko pulled her to him again. "*Chérie,*" he crooned. "*Chérie. Calme-toi, calme-toi.*" She let herself sink against him then and sobbed and sobbed against the rough fabric of his coat. When at last he loosed his arms and led her gently toward her bedroom, she went unresistingly.

Lying alone in her rumpled bed next morning, Joanna was stern with herself. "This can't go on," she said aloud, as though she were talking to someone else. "I've got to stop seeing him."

Branko didn't come to her that night. Or the next or the next. When ten days had gone by, Joanna knew he would not come again. She told herself it was just as well, that it couldn't have gone on. Then she burst into wild tears. It was the weekend, and for two days she stayed in bed in her flat, muffling her sobs in the pillows. She didn't sleep. She didn't eat. And she left her bed only to go to the bathroom or creep to the kitchen to fix herself a cup of tea.

On Monday she got up, dressed, and went to her office. Yasna and Gordana were there, talking about a play they had seen that weekend. Ivana brought them all coffee, and they sat at their desks sipping the hot, sweet drink. Selma came in, her face puckered with pain. It was the wind, she said, the south wind. Her migraine had returned, and every step she took sent daggers of pain through her head.

"Yes, it's terrible," Yasna agreed, and her dark-ringed eyes were clouded. "My back ached all night."

"And mine, too, " Gordana sighed. "Oh, it's terrible, that wind. We all suffer so." She turned to Joanna, who was taking papers from her briefcase. "But you don't feel it at all, do you, Joanna?"

Joanna considered. She could have lied. She could have told them her listlessness and the dull pain she felt came from the wind. Then they would have hurried to comfort her. The south wind was her passport to their world, to Branko's world. She could have shared their sympathy and their condition. Instead, shook her head. "No," she said. "It doesn't bother me."

From then on Joanna continued to teach her classes and go for coffee with her students. Yasna continued to endure her lonely marriage and perform small services for her, and Selma continued to invite her to dinner from time to time. Gordana told her malicious stories about their colleagues as usual, and Joanna often saw her smoking with Pjetar in the dark corner of a coffee shop. Ivana's schedule changed, and she stopped bringing Joanna coffee, but Slobodan took up the task, plying her with compliments and taking great interest in the size of her flat.

The south wind was blowing the day Joanna boarded the plane that would take her to Belgrade for her flight home. Yasna drove her to the airport, cutting in and out of traffic and passing on blind curves, all the while complaining about the wind. Joanna felt sad. Already she was a little homesick for Sarajevo. She would miss Yasna and her sorrow. She would miss Selma's disapproval and Gordana's malice. She would even miss Branko. She could think of him now with neither anger nor regret. As she walked across the tarmac to her plane, the wind billowed her skirt around her thighs, and a man who bore a striking resemblance to Branko stared unabashedly at her legs.

"I never really did learn Serbo-Croatian," she thought.

The plane spiraled up over the trees and turned toward the narrow pass in the mountains which led toward Belgrade. Joanna pressed her face to the window. The city lay below in the summer haze. She stayed there, watching the jumble of red tile roofs with their counterpoint of minarets fall away until they were only a memory. Most of all she would miss that city of passion and desire.

Now, watching the horror in Bosnia unfold on the nightly television news, Joanna tries to hold onto that last sunny, God's eye view of Sarajevo while the cameras pan the rubble and flash on hunched figures dodging sniper fire in their search for water and fuel. She tries to identify streets where she walked or the buildings she passed each day on her way to work, and she searches those fragmentary scenes for familiar faces, half afraid she will recognize one of the forlorn corpses lying stiffly in the ruins or see a friend among the sorrowing women stretching out their hands for help that never comes. The south wind must blow all the time now, she thinks sadly.

One day as Joanna is driving to work, NPR features an interview with a woman from one of the Bosnian refugee camps. She has been raped — relentlessly, again and again — and she describes those repeated violations in the dead, flat voice of one for whom emotion is an unimaginable luxury. For a minute Joanna thinks it is Mirjela, and she pulls over to listen. Then the announcer addresses the girl as Nena, and Joanna drives on. That night, on an impulse, she picks up the phone and dials Selma. The phone rings and rings until, finally, she is cut off. She tries writing — to Yasna, to Gordana, to Dzenana and Dijana and Biljana — but there is no answer. She can no longer reach that city she thought she knew so well.

Hearts remote, yet not asunder. - Shakespeare

TATTOO BIRD

by Brenda Webster

Anna raises herself on one elbow in the crumpled bed and gives John a queasy smile. "You've been enough of a Red Cross knight this morning. You brought me tea and toast, washed my face, even changed the sheets."

Her green eyes narrow, appraising him as he stands beside the bed holding her hairbrush. "You're going to start hating me." He opens his mouth to protest but she cuts him off, gesturing impatiently as though she is shooing away a cat.

"Go into the city and try out your new camera, practice for the big event."

John sits down on the edge of the bed and lifts a strand of matted blond hair away from her mouth. What self-tormenting irony had possessed him to say he was going to shoot the birth? All he wants now is to try and forget it.

"I don't like leaving you like this." He glances restlessly out the window at the sailboats scudding across the bay, then back at Anna. "Besides, I have six months to practice." Her skin feels clammy under his mechanically stroking fingers. Is he imagining it or is it getting darker? There is a shadowy patch like a racoon's mask over her upturned nose. Since she has gotten pregnant he almost doesn't recognize her.

"Go on," she repeats, "you know you want to. I'll be fine."

He kisses her forehead, avoiding her eyes. Seeing her now, he would never guess she was a designer of elegant dresses. A chic, modern woman. She looks like some nesting feral animal curled up in her burrow of blankets. Nibbling toast. And all the while that thing is battening on, clamping itself to the wall of her womb. He imagines reaching inside to pluck it out and flushes with shame.

"Remember, you're my precious love," he tells her, thinking what a bastard he is. He picks up his Armani jacket from the chair, blows her a kiss and slips out the front door with his camera equipment in a metal box. He half expects a policeman to be waiting for him on the lawn. Arrested for murder in the heart.

Speeding along the bay towards San Francisco, seabirds swooping and soaring alongside, he replays the awful night of Anna's revelation. She'd been lying warmly ensconced in his arms and out of the blue she'd said, "I hope he has your eyes."

"What?" he'd asked, breathing in her wild-flower smell, still dazed by their lovemaking. "Who?"

She'd laughed a light, tinkling laugh. "The baby. We're going to have a baby." Her laughter cut into his exposed skin like glass splinters from a shattered windshield.

Now, watching the speedometer edge towards eighty, he wonders why he is so undone by this pregnancy. After all, he is an adult man, not a mewling child. When his brother was born, he'd cried inconsolably for his mother and wouldn't sleep until his father took him into his bed. His grief had vanished from his memory but the humiliating image lasted of himself, face pasted with snot and tears, clinging like a monkey to his father's chest. "Sissy," he tells himself in his father's voice. "Namby-pamby mama's boy."

Maybe it is because the idea of the fetus growing in the rank blood-sodden soil of Anna's womb unnerves him that John decides to photograph skyscrapers. He is hungry for clarity, brightness, clean lines. He parks in a garage on Union Square and walks over to the financial district. Offices are closed because it is Saturday and the streets are quiet, relatively free of people. He breathes deeply, the nervous pains in his stomach quieting.

After a few minutes of pleasantly aimless wandering, he is struck by the Trans-Am building, a broad-based steel and glass structure tapering to a needle point. It pleases him by the cocky way it is set off from the others. He plants his tripod on the sidewalk and then, afraid that someone will walk off with his equipment while he is concentrating on his pictures, chains his metal box to a parking meter.

The surge of bitter liquid in his chest when he thinks of being ripped off reminds him how his mother pressed a handful of quarters into his palm, his last trip to Miami, "So you shouldn't get a ticket." What she meant was that he shouldn't forget himself and have fun. Not even for an hour. Reflected clouds drift over the surface of the brown glass building. He wonders if his mother had ever had a pleasure not contaminated by worry.

Sex with Anna was that pleasure for him, he thinks, taking out his 28-millimeter lens. Though he still wasn't sure how she had broken down his defenses and persuaded him to marry her. Part of her appeal had been that, though bursting with youth and beauty, she didn't want children. That he was enough for her. Damn! Why was she doing this to him?

He screws the wide-angle lens angrily onto the camera and bends to focus. Only half the glass skyscraper is visible. He moves the tripod back but it doesn't help. If he moves any further he'll have nothing but street traffic in his picture. He unscrews the camera from the tripod and leans backwards trying to get the full sweep of the building, its soaring effect, but no matter how he contorts himself, he can only get half of it into view.

For a minute he wishes he was back in his office in City Hall. Being District Attorney was stressful, but at least he knew what he was doing. He frowns, thinking of his latest case. Did that dumb kid really think he'd pull off a stick-up like that? No getaway car. No back up. Just running until they trapped him in an alley. What was happening to kids these days? First drugs, now guns. The controls he grew up with just didn't seem to

293

function anymore. He presses his eye against the camera again and resignedly shoots the lower half of the building.

Just as he is pressing the button, someone walks in front of him.

"Watch it," John says, annoyed.

"Cool it, man," the boy shoots back. "You're the one in the way, cluttering up the street with your stuff." He has dark hair with short bangs, high Indian cheek bones, a square jaw and full pouting lips. Almost too pretty for a boy. As he goes by, he swishes his butt provocatively at John. Dismissing the slight embarrassed flush he feels spreading up his neck, John aims his camera again and takes the upper half of the glass building, tip impaling a cloud.

Late that night, he wakes up in a sweat, dreaming of earthquake, gets out of bed quietly so as not to wake Anna and spreads his photos out on the big rosewood desk in his study. Most of them are terrible. Truncated buildings. It occurs to him that if he pastes the top and bottom parts of the glass skyscraper together he'll feel a lot better. He wants to see it rising in front of him the way it did on the street, confident, whole, reassuring. He imagines a whole block of photo buildings, absolutely straight. Maybe he can even construct it in his study. Make it three dimensional, have a real block you can walk around. Why he wants this he doesn't know. Hunching over, unconsciously holding his breath so as not to jiggle the paper, he glues together the two halves of the building with crazy glue. But the color doesn't match — the top is much browner than the bottom — and the sense of power he hopes for isn't there.

Feeling as disappointed as he did when his father forgot his birthday, he goes into the bathroom and stumbles over a book next to the toilet. *The Growth and Development of the Fetus.* The fetus stares blindly up at him with its protruding frog eyes. It is shocking pink with a huge bulging umbilical and a skeletal face like a wizened old man. Disgusted, he pushes it away with his foot, sits down and starts thumbing through his discount catalogue looking for the perspective correcting lens he'd read about. With the right technical help he is sure he can capture the elusive glass building.

* * *

By the time Anna is six months pregnant her morning sickness is long past and she radiates energy. She not only decorates the baby's room, but she does an exuberant series of spring dresses, restores an antique cradle, and makes two wall hangings and a quilt. The only thing she seems lukewarm about is lovemaking. She strokes John languidly as though she is moving underwater. Once, afterwards, she draws his hand down to the curve of her belly.

"You never touch me there anymore," she says. "It's all right, you know. He's not fragile. You've got to start getting acquainted."

He feels her stomach heave violently against his palm.

"He's kicking me." He recoils as though he'd touched a cactus. "The little bugger wants me to take my hands off you."

"Nonsense," she says sharply, and then, more gently as though explaining things to a child, "he's active, that's all. It's boring being cooped up with no T.V." She smiles, encouraging him to smile, too, but he can't. Her belly bulges ominously like a time bomb in an old cartoon.

"It was a kick," he says stubbornly, "a hostile kick. I felt it."

She pats her belly affectionately. "Maybe he's going to be a soccer player and win the world cup."

"Great," he says, "I love competitive sports." He hates them, in fact, has no hand-eye coordination. His brother is the athlete.

She tousles his hair, pulling at it a little too hard. "Hey, lighten up, this is supposed to be fun."

"Maybe for you." He hates the plaintive whine in his voice. This isn't the way he acts. He doesn't know what is happening to him. It is like being stuck in a time warp. Helpless, impotent. Two years old.

A few days after his conversation with Anna, John begins to photograph store window mannequins. He'd bought the perspective correcting lens and constructed a whole block of buildings but once he'd overcome the technical difficulties, he found to his distress that the skyscrapers no longer held his attention. Nothing happened, nothing moved. Especially now that Anna is so involved in preparing for the baby, he needs something more substantial. Something he can get his teeth into.

At first it is kind of a joke. He sees a pretty mannequin in I. Magnin's window that reminds him of Anna and he feels an irresistible urge to take her picture. He pretends to be interested in a Harley-Davidson parked at the curb while he glances up at the window surreptitiously. He is afraid people will think he is ridiculous, a distinguished middle-aged man with gray at his temples wearing an impeccably tailored Italian suit. What is he? Some kind of voyeur? But when he finally stations himself directly in front of the model and starts shooting, some girl comes up to him and tells him quite seriously that another window down the street has great costumes. To his surprise, he realizes that she respects his craft. The camera is my cover, he thinks with a start. I could do almost anything now.

Since he started to photograph, he has kept a notebook recording the film, the exposure speed and the filters. Now, because for some reason it amuses him, he begins to write as though he were a fashion photographer with real models in the window-settings instead of plaster figures. He gives the mannequins names. "I shot Gilda again today," he writes, "the smashing red-head with the great legs." Or, "I'm going to use the blue filter on Tina tomorrow. It makes her look as if she's carved of ice."

Gilda is his favorite, the Anna look-alike. He shoots her on Valentine's day when her hair is swept back on one side to show off a delectable sea shell ear pierced by a huge dangling earring. Ruby red. Her evening dress is heavy, metallic silk with enormous flowers in gold and dusty pink and she is perched on the edge of a brocade seat.

296

He has to admit that the seat gets to him. It has a fantastically curved back like an unfurling leaf, or better still, like an elephant's white head and she's sitting and leaning back against his upraised trunk still curled at the tip. What excites him is the way she sits on it as though she weren't aware of all that power under her, looking out into the street. She leans forward slightly, her left arm resting on the seat, and her dress slipping off one white shoulder. She should have a necklace around her throat, John thinks. Something barbaric. Thick rows of heavy beads in gold and pink. He wants to walk into the window and shake her until that preoccupied expression gives way to recognition, passion. This thought gives him an erection and he bends further over the camera to hide it.

There is a large oval mirror to the girl's right, surrounded by white sculpted waves. In the mirror, he sees her back, and behind that, the reflections of a bulging white building with a black door gaping wide. It disturbs him. He tries to shoot so he doesn't get the gravid, white building in the picture but now that he knows it is there somehow it spoils his pleasure. While he studies the reflections through the camera, a figure comes out of the door and reappears next to the model's hip where the fabric is pulled tight. John sees the figure's face. It is that boy with the full lips John saw his first day photographing. Now he sees the boy's square jaw is the same as the model's. The planes of his face mimic hers. For a minute John isn't clear whether the boy is outside in the street or inside with Gilda.

John turns around sharply and sees the boy watching him shoot. He is wearing a black silk shirt open at the neck to show a gold chain. John wonders whether he carries a knife. Or a gun, like his stick-up case. That kid had a pretty face too. "Want to buy some coke?" the boy whispers, fishing for something in his pocket. "I can give you a real good price." When John hurriedly says no, he gives him the finger, and slips away into the crowd. Again John feels his neck flush but this time it covers his chest as well. That night he dreams of fondling the boy's slender brown penis.

Side Show 1995

* * *

At nine months, Anna can't find a comfortable position to sleep in. She is swollen as if she has dropsy and waddles like a duck. The doctor says she is already three centimeters dilated and the baby's head has dropped. Shipping out, John thinks. Restless, she walks around in her robe. She has been converting some of her dresses to nursing dresses, making flaps and hinges to let her breasts out. He surprises her trying one on in front of the mirror and she lets her robe fall open and holds her breasts out to him. The blue veins on the surface are rich with blood.

"Look, aren't they great? I never thought I'd be a C cup." She laughs. Her laugh is getting lower, like a smoker's.

Soberly, he studies her. For a minute he sees her magnificence the way a primitive man might have seen it. Swelling with life. Ripe, the skin stretched taut over her belly. But it is somehow too much for him. Too full. He studies her soberly, concentrating on a detail. The dark blond line of hair running down from below her breasts to her pubis.

"I brought you a present," he says, making himself look into her face, away from the fascinating furry trail. While she takes the box in her hand, he closes her robe and ties it.

Anna undoes the shiny red paper and gasps when she sees a gold choker wound with lapis.

"So that's what you were up to. Going out with that secretive look. I almost thought you were having an affair in the city." She is smiling but he notices her voice quivers.

"I'm surprised you noticed," he blurts out. "I'm not much use to you now. Just a royal pain in the neck."

"Is that it? Is that why you've been so ..." she hesitates a fraction of a second, searching for an inoffensive word, "quiet?" She means cold.

298

"I've been working at it," he offers wryly, "trying to make myself into a comforting presence." He thinks what she needs now is a feather pillow, not a man.

"It's not that kind of quiet," she says putting her arms around his neck. "You feel neglected."

He detects a note of condescension and stiffens. "On the contrary," he says coolly, wishing he were the kind of person who could kneel and put his head against her legs. Beg her to keep on loving him. "You're unfailingly sweet and cheerful."

"You make me sound like a convalescent nurse," she nuzzles his cheek softly and he smells her light, fresh perfume. "Can't you kiss me?"

The perfume gives him a pang of remembered nights. He brushes her lips. A cousin's kiss. Less than kind. "Here," he takes the necklace from her hand. "Let me put it on for you." She sighs and bends her head forward. Not enjoying the present any more. As he fastens the heavy strands around her throat, he thinks of the baby's umbilical cord swollen like a leech. Bulging and twisted and blue. How easy it would be for the thick cord to wrap around the baby's scrawny neck. It happened sometimes. He pictures Anna weeping in his arms. How sweetly he would comfort her.

Next time he sees Gilda, he thinks she has a disdainful expression. He has taken hundreds of pictures of her by now but he has never seen her so harsh. He puts on a blue filter and shoots her face. The skin shines like the white underbelly of a dead fish. Her gorgeous gown is gone. She's wearing a fantasy costume. A red tulle skirt and a gold bustier laced tight up the back covered with tiny glittering scales. On her head is a crown of playing cards. Hearts. She looks as if, if you played with her and lost, you were going to get the big one. She has blood red lips and there is a glittering bottle in her hand that looks to him like a huge hypodermic. From this angle she seems to be staring at him, needle poised.

He imagines that there is a man coiled up in pain at her feet. That reminds him of his witness in the stick-up case. Yesterday when they finally got to court after months of delay, she told how the boy forced her to lie on the floor, gagged her and put a gun to her head. John had cautioned her to speak softly, to be sure not to leave out any details, to make the jury understand the ordeal she'd been through.

"He gave me sixty seconds to open the safe," she said, "before he blew my brains out." Her voice broke telling it. The jury was mostly female. John passed the gun around wrapped in a white cloth. He made them feel its weight, hold it in their hands. Up until now they had sympathized with the boy: he was so young, frail, almost a child. But the gun made them think again. He could see he'd won from their faces. Now he imagines Gilda's red lips round the black muzzle. Toying with it. This had been the kind of thing that obsessed him before he married. Before he fell in love with Anna. He pushes the image out of his mind and shoots another picture with a pink filter. Suddenly he sees the gun in Anna's mouth. Her face is distorted with fear. Trembling, he dismantles his camera and hurries back to the car. Locked in the safety of the garage he opens his pants and fingers himself, hunched over, pretending to be reading a paper spread on his lap. Once he looks out the window and catches the eye of a woman going back to her car. He comes imagining what her face would look like if she saw what he was doing.

When he finishes, he feels an intense pressure to go out with his camera again, photograph something new. He drives over to the Tenderloin district, parks and begins prowling up and down the seedy streets. He shoots quickly as the mood strikes. A giant mural of an ad for Yes Clothing. A girl with a purple dress up to her thighs, ass protruding, her fingers around in back as though she's looking for a place to stick them. Two semi-nude men in jockey shorts advertising safe sex. A high, narrow window in a shabby brick building with a mannequin in black garter belt and stockings and a sign at her feet saying "Sorry, we're CLOSED."

He moves fast, not giving himself time to think. Not wanting it to start all over again. The crazy wants, the fantasies, that he hadn't allowed himself to give in to, that had finally driven him to take a wife. He is horrified at the thought. No. That wasn't why he married. He loves her. Finally he comes to a red door with a poster of Marilyn Monroe standing on a grate in a white dress, laughing as she tries to hold it down, hands right there. The interior of the store is dimly lit and at first he doesn't see that it's a tattoo parlor. Then he sees that the walls are covered with photos of bizarrely decorated bodies. There is a sign on the counter that says "YES, IT HURTS."

He stands for a minute letting his eyes adjust, taking in the low couch covered with towels. There is a man cleaning some equipment next to what looks like a stack of bandages.

"How much for a tattoo?" he asks, wondering what the judge would say if she saw him in a kinky place like this. He makes his speech clipped, East Coast, respectable. To show he doesn't really belong there.

"It depends on the size. A small one on your arm, say a heart or a flag, is fifty. A big piece, say, on the back, could run up to fifteen hundred. Check it out." The man hands him a book with ideas to choose from. Women with butterflies and bracelets. Women covered with jungle flowers or dragons. Men with bloody vampire mouths or skulls. All I need is a woman with fangs on my arm, he thinks, and coughs to cover a snort of laughter. He wonders if he is coming apart. If he's going to end up in Napa. Driven mad by his wife's pregnancy.

One man has a tapestry of interwoven vampires covering his whole back. Wall to wall bloodsucking, he thinks and snorts again. He makes an effort to control himself.

"Something like that must take all day," he says carefully to the man.

The man yawns. He is awfully clean cut for this place: blond, blue-eyed, he looks like a college student. "You can't do it all in a day. The skin won't take it. You need at least four sittings, maybe five."

"And the smaller ones?" John stretches his thumb and his index finger apart. The distance between them is about five inches. "A couple of hours. See anything you like?" He seems to assume that John is going to do it.

John glances down at the counter and sees a tattoo bird with a gorgeous plumed tail, half peacock, half phoenix. "This," he says impulsively. He feels as though chunks of ice are breaking up inside. He doesn't know whether to laugh now or cry.

"No problem," the man says. "Where do you want it?"

He wants it on his chest with its wings spread over his heart but then he'll never be able to wear shorts or a bathing suit again. Unless he swims with a shirt. It occurs to him that he is a very hidden person. Except to Anna, he never shows what he feels. And even she doesn't know much about his awful childhood. For an instant he can imagine what its like to be her. Heavy, vulnerable, needing him, while he's off in space somewhere.

"Here." He pats his belly, picturing the bird rising from the nest of his pubic hair, beak stretching towards his navel. That way only Anna will know. As he takes off his trousers and lies down on the couch, he wonders if she'll mind. Or worse, laugh. He sees her in her maternity dress, laughing, and begins to sweat. Then he remembers her hair is still brittle from dyeing it pink when she was sixteen. "Incipient signs of my future career," she told him with a touch of pride. "I was designing myself." Her acceptance of herself relaxes him. She doesn't judge. He realizes he trusts her.

The man studies the photograph and then turns on the machine. It emits a low steady buzz like a dentist's drill. John can see the tip of the needles barely emerging from the sheath, like a cat flexing his claws. Then he feels a stinging pain. Not too bad. He pictures the colors flowering on his skin and thinks about Anna. Everything about her is becoming more violently colored, darker. Her swollen nipples dark as wine. He remembers how she held them out to him the other day and suddenly strangely it's all right, he wants her again. He has to add a column of figures in his mind to stop himself from getting an erection.

Just as he is finishing, the boy with the Indian cheekbones walks in. Somehow John isn't surprised. He feels almost as if the boy is a kid brother. He notices for the first time that he has a slight limp.

"Hey, that's a cool bird," the boy says, staring down at John with uncontained curiosity. "Too bad you couldn't get it right on your dick." He laughs, not unpleasantly, climbs up on the table next to him, and takes off his pants.

For a minute John thinks of getting up and leaving, but then he relaxes. The boy isn't so sinister really, just young. Macho. Frightened. He has a heavy black outline covering his whole leg.

John is curious despite himself. He tries to figure out the design's intricate interlacings.

"It was a bitch to get this thing right," the boy says, "so much depends on the movement. It's a tribal." He beats an imaginary drum shaking his shoulders.

"Yours is more artistic," John's tattooer whispers to him, "more room for improvising."

The boy glances at himself in the mirror over his couch, flexing his biceps. "I'm going to have a leg that's solid as a totem pole."

"He's going to an Iron John workshop" John's tattooer explains. "If those guys take to tattooing, it'll be great for business."

John remembers reading something about men beating tom-toms in the wilderness. Dancing in circles. He thought it was childish, but maybe better howling and sobbing in company than jacking off alone. "You'll knock 'em dead," he tells the boy.

"If you ever need a model," the boy starts, "I'm good. I do movies, too."

John shakes his head, fending him off. The boy has a bruised look around the eyes. A naked hunger. John feels an involuntary response, a flash of desire. Then, just as clearly he knows this isn't what he wants. He wants Anna. Her special warmth, her body. She is the best thing that's ever happened to him. He prays

303

it isn't too late. That he hasn't ruined everything. The tattooer smoothes some neosporin ointment on the wound and covers it with a gauze bandage.

Later, John is sitting at his desk at home pretending to work, trying to think of how to talk to Anna.
"Come to bed and make love to me," she says, tugging at his hair. "It'll bring on the contractions. I want this baby born."
He feels insanely happy. She is tired of the baby, wants no more of the baby, wants him expelled. She is going to come back to him. He follows her to the bedroom, holding her hand the way he had the night she told him she was pregnant.
"What is this?" she touches his bandage. "Did you hurt yourself?"
"It's nothing. It's a tattoo. It has to heal."
"A tattoo? Not a heart with my name on it?"
"Don't laugh. Okay? Just don't." He touches her lips with his fingers. "It's a phoenix." Rising from the ashes, he wants to say. Us. Starting over again. Instead, he turns her on her side, grips her hips and pushes himself into her as far as he can. It is so delicious he doesn't want to leave. Ever. He thrusts. Draws back reluctantly. At the next thrust he thinks he feels the womb opening and something reaching out, pushing against his penis. He pushes back. "En garde mon fils." he thinks, "You're vacating now. Time's up."
"Harder," Anna whispers, reaching her hand back to stroke his thigh.
"I don't want to hurt you."
"Don't worry," she pinches him lightly, goading him.
He thrusts again, spiralling around the edges of her, mining, digging like a dog down a burrow. Sparks flare in back of his closed eyes. Washes of red and purple. He imagines the baby crouching just out of reach of his spade like a terrified rabbit. Little trembler, little pinknose, fuzzy ears. How could I have been so scared of him, he thinks. Why he's nothing. He's going to be flat on his back in a diaper in a few hours. It increases his

pleasure to imagine puny hands flailing the air, unable to do anything without help. While he has this perfect, this peerless pleasure. This is his, anytime he wants, this velvet sheath to tuck into. To burrow in, to warm himself from the cold.

At his next thrust a great burst of liquid floods down his legs. At first he thinks he has urinated. Or she has. He can't tell the difference between them anymore.

"That's it, the water," she breathes, exultant. "It's started." She reaches behind to pat him.

He struggles back to consciousness. "What shall I do? Pack? get the car?" He feels close to her again. Shrunk and tired but tender.

"In a minute." She takes a big watch and starts to time the contractions. "Just hold me a minute more."

"We're going to be all right," he says against her ear. But he is thinking of the child. He doesn't want his son to grow up the way he did. Without feeling for so long. Frozen. He feels a deep sadness where the hatred had been. A swamp of unshed tears.

Anna is intent, counting under her breath.

"Five minutes apart," she says. "We ought to go."

He pictures the baby lying beside her, wrapped in his blue receiving blanket. Sees her gently offering her breast. Then he puts his face against her warm back and, just for a minute before he goes to get the car, he lets himself cry.

Notes about Contributors

Lee Blackcrow (Second Prize) married an Oglala Sioux in 1977 and moved to Wanblee, South Dakota, where she raised a sacred herd of buffalo and taught at the Oglala Lakota College. She is now an editor at *Calyx*, a quiltmaker and a frequent contributor to literary magazines. Her story in last year's *Side Show* was a 1994 Andres Berger Finalist in Short Stories.

Dorothy Bryant is well known for a line of distinguished novels, including *Ella Price's Journal*, *Kin of Ata* and *Madame Psyche*. Last year she published *Anita, Anita* about Garibaldi and his wife in South America. She has recently turned successfully to playwriting and has seen two plays staged to glowing reviews. *Dear Master* won a Bay Area Theatre Critics Circle Award. *The Panel* is her latest.

Colleen Crangle (Honorable Mention) grew up in Zimbabwe and South Africa. Since arriving in America, she has written a collection of short stories about life in South Africa. She also runs her own small software business. A story of hers is due to appear in *Confrontation*.

Charles Fenno lives in San Francisco with a posselq ('significant other' in Census Bureau argot) and the ghost of their departed cat.

Margot C. Kadesch (Honorable Mention) spent 1980-81 teaching at the University of Sarajevo as a Fulbright Junior Lecturer. She now lives in Salt Lake City where she is an administrator in a small liberal arts college. The story appearing here is her first published fiction, although she is a restaurant reviewer and the co-author of two textbooks, and has published a number of articles. She is currently at work on a novel.

Martha Kent lives in Bolinas, California, where she went to live after a career as an editor and a congressional assistant. She is now embarked on a project building a residential cooperative in Point Reyes for retired people.

Elisa Jenkins' work has appeared in small literary magazines including *The Sun: A Magazine of Ideas*. She is the recipient of 1994-95 Individual Artist Master Fellowship from the Indiana Arts Council, with the support of the NEA. She won first place in the 1994 Hemingway Short Story Competition.

Electra Long (whose painting appears on the cover) is a San Francisco artist who specializes in commissioned oil portraits. She teaches at the Academy of Art in San Francisco. She studied at the Art Students League in New York and has won many awards. She lives with San Francisco architect, **Lawrence Cannon**, who designed our cover.

First Prize Winner **Carol Ann Parikh's** stories have won awards including a Massachusetts arts council fellowship and first prize in last year's *Indiana Review* fiction contest. In 1992 "The Turtle" took first place in the Hackney Literary Awards.

Paul Pekin (Honorable Mention), in addition to winning third prize in last year's *Side Show*, has had his work appear in *Best American Sports Writing of 1991* (Houghton Mifflin) and has been extensively published in mainstream and literary venues. Before becoming a writer and teacher, he spent 10 years as a police officer for the Cook County Forest Preserve District and he now resides in Chicago where he directs the Storyarts writing workshop.

Paul Perry won second prize in the first *Side Show*. He lives in San Antonio, Texas, with his wife, Toshi. He recently retired as Assistant Professor of English at Palo Alto Community College, although he continues as an adjunct faculty member. After 20 years in the Army, he returned to college, earning his B.A. and M.A. His stories have been published in both mainstream and literary publications. He is now looking for a publisher for a novel.

Anne Raeff (Honorable Mention) grew up near New York City. She now lives in New Mexico with her significant other and teaches at Albuquerque High School. She is working on a novel and the story in *Side Show* is her first publication.

Kal Rosenberg lives in Gainesville, Florida, with his wife. He is a historian and political activist who began writing in his 55th year.

Gary Earl Ross (Honorable Mention) teaches writing at the University at Buffalo Educational Opportunity Center. He has been widely published and he is now finishing a collection of short stories.

Susan Segal, our Third Prize winner, was born in New York and now lives in Costa Mesa, California, where she teaches creative writing. She has published stories in *Redbook* and *Snake Nation Review* and other literary magazines. She is working on her first novel.

Laurell Swails won first prize in last year's Side Show. She has also received a fellowship for fiction from the Oregon Institute of Literary Arts in 1993. An Oregon native who has been widely published in small magazines, she was a 1980 recipient of a NEA fellowship for her fiction.

Lee Vining lives, works and writes near Death Valley.

Brenda Webster has published a novel, *Sins of the Mothers* (Baskerville 1993). In addition to publishing books of criticism, including *Yeats: A Psychoanalytic Study* (Stanford Univ. Press), she has worked a co-editor and translator. She is president of PEN American Center (West) and a member of the board of directors of *Zyzzyva*. She lives with her three children and her husband in Berkeley, California, where she is at work on another novel.

Susan Welch was a Wallace Stegner fellow at Stanford University. Her fiction has appeared in *The Paris Review, The Pushcart Prize* anthology and in other publications. She lives and writes in Minneapolis, Minnesota.

ORDER FORM

Yes! I want to order *Side Show*. Send me:

_____ copies of *Side Show* 1995 at $10.00 (+ $2.00 postage and handling (Calif. residents add $.83 sales tax per book) (ISBN 0-9630563-3-6)

_____ copies of *Side Show* 1994 at $10.00 (+ $2.00 postage and handling (Calif. residents add $.83 sales tax per book) (ISBN 0-9630563-2-8)

_____ copies of *Side Show* 1992-93 at $12.50 (+$2.50 postage and handling) (Calif. residents add $1.03 sales tax per book) (ISBN 0-9630563-1-X)

_____ copies of *Side Show* 1991 at $10.00 (+$2.00 postage and handling) (Calif. residents add $.83 sales tax per book) (ISBN 0-9630563-0-1)

Buy all four annuals for $25.00 (plus $3.00 postage and handling).

Send book(s) to (please print or type):

Name _____

Address _____

_____

Phone _____

I'm enclosing my check for $_____. Sorry, no credit cards accepted.

somersault press
P.O. Box 1428
El Cerrito, CA 94530-1428
(510) 215-2207